I0687717

CRISTO

Frances Buzzell

Copyright   2018 Frances Jean Buzzell

This book is a work of fiction. All characters have no existence outside the imagination of the author and have no relation whatsoever to anyone bearing the same name or names.   They are not even inspired by any individual known or unknown to the author, and all incidents are pure invention.

All rights reserved. No part of this book may be reproduced or transmitted in any form whatsoever.

ISBN 13: 978-0998912103
ISBN 10: 0998912107

This book is dedicated to my husband, Jim.

Prologue

The coast of Italy

A warm summer wind swirled around the tiny cove. Moonlight lit up the tips of waves as they crashed on shore. Bright stars filled the sky.

Steve Crawford, a U.S. federal agent, bent down and rinsed his goggles in the Tyrrenhian Sea. He turned his head to the left and stared at the lights of Positano.

"I think it's been long enough," he said to his partner standing next to him.

Peter O'Brien adjusted his scuba tank. "I'm ready."

A light blinked from several hundred feet off shore. Steve reached for his flashlight and returned the signal. "Let's go."

He waded out into the sea. When the water rose above his waist, he gave a thumb's up sign to Peter and disappeared beneath the waves.

Fifteen minutes later, Steve and Peter surfaced at the rear of a yacht. They stowed their equipment in a net and secured it to the side of the boat. Once on deck, the two agents hurried to the salon entrance.

A man stood in the doorway. Steve recognized Carlo, the steward.

"The Di Biasi's and their guests are sleeping," Carlo said.

Steve nodded and turned to Peter. "I'll signal the boat."

Carlo and Peter moved through the salon and disappeared down the stairs that led to the rooms below.

Steve signaled the Agency boat. It took a few valuable minutes to make this contact and he swore under his breath, as he ran to catch up with Peter.

Carlo waited at the bottom of the stairs and Steve followed him to the first room down the hall. The door was open wide. Two men lay on a blood soaked carpet in the middle of the room. Peter stood above them pointing to a large wooden chest several feet away. Steve consulted his watch. Ten minutes until help arrived. "Let's get this thing on deck," Steve whispered. "Set it close to the railing.

Peter and Carlo carried the cache out the door and up the stairs to the salon. Steve helped them outside and led them to a spot that would allow cover from the salon windows. He turned and looked back, checking the yacht for any movement. There was none.

He stood above the chest, his eyes scanning the surface. He shook his head. "Somehow I thought the cache would be bigger. This may only be a portion of it. Let's see what's in it.

Steve's hands shook as he reached for the latch. Cristo was known to set booby-traps. After taking a deep breath, he slowly lifted the lid. His eyes opened wide. Lying on top of the gold and jewels sat a ticking device with blinking green lights. The red digital numbers read five minutes.

Sweat broke out on Steve's forehead. His pulse raced. "Shit! This thing's going to blow in five minutes!

"Where the hell is the boat?" Peter asked.

Steve glanced at his watch again. "It should be here in seven minutes. Any ideas?"

His partner shook his head.

"I'll send a second signal to come full speed ahead." Steve stood and a bullet zinged close to his ear. He took cover and saw movement in the salon.

Two more shots rang out. Peter and Carlo crouched behind the chest.

"You need me, Steve!" Cristo cried.

Another shot from the salon. Steve saw the terrorist move closer to the door.

"The device has already become a bomb," Cristo said.

Steve returned fire then glanced at Peter. "What time does the clock say?"

"Four minutes."

Several bullets hit the railing above the chest.

More movement in the salon crossed Steve's line of vision.

The countess, Alissa Di Biasi, took cover behind a couch. His heart wrenched. How could he save her? Did Cristo know she helped him?

"We won't give up the chest!" Steve yelled. He didn't take his eyes off the salon. "Peter, how much time left?"

"Three minutes."

"Set the chest on the railing, and when it hits two minutes throw it over."

Steve reloaded.

Peter and Carlo struggled to set the chest on the railing amidst another round of fire. Both men fell to the deck.

"I'm hit!" Peter cried.

Steve emptied his clip.

Peter pulled himself up far enough to push the chest over. Blood oozed from his wound as he collapsed.

Carlo lay on the deck, blood flowing from his head.

Signal or no signal, now was the time to move.

Steve fired as he rushed to his partner and lifted him over his shoulder.

With a grunt, he jumped..

Steve surfaced, clutching Peter's wetsuit. He spotted the Agency boat. As he swam toward help, the yacht exploded.

ONE

Five Years Later

Steve Crawford stepped out of a trattoria and into the warm Italian sun. He reached into his shirt pocket for his sunglasses and began walking toward Campo de Fiori, located in the center of Rome. His steps were brisk, his expression grim.

The news he had just heard was dire. A major terrorist group in Italy planned to kidnap someone in Rome within the next week. His contact had no idea who the person could be, but Steve had a long list of prospective victims swirling around in his head.

A few minutes later, he entered Campo De Fiori and became lost among the crowd of shoppers in the busy produce market. He bought fruit and vegetables, and then headed for his hotel set deep in the tangled back streets a few blocks away.

He passed the statue of a heretic who was burned in 1600 for believing the world was round and not the center of the universe, and paused at a building of ramshackle apartments on the edge of the square. He leaned against a wall and pulled an apple from his shopping bag. As he rubbed the fruit on his shirt, his eyes darted around watching the crowds of people. He froze. He had a tail. A man wearing a blue shirt stood at the base of the heretic's statue, a man Steve had seen earlier outside the trattoria.

He finished his apple and tossed the core in a nearby trash can. His long stride served him well as he hurried down the busy street next to the apartments and hailed a taxi.

Sometime later, the cab pulled up to the Vatican museums and Steve got out. He quickly blended into a small crowd walking toward St. Peter's Square.

Steve casually turned his head and saw the blue shirt stepping out of a cab behind him. He picked up his pace and passed the crowd of tourists, his destination the small escape wall that runs from the Vatican to Castel d' Angelo. A grand medieval hotel set in the shadow of this wall offered a good cover. He would check in and wait for dark.

Peter O'Brien, code name Apollo, walked out of the airport terminal. He stood at the curb and waited for his contact. Within minutes, a car pulled up and he recognized the thick dark hair and patrician nose of Vittorio de Luca.

He opened the door and sat in the passenger seat. The Italian smiled and eased the car out into traffic toward Venice six miles away.

"How was your flight?" Vittorio asked.

"Long! I'm so exhausted; I just want a hot shower and a bed." He eyed Vittorio and knew the shower and bed would wait. "What have you got set up?"

"We go to the hotel. You have your shower and dress for a meeting. Later we go back to the hotel and you have a siesta. Tonight we meet Bruno."

Peter tried to process everything with his jet-lagged mind. Something gnawed at him. Five years ago, Bruno Caminetti had been one of Cristo's enforcers.

He rubbed his jaw. "Do you think we can trust him?

The man used to work for some ruthless people."

"His information has been good in the past. We have worked together often."

Vittorio paused and shrugged his big shoulders. "But of course, one cannot be too careful."

"Who are we meeting?"

"One of my co-workers, Daniella Franco."

Peter recognized the name. She and Vittorio worked for the Italian government. He leaned back in his seat and relaxed.

"I've worked with her."

"Good," Vittorio said. "With her help, perhaps we can both go home early, eh?"

He turned his head and met the Italian's gaze. "Can she work miracles?"

Vittorio's deep laugh echoed in the car.

The hotel, once a fifteenth century palace, stood on the best romantic real estate in Venice. From his second story window, Peter enjoyed a view of the terrace garden below and the shops and cafes located in the heart of the city.

He thought of Carrie, his wife of three years, and saw her dressed in a pink lace teddy. Her blonde hair pulled high on her head, blue eyes sparkling, arms outstretched in an invitation to life's pleasures. His thoughts changed to the baby inside her.

Happiness filled him when he remembered that seven months from now he'd be a dad.

The alarm on his watch vibrated. He pulled away from his daydreams. In his line of business, not focusing completely on matters at hand could cost him his life. He hurried toward the door, mentally checking for his gun, phone, and small dagger.

Vittorio met him in the lobby. Peter followed him outside and into a waiting water taxi.

They rode the Grand Canal toward Piazza San Marco. Peter loved this part of Venice the best. Old palaces, dating back to when the city was the richest in the world, lined the waterway. Over the years he'd never tired of the beauty.

Today, he didn't see the old world charm. He could only think about his current assignment. Bruno was bad news and he didn't trust him. How could he convince the Italians to abort the meeting tonight?

The taxi pulled up to the dock near the piazza. Peter followed Vittorio past a line of black gondolas, and into the famous square seen for decades in the movies and on millions of postcards.

They waded through the hordes of pigeons in front of St. Mark's Basilica, before entering a narrow alley full of tourists. Vittorio increased his pace. Peter stayed close until they came out onto an avenue and mingled with more tourists. Half-way down the street, the two men entered a shop.

The small store, loaded with jewelry and souvenirs, held a soft scent of perfume.

A sales girl approached Vittorio. He smiled and pointed to the window. "Please, I would like to see your cameos."

While Vittorio held the girl's attention, Peter wandered to the back and turned left into a small alcove. A woman stood at a counter holding two Carnevale masks adorned with feathers and glitter. She furrowed her brow as she looked at one and then the other.

He stopped next to her and studied postcards on a nearby rack. He'd found his contact and the source of the perfume. They were alone.

"Buonasera, Peter," Daniella Franco said softly. She covered her eyes with the gold mask and looked into a mirror.

"Hello, Daniella, nice to work with you again. Is

everything set on your end?"

"Yes. Vittorio will put a wire on you. I am suspicious about the nature of this meeting. Bruno knows more than he is telling us."

She turned and held the masks up for him to see. Her long brown hair hung past her shoulders and framed an exotic face with large dark brown eyes and creamy skin.

Peter stared at her for several seconds. He'd forgotten how beautiful she was. "Bruno met with a reliable source in France last month. He is prepared to give us new information on the laundering of money for the terrorist cell."

She still held the masks for his regard. He pointed to the gold. She set the black one down and met his gaze. "I am still suspicious. My superiors disagree. I can only go along." She smiled and a dimple appeared near the left side of her mouth. "Vittorio will fill you in on the rest. Good luck tonight. Ciao."

Peter followed her as she walked into the other room and stood at the cash register.

"There are too many beautiful cameos," Vittorio said. "I must bring my wife to choose one."

The salesgirl smiled and closed the case. She saw Daniella and hurried to ring up her mask.

Vittorio left the shop.

Peter scanned another rack of postcards and selected a few. After Daniella left, he paid for his cards and met Vittorio down the street in front of a MacDonald's restaurant. He chuckled. "Are we having lunch?"

Vittorio turned and walked two doors down and entered a trattoria.

Peter followed and a waiter led them past a long counter featuring pastries, sandwiches, pizza, and other Italian dishes.

They sat down at a table in the back of the long

narrow café. Vittorio ordered two espressos. They sat in silence for several minutes until the waiter returned with the espresso.

The Italian's piercing brown eyes scanned the room. Satisfied, he leaned forward. "How did it go?"

"She's suspicious," Peter said. "One thing I remember from working with her, she has good instincts. I think we should reconsider the meeting tonight."

Vittorio picked up his cup. He appeared deep in thought. A frown creased his forehead. "I know Bruno can help, but if Daniella is concerned, I will meet with the others at the hotel. It will not hurt to review our facts."

Peter's body stiffened. Vittorio was being polite. The Italians wouldn't change their minds. Besides, this issue with Bruno was personal. He remembered the day five years ago when the Agency fished a female agent's body out of the sea. She had been undercover in Cristo's organization. Her last contact, a note written quickly and stashed in a secret hiding place, said Bruno would be taking her to Positano for a meeting with the boss.

She had been a good agent and didn't deserve to be beaten and raped. He would be the judge of Bruno.

Lights from the bridge reflected on the water of the canal. Peter leaned against the white stone railing. Apprehension sent prickles up his spine. Bruno was late.

Two minutes later, he saw the man walking toward him. The years had been kind. His body still slender and athletic, his wavy hair neatly combed, expensive shoes and clothing. Peter almost laughed. The asshole appeared to be distinguished.

Bruno stepped onto the bridge, crowded with people

enjoying the night air.

Peter turned and faced the canal.

"Sorry to be late," Bruno said. "Someone followed me. I lost him."

Vittorio would have a man on Bruno.

Peter shrugged. "Let's walk."

They stepped onto a sidewalk and moved away from the bridge.

The balmy air smelled of pasta and sauce as they strolled past outdoor restaurants. Tourists flocked around the shops. Two blocks later the sidewalk ended at a canal.

He scanned the immediate area and saw no one near them. "Okay, what do you have for me?"

"The group will drop off money at a bakery in Rome. I can take you to this place."

"How much?" Peter asked.

"Two-hundred-thousand American dollars."

Peter stared out on the waterway. Either Bruno was crazy or his balls were awfully big. How could he ask for that kind of money? And would the payoff go into the pockets of the terrorist organization?

He didn't have a choice. The Italian's wanted to see this thing through. "Okay. When will the money be dropped off?"

Bruno's small dark eyes darted from the canal to Peter and back to the canal.

"Not tomorrow night. Next night."

Peter shrugged. He had two days. "I'll call you after I check into my hotel in Rome. Vittorio has your number?"

"Si."

Being with Bruno made him feel dirty and Peter wanted to get as far away from this guy as possible. He turned his back and walked briskly to a nearby water taxi.

The boat pulled away and out into the canal,

accelerating into traffic. Peter thought about the man and his plan. He slowly turned and glanced back. Bruno stood on the bridge watching him. Peter had a strong feeling of dread.

Daniella's suspicions are correct.

Once back at his hotel, he showered and slipped on a robe. Tight muscles were relaxed, but the mind continued to worry. Exhaustion overwhelmed him. He stretched out on the bed placing his head on the propped up pillows.

His eyes closed and he visualized Carrie smiling at him holding her spoiled dog. His heart ached for her and the small red cocker spaniel. She would be sitting behind her desk at work about now. Impulsively, he gave in to the need to separate himself from the danger and intrigue of his job. He reached for the phone and dialed.

"Carrie O'Brien."

Hearing her voice gave comfort and he smiled. "*Caio, bella Carrie.*"

"Peter! Are you in Venice?"

"Yes, I'm here and ready to get some sleep. I've already been out admiring the beauty of the canals and stepping around the pigeon poop. I just wanted you to know that I got here and I love you."

"I love you too. I miss you already. Pigeon poop?"

Peter could hear the emotion in her voice and hoped she wouldn't cry. He hated it when she cried. "I miss you too, honey. The pigeons in St. Mark's Square. Remember? We looked at the pictures in the travel brochure."

"Yeah."

He heard her sigh and his heart tightened. "Are you feeling okay?"

"Most of the time. I was sick this morning, but I ate a few crackers."

"Good, how's Penny?"

"She's doing better. I took her to the vet yesterday and he gave her some pills for her stomach. He said she's probably not sick. I have to limit her 'people' snacks. He mentioned something about sympathy for my condition."

Peter chuckled. "Sounds like your spoiled dog. Is she taking the pills okay?"

"So far. I wrap them in hamburger. It makes me gag, but then I eat a dill pickle and feel better."

"You had ice cream with that pickle didn't you?"

"Doesn't everyone?"

They laughed together.

"Sounds like you have everything under control." He yawned and sighed. "Well, have to go. I'm beat. I'll call you tomorrow night from Rome."

"Okay, my darling. Bye, love you!"

"*Caio, mia amour.*" He hung up the phone with a heavy heart and slipped beneath the covers.

He thought of Carrie and her unusual diet. Crackers and pickles. Thank God for her and their life together in Dallas. At times, it kept him in the realm of sanity.

Someone knocked at the door. Peter jumped up and grabbed his robe and weapon. Who the hell was this?

He opened the door with caution.

Vittorio stood in the doorway. "Forgive the inconvenience."

Peter motioned for him to sit and the big man settled into a chair close to the door.

"The reservations are made. Dimitri will be in a room across the hall from you. I called Daniella and she will send a team to watch the hotel. When you know where the bakery is located, she will send her people inside.

If Bruno will only drive you past the bakery,

Dimitri will follow you. Either way, you have protection."

Peter sat on the edge of the bed. Just as he knew they would, the Italians were sticking to their plan. His superiors in Washington wanted him to cooperate. The space between the rock and the hard place just got smaller. He shook his head.

"I still have a bad feeling about this whole thing."

"Bruno gave us good tips in the past. We will be careful, okay?" Vittorio shrugged and rose from his chair. "I will see you in Rome. Dimitri will be on the same train. If you have a problem, find him.

Sunday evening, Peter stood at the window of his hotel in Rome. He scanned the street below as his mind went over his plans. Daniella's team sat in a blue van parked half-way down the street. Two American special agents were in a car near the front of the hotel. Everyone in place except Dimitri.

He turned and started to unbutton his shirt. A quick shower and then a dinner date downstairs with Daniella. Tomorrow, a meeting with Bruno outside the hotel. If all went well, two days from now he'd be home with Carrie. Should he call her now?

A loud knock at the door echoed in his room.

TWO

Lightning lit up the dark sky and a peal of thunder, loud and strong, shook the ground. Carrie O'Brien felt the vibration as she stood in the foyer of her home in Dallas. This thunderstorm wouldn't ruin her plans to work on the nursery. She grabbed her keys and hurried into the garage.

The big door closed behind her as she pulled her silver BMW out of the driveway and headed for the boulevard. The rain started to come down fast and heavy, so she turned on her windshield wipers. Visibility, nil.

This was not a good idea.

At the intersection, the light changed from green to yellow and she hit her brakes. The car skidded. Frightened out of her wits, her pulse quickened and she longed to be home.

Stop being such a ninny. If Peter were here he'd tell you to calm down. You're still alive.

Thoughts of him flowed through her mind, causing her to smile. She missed him so much when he went on trips. Even though he told her not to worry, she always did. This time he said it was just routine, a visit to his mother's banker in Rome and a little job for his "friends." Jobs for his "friends" were dangerous. She should know

Three years ago she'd been pulled into a web of money laundering and stolen jewels when a co-worker sewed a coded letter into her tote bag.

Unknown to her, she'd been stalked for days.

Finally, the stalker tried to kill her, but Peter saved her. He had been the agent in charge of investigating the stolen jewels. She owed him her life.

The light turned green. She drove through the intersection and made a quick turn into a strip mall. Once inside the hardware store, her slicker and umbrella dripping heavily on the floor, she found the paint section and scanned the choice of colors. An eerie feeling passed over her as she knelt to read the labels.

She shuddered and looked up at a tall thin man standing to her right, holding a can of paint. He turned his head and their eyes met.

Thunder roared and the ground shook. The lights blinked. Chills ran down her spine.

She grabbed a pint of mauve paint and hurried from the department to the check out.

Her heart palpitated and sweat broke out from the fear of a panic attack.

Get hold of yourself.

With shaking hands, she paid the cashier.

At her car, the eerie feeling swept over her again. Someone was watching her. The man in the store came to mind, and her hands trembled as she started the motor.

The rain stopped when Carrie turned onto her own tree lined street. She sighed with relief. Most of the time when Peter left on a trip out of the country she did okay. Why did the creepy man bother her?

He's just a tall, thin man with intense brown eyes. The thunder and lights in the store created a scary atmosphere.

See, you are over-reacting.

Her house sat only a block away. She smiled and

gazed into her mirror one last time.

A gray sedan followed close behind her. Carrie's brows knit together.

Don't even bother thinking about that car. It's nothing.

She pulled into her garage and turned off the motor. She pushed the garage door button and glanced in the rear view mirror again. The gray sedan sat at the foot of her driveway.

The driver's eyes dark and piercing.

The garage door came down with a thud and Carrie hurried into the house, her heart beating fast. She punched in her code and enabled the alarm before rushing to the living room window. The gray sedan was gone.

She ran upstairs and sat on the edge of her bed. A feeling of being watched haunting her.

Peter's only been gone three days and already you're a basket case.

The phone on the bedside table rang. She jumped and read the Caller ID. Her brother. Relief flooded through her.

"Hi, Steve."

"Hey, little sister! How 'bout we go to dinner this evening? My treat."

"That sounds great!" Carrie couldn't believe her luck.

Getting out would help her forget her fears.

Steve towered over his sister as they stood in the foyer of her home. He looked her over from head to toe searching for signs of distress. Carrie, known in the Crawford family as the "emotional one," had a stockpile of strength when needed. He just wanted to make sure she was using it.

"You're making me feel like a specimen in some lab," Carrie said. "I'm okay."

Steve laughed. "It's been a while since I saw you. You look good."

"Thanks, but you're different." She studied him for a few seconds. "Your hair's shorter!"

"Don't look too closely. My hairline is receding and you know how vain I am!" He glanced at the rooms off the foyer. "I like your new house."

"It's a lot bigger than the other one and closer to my store in Plano."

Penny jumped up on Steve's leg.

"Hey, Penny the Pest! How are you girl?" He picked up the dog and hugged her squirmy body. She licked his face and he put her down. "She hasn't changed much has she?"

"No."

"Are you ready to go?"

She nodded and grabbed her yellow sweater off the table in the foyer. They walked out to Steve's Vette and he drove toward the freeway.

"Where are you taking me?"

"We're going to one of our favorite places, Pepe's Paradiso."

"That's great! I haven't been there in a long time."

He entered I-75 going south then switched to the LBJ freeway. Steve exited MacArthur in Irving and a few minutes later they entered their old haunt.

Steve watched Carrie take a deep breath and chuckled. "You already know what you're going to order don't you?"

She laughed and nodded.

They sat in the back and he scanned the room for any "friends" or "enemies." There were none. The waitress took their order and left chips and salsa. A Mariachi band began to play a serenade.

"In the old days, I used to eat here almost every week," Carrie said.

"I come here pretty often. It's a nice drive from Fort Worth." He looked around the room. "I've always liked the decor. It's like early hacienda."

His little sister laughed. She always found humor in his corny jokes.

The waitress set their food in front of them. Carrie lifted a taco from her plate and started to take a bite.

"I see your pregnancy hasn't affected your taste for tacos," Steve said.

Carrie dropped her food onto her plate. "How did you know? I only told Mom and Dad."

Steve shrugged his shoulders. "I called them last night and they couldn't wait to tell me the news. I thought you would have told me earlier at your house. Why the big secret?"

"I was going to tell you at the party on Saturday. It's no big secret, but Peter hasn't told his mom yet."

"Will she be at the party?"

"We don't know. She released a new book last week. You know how busy she gets. But it's her only son's wedding anniversary."

Steve picked up his chili burger and took a bite. His eyes opened wide and he grabbed his water glass.

"When they said 'chili' that's exactly what they meant!" he croaked.

Carrie laughed. "You've always been such a comedian!"

He ate more of his burger then pulled out his handkerchief and wiped his forehead. "Is my face red?"

Carrie rolled her eyes.

They left a while later with Steve vowing never to get the chili burger again.

He pulled onto MacArthur and headed for the LBJ

freeway. A light gray sedan followed him out of the lot.

This car was also in back of him when he entered the on-ramp of the freeway. Hmmm.

Steve accelerated and changed lanes. The sedan sped up. He accelerated again and exited the freeway cutting off several other cars in the process.

Carrie gasped. "What's wrong? You never drive this fast!"

"Just taking a short-cut."

She turned her head and looked out the back window. "Do you have a tail?"

Steve laughed. "Peter's been teaching you a thing or two. Yes, someone seems to be following us. I want to see who it is."

They raced down a busy boulevard catching all the green lights. When he looked into his mirror, the sedan was still with them. He entered a residential street and pulled over to the curb. The sedan whizzed past. He memorized the license number and quickly made a u-turn heading back for the freeway.

A few miles later, the sedan came up behind him.

"This guy is definitely following us and he doesn't try to hide it."

"What kind of car is it?" Carrie asked.

"A gray sedan, like a Honda or Ford."

"Oh, no! That's the car that's been following me! I think it belongs to that nasty looking man I saw in the hardware store today."

Steve took his eyes off the road for a minute to glance at his sister. "What man are you talking about?

Carrie told him about her experience.

He knew his sister could just be over-reacting. She did have a great imagination. The incident didn't sound like much.

"I know what you're thinking," Carrie said. "You

think the man was looking at me because he thought I was pretty or something."

He turned onto her street and stopped in front of her house. "That is the most logical assumption. You can be kind of cute at times."

Carrie stared at him. "It wasn't like that."

Steve killed the motor. "Let's wait a few minutes and see if the sedan shows up.

Vittorio stood on a bridge and stared into the water below. He tried not to panic. Two of his men rowed toward the body of a man floating in a Venice canal.

A feeling in the pit of his stomach told him the body was bad news. He watched them haul the corpse into the boat and head for the corner of the bridge. The bad feeling got stronger. His stomach knotted when he recognized the clothing.

He coughed a few times to release his emotions. A man in his position saw many horrible things, but this by far was the worst. They had once been partners working many famous cases together.

What had happened? He turned and walked toward his car forcing himself to think about the present. Daniella had been right.

THREE

The ringing woke Steve. He groped in the dark and found his phone.

"The park. One hour."

Steve pushed off the couch and slipped on his jacket. He grabbed his gun and stuck it in his pocket. As he opened the front door, he felt sick to his stomach. The chili burger.

It was a short drive to the park. The overhead lights gave off an eerie glow. He stopped the Vette at the entrance and scanned the lot. It was empty except for the contact's car near the rendevous point.

He hurried down the walkway, but stopped at the sound of a motor. A small foreign sedan drove into the lot and parked near his Vette. The hairs on the back of his neck prickled. Steve ran to the swings and punched a number into his cell phone, then hung up.

A man got out of the small sedan and walked to a trash can.

"Think you were followed?" A voice behind him asked.

Steve turned and gazed at his contact. "Don't know. I was careful. This city never sleeps, it could be anyone."

The man returned his pager to his coat pocket and pulled out his weapon. "Why did you call?"

"Someone's following Apollo's wife. Do you know anything?"

The man sighed. "There is no trace of Apollo in Rome. We think he's been kidnapped. The Italians said he was supposed to meet with Bruno Caminetti."

Steve froze. Peter kidnapped? Impossible. Was this the kidnapping his contact in Rome had referred to?

"Are you sure about this?" he asked as he ran a hand through his blond hair and stared at the ground. "Of course you are." He took a deep breath and lifted his eyes to meet the contact's gaze. "I do recognize the Caminetti name. When Apollo and I used to be partners, Bruno was connected to ETA, a terrorist organization."

His contact shrugged. "This could be terrorist related. The Italians found a body in one of the canals in Venice. We're hoping it's not ours."

Steve felt physically ill. The impact of the man's words went far beyond work. His sister's husband could be dead. Sweat broke out on his face and palms. He wanted to throw up. But of course he had to be in control. After all, he handled cases like this from time to time. But this one involved his old partner... his buddy... his brother-in-law. He took another deep breath to gain composure and wiped his forehead with the back of his hand.

"I want to be in charge of this investigation."

"We figured that," the man said. "You'll take care of his wife?"

A picture of Carrie earlier this evening grinning at the news of her pregnancy flashed through his mind. His heart ached. "I'll put a team on it right away and find a safe house. What's her code name?"

"Venus."

"Usual number for this?"

"Yeah, until further notice." The man turned and vanished into the night.

Steve saw the foreign car leave the lot. He forced

himself to move toward his Vette.

His mind raced through all kinds of possibilities. He needed more information, and he knew where he could get it. Italy.

He had to go.

What should he tell Carrie? His eyes moistened and he fought his emotions. He couldn't tell her anything. It was the rules. Hell, he didn't know anything anyway.

Inside the car, he started the motor and picked up his phone. Juan Castillo answered.

"Juan, you and Walker stake out Peter O'Brien's house in Dallas. Something's going on and you two are on my team."

"We're on it," Juan said.

Steve held the phone in his hand as he thought about his next move. Should he call his sister? No. She would only ask questions he couldn't answer.

He headed for home.

The phone rang as he stepped into his apartment. He checked the Caller I.D. and let the message go on the machine.

"Steve, it's Jessica. Sorry to call so late. I have to cancel tomorrow night- or is it tonight? Anyway, can't make it. It's a shame, too. I had such plans for you!"

Steve smiled and thought about her plans.

"Another time, Jessica," he whispered.

Grabbing a suitcase out of the closet, he packed enough clothes to last a few days. He hurried to the bathroom for his toiletry case and set it in the suitcase. He smiled down at the ratty old leather thing. This item had been traveling with him since his first trip to Italy. He always felt it was like a good luck charm; safe trip, catch the bad guys, safe trip back home.

The phone rang again. It was Juan.

"Hey what's up?"

"We're parked outside the pizza parlor. Would you like one large pepperoni or two?"

"One should do the trick."

"Okay. See you later."

Steve hung up and went into the kitchen for a bag of popcorn and a beer. He carried them to the couch in the living room and turned on the television to the news. Juan and his partner were set up outside the O'Brien home. They would make one sweep of the property every hour. Carrie should be fine until he made arrangements for a safe house.

He stuffed his mouth with popcorn and thought about the Agency meeting in Austin yesterday. A European terrorist group had set up a small cell somewhere around Florence. Could Peter's disappearance have anything to do with it?

Highly unlikely.

Maybe his old buddy stumbled into a bad situation. Again unlikely. Always cautious, Peter had good instincts. He took a sip of the beer and swished it around in his mouth to get rid of the popcorn stuck in his teeth.

Still. He could have been forced by others to compromise his safety... Very Likely.

There were just too many possible scenarios.

Peter and Steve belonged to a government agency tucked away under one of the larger groups within the government spy system. The agency didn't have a name, but were often called EUS, short for European Underground Surveillance. The people in his group referred to themselves as the "Agency." Steve first met Peter in college. They had the same history class their second year and became friends. When Steve told Peter he was going to apply to be a government agent, Peter decided to do the same. Steve went in first and was sent to Italy. When Peter came in, they sent him to Rome to be Steve's partner.

Their first case together was one that involved Cristo and his organization called the ETA.

At the time, this group supported many terrorist factions across Europe. Today they were even bigger,and their influence was felt across the globe.

The news ended. Steve turned the set off and crossed the room to his desk. He went on the internet and made his plane reservations for Milan. In two days he would meet with the Italians and be deep into the investigation.

Daniella stood in the lobby of a hotel in central Rome. She couldn't believe what had happened. She had been sitting in the restaurant of this hotel while Peter was kidnapped. Worse yet, Dimitri was dead. She pulled her purse higher up her shoulder and crossed her arms. She knew who was responsible for this. Bruno. Vittorio and the others should have listened. But it was useless to blame them.

Her team now questioned the hotel guests and staff, again. She would not stop until some clue was found.

Vittorio came through the front door. She could see his grief in the way he walked and the sadness haunting his eyes. He joined her and they stepped into the elevator.

"I am sorry about Dimitri," she said.

His big shoulders sagged. "It happens in this business."

They got off on the third floor. A man stood outside Peter's room. He nodded at Daniella and opened the door. Peter's bags sat on the floor untouched. There was no evidence of a struggle. The room was perfect.

"They cleaned up before they left," Daniella said. "We have gone over the room for fingerprints and of course found none."

Vittorio nodded.

"Who do you think did this?" Daniella asked.

"Bruno. We will find him. I have contacted Peter's superiors in the U.S."

Daniella stared up into the ruddy face of her co-worker. "They will send another agent."

Vittorio shrugged. "We will accept their help." He walked toward the door. "I go to the morgue. Dimitri was a good agent and a good friend. We will find the bastards."

Steve sat in the Vette at the rendezvous point. The passenger door opened and his contact got in.

"Start driving," the woman said.

"Any place in particular?"

"No. Apollo is still missing. The body found in the canal was an Italian agent."

Relief flowed through Steve. Peter is alive.

"We know more about Bruno Caminetti," the woman continued. "He had information concerning one of the terrorist splinter groups that formed after Cristo died. This organization has become powerful. Apollo was investigating money laundering connected to them and Bruno was to point out a business involved."

Steve stopped for a traffic light. "I know the organization you're talking about. They are ruthless. Aside from that, how could this situation have happened? He is always careful and this case sounds so routine."

"The Italians think it has nothing to do with the splinter group."

"What do they know that we don't? Any ideas who

could be behind this?"

The woman shook her head. "Not a clue. Turn left at the next corner and let me off at the gas station. Here's a file on the splinter group." She placed a folder on his lap.

Steve pulled into the lot.

The woman reached for the door handle.

"Start packing your bags."

"I've already made arrangements."

"Figures." The woman got out and walked down the street toward a shopping center.

Steve returned to his apartment. He grabbed two beers from the refrigerator and drank one down quickly. He paced up and down the living room, deep in thought. Questions kept repeating over and over in his mind. Why did the kidnappers kill the agent and not Peter? If it's not the terrorist group, what could be the motive? Who would want his old partner?

Peter opened his eyes. His mind was groggy and his head hurt like hell. It throbbed in time to a noise. And a swaying movement.

His mind cleared. I'm in a car.

Another sound blended in with the car noise. Someone was snoring.

He turned his head and realized he was in the backseat, and the snoring came from the front seat.

Who are these people?

"Bruno, wake up."

Peter didn't recognize the female voice, but she answered part of his question.

The snoring continued.

"Bruno, wake up!"

The snoring stopped. Bruno moved around in the front seat. "What do you want Mara? My dream was great."

"The man in the back should be waking up soon. We will stop ahead and get fuel for the car. I am hungry. You buy food for us."

"How much farther do we have to take him?"

" Hundreds of miles."

A few minutes later, the car stopped.

Peter closed his eyes and pretended to sleep. He heard the car doors open and felt a blanket covering him. Someone opened the fuel tank and he smelled gas and heard it going into the trunk. There were voices and since he spoke Italian, he could understand everything.

Mara and a man who worked at the gas station were having a conversation. The attendant was coming on to her and the woman was cold. The attendant only stayed long enough to collect the money and then Mara sat behind the wheel again. Bruno returned a few minutes later and the car pulled out.

"What did you buy?" Mara asked.

"There was only snack food. I bought drinks and a bag of potato chips. The American should like that. Their diets are bland and greasy."

"We will stop ahead for sandwiches," Mara said.

They drove on and Peter fought to stay awake, but lost.

Sometime later, he felt himself being pulled from the car and thrown over a shoulder. Peter knew it was Bruno. He recognized his scent, a combination of body odor and sweet cologne. His stomach lurched. When the Italian set him on a large rock, he looked into the face of his abductor.

Bruno sneered. "Mara! He is awake!"

The woman rushed up the hill from the car.

"So, Senor, we meet. Sorry we cannot offer a full

course meal." She laughed and gave Bruno a signal to untie their captive's feet.

As the ropes were cut, Peter could feel the blood going back into his numb feet. Then, he felt the pain and resisted making any sound. It was hard not to moan.

"Your feet do they hurt?" Bruno asked. He raised his eyebrows and laughed.

Peter wanted to push his ugly face into the rock, but his hands were still tied.

"Take him around the rock and let him relieve himself. Walk him for a few minutes and bring him back to the car."

She gestured and Peter could see the food set out on a blanket. When did they make that stop? He also realized it was evening, now. He must have been out for hours.

Bruno grabbed his arm and dragged him off the rock. Peter tried to stand, but tingles in his feet were like sharp knives cutting through him. As he was pulled forward, his feet gave out and he fell against Bruno. The man cursed and brought his body upright again.

"Walk, you piece of shit. I will not carry you."

"You have learned some bad English words, Bruno. You'd better clean up your mouth before your mother, Mara, spanks you."

"Shut up! I will beat you!" He snarled and pulled Peter forward.

"So, what happened? Did our deal fall through or is this something different?" Peter knew the man wouldn't hurt him. If that had been the objective, his body would have been covered with bruises and hurt like hell.

Bruno's expression changed from sneering to sinister. "You will find out soon."

Peter's feet felt like rocks on the end of his legs. But he could balance his body better.

"Mara!"

Standing at the car, the woman turned and looked up the hill. "What do you want now? "

Bruno pulled a gun out of his pants. "Come up here. I do not want to help him take a piss."

She hurried up the hill. Her body language saying so many things. If looks could kill, Bruno would be dead.

FOUR

Carrie washed the last of the dishes and set them in the drainer to dry. With Peter gone she didn't even bother to cook or use the dishwasher. Today, after leaving the store, she'd stopped for Chinese take-out.

She walked into the family room, turned on the television, and plopped onto the couch next to Penny. The dog jumped onto her lap and Carrie stroked her fine silky hair.

The interior decorator was due any moment. Somehow her heart wasn't in it. The house was so lonely without Peter.

He didn't call when he got to Rome.

The doorbell rang and Penny barked. Carrie scooped the dog up into her arms and hurried to the door. A woman stood outside, her arms loaded with swatches and notebooks. Carrie smiled as she opened the door.

"Mrs. O'Brien?"

"Yes."

"I'm Shelley from Baby Bunting Interiors."

Carrie opened the door wider. Penny squirmed to get down. "Come inside."

Shelley stepped into the foyer and Carrie shut the door with her hip before she set the dog on the floor.

"Oh, what a lovely home, Mrs. O'Brien. Mind if I set these things down?"

"Not at all. Let's put them in the living room."

The women went into the living room and the

interior decorator set her items on the floor next to the couch.

"Would you like tea or coffee?" Carrie asked.

"If you wouldn't mind, I'd like to see the baby's room. I don't have a lot of time this evening and I want every minute to count."

Carrie smiled. Great. We'll get this over fast.

They went upstairs and into the first bedroom on the right. The interior decorator looked around the room. Her eyes fell onto the bay window facing the street. "What a beautiful window. I've always liked window seats. They're so charming. Do you have colors in mind or a theme?"

"I want to feature characters from childhood classics instead of all this princess and macho-man stuff the kids are into today." Carrie opened the closet door. "This space should be painted the same as the room. No decorations. I haven't any ideas on colors yet."

The interior decorator clutched her small notebook firmly against her chest. A frown creased her brow. "You don't look very far along in your pregnancy. Don't you want to wait a few months before you decide on colors and a theme? You'll know what sex the child will be by then."

"I'm not having the test done," Carrie said. "I want to create a room that would suit a boy or a girl. More importantly, a baby."

The woman's eyebrow's rose. "Oh. Well. I just need to take the dimensions of the room and make a sketch.

Carrie waited in the hall as the woman measured the room. Family pictures lined the wall. Her eye caught a photo of Peter water skiing last June, when they'd visited his mother in New Jersey.

His tall lean body was tanned and he was waving at her as she stood on shore taking pictures.

His big smile told volumes. Her eyes moved to their wedding picture. He looked so handsome in his tux.

His black hair gleamed in the candlelight from the altar. It had been a perfect day.

Worry began to gnaw at her. This situation was so unusual. Should she call Steve now? Or wait another day?

Steve rang the doorbell. Penny barked. Her bright brown eyes peeked out from the glass on the side of the door. Her barks increased, but the tone changed. Her tailed wagged. Steve smiled at the crazy dog.

Carrie opened the door and grinned. "What a surprise! Just when I was feeling lonely and sorry for myself, you show up. Great!"

Steve closed the door behind him. "Can you go for a little ride?"

His sister gazed up into his face and he saw her fear. She's worried about Peter.

"Yeah. The Baby Bunting lady just left."

She grabbed her purse off the small foyer table and Steve followed her out the door and into the Vette.

He headed for the boulevard. His sister gripped the door like she thought she would need to jump out any minute.

"The Baby Bunting Lady?" he said dryly.

Carrie chuckled. "They're going to help me with the baby's room...okay, what made you drop by? Is it about Peter? He was supposed to call me from Rome and he didn't."

Steve felt bad. He didn't want to tell her.

"I've checked into a hotel nearby. I have people watching your house."

His sister turned her head toward him. "Why are

there people watching my house? Is it about the tail the other night?"

Steve shrugged. "That's one of the reasons...do you mind going to the hotel with me? I want you to know where I'm staying."

"No. I don't mind. But you'd better have some snacks handy." She grinned. "Pregnant women like to eat. Often."

Steve turned into the parking lot and found a space outside the side entrance and away from the street. They hurried up the stairs and to the second floor. He scanned the room quickly as they stepped inside, and then dead bolted the door behind him.

Carrie glanced around the suite. "This is pretty nice. All the comforts of home."

"Would you like a drink? I even have those snacks you mentioned." Steve gestured toward the mini-refrigerator. Sitting on top were bags of pretzels and chips.

She shook her head. "I don't need anything right now. Thanks anyway. Why don't you tell me the real reason we're here? It isn't just about the tail is it?"

"Why don't we sit down? I've had a busy day."

Carrie sat on the couch and Steve sat in the chair across from her.

"That's pretty pathetic," Carrie said. "I'm the one that's supposed to be tired."

He laughed. "You're right. How are you feeling?"

"I'm feeling fine. What's going on with my husband?"

Steve could see her hands knotted in her lap. This wouldn't be easy. He sighed. "I'm afraid it's bad news. We think Peter has been kidnapped."

His sister took in a huge amount of air and held it a second before blowing it out. He saw the horror register in her eyes and he felt terrible. Maybe he shouldn't have blurted it out like that. He hated himself. "Can I get you that drink now?"

Carrie stood up. Her hand went up to her mouth and she could feel her trembling lips. "I'll be right back."

She ran to the bathroom and locked the door. Tears streamed down her cheeks and she sniffed. Grabbing a tissue she looked in the mirror and wiped her mascara from under her eyes. She took another and blew her nose.

"Get yourself together," she croaked. "He didn't say Peter was dead. Just missing."

She threw the tissues away and pulled her pants down. Time for another pee. As she sat on the toilet, the tears returned and rolled down her cheeks.

A few minutes later, she returned to the living room and sat on the couch again. Her brother still sat in the chair. His eyes seemed to search her face. She could see the worry hiding behind his gaze. There was also love.

"Would you like a cup of tea?" He gestured toward a coffee pot sitting next to the refrigerator. "There's bottled water. I know how you don't like tap water."

She gazed at him and forced a weak smile. "No on the tea and yes on the water. A small glass would be nice."

He brought her the water and she sipped it. She tried to smile again to reassure him she was okay. After all, it wasn't his fault her husband was missing.

"I'm sorry. There just wasn't any other way to tell you. Maybe I could have said it better."

"Steve, I'm fine. Tell me about Peter." She had to know everything.

"All I know is that he's missing. Everyone in Italy is looking for him. The good news is that I'm in charge of finding him. You know I'll do whatever it takes to find him."

"I know you will. You have people watching my house. Does that mean you think whoever it is will want to kidnap me too?"

Steve stood up. He stuck his hands in his pants pockets.

"We don't know. I'm taking no chances. Let's go get something to eat, I'm starved."

Carrie smiled. "It's nice when someone else is starved too."

Steve opened the hotel door. "When I take you home, I'll search your house and make sure it's safe. Also, there's always the chance your phone is bugged."

Carrie's heart sank to her stomach. Her house wasn't safe? Her phone might be bugged?

Darkness enveloped him. Instinctively, he listened for any sound of people moving around. Only silence. Peter turned his head. A dull light lit up an area several yards away. His hands and feet ached, stomach too.

Where am I? It couldn't be hell, too cold and dark.

He felt underneath him. A mattress. And his hands and feet were not tied. Good.

Peter sensed he was alone and tried to sit up, but fell back down. His head swam and he groped for something to steady the movement. He wanted to cry out in frustration.

Why was he here?

His eyes closed and he forced himself to concentrate, searching for memories. There were none.

After taking several deep breaths and blowing them

out slowly, he tried to sit up again. This time he didn't fall back onto the bed. His head still swam, but objects in the room became more distinct.

He sat for what seemed an eon, feeling nauseated and staring at the dull light across the room. Then, something remarkable happened. His head cleared and he could remember things.

Bruno and Mara were his abductors.

This memory only produced more questions.

Why did they bring me here? Who are they working for? Or are they acting alone? And finally, what do they want?

He moved his body around and let his legs dangle off the bed.

"Let's try to stand up," he whispered.

His feet landed on the floor, but his legs wouldn't hold his weight and he plopped back on the bed. The springs squeaked. He cringed and hoped no one heard it.

Fighting a feeling of hopelessness, he forced himself to think of something good. An image of Carrie appeared in his head. He almost cried. Would he ever see her again? Would he ever hold his baby in his arms?

He swallowed hard and shook his head to get rid of the sentimental thoughts.

Focus on the matter at hand, his inner voice insisted. You will see Carrie again and you will hold your baby in your arms.

Peter waited a few minutes. Again, he tried to stand up. This time he didn't fall. He gingerly took a step and fell flat on his face. A moan escaped and echoed in the room. Shit, his mind screamed.

He began the job of crawling back to the bed.

Mara awakened with a start. Bruno snored and his

mouth blew a foul odor toward her. She shook him to wake him up. He turned over and snorted.

He is such a pig.

She slipped out of the bed and left the room to walk down the hall to the American. Her body leaned forward and she pressed her ear against the door. Only silence.

The drug is powerful. It will take him hours to get control of his body.

She shivered from the cold and silently cursed Bruno for not turning on the heat. Her flimsy nightgown gave no warmth. She hurried away and heard the snoring before she reached the bedroom door.

It cannot be louder. But it was.

Frustration made her want to wake him up. Her hands shot out for his head, but common sense took over.

He will only want to talk.

Peter lay on the floor and listened to the footsteps fade away. He knew it was Mara. At first, he fought panic at being discovered. Now, he was overjoyed that she didn't come inside.

He didn't care about the window across the room. It was probably nailed shut. His mind wanted to think about how he got to this place and his body needed rest before he pulled himself back onto the bed.

Memories flooded in. He remembered meeting Bruno on the bridge and following him to Rome. Everything became blank after that, except for the sandwiches. He remembered eating lunch with Bruno and Mara. Was that today? Or yesterday? Hell, it could have been a month ago. This was so damn frustrating.

Dimitri.

His room was across the hall.

What happened to him? Could he be somewhere in this house? I have to help him.

Emotions surged and he willed himself to get control.

His arms pushed his body up and he pulled himself onto the bed. A huge sigh of relief escaped. Joy filled his every being. Energy returned.

He reflected on his situation. The Agency would be looking for him by now. Help could arrive at any minute. Great- now get moving, he scolded himself.

He stood and took a step. When he didn't fall, he grinned and walked gingerly to the window.

It was nailed shut.

Stifling a laugh, he ran a hand across the pane. The glass was covered with paper. He made a little hole in the corner and squinted to look out. Nothing but darkness. He blinked several times and waited for his eyes to adjust.

Water glistened in the pale moonlight far below the window. This house was on a cliff? I'm on the coast of Italy.

"You idiot," he whispered. "It could be any coast, anywhere in the world."

As he started to walk back to bed, he felt tired and fought something foreign to him. Depression.

FIVE

Carrie pulled her nightgown over her head and propped up the pillows on the bed. She grabbed a book and slipped under the comforter. After a few minutes of reading the same paragraph over and over, she set the book back on the side table next to the lamp.

Tears formed. She couldn't concentrate on anything except her husband. Not only did she miss him, but she was worried sick about him.

Who would kidnap Peter?

She didn't like to think of the work he did. He never talked about the danger, but she knew it was there. Steve didn't have to tell her that the kidnappers could be anyone her husband had to deal with in his career.

There would be hundreds of suspects.

She wrinkled her brow and picked up her book again.

This time she couldn't get past the first sentence. Her mind wouldn't leave her alone. A memory of the day Peter left for Italy haunted her. She closed the book and eased back into the pillow.

They had sat across the kitchen table from each other eating breakfast and reading the morning paper. Peter spread jam on his wheat toast and smiled.

"When I get back, we're going on a two week vacation. Start making the arrangements!"

She was excited. "What kind of vacation?"

"I think we should start with a week in New Jersey. Mother will be so excited about the baby. From there we'll fly to the Bahamas and spend a week on the Beach, where I'll have you all to myself with no interruptions."

His dark brown eyes had sparkled.

Tears ran down her cheeks, now. She wiped them away with her fingertips. She loved him so much.

Setting the book back on the table, again, she turned out the light. Loneliness pressed into her in the dark room. She felt Penny jump up on the bed and lay against her legs. She stroked the dog's back.

A car drove past the house and she thought of the man in the gray car. Her pulse raced. Throwing the covers back, she rushed to look out the window. The car she had heard was now turning into a driveway across the street.

Her fingers grasped the curtains and squeezed hard. She took a few deep breaths and willed herself to calm down.

A dog barked. The sound caused the hairs on the nape of her neck to stand up. She instinctively moved away from the window. Steve said he had someone watching the house. Could there be others?

Around two in the morning, Juan Castillo adjusted his night vision glasses and panned the street.

"Everything looks good here, Walker. I'm going to check the back now." He turned around and faced his partner. The two agents sat in a van a few doors down the street from Carrie O'Brien's house.

Walker removed his headphones from his bald head and picked up his walkie talkie. "Okay."

Juan jumped out of the van and closed the door. He wore dark clothing and a black baseball cap covered his short black hair.

Crouching down, he hurried to the safety of the bushes a few feet away. When he thought it was safe to proceed, he quietly skirted the houses and ended up in the shadow of a big tree on the other side of the O'Brien's garage.

A car turned the corner and drove toward him. Juan crouched down lower. The car stopped two doors away and the driver killed the lights. Juan hurried toward the yard and jumped over the locked gate.

He paused and listened to the teenage voices and laughter floating down the street. He hoped they'd be gone by the time he finished the backyard.

As he kept to the bushes along the side of the fence, he noticed the lights were off in the back of the house. He used the night vision glasses to pan the backyard. Nothing back here.

His nerves were suddenly on alert. He thought he saw movement out of the corner of his left eye, but was too late to defend himself. Volts of electricity coursed through his body and he fell to the ground.

The intruder paused only a second before he rushed to the back and disabled the alarm system. Of course, he had known someone would be watching the house. He figured it was the van parked a few doors down.

The agent would be out long enough for him to grab the woman. Without a sound, he tried to open the sliding glass door off the patio. There was a stick in the glider. He frowned and hurried to a nearby window. Another stick. He chuckled softly as he reached into the pocket of his jacket and pulled out a glass cutter. Using precious minutes, he returned to the glass door. He knelt down and cut a large hole. After removing the stick, he jimmied the lock and slid the door open.

The house was quiet. He didn't know the layout, but knew the woman's bedroom overlooked the street.

He pulled a knife from his pocket and gripped it tightly as he walked up the stairs. The dog would have to be dealt with swiftly.

The first bedroom was empty. The second room, an office. As he approached the third room, he heard the dog growl.

His footsteps were quick as he found the side of the bed, close to the window. The bed was empty. Where was she? Did he have the wrong room?

A sudden jarring pain in his shoulder caused him to turn. He reached toward his attacker, but cried out instead from a sharp stabbing pain in his left ankle.

He grabbed the woman's arm. Her high pitched scream broke the silence of the night. He looked down and saw her dog's teeth sunk into his ankle.

The woman struggled and he tried to steady her while he dealt with the dog. The mutt growled and pressed its teeth in deeper. He lunged with his knife to kill the animal, but the woman dug her fingernails into his neck.

He smacked her face.

She screamed louder.

"Shit!" he said in Italian. His instructions were to not harm the woman in any way. She was making that order difficult to follow.

He threw her down. The dog let go. He ran down the hall and took the stairs three at time.

The dog nipped at his heels and the woman screamed louder as he ran into the foyer. Seconds later he was outside running toward the back of the yard with the dog close behind. When the lights came on in the house, he went over the fence and became lost in the dark.

Agent Bart Walker heard the screaming and barking. He picked up his walkie talkie.

"Juan."

No answer.

"Juan."

Walker checked his weapon, picked up his flashlight, and put on his ball cap. He opened the van door and scanned the immediate area. All clear. Crouching down, he ran to the gate at the side of the O'Brien's house.

He shined the flashlight over the gate and around the side of the yard. He saw the still form of his partner lying nearby.

After jumping the gate, he knelt down and felt for a pulse then checked for injuries. He lifted Juan, opened the gate, and ran to the van. As he drove away from the house, lights came on all over the neighborhood. He glanced at the O'Brien's and saw a man dressed in sweats banging on the front door.

One street over, he passed a black and white heading for the house. Once on the boulevard he picked up his phone.

Steve reached over and answered on the fourth ring.

"Yeah," he breathed.

"Someone got past the security system and broke into the home."

He recognized Walker's voice. "Is Carrie okay?"

"I think so; the police just passed me on the way to her house. Juan is injured. The intruder attacked him when he entered the backyard. I'm taking him to the hospital."

"I'll be at the house with Carrie. When you know

something, find me."

Steve sat on the edge of the bed. The surveillance had been justified, and not a minute too soon.

The phone rang again. He picked it up and didn't have a chance to answer.

"Steve! Someone broke into the house!"

Her anxious teary voice told it all. She had been terrorized.

"Stay in the house, Carrie. I'm on my way over."

The lights from the cruisers bounced around the neighborhood. Carrie stood at her bedroom window and watched the drama acting out in front of her house. Two squad cars were parked in her driveway, a few minutes ago the ambulance left and right now two more cars pulled up to the curb. Her hand flew to her mouth when she saw her neighbors huddled in a group watching the police.

She turned and sat on the bed slipping an afghan around her shoulders, trying to get warm. Her hands trembled. She knew the intruder was gone, but her body felt like he was somewhere outside watching her.

Penny jumped on the bed and Carrie pulled her close. "You're my heroine, Penny." She gave the little dog a hug and set her on the floor. "Let's go downstairs and wait for Steve."

The dog followed Carrie down the stairs and into the foyer. She glanced into the family room and saw someone standing at the open sliding glass door. The light was on in the yard, and a uniformed officer stood at the back fence. Two others were at the front door, as if guarding her from the world.

Melancholy shot through her like poison from a dart. She needed Peter to be here with her. Where was he?

Penny ran into the living room and she followed her

to the couch. The dog jumped into her lap. A moist tongue licked Carrie's hand, the nervous tension started to ebb.

Steve walked up the steps of the house and presented his I.D. to one of the patrolmen standing at Carrie's front door.

The officer passed him in and Steve stopped in the foyer taking in all the activity.

He glanced into the living room and saw his little sister on the couch, clutching her dog as if it was a life line. Her sunken shoulders made his heart lurch. She turned her head and their eyes locked. He walked in and sat next to her on the couch. Tears ran down her cheeks, he drew her against his chest

"Tell me what happened," he whispered.

"A man broke into the house," started Carrie. Her voice cracked. She paused to swallow. "Penny growled when the man started up the stairs and it woke me up. I grabbed her and the lamp. We hid in the closet. He came into the room and bent over the bed... I stepped out with the lamp and swung it at him. I aimed for his head, but he was so tall I struck his arm or shoulder."

Her hands trembled. A crumpled tissue dropped into her lap and she picked it up to wipe her nose. "Penny wouldn't let go of him and when I screamed, he grabbed me. Then he hit me. He said something in a foreign language as he ran out the door. Penny followed him. I dialed 911."

Steve saw the bruise on her face where the man had struck her and vowed to find the low life that did this to her.

"I'm glad you're okay, Sis. Sounds like you and Penny did a good job of protecting yourselves."

He glanced toward the foyer and saw Walker standing in the living room doorway.

"Sweetie, I'll be right back."

Steve and Walker stepped outside and stood away from the house.

"How's Juan?"

"The doctor said he'll be okay. He has to spend the night in the hospital. Juan said the guy used a stun gun."

Steve narrowed his brows. This wasn't a random burglary. It was as he suspected, whoever took Peter was also after Carrie.

"Find a safe house."

Walker left and Steve went inside and stood above his sister. His jaw tightened as he held his hand out to her.

"Let's go upstairs and pack a bag. You're coming with me."

The tall thin man dialed the number. When the caller picked up, he recognized the man's voice.

"I could not get the woman. The police had her house staked out and her brother is with her. He is too close for me to try again."

"Come home. I will use others now. There is another job for you to do."

Lorenzo hung up and thought about the situation. The agent would go to Italy soon, and take Peter's wife.

The old black and white movie from the forties droned on. Steve sat in a recliner and stared at the television. He had no idea what the story was about. The only thing on his mind was smoking a cigarette.

It had been years since he had smoked one, but tonight had really unnerved him and the only thing he could think about right now was a lousy cigarette.

He turned his head and glanced at Carrie sleeping soundly on the bed with her dog curled up beside her. No one else would get the job of protecting her. He'd see to that.

Where in the hell was Peter?

This situation was becoming more and more complicated. The same people had to be responsible.

He stuck his gun under a pillow and lay down.

Once he turned the television off and covered himself with a blanket, he fell into a deep sleep. There was a man outside the door and two in a car in the lot; he could allow himself this indulgence.

SIX

Early the next day, after dropping Carrie and her dog at a safe house on Inwood Road, Steve turned onto Mockingbird Lane and headed for the LBJ freeway. He was on his way to Fort Worth to take time off work, and meet his contact.

He knew the editor at the Fort Worth Daily Register would gladly let him off. The job was a good cover. Steve suspected the man was somehow connected to the Agency.

He entered the freeway and maneuvered into the fast lane.

His mind switched to the attempted abduction the night before. He frowned. The case was heating up. He knew his final destination would be Italy, but his sister's situation weighed heavily on his mind. He spent the next ten minutes thinking about his options.

At the Stockyards in Fort Worth, he parked in the lot and walked into the old historical district where he entered a novelty store near the train tracks. The middle-aged man behind the counter moved to the other side of the store to help another customer.

Steve hurried to a souvenir rack close to a window that had a good view of the train tracks and the street outside. A man wearing a brown leather jacket and carrying a newspaper walked past the store and stopped in a shaded area near the street. Steve grabbed an armadillo key chain off a rack and hurried to the counter.

The middle-aged man appeared and rang up the sale.

"A pack of cigarettes too," Steve said. He pointed to the ones he wanted.

He paid and put the key chain in his pocket.

Once outside, Steve waded through a crowd gathered to watch the longhorns walk to their pens at the other end of the street. Vaqueros rode next to them. Tourists snapped pictures.

Steve stopped next to his contact and pulled a cigarette out of his pocket. "Excuse me, do you have a light?"

The man turned and smiled. He lit Steve's cigarette. "I thought you gave those up a long time ago."

"I did. Do you have any news?" He turned his head and blew a plume of smoke into the air. His eyes scanned the immediate area.

"Apollo hasn't been found. We have a team outside his mother's estate and one outside your sister's house in California. We're investigating the incident with Venus. It's time for you to go to Italy."

The man walked away, following the steers down the street. Steve hurried to his car. As he headed for the newspaper office, Carrie's dilemma continued to haunt him.

Several hours later, he opened the door at the safe house. Carrie sat on the couch watching television and eating a sandwich. She glanced at him as he came through the door.

"How do you like your new home?" Steve asked.

Carrie scowled. "I hope we don't have to stay here a long time. Where's Penny?"

"Walker took her to your vet."

She stood up and sucked in a huge breath. "Is she sick? You didn't tell me she was going to the vet."

He cursed himself for being so stupid. "Calm down, Sis. She's not sick."

"Why did she go to the vet?" Carrie sat back down on the couch.

"They're going to board her for a while. We may have to leave this house on a moment's notice. It isn't fair to Penny to put her through all that. When we're settled, we'll get her."

Her eyes teared up.

Uh-oh, here it comes. He knew his sister wouldn't let it rest.

Steve hurried to the kitchen and opened the refrigerator. Which beer should he have and should he have more than one?

"Can I see her later? Or is that risky?"

He took a beer out of the fridge and shut the door. Carrie stood in the kitchen doorway, staring at him.

"Yeah."

He walked into the living room with his sister on his heels.

Mara shut the door of the small peach-colored house and walked downhill toward the street that would take her into town. She could hear the waves breaking on the rocks below and the gulls crying as they flew above her and out over the Ligurean Sea.

She smiled, something she didn't do very often. She loved it here. Her grandmother's house sat at the end of a street of houses perched on a cliff. Happy memories from her childhood came flooding back, but she only lingered on them for a few minutes, her thoughts had to be on business only.

The smile vanished.

Bruno was off somewhere with secret instructions from the boss. Mara laughed inside. He was such a stupid man. She could not understand how he had been of such importance several years ago in the south of Italy. She was much smarter.

He had a tendency to drink too much.

He could be surly and uncooperative, but Bruno had one redeeming quality; he followed orders to the letter. That was why she had agreed to work with him. At the intersection, she turned and headed toward the grocery store located close to the railroad tracks. Off to her left, the surf softly hit the beach. This would be a great day for a swim. Too bad she had to babysit the American.

I am tired of playing the role of jailer. She fought a strong feeling of resentment. Bruno should be here and she should be with the boss.

Several feet later, she entered the tunnel leading to the old part of Monterosso al Mare, a city located in the Cinque Terra on the northwest coast of Italy.

She grabbed the shopping list out of her purse. Tomorrow they would move the prisoner again, but tonight she would cook a traditional meal for him and Lorenzo. The tall thin man had arrived an hour ago with instructions. Bruno had been surly to Lorenzo.

Mara smiled. He did not know how dangerous his actions could be.

Peter watched Mara from his window high above the street. He felt helpless. This morning, Bruno had put leg chains on his ankles while Mara held a gun with a silencer. He remembered the look in her eyes. Although he felt whoever was behind his abduction wanted him alive, he was certain Mara wouldn't have hesitated to wound him, and a wound would only complicate his problem.

About an hour ago, Bruno left in the van. He had

returned a few minutes later with a stranger. A tall thin man with long hair.

Could this new guy be a sign that the mastermind of this fiasco wasn't too far away? He must have brought orders with him. Bruno left within minutes.

Who could be behind this operation?

He knew it wasn't Bruno or Mara. He searched his brain trying to remember past cases in Italy where his cover had been compromised. His effort was fruitless.

His attention returned to Mara. He noticed she had a naturally seductive walk that many men would find alluring. She reminded him of someone he had not thought about for a very long time, Alissa DiBiasi.

He remembered her long, luscious black hair and her deep sensuous eyes. Of course, her beauty had been far greater than Mara's. Many men had found her voluptuous body arousing and she had known how to use that to her advantage.

Alissa had been more than just a beautiful woman, she had been a spy. Over the years he had always hoped that she had survived the explosion on the yacht. He liked to think of her having fun and seducing half the men in Europe. He smiled and turned away from the window.

He gazed around the room, his prison.

His feet shuffled back to the bed. Fatigue washed over him.

It's all those damned drugs they've been giving me. He wanted to punch something, but didn't have the energy.

Carrie stood in her dark bedroom and slipped on her robe. It had been hours since they ate and she was hungry. She couldn't help it if it was the middle of the night.

She tiptoed down the dark hall toward the kitchen. Passing Steve's door, she noticed his lights were out. Good, he's getting some sleep. If anyone needed to sleep, it was her brother. This incident had shown her how hard he worked and how stressed out he could get.

She entered the kitchen, not turning on the light. Her hand clasped the refrigerator door.

The hairs on the back of her neck stood up.

Someone is watching me.

She couldn't move. Fear held onto to her and wouldn't let go. Tears welled up in her eyes. She got mad and forced herself to turn toward the small kitchen window.

Her hand reached over and pulled the curtain aside so she could look out into the darkness. The street appeared deserted except for a car's tail light leaving the front of the house.

"Close the curtain, Sis."

Her body jumped and a tiny scream escaped. Her hand flew up to her chest. She turned toward the voice and saw Steve standing at the kitchen doorway.

"What's going on? Why are you standing in here with the light off?" he asked.

The heartbeats slowed down, but the anxiety didn't. Anger came forth from some foreign place. She hardly ever showed anger.

"You scared the life out of me! I'm still shaking. You could've hurt my baby!"

Tears ran down her cheeks. She didn't care.

Steve rushed over and closed the curtain with one hand while he pulled her close to him with the other.

"I'm sorry, Carrie. The window has to stay closed for security reasons."

"But you have men outside taking care of us, don't you?"

"Yes. But they don't control who comes up and down the street."

Carrie didn't want to talk anymore and she was even hungrier. She opened the refrigerator door. "I'm starving. I didn't want to wake you up."

Steve gently touched her shoulder.

"Sit down. I'll make you whatever you want ... I need to talk to you."

He turned the light on and took a small bottle of water off the counter, tossing it to her. "Drink some of this to start. It'll help calm you down. Sorry I frightened you."

She caught the water and sat down at the kitchen table. Her fingers threaded through her blonde silky hair. "I'm so bored. I miss Penny and my business is faltering!"

Steve stared at her. "Have you called your office?"

"No. You told me not to... But I've been tempted."

"Walker's been keeping an eye on your store. It's doing well, even though you may think it's not." He sighed. "We've been over this a few times, Carrie. What's really wrong?"

Steve took eggs out of the refrigerator along with cheese. Sometimes he practically lived on omelets. His sister hadn't answered his question yet. Without looking at her, he knew from past experience that she was carefully thinking about her response.

"How much longer do we have to hide?" Her voice sounded strained. "Do you think that awful man is still out there waiting to kidnap me?"

He glanced over his shoulder. Her eyes were huge and full of fear. At that moment he knew he couldn't leave her. If something bad happened, he'd never forgive himself. But it would be risky to take her along. His only option was one that he'd been gnawing on since meeting with his contact earlier. He quickly formed his plan.

The eggs were done and he slipped them on a plate and reached for the toast. He turned around and smiled at her. "This safe house was a good idea, but I think we can find something better."

Carrie stiffened. "Are we going somewhere else?"

Her soft voice was filled with apprehension.

"Yes. Tomorrow morning I'll take you home to pack more of your things. On the way we can stop at the vet and you can see Penny for a few minutes. Then, we're flying to your mother-in- law's estate in New Jersey."

Carrie froze. She wasn't going home. Her business might collapse, and Peter could be dead. Her life wasn't hers anymore.

She felt lost.

Gathering as much strength as she could muster, she sat straight up and eyed her brother.

"I'm ready."

Steve bent over and grabbed her hand.

"I'll help you through this," he whispered.

SEVEN

Marian O'Brien stepped out of her bedroom dressed for a book signing. The limo had arrived a few minutes ago; she'd seen it from her bedroom window. She needed to talk to Raoul before she left. Carrie and Steve would be here in the early afternoon and she wanted to make sure all was taken care of for their stay.

She sighed and walked toward the end of the hall. This business with Peter being missing and two or three agents outside her house, and now the unexpected company, added to her stress. She didn't like stress. It curbed her creativity.

Raoul Ortiz, her personal assistant, met her at the foot of the stairs. His dark eyes bore through her. Marian loved it when he did that. She felt like he had ex-ray vision, checking to see if she was physically well, mentally alert.

She smiled. "Good morning, Raoul, everything covered for our unexpected guests?"

He grinned and her heart melted. He aroused so much passion in her. "Yes, my dear, all is under control. You go off to your book signing and sell lots of novels. I will take care of everything."

"I'll be back in time for tea

He took her arm and walked her to the door where her large briefcase sat waiting for her. Raoul thought of everything.

He pulled her into his strong arms and kissed her. It was a sensual kiss. Marian felt it go through her body all the way to her toes.

She had described this many times in her books, but had never experienced it until Raoul had come into her life. She returned his kiss and he eased away, giving her a little nudge toward the door.

"Your limo is waiting; we don't have time for this stuff." His brows lifted. "We'll finish this tonight." Raoul opened the door and she went out onto the porch of her mansion. It was a sunny day and she was glad. Too much to deal with in her personal life for the weather to be bad. Hal, her regular driver, opened the car door for her.

"Good morning, Hal." She slipped onto the back seat and the driver set her briefcase next to her.

"Good morning, Mrs. O'Brien. Nice day to meet your public!"

Marian chuckled as he closed the door and went around the back to get in on the driver's side. He slipped behind the wheel and started the motor. As he pulled out and headed down the drive, Marian looked back and saw Raoul going inside the house. She felt so lucky to have him.

When he turned off the drive, Hal tipped his hat at the federal agents sitting in a car on the street. Marian cringed. She already wanted this all to end.

Peter paced up and down his room, hands on hips, brows furrowed. A few minutes ago, as he watched from the window, Mara and Bruno loaded luggage and groceries into a different van. This one was blue. The tall man stood nearby supervising the project.

Who is this new guy? He and Bruno were definitely not friends.

When the Italian had returned earlier, the new guy had met him in the yard. The body language between them had told Peter a few things. Number one, Bruno was afraid of this man.

Footsteps on the stairs caused excitement to flow through him. They're coming for me.

He sat on the bed and waited. Seconds later, the door flew open and his eyes locked with Bruno's.

"Are we going on vacation?" Peter asked.

Bruno's lips pulled back into a sneer. "Stand up and turn around."

Peter did as he was told, placing his hands behind his back. He tried not to grimace as Bruno tied them tighter than necessary and grabbed his arm, pulling him toward the door.

"Who's your new friend? He's better looking than you. Will you lose your place in Mara's bed now?"

"Shut up!" Bruno squeezed Peter's arm like a vise. "I will gag your insolent mouth if you do not shut up!"

Peter stifled an urge to laugh. He knew Bruno wouldn't hurt him. The man would have done so by now.

They walked down the stairs and out the front door. Mara was behind the wheel with the tall man in the passenger seat.

Peter kept his eyes away from the new person, but he could feel his coldness as he passed the window. Bruno shoved him into the van and he settled in the back. The strength and cruelty of the tall man hung in the air.

Bruno jumped inside and shut the door as Mara started the motor. She pulled out of the driveway and headed down the street toward the intersection. Peter stared out the window at the water and gulls. He didn't recognize this place.

His kidnapper crawled into the back with him. The

Italian's cold black eyes held a fiendish amusement. Peter braced himself. Bruno stuck a needle into his arm.

"How much longer?" Carrie asked. "This day is wearing me out and if I don't get there in the next five minutes, you'll have to hunt down a bathroom."

"Five miles, Sis."

"Thank you, God," Carrie said under her breath.

Ten minutes later, Walker turned onto the drive of the O'Brien estate. Steve whistled. "Wow! Trashy romance novels must be in great demand."

Carrie nudged him in the ribs. "Don't say that. Marian's books are popular. She gets a lot of writing awards."

Steve laughed. "Walker, park at the front door. Then go down and tell those other guys to go home for a couple of days. I've already cleared it with their superiors."

"Will do, Boss."

The car pulled to a stop and the front door was opened by a muscular Hispanic man of average height.

"That's Raoul," Carrie said.

Raoul held the door open wide and Steve followed Carrie into the foyer. "Marian is upstairs changing clothes. She just got back from a book signing."

Steve held out his hand. "I'm Steve Crawford. Carrie said you're Raoul?"

The man clasped his hand. The handshake was strong and firm. The eyes were piercing and vibrant. Steve was immediately on alert.

"Yes." He gestured toward a room off the foyer. "Please have a seat in the living room. We'll serve tea in a few minutes. There's a restroom down the hall if you'd like to wash up."

Juan set the luggage down in the foyer.

Carrie headed for the bathroom.

"Raoul this is Juan. Where should we put the luggage?" Steve asked.

"Upstairs." Raoul reached down and grabbed several bags and began to walk toward the stairway. "I will help. You and Carrie get settled for tea."

Juan raised his eyebrows as he picked up the remaining luggage. He mouthed the words, "you owe me" as he passed Steve and followed Raoul.

Steve grinned.

Walker strolled into the foyer. "The men left. Charlie's here. Left him down at the foot of the drive for now."

"Good. We'll start the watch as we planned. There's a restroom on this floor and the bedrooms are upstairs. You and Charlie take the first watch."

Carrie came out of a room down the hall and Walker headed toward her. "Will do. Better take care of business first."

Steve waited for his sister and they stepped into the living room. He wanted to let out another whistle, but held himself back. Even though he was independently wealthy himself, having inherited a sizable amount of money from his paternal grandfather, he didn't live in this kind of splendor.

The room had a large window which looked out on the grounds.

Steve walked closer and stared out at the beautiful landscaped estate. He went behind the bar in the corner and checked out the liquor. Well stocked.

"Steve!" Carrie said. "Don't you think that's rude?"

He turned to her and laughed. "Maybe."

She sat down on the couch that faced a granite fireplace. He walked over and sat in a large chair nearby. The room was cozy yet opulent.

Marian pulled on her riding boots. They were new and a little too tight.

She stood up and walked a few steps around the bedroom.

Her book signing had been great. One of the book clubs in the area had shown up and people from her fan club, too. Lunch had been set up at the back of the store and it had been fun, but hectic. She glanced at her watch. Tea first and then a ride. She was looking forward to seeing Carrie again, even though the circumstances were awful.

Two raps on the door. Raoul stepped in wearing his riding clothes. Marian smiled.

"Am I having company today?" she asked.

Raoul slipped his arm around her shoulders and lead her into the hall and toward the stairs.

"I thought you needed a treat today. How did things go at the book store?" He kissed her hair.

"It went well. How's Pamela holding up in the kitchen for tonight's dinner? Has anyone canceled?"

"Pamela is doing her usual stuff. Because of the special circumstances, Vince has agreed to stay and help."

"What will we do with our guests?"

"How about the conservatory?"

"Oooh, I like that idea. It's one of Carrie's favorite places in the house. And she isn't always here at this time of year. Great. Everything is covered."

"Well, not quite, my dear. You need to talk to Steve about tonight and especially tomorrow night. He may not know about our plans."

"Ummm. Good idea."

They reached the bottom step and Marian turned.

Raoul's lips brushed hers.

"I'm looking forward to our ride," she said.

"Me also. You join your company. I will get Pamela to serve the tea now."

Steve stood when Marian entered the room. He was surprised to see her in riding clothes. He hoped there weren't too many other surprises.

But then, what did he expect? He had just thrown himself and Carrie and the others on her at the last minute.

Marian rushed to her daughter-in-law on the sofa. "I'm so happy to see you." She sat down and pulled Carrie into her arms. "It's awful about Peter's dilemma. I know things will work out well for him."

Carrie's eyes watered. "Thanks, Marian. It must be hard on you too."

She dug into her purse for a tissue.

Raoul entered the room and sat in a chair close to Steve.

"It's too bad you had to cancel your party for Saturday," Marian said. "I was looking forward to seeing your family again."

"It isn't as bad as what Peter's going through right now." Carrie wiped her nose.

A middle aged woman with ample hips and long blonde hair entered the living room with the tea service. She set it on the large coffee table in front of Marian.

"Thanks, Pamela," Marian said.

Steve watched the woman leave the room and wondered how many other servants Marian employed.

Their hostess picked up a cup. "Carrie would you like tea or coffee?"

"Tea, please. Only lemon."

Marian handed her the tea. "Steve?"

"Coffee, black."

As Steve took the cup, their eyes met. "By the way, Steve, I'm not sure you know, but we're having a dinner party tonight."

Steve's eyebrows flew up. "Really?"

"It was approved by the other security people," Raoul said.

Steve turned to face Raoul. "Anything else I should know?"

Raoul waved off a cup of coffee from Marian. "Yes. The dinner tonight is for seven people who have all been approved by your security. The reason for the dinner is to go over what will take place tomorrow night, at the gala. There will be close to three hundred people here, roaming the grounds."

Steve couldn't believe his ears. If the other agents had approved tonight, then tomorrow must also be approved. What could he do? "We need to talk about this."

Raoul nodded.

"Well, since you have such nice surprises for me, I think Carrie has one for you. Don't you Carrie?" Steve stared at his sister.

Carrie grinned as she set her cup down on the table. "Yes. I'm pregnant."

Marian sucked in air. Her mouth formed an "o". She threw her arms around her daughter-in-law again. Her smile was radiant. "That is such great news. Does Peter know?"

"Yes, he does," Steve said. He had to answer for his sister because Marian hadn't let up on the bear hug. And from where he sat, it looked like a pretty tight squeeze.

Raoul, wearing a big grin, went to the bell pull on the wall. "This calls for a celebration."

A few minutes later, Pamela wheeled in a cart with a huge white cake decorated in pink and blue. "Happy Pregnancy" was written in the middle of it.

Carrie's hands flew up to her face. "How did you know?"

"Peter called when you first found out. Swore me to secrecy. When you canceled your party and were coming here, I ordered the cake." Raoul grinned at his boss.

Marian's eyes lit up. "Thanks, Raoul."

After everyone was served, Steve placed his coffee cup on the table. "That was good cake. Can I have two pieces to go?"

Everyone laughed.

A few minutes later, armed with two pieces of cake, he was out the front door headed for Charlie sitting in the car at the foot of the driveway.

His mind raced. These new details disturbed him. If the man that broke in at Carrie's house had followed them here, tonight and tomorrow night could leave them all vulnerable. Had he put his sister in more jeopardy and added more work for himself and his team?

Charlie Wong rolled down his window as Steve approached. Steve was glad to have Charlie; he had proven himself invaluable a number of times since joining the team two months ago.

Charlie took the cake.

"Any problems?" Steve asked.

"Nope. There's a substantial amount of traffic, but no one has even slowed down when they passed the estate. Where's my fork? Is someone having a birthday?"

Steve grinned. He took a fork out of his pocket and handed it to Charlie. "No birthday. They're celebrating Carrie's good news... we'll be having company this evening. Think we can handle seven dinner guests?"

Chewing a big mouthful of cake, Charlie nodded.

"Here's a list of the guests. They'll start arriving in three hours. Before that, leave the car on the street and stand at the door. Check everyone's I.D. and compare it to the list."

"Where's the coffee?" Charlie asked before he stuffed more cake into his mouth.

Steve could see water bottles sitting on the passenger seat of the car. "You'll have to get that later."

He left Charlie to enjoy his dessert and walked to the back of the estate. Walker sat near the pool in the shade.

"I see you don't want to get that bald head of yours sunburned."

Walker took the cake. "Yeah, forgot my hat."

"Did Mrs. O'Brien and her assistant come out here?"

"Yes. They walked to the stables and rode off a few minutes ago. Somebody having a birthday?"

"No... We're having company tonight. Seven guests. Keeping to our schedule. Tell Juan when he relieves you and remind him there's cake in the kitchen."

Steve checked his watch as he headed for the house. In two hours he had to relieve Charlie for an hour. Right now he had to call his contact.

Marian's library was across from the living room at the front of the house. The safe line had been installed in that room. He stepped inside and dialed the contact's number. The man answered on the third ring.

"It's about time you called. What's going on?"

"We got here without an incident. I sent the other security home. But now have a new situation. There's a dinner party here tonight and some sort of big gala thing tomorrow night. This complicates everything."

"I agree. What do you need?"

"We should be okay tonight. Tomorrow we'll need the other three agents back here and they can leave after the shindig is over. Anything new on Peter?"

"No, the trail is cold. The Italian's are waiting for you in Milan. I'll send help for tomorrow."

The man hung up.

Marian led her horse down the first trail. She glanced over at Raoul and smiled. He never went along on her rides, allowing her to have free time.

She usually came up with new ideas for her stories when she rode alone. Her mind was already churning. Her assistant had a gun beneath his jacket. She had felt it when she embraced him in the study before coming out to the stables. She didn't know why the gun would surprise her. She was always finding out new things about him.

"Do you remember the first day we met?" she asked.

Raoul stared straight ahead. "Yes, my dear, you were signing your books at the mall. I offered to buy you coffee. You refused."

Marian laughed. "I'd never been to Tampa Bay before. The whole trip was eye opening. I refused everyone's invitations."

"Yes, but I didn't take no for an answer."

"You were sneaky. Calling my son to get a date!"

"Lucky for me, Peter was accommodating. Our dinner together that night was entertaining." He turned and grinned. "You were so shocked to see me turn up at your table. And when I asked you to sign the book I bought that day, you laughed."

"That's because it was the only one I sold! And you bought it while I was gone to get a latte. Maybe I would have had coffee with you if you'd asked me to sign your book before I left the store."

"You still would have refused me. You thought I was a serial killer or a rapist."

Marian laughed again. "I did say that, didn't I? I'm so glad you persisted. My life just wouldn't have been as exciting without these last few years."

"Or mine so entertaining. I think you said that stuff about the rapist because you were already lusting for me."

Marian gasped. "You are so full of yourself, Raoul. Every woman in the world isn't in love with you."

But, Marian thought, every woman in the world would find something about him to like.

He was all man.

Most women would have brought up marriage by now. The subject had been discussed once, and both had rejected it. Marian had such a horrible divorce experience with her ex-husband; she wasn't ready to take the big step again. And Raoul's wife of thirty years had died in a car crash two years before she met him. He seemed to like being a bachelor.

"The weather is cooperating today," Raoul said.

Marian looked around at the grass and the squirrels. The sun was filtering through the trees that lined the trail. She felt cheery.

"Yes, the day is beautiful. Warm enough for a little dip in the pool."

She glanced at him and their eyes met. She loved him very much. He had been the best thing that had ever happened to her, besides her children. She remembered in bed last night when they had made love. That was one of the things they had in common. Lust and sexual appetite. Of course, it wasn't like when they were twenty. Everything changes when you hit your fifties.

"Get your mind out of the bedroom, my dear. We need to discuss the dinner party you have scheduled for tonight."

Marian laughed. How did he know what she'd been thinking? "Do we need to go over it again? You've taken care of everything, right?"

"Yes, I have. So, we will talk about your son. You are worried about him. He will be fine. Steve and the government agency he works for will find Peter and bring him home soon."

"My mind knows this, but my body just wants to cry." Marian said.

Tears appeared and ran down her cheeks. She quickly wiped them away. "I always go through this when he stays a little longer on a trip. It's worse now, because he's missing."

"I know, my love. Your emotions get the better of you. That's why you are such a gifted writer."

He raised his reins and grinned. "Let's give these horses a run today. I know I can beat you to the pond."

Marian spurred her horse faster down the trail, trying to catch up with Raoul. She soon forgot her melancholy as a new idea for her latest novel popped into her mind.

EIGHT

In the kitchen, located at the back of the mansion, Pamela poured ice into a silver bucket and put the lid on it. She turned and faced Raoul. "The ice is ready."

Dressed in a tux for the special occasion, he stood at a nearby counter placing hors d'oeuvres on a tray. His mind was going over everything that had to be done.

Pamela cleared her throat.

Raoul put the last hors d'oeuvre on the tray and raised his head. A frown creased his brow. "Okay, Pamela." He crossed the kitchen and picked up the bucket. "Let me know if you need more help. I'll send one of the security guys."

Pamela laughed. "Don't bother, I'd rather do it all myself... While you're there, check the trays in the living room."

Raoul nodded. He headed out of the kitchen and down the main hall. Vince stood at the front door greeting guests and showing them into the living room.

"Vince," Raoul said. "Take the ice."

The houseboy grabbed the bucket and Raoul followed him into the living room. He stopped at the coffee table and watched Vince continue on to the bar.

While switching all the food to one tray and filling the empty one with dirty glasses and napkins, Raoul saw Vince set the ice bucket down and return to the front door.

One swift look around the room and he picked up the tray and returned to the hall.

"Vince, take this to the kitchen and help Pamela."

The houseboy took the tray and hurried down the hall.

Raoul greeted a few guests and wondered what was keeping Marian. Time to check on her. He turned and stepped away from the door leaving the new arrivals to fend for themselves. He stopped when he saw her standing at the foot of the staircase. She shortened the distance between them.

"Dinner is on schedule," Raoul said. "You look beautiful, my dear." He admired her black lace cocktail dress and the astonishing new necklace she'd bought last week.

"Thanks." She touched the white gold pendant with three carats worth of diamonds. "I love my necklace."

"You should, it cost a small fortune." He grinned. "But you can afford it."

Marian squeezed his arm. "See you later."

She took her place at the door and Raoul rushed to the kitchen.

Carrie sat at a table in the conservatory admiring the beautiful flowers and plants. This was her favorite room in Marian's huge house. But even the ambiance couldn't cheer her up.

She was so bored. She'd spent the entire day in her bedroom reading and watching movies. Besides missing her husband and dog, she also yearned to be at her store. And not being able to have communication with her employees was grating on her nerves. Her eyes scanned the table setting. It was Almost romantic, with candles and beautiful china.

She thought about her husband and her heart ached. Not only was she worried about him, she missed him so much. Forcing back her emotions, she picked up her crystal glass and took a sip of sparkling water.

Footsteps sounded on the mosaic tile.

"Wow, this is beautiful."

Steve crossed the floor and joined Carrie at the table.

Her brother looked handsome tonight. His short blond hair was combed into an actual style and the dressy clothes made him look like a male model. She'd forgotten just how handsome he could be.

"It is beautiful. Have all the guests arrived?"

"Yes. They're gathered in the living room eating munchies and swigging down the booze."

Carrie laughed. "You sound so crass. Marian probably serves the best money can buy."

"She certainly appears to have the money."

"Well, three of her books were made into movies."

Steve whistled. "That would buy a lot of canapes and wine."

Raoul cleared his throat as he entered the room.

Carrie turned her head and smiled. "Raoul, what a great choice of scenery for dinner. Thanks."

Her mother-in-law's assistant smiled. "Vince is on his way with the cart. The guests will eat their meal in half an hour, and then will come in here for their coffee and a meeting."

"We'll be long gone by then," Steve said.

Vince wheeled in the cart and started serving the dinner. Raoul helped him and the two of them left.

Carrie took a bite of the roasted capon. She wanted to ask about Peter. Should she do it now, or wait until after dinner?

Her brother picked up his wine glass and took a sip.

His forehead creased and eyes squinted when he set the glass down. She knew he was about to tell her some bad news.

Steve's frown deepened. "There isn't any news of Peter...But in a way that's good."

"And in other ways, it's bad?" Carrie felt like her heart was being squeezed by a vise. She didn't want to allow her mind to dwell too much on her husband's situation. She conjured up too many tortuous things.

"Sis, don't worry so much. I'm going to Italy soon. Would you mind staying here with Marian? I think she'd probably love to have you."

Carrie thought that if she couldn't be at home anymore, than this would be a great place to stay. "What about Penny?"

"You'd better ask Marian about the dog. But wait until I've asked her to let you stay. That way we won't be putting her on the spot."

Throughout her young adult life, Carrie had heard Steve talk about the various countries he'd traveled to for fun and for work. He'd never told any personal accounts about those trips. This might be a good time to press him for more details. "So, you're going to Italy? When was the last time you were there?"

"You know I can't tell you that bit of information."

"Do you have a girlfriend over there?"

Steve almost choked on the chicken he was chewing. Carrie found that amusing, but didn't let him know.

"I don't have a girlfriend at the moment," he said.

"Does that mean that you've had one in the past? Lord, I would hope so."

Steve raised his eyebrows. "Getting a little nosy aren't you?" He grinned and took another sip of his drink. "I did have a pretty serious girlfriend, once. We almost got married."

Carrie put her fork down on the table. "You never mentioned her to me or the rest of the family. Who was she?"

"She worked for the Italian government. Circumstances got in the way of our relationship."

"What kind of circumstances?"

Vince walked into the room and stood next to the cart.

"Have to tell you another time. It's a long story. Are you finished?" Steve looked at her plate. "I can't believe you ate as much as I did tonight!"

"Very funny. I'd like to eat my dessert upstairs." She picked up her cream puffs and followed Steve out the door. "Don't think you're getting off about the girlfriend. Now that I know about her, I won't let up."

She heard him sigh, and smiled.

It was dark. Why was he always opening his eyes to darkness? He was lying in the back of the van and could feel cool air on his body. The smell of the ocean filled his nostrils. He heard the surf crashing against the shore.

We're still along the coast.

Low voices drifted in. Peter pulled himself to a sitting position and stared out the window. Bruno and the other man were a few feet from the van smoking cigarettes.

Bruno threw his on the ground and turned to walk away.

The tall man lifted his arm and hit Bruno on the head. He staggered and fell. The man pulled a knife out of his pocket and pounced on Bruno's back, stabbing him over and over again. The brutality of the act surprised and horrified Peter.

Who is this guy? Am I next?

Mara stepped out of the shadows. She grabbed one of Bruno's arms and helped drag the body out of sight.

Adrenalin rushed through him. Now was the opportunity he'd been waiting for. He tried to rush for the back door. The drugs had weakened him to such a state, he fell flat on his face.

With a sinking feeling, he realized he wouldn't get far before the other two overtook him.

There wasn't anything to do except lay down and wait for them to come back.

The next morning, Steve found Carrie in the game room playing solitaire. She glanced up as he walked into the room.

"Good morning Sis, you're up early."

"Yeah, I've even had breakfast. Can't believe I was hungry after all I ate for dinner and dessert."

Steve raised his eyebrows. "You must be feeding a linebacker." Guilt grabbed him. "Although you don't look like it."

She grinned. "Thanks, I think. You got up early, too. I saw you out front with Juan. How did everything go last night?"

"The whole evening was great. No problems. Have you seen Marian or Raoul?"

"Raoul is downstairs somewhere. I saw him go past the door a few minutes ago. Marian is still upstairs."

"Somebody mention my name?" Raoul stood in the doorway. "Did you sleep well, Carrie?"

"Yes, I did. Is my mother-in-law up yet?"

"She is having breakfast upstairs before going off to a speaking engagement."

"I imagine you have a lot to do today, Raoul," Steve said.

Raoul shrugged. "There is much to prepare. Marian

has invited you both to the gala this evening. Would you like to attend? She can have several dresses sent out for Carrie to try on and we can order a tux at the same time. It would be her treat."

Carrie frowned. Steve could tell that the gala was the last thing she wanted to do.

"I think I'll pass. I'd rather camp out in my bedroom and watch the rest of the movies Marian left for me."

"I'll have to pass too," Steve said. "I'll be too busy making sure there are no problems with unexpected guests."

"As you wish." Raoul leaned on the door jamb and examined his fingernails. "Steve there has been a change in our plans for the party."

Uh-oh. Another problem? He gave Raoul his attention. "What's up?"

"I have checked the weather reports and rain is forecast for this evening. Possibly a storm. So, the tent is out. We will all be inside."

It had been such a simple plan with the tent. Now, the focus would be on the house.

"I'll get back to you a little later on my security plan," Steve said.

"What are you doing today, Carrie?" Raoul's smile was exceedingly charming.

Carrie glanced up from her card game. "Not much. Do you need some help?"

"Pamela is overloaded in the kitchen. Although we have a caterer, she does make her own specialties, too. She would be happy to have you join her."

Carrie smiled. "That sounds like fun."

"Just step inside the kitchen and let her know. You can work things out with her yourself."

A bell rang somewhere down the hall. Raoul smiled. "Aw, that is my boss wanting me to fill her in on every detail." He looked at his watch. "She will leave in an hour and will be gone until about three this afternoon. Anything you need to tell her, Steve?"

"Not that I can think of at the moment."

"I will see you later."

Raoul left and Steve could hear the bell ringing again. He almost laughed. Marian had her assistant jumping through hoops sometimes. But Steve knew that Raoul ran the whole show.

He headed for the door. "I'll check on you later, Sis. If you need me, call me on my cell."

A few minutes later, Steve walked outside and gazed up at the sky. No rain in sight. Maybe the storm would pass them by.

Juan sat in the car halfway up the driveway. Steve reached into his shirt pocket and pulled out his memo sized notebook. The window of the car came down. He bent and rested his arm on the car door. "Everything okay?"

Juan nodded. "Yeah...change of plans?"

Steve nodded. "It's supposed to rain tonight. Raoul has shifted everything inside. Make sure you and Charlie have your layouts of the house."

"Will do."

"With the tent we could have confined the guests to the back of the property. Since there's a terrace off all the rooms on the ground floor with doors leading out, I'll request, again, that Raoul lock the doors of the dining room, Marian's office, and the breakfast room."

"So, just like last night, there will be no one allowed in the back by the pool and stables?" Juan asked.

"Yeah. Except the caterers will be here around four and will park in the back for easy access to the kitchen."

Juan nodded. "I'll tell Charlie."

Steve stood up and glanced around the estate. "The

extra agents should be showing up soon." He ran a hand through his short hair. "I hope we don't have too many problems."

In the early evening, rain clouds hovered in the west. A moist breeze swirled around the stables. Steve saw Charlie come out of the barn and waved at him. The two met at the corral fence.

"How's it going?"

Charlie grinned. "Just fine except for the horses. They keep snorting. When Raoul came out an hour ago, he said they can feel the storm coming and not to take it personal. The stable boy put them inside when he left a few minutes ago. No more snorting, but when I go inside, that big brown one in the back paws at the ground."

Steve rolled his eyes. If this was Charlie's only problem tonight, it would be a miracle. "You don't have to stay in the barn unless it rains or storms. Stake yourself out close to the trails. Pick a spot where you can watch the barn and corral, too. When Walker relieves you, tell him to do the same. Oh, and someone is stationed close to the pool."

"Okay." Charlie raised his eyebrows. "Is it the female agent?"

Steve laughed. "No. There's food in the kitchen for you, don't waste your break on flirting with the woman. I already checked, she's married. Any questions?"

"No."

"Good. See you later." Steve watched Charlie walk away. His instinct told him the trails were their weak point. He made a mental note to check on this area every half hour.

Raoul stepped out of the game room. He turned and

hurried toward the living room to find Vince.

He saw Marian standing in the foyer greeting her guests as they came through the door. She almost took his breath away. This evening, his five-foot-six sex goddess was wearing a beautiful off the shoulder gown.

This lavender creation hugged her slender body. At her age she could get away with this because she worked out with her personal trainer three times a week and she had a personal dietician that Raoul and Pamela had to deal with on a daily basis. All to keep this goddess looking beautiful. He watched her touch her reddish brown shoulder length hair. How could she know if it was out of place? He remembered the amount of hairspray she put on it and almost laughed.

Marian turned and saw him. A question in her eyes. No one was coming through the door right now, so he took her aside.

"You look ravishing, my love," he whispered.

She squeezed his hand. "Thank you, Raoul. The nap this afternoon helped."

"Did you spend any time with Carrie?"

"Yes, before I got dressed, I found her in the kitchen helping Pamela. I love her so much, Raoul. She looked so healthy and vibrant, laughing and cracking jokes with Pammy. Hard to believe I'm going to be a grandma."

He raised a hand to his lips and caressed it. "And what a gorgeous grandma you are. Peter will be coming home soon, too, my dear. Do not worry."

"I won't." A couple stepped into the foyer and she broke away from him. "Duty calls. See you later."

Raoul scanned the living room. From the doorway he could see the refreshment table. Still fully loaded, but no Vince attending to the guests. So, the houseboy was not in the game room, the living room or the kitchen. Where was he?"

Half-way down the hall, he saw the young man's white jacket come out of the conservatory.

"Vince!"

The houseboy hurried to him and Raoul rewarded him with a glare. "Where have you been? The cocktails need refreshing and more canapes in the game room and living room."

Vince smiled. "Sorry, Mr. Ortiz, I helped Mrs. Carrie up the stairs and then brought her a tray of goodies to last the night. The conservatory is now ready for the guests to use and mingle outside onto the terrace. It is not raining yet."

Raoul frowned. He had forgotten about Carrie and Steve eating their dinner in the conservatory. And half of the guests would be using that room's terrace to eat their meal soon. Vince was on the ball.

"Good job, Vince."

"I'll hurry to the game room, now, sir."

Raoul stepped into the conservatory. The tiny lights twinkled in the room and outside on the terrace giving the impression of a wonderland. Tables were set up inside and outside to accommodate the guests. He walked to the French doors and gazed at the weather. It was holding up. Hopefully, the rain would not start until the meal had been served and the guests finished. He looked at his watch. In an hour the band would set up, but now he had to return to the kitchen and help Pamela and the caterers.

He entered the hall and turned toward the kitchen. It was then he heard the crash in the dining room. Now what?

He mumbled a vile curse in Spanish as he increased his pace.

NINE

Around eleven-thirty, Steve knocked on Carrie's door. He had to make sure his sister was taken care of before he took a nap.

Carrie opened the door and stared out at him. "Is the party over?"

"Just about. How are you doing?" He pushed his way into her room and walked to the window. It was locked.

"I'm about to turn off the TV and go to bed. I've had enough movies to last me a year."

He turned and patted his sister on the shoulder. She looked tired, but otherwise fine. "Be sure you lock this door, and don't open it for anyone except my guys, Raoul, or Marian. Understood?"

She sighed and nodded her head. "Understood."

"Well, good, then I'll see you in the morning. This party will break up in about an hour."

"Goodnight."

Steve pulled the door closed and heard his sister turn the lock. He hurried down the hall to his own bedroom and locked the door. His clothes were off in seconds, the alarm on his watch set to go off in three hours. He fell asleep when his head hit the pillow. The extra man power would leave at one o'clock. He needed to be fresh to help watch the house.

Raoul found Marian sitting in the living room,

head resting on the back of her chair, and staring at the ceiling. She looked exhausted and stressed out.

"Let's go to bed, my dear."

Marian raised an arm. "Please help me up."

He walked over and bent down, kissing her on the lips. "You were wonderful. Did your guests have a good time?"

He slipped his hands underneath her arms and lifted. Marian stood, but leaned into him. "They loved the food. Be sure to let Pamela know."

They walked slowly toward the stairs. "That will please her…. Marian, perhaps you should consider taking a vacation. We can bring along your writing. It would be good for you to get a rest."

They reached the steps and started going up one at a time. Marian sighed. "You're right, as usual. I do need a rest. We'll talk about a vacation. I wasn't stupid enough to schedule something tomorrow, was I?"

She turned her lovely head to him and he smiled. "No. You don't have anything scheduled until Monday."

Her lips twitched to form a weak smile. "Great."

"But you do have a deadline on the ghost story. Only a month until you have to send it in."

"And I haven't started to polish it yet." She sighed as they took the last step up on the landing.

He pulled her close and pushed her head onto his shoulder.

They reached the bedroom door and Raoul led her across the room. Her nightgown was close to the pillows, her slippers on the floor below.

He reached in back of her and unzipped her dress, letting it fall to the floor. She sat down on the bed. His mouth covered hers. It was a gentle goodnight kiss, but his sex goddess started to come to life.

He pulled away and picked up her dress, arranging it on a chair.

"Is your alarm set?"

She glanced at her bedside table. "Yes, I did that earlier."

"I'll see you in the morning, my dear."

He left her to get herself to bed and hurried to the doorway. All the lights were out downstairs. Vince had gone around and picked up the trash and dishes. Raoul had put away the food and loaded the last of the items in the dishwasher. The caterers had cleaned up their own mess. Tomorrow morning, Pamela would finish up the cleaning.

Exhausted, he crossed the hall to his bedroom. One hand shut the door while the other tugged at his tie. He sat in his valet chair and removed his shoes. He needed a drink. No, he desperately needed a drink.

His body protested when he stood up and crossed the room to his armoire. Inside was a little bar. He poured himself a scotch and downed it in one gulp, then licked his lips. Yes, that will do the trick.

By the time Raoul hung up his suit, he was ready for bed. Tomorrow, he would convince Marian to take a vacation. He really needed one.

"Steve, Steve come in...Steve, Steve come in."

He reached over for the walkie-talkie and glanced at the clock, one-twenty-five.   "Yeah."

"Steve, it's Juan. Walker didn't make his check-in call and I've waited an extra five."

"You and Charlie come up to the house... And be careful! I'll meet you at the front door."

Steve pulled on his pants and slipped into his shoes. He shoved his gun into his pants pocket and grabbed his shirt and jacket as he went out the bedroom door.

Taking the steps two at a time, he felt his watch alarm go off.

His index finger pushed the button to shut it off as he finished getting dressed in the foyer.

He could hear faint noises outside and pulled out his weapon. Gazing through the window next to the front door, he saw Charlie and Juan in the shadows of the porch. He rapped on the window as they approached.

"I tried Walker again, but no answer," Juan said, as he came inside.

Steve reset the house alarm. "Okay, Juan, you stay here. Go upstairs and wake up Raoul, tell him what's going on. Let Carrie know there could be a problem and guard her door. The servants don't sleep on the premises; we don't have to worry about them. Keep eyes on the stairs for anyone coming up. I'll take Charlie and check on Walker."

Juan nodded and headed for the stairs.

Steve and Charlie ran toward the kitchen. There was a light on over the stove and Steve turned it out. They slipped outside, making sure the door was shut and the alarm reset.

"You go on back to the barn; I'll look around the pool. Stay down low," Steve whispered.

Charlie took off for the back of the estate. Steve walked around the pool, and then headed for the gazebo nearby.

He raised the walkie-talkie and made contact with Charlie.

"Anything yet?"

"Yeah, I've found Walker. We're in back of the barn close to the trails."

"I'm on my way."

Steve hurried to the barn and found Charlie.

"He's over here in the bushes." Charlie led him to a

spot close to the trails.

Walker was curled up in a fetal position with his hands and feet tied together. Steve felt his neck. "He's alive, but his pulse is strange. He could be drugged."

Charlie shined his light around the area. "Looks like he was attacked from behind."

Steve used his cell phone to call headquarters for an ambulance while Charlie untied Walker.

"Stay with him, Charlie. The ambulance will come here. I'm going up front."

Raoul stood behind Juan at the top of the stairs. He could hear shuffling noises at the front door.

"They're coming in," Juan said.

"I'll stay with you. There is no way anyone can get to Marian."

A loud banging noise began.

"They're going to ram the door," Juan said.

After three attempts, the door splintered.

The alarm sounded and Juan opened fire. The intruders entered the house. Raoul emptied his own clip. Juan reloaded. One of the three men fell.

"A man is outside my room setting up a ladder!" Carrie yelled from her doorway.

Raoul rushed to Carrie's room and looked out. A man dressed in dark clothing started to climb a ladder that reached up to Carrie's window. Raoul reloaded, opened the window, and fired.

"Go to Marian and bring her back here," Raoul said over his shoulder.

Carrie hurried out of the room.

The man at the foot of the ladder turned and ran for the front door holding his arm. Raoul didn't want to waste valuable ammo, so he let him go.

When he rushed back to help Juan, the agent was

flat on the floor exchanging shots with one of the intruders. Raoul crouched against the wall and scanned the area below to locate the other men. Someone stepped out from a doorway and fired.

Juan scooted backwards, away from the stairs. Blood oozed from a wound in his arm.

Raoul took his place and emptied his clip. Juan reloaded.

The intruders headed for the front door. One man carrying another. Juan managed to get off a few shots before they were gone.

Steve made it to the pool before he heard the shots. He called Juan. No answer. He ran for the house. Near the back door, figures emerged from the shadows. He crouched down and waited.

They took off running in the direction of the stables.

"Stop, federal agents!" Steve yelled.

One of the men turned and fired at Steve while the others continued to run.

Steve looked for a place to take cover. There was none. He fell onto the ground. The lone man took off toward the barn.

Shots rang out close to the stables. Steve ran to help Charlie. At the barn, he crouched in the dark shadows close to the door. He could see Charlie behind a water trough at the edge of the corral. His fellow agent was exchanging fire with a man hiding behind another trough on the other side of the corral.

Steve was too far away to help Charlie. He crouched and hurried down the side of the barn to the trails. A car was parked just past the stables near a huge hedge. Men were getting into the car.

Shit! He was too far away to do any good.

The man from the corral area rushed to join his

buddies. He barely made it inside before the car started down the trail away from Steve.

Charlie came up next to him. Steve pumped out what was left in his clip at the fleeing car then reloaded.

"How's Walker?" He turned his head toward the bushes.

"Still alive," Charlie said.

"Stay put. I'm going up front."

Charlie left and Steve moved toward the house.

Juan's voice came in over the walkie-talkie. "Steve, we need you up front."

"I'm on my way." He felt a jolt of relief. Juan was okay.

There wasn't a door when Steve stepped onto the front porch. He entered the dark house and stopped at the stairs. "Juan, I'm coming up."

Taking two steps at a time, he stopped at the top and scanned the hall. A man was propped up against the wall, legs spread out. Someone stood above him.

"Juan's been shot," Raoul said. "Carrie, turn the light on."

The light from Carrie's bedroom, cast brightness into the hall.

Steve rushed to Juan. Sweat poured down his fellow agent's face. The sleeve of his left arm was soaked with blood.

"I'm okay, Boss. Just a nick."

Steve raised his walkie-talkie. "Charlie is the ambulance there?"

"I can see the lights coming up the trail."

"Send them here when they're finished with Walker. Juan's been shot." He looked at Juan. "What happened?"

"They busted the door down. Raoul and I held them off."

Steve glanced at Carrie's doorway. Marian stood with his sister. He was relieved that the women hadn't been hurt.

"They knew the layout of the house," Raoul said. "They only left after we hit a couple of them."

"How many were there?"

"Four," Juan said. "One of them was so bad, he had to be carried. Raoul went downstairs and followed them out the door."

Marian's assistant shrugged. "I saw them turn the corner toward the pool. Juan needed me more, so I came back."

"He also shot a man trying to get to Carrie's room with a ladder," Juan said.

Steve stared at Raoul. Who is this guy?"

Sirens sounded outside and Steve rushed to Carrie's window. Three squad cars pulled up out front.

Charlie's voice came over the walkie-talkie. "Steve, we've got company. The local police are behind the ambulance."

Several hours later, Steve sat on the couch in the game room. He sipped coffee and stared at the flames in the fireplace. He could hear Vince running the vacuum in the living room. Pamela was busy in the kitchen. The Agency forensic team had come and gone.

The incident had made the morning news. The local police had done a good job with traffic control of all the gawkers passing by for a look at the house.

Only two squad cars remained. One in front and the other in back. He had no choice but to accept their help. They didn't want another incident, and he didn't blame them.

Headquarters had given him and ultimatum. Go to Italy now or get off the case. Everyone had to leave this house. No one was safe.

Raoul walked in and sat in a chair close to him. Steve marveled at the man. When does he sleep?

Now was as good a time as any to have a heart to heart with Marian's assistant. He cleared his throat. "Raoul, after last night, Marian should cancel all her scheduled appointments for at least a week. The men were after her, too. And she should leave this house."

"You are right. With all the publicity, her life would Be hell. Will you provide security for her?"

"Yes."

"I know of a place in France and also another in Italy where we can go. She likes to ski and there should be snow."

"Write down all the details about it. I'll see if it will pass."

Raoul's idea was good. Steve ran a hand through his hair. Earlier he'd come to a hard decision about Carrie. He hoped it was the right one.

His sister stopped in the doorway of the game room and waved. "I can't rest. Thought I'd eat breakfast and help Pamela."

"I'll join you." Steve went into the hall with Raoul on his heels. "Are you coming with us, Raoul?"

"No. I will take a breakfast tray to Marian. When I tell her the news, she will not be happy." Raoul continued toward the kitchen.

Once seated in the breakfast room, Steve ate heartily. He watched Carrie sip her tea. The bags under her eyes were obvious. Last night was pretty bad for her. Heck, it would be bad for anyone. It was a shame he had to tell her now about the new plans.

"Sis, we can't stay here. You and I will go to Italy."

Eyes open wide, Carrie's trembling fingers grabbed a piece of toast. "What about Marian?"

"Raoul will take her somewhere safe."

Marian and Raoul sat in the small sitting area off her bedroom. The breakfast tray was on the table next to her. She hooked a finger around the handle of her cup of coffee and took a sip. The hot liquid felt wonderful as it slid down her throat. It was her favorite blend and she closed her eyes relishing the deliciousness of it.

"My dear, we have to leave the house."

Her eyes snapped open. "Why? Is it because of last night?"

"Yes. We have to go where you will be safe. Steve will arrange protection for us."

"What about Carrie?"

"Before I came up, I talked to Steve in the kitchen. He and Carrie will go to Italy. He has to find Peter."

She was not happy, but last night was awful and she didn't want to go through that again in this lifetime. "Where will we go?"

Raoul smiled. "I will make the reservations. Do not worry. Start packing for a long trip. And take your skiing clothes."

Marian smiled. Time with Raoul on the ski slopes sounded like heaven.

"We need security for Mrs. O'Brien and her assistant. They'll be leaving the house this evening," Steve told his contact. He stood in the library gripping the safe phone, hoping the Agency would come through with support.

"Two men are on their way now. Should be there this afternoon. Do you know the destination?"

"No. Raoul says he will make the arrangements. I trust this guy's instincts. What about us?"

"Your tickets are waiting at the airport. You leave in three hours. By the way, we canceled your earlier flight."

Steve processed what he said and sighed. "Thanks, forgot about that... You'd better put protection on my sister in California and my mother and father in Fort Worth... Oh, yeah, and Peter's sister. I'm not sure where she lives."

"Already done. Peter's sister has protection. Your sister and her family are in a safe house. We've moved your parents to the O'Brien home in Dallas. The security is better than at their home on the lake south of Fort Worth. The local police are helping. And we picked up the O'Brien dog. Heard she was a good watch dog."

Steve chuckled. "That she is. I'll contact you when I get to Milan."

He hung up the phone and glanced at his watch. The flight from New Jersey to New York left in three hours. The eight hour flight to Rome and then a connecting flight to Milan would eat up a good portion of the night. He hated to put Carrie through such a long ordeal. Maybe they should spend the night in Rome and finish the trip tomorrow.

He sighed.

Not a good idea. Too big of a risk.

The van turned down a residential street in Milan. Peter sat in the back and gazed at the homes. His captors hadn't given him any drugs since yesterday. Every nerve of his body was on edge and he knew it was withdrawal. And now, here he sat in plain view of the people on the street. Why?

Yesterday, he had also learned that the tall man's name was Lorenzo. He'd been searching his mind for any memory of the person or the name. Nothing so far. And not a word from his captors about Bruno.

Mara pulled into a driveway. The house had many steps and there was no garage. So much for hiding me from the world.

Lorenzo turned in his seat and his dark eyes bore through him. "You will follow Mara and make no trouble."

Mara got out of the van and hurried to open the front door. Peter followed. The tall man walked behind him.

They stepped into a large living room full of antique furniture. An ancient television sat in a corner. Mara walked to the foot of a stairway where she turned and waved her gun at him. "Come. Hurry."

Peter took the first step and Mara shoved him.

"Go. Waste no time." At the top of the stairs, she grabbed Peter's shoulder. "Stop. Go in there."

He stumbled into a small room with a window looking out onto the street. The door slammed shut and he could hear a key in the lock. Peter rushed to the window. He watched Mara and Lorenzo emerge from the house to unload the luggage and boxes.

Whoever is behind this wants reports of my having been in this house. Why?

He shook his head. Too many "why's" to make any sense of this whole thing. Since he himself was confused, it made sense to assume the rescuers would be confused.

The person behind this abduction was a master planner.

Vittorio's eyes darted from person to person as hundreds of people milled around his car and the other vehicles surrounding him. He felt uncomfortable and glanced at Daniella sitting next to him in the passenger seat. "It is time to go. The informant is not coming."

They sat in his car on a hillside above Florence. This large parking area was full of tourists. It gave the best view of the city.

"This was a waste of time, Vittorio. Someone is toying with us."

Vittorio nodded his head. "I agree." He shrugged his big shoulders. "We had no choice. The source was reliable. Every clue should be investigated."

Daniella opened her purse and found her compact. She lifted the lid and gazed at herself. "Who do you think is behind all of this?"

Vittorio started the motor and pulled out slowly, careful of the crowd. He wondered if the tipster was watching.

"It must be someone with a grudge. There is no ransom note, and no body. The Americans will have to figure this out. They are sending one of their agents to Milan. Steve Crawford. Can you meet him at the train station tomorrow at four?" He glanced at Daniella hoping she would cooperate.

She dropped her compact back into her purse and took out her small date book. Her mouth tightened as she turned her head to glance out the window.

"Yes, I can meet him. Let us hope he knows more than we do."

TEN

Carrie stood in the foyer, next to the luggage. She chewed on the tip of her little finger and thought about last night.

Along with visions of Juan and Raoul shooting their weapons, she could hear the deafening sound of the bullets and see the blood oozing from Juan's arm. Her body shivered as if a cold arctic wind had blown over her.

"Carrie, I'm so sorry we have to leave! What a horrible night."

She pulled herself away from the traumatic thoughts and folded her trembling hands. Out of the corner of her eye she saw movement and turned to see Marian coming toward her from the stairs. Her mother-in-law's shoulders were hunched, her hair wasn't combed, and she wore her bathrobe. Carrie had never seen Marian in such disarray.

The two women embraced.

"Thanks for having us here," Carrie said. "I was looking forward to staying with you until Peter came home, but-"

Marian grabbed her hands and squeezed them. "This whole thing is so scary. My son must be going through hell and here I am freaking out over a little gun battle." Marian sniffed and pulled a hankie out of her robe pocket.

"Do you know where you're going?" Carrie touched

Marian's sleeve.

"Raoul won't tell me. He said he isn't telling anyone. He doesn't want to take any chances that there's a mole in the organization. He doesn't know what he's up against yet."

Carrie's head started spinning. What is she talking about? Mole? Organization?

Marian hugged her, again. "Take care of yourself. Remember, you're carrying my grandchild!"

Steve and Juan walked through the front door. Carrie noticed Juan had his arm in a sling. She supposed the agents had to be on death's doorstep to be excused from a mission.

"Hey, Sis, you ready to go?"

Her bother slipped his arm around her and Carrie felt more relaxed. She nodded and picked up her purse off the suitcase. "Where's Raoul?"

"He's in the library making his reservations," Steve said. "The man is something else, Marian. He won't say a word about his plans."

Marian's face lit up. "I'm discovering all kinds of new things about him. He's been carrying a gun for days."

Steve raised an eyebrow. "We were lucky he was here last night." He gave Carrie a little push. "C'mon, let's go."

"But I didn't say goodbye to Raoul."

Her brother picked up her suitcase and overnight bag. "Sorry, we don't have time."

She walked outside with Steve on her heels and got into the car. She waved at Marian standing in the doorway and tried to hold back her emotions. Before the last two weeks, Italy had always been a romantic place in her mind. Now, the thought of going there, frightened her.

An hour after Carrie left, Marian put the last of her

clothes into her suitcase and zipped it. She grabbed her sweater and tote bag for the plane. Her tiny purse sat inside the bag along with her writing and reading material. She knew it would be a long trip wherever they were going.

"Are you ready, my love?" Raoul walked into the room and stood in front of her.

She saw the worry lines on his face. Had he slept at all the last few days? Guilt engulfed her. Marian felt so selfish. She relied on him far too much.

Her arms went up around his neck and her cheek pressed against his face. "Thank you for everything, Raoul."

"Marian, please, not too tight."

She pulled back. "Sorry, I do get carried away."

He bent down and lightly kissed her lips. "I love it when you get carried away. We soon will have time to relax and enjoy each other's company."

They walked out into the hall. Vince came up the stairs and passed them.

"Do you have everything, my dear?" Raoul asked.

"I'll just buy what I don't have."

"Good idea."

They went down the stairs together. Pamela waited at the bottom.

"Say goodbye to Pamela," Raoul said.

Marian hugged her housekeeper/cook. "Have a nice vacation, Pammy. Say hi to your mom for me. She'll just roll her eyes when you tell her all that went on. My life hasn't changed so much since we were friends in high school. Odd things happened to me back then too."

Pamela wiped a few tears off her cheeks. "Bye, Mrs. O. see you in a couple of weeks."

Raoul steered her toward the kitchen.

"Where are we going? Is the limo here yet?" Marian was confused. They usually went by limo to the airport.

"Not going in the limo."

"We're not?"

In the kitchen, the door to the garage stood open.

"Oh, we're taking one of the cars?"

"Yes."

He helped her into his old restored Pontiac Le Mans. A man came in from the house and got in the back behind her. Vince put the luggage in the trunk.

Raoul popped in behind the wheel and backed out of the garage. When they reached the end of the driveway, a car fell in behind them.

"See Marian, that's more protection behind us."

She shifted in the seat and looked back. "Great. After last night, we need all the protection we can get."

Half-way down the street, her hands flew up to her face. "Raoul, I didn't say goodbye to Vince!"

Her assistant glanced over at her. "We're not going back. I said goodbye for you."

Marian's heart sank. When would she come back to her haven? Would her peaceful life ever return?

Raoul squeezed her hand. "It won't be long until we come back."

Marian frowned. Did he read my mind or did I say that out loud? "Where are we going?"

"You will find out soon enough. Do not worry anymore. You will be pleasantly surprised."

Marian raised her brows.

Raoul grinned. "I cannot tell you. Security reasons."

"So, we're taking this car, because?"

He laughed. "It is inconspicuous. I took the idea from one of your books."

Late Sunday morning, Steve grabbed Carrie's arm

and hurried down the concourse in the Milan airport. He saw Charlie standing several feet ahead. As he passed his fellow agent, they didn't make eye contact, but Steve knew everything was okay. The car would be waiting and Charlie would get their luggage.

They stepped outside into an overcast sky with a threat of rain. Steve's eyes scanned the immediate area and saw a car with Juan in the back seat. He opened the passenger side door and helped Carrie inside. Once at the wheel, he eased out into traffic.

The ride through the streets of Milan took half an hour.

At the safe house, Carrie clung to his arm. They stood in the foyer facing a balding middle-aged man with a rotund body and double chin.

"Carrie, this is Kevin our host," Steve said.

The man grinned and pushed a hand out to Steve.

"Hello," Carrie said.

Kevin withdrew his hand from Steve's and grabbed Carrie's.

"Nice to meet you," he said. "My wife, Gina, is in the kitchen preparing a light brunch. We don't employ servants, so if you see a thin red-haired woman with freckles and a big smile, it's her. If she isn't smiling, you'd better be careful. The wrath of Gina can be brutal."

He shuddered as if afraid, but his hazel eyes sparkled.

Steve and Carrie laughed.

"If you would like to step into the living room and wait a few minutes, we'll serve the brunch." Kevin gestured toward a big room off the foyer and hurried toward the back of the house.

Steve sat on a couch facing the fireplace. His sister took the opposite end. Brightly colored rugs covered the wooden floor and were spaced around the large room. Two windows overlooked a garden and another faced the street in the front of the house.

He leaned his tall body into the soft cushions and rested his arm across the back of the couch. "Kevin's gone to wait for Charlie and the luggage. I stay here every time I come to Milan. They're wonderful hosts."

Carrie nodded and stared at the fire.

"Are you okay, sweetie, you're quiet."

She laid her head back on the couch. "Everything is so surreal. I feel like I'm in a dream." She turned her head and stared at him. "I'm okay. Just really tired. After brunch I want a nap. I didn't sleep much on the planes."

"I know how you feel." It occurred to Steve that Carrie probably would rather go to her room right now instead of later. It was so unusual for him to travel with people and think of their every need. His life was always centered on himself and his current assignment.

Gina Garrison walked into the room. She was just as her husband had described her, right down to her smile.

"Welcome to Milan, Mrs. O'Brien," Gina said. "Steve, it's great to see you again."

He nodded. "It's been awhile. We hope we're not going to be here too long."

"Brunch is set up in the dining room."

Steve cleared his throat. "Gina could we bother you to serve trays in our rooms? I'm tired." He turned his head toward Carrie. "How about you, Sis?"

Carrie didn't lift her head off the back of the couch.

"Sounds good to me."

Gina smiled. "Your rooms are ready. Wait a few minutes before going up there, it won't take me long to fix the trays."

She walked across the foyer to a brightly lit dining

room.

"I hope that was okay with you, Carrie." He turned his head and stared at her. Now, her eyes were closed.

Would he have to carry her up the stairs?

"That was a great idea. What do you think she made for us?" Her voice was barely above a whisper.

"Probably the same thing she always makes for me when I come here. Eggs and biscuits and fruit."

Carrie chuckled. "Eggs. I should have known." She opened her eyes and sat upright. "Seriously, Steve, is that all you eat or know how to cook? I didn't want to say anything at the time, but before we went to Marian's I was getting tired of them."

"Hey, eggs are good for you! And... They're easy to fix." There was a noise out in the foyer. "Sounds like our luggage is here."

A few seconds later, Kevin and Charlie went up the stairs with their things. Gina followed with a tray.

Steve stood up and extended his hand. "Let's go upstairs and get settled."

Carrie grabbed his hand and he pulled her up off the couch. She took a few steps and he touched the back of her shoulder and guided her toward the stairway. Fatigue hit him hard. He was glad he didn't have to go outside and check on Juan and Charlie. Kevin was in charge of securing the house.

They walked up the stairs in companionable silence. Steve was deep into his own thoughts. At the top, he noticed Gina and the men going down the back stairs at the end of the hall. He stopped at the first room. Carrie's suitcase sat at the foot of the bed. Her repast sat on a small table near the window.

"This is it, Sis. Have a nice rest. There's an intercom system, so you can call down to Gina if you need anything. I'll be across the hall."

"I can hardly wait to put my head on the pillows," Carrie said. "See you later." She stepped into the room and waved at him before closing the door.

He didn't waste any time. He closed his bedroom door, fell onto the soft mattress, and drifted off instantly.

The alarm on his watch woke him around three. He drank a little of the cold coffee and ate two mouthfuls of biscuit and egg, then rushed to shower and shave.

At five minutes to four, Steve walked into the train station across the street from the Pirelli building in Milan. He scanned the lobby for his contact and saw her sitting on a bench reading a magazine. He bought a newspaper and his eyes scanned his surroundings as he walked across the room. Feeling okay about the security, he casually sat down on the bench near her. She didn't look up.

He opened the paper to read the headlines. "It's been a long time, Daniella."

She turned a page of her magazine. "I think it has been four years since we last had our little fling on the beach in Nice."

"Can you ever forgive me for leaving without saying good-bye? After all, I did send you flowers."

"I hated you. But now I am glad to see you again." She closed the magazine and stuck it into her large purse.

"Maybe time does heal all wounds," Steve muttered. He stole another look at her. How could he have left such a beautiful woman? Well, she did have a temper. She turned her head and their gazes caught. Steve could tell that she had not forgiven him.

"Is the bird in its nest?" Daniella asked.

"Yes. Can you meet me tonight at our old hangout? Say ten o'clock?"

"No. I can meet you at eight at the restaurant

where you proposed to me."

"Eight, it is."

Steve stood and walked out of the building, fighting the urge to look back at her. He hurried across the street and pretended to window shop. As he watched her leave the station, he realized tonight would be an even bigger challenge than he had anticipated. She was always in his thoughts and at times haunted him. Minutes ago, when he had looked into her dark eyes, he had fought a strong urge to pull her into his arms. His feelings for her were as strong as ever.

Carrie woke from her nap and had a long luxurious bath. She dressed and went downstairs, feeling lonely and trying not to let worries consume her.

She missed her dog and her business, and now her husband had been missing more than a week. Would Steve be able to find him? She pushed back the approaching anxiety. She didn't want to think about what was happening to Peter. Her stomach growled as she sat down on the couch in the living room. She took a deep breath. Gina was cooking again. If the food was as good as it smelled, she knew she'd stuff herself.

The windows off the garden caught her attention. It was still light enough outside to see flowers and shrubs clearly. She smiled when she noticed white roses close to the terrace. They were high on her list of flowers she loved.

"You look rested. Can I join you?"

The voice startled Carrie. She turned her head and saw Steve standing at the foot of the stairway. "Of course. And yes, I'm feeling a lot better. This place is really nice. Much better than the other safe house."

"I think coming here was a good decision," Steve said. "We should be able to relax a few days until I know more about where this case is taking us." He left his spot and headed her way, stopping at a bar in the corner of the living room.

"Would you like a before dinner drink?"

"Sure," Carrie said. "Do they have sparkling apple cider?"

"Of course!" Steve bent down and came up with two flutes filled with what looked like champagne. He crossed the room and set a flute in front of her.

She lifted the glass and took a sip. "This "champagne" is excellent."

Steve grinned. "It sure feels great to let go of the stress doesn't it? And you're right; this is not your ordinary safe house. It has its own wine cellar. I've stocked it with some of my favorites and this is one of them."

"What makes this place so safe?"

"Don't let the beauty and serenity fool you. Gina and Kevin are here to protect us as well as serve us. Both work for the Agency and are excellent shots. In addition, Juan and Charlie are on guard outside. Security is guaranteed."

He winked at her.

Carrie raised her glass. "A toast to all of our protectors."

Steve grinned and touched his glass with hers.

"I'm going outside and check on things." He finished off his champagne and left her to her thoughts.

Carrie watched him leave and heard the front door shut. She picked up a fashion magazine off the coffee table and turned the pages admiring the essence of Italian glamour. She smiled when she realized that she felt better, now. But, then, her big brother had always been able to lift her mood.

Steve approached the car in the driveway. Juan sat behind the wheel. This was his first opportunity to talk to his team since they arrived. Earlier, when he left to meet Daniella, he had been pressed for time. And when he returned, Kevin had met him in the driveway to discuss security for tonight. Now, even though he trusted Kevin to do an excellent job, he wanted to be assured that his team was okay.

"How's it going?" Steve asked. He looked around and decided that his fellow agent had a good view of the front of the house and the street.

"Looking good." Juan lifted his binoculars using his good arm.

"Did they feed you earlier?"

Juan chuckled. "Yeah, I had ham and biscuits. It sure beats the safe house in Dallas when you were doing the cooking."

"Carrie said basically the same thing," Steve said dryly. "My cooking couldn't be that bad!"

"You have to like eggs," Juan said.

They both laughed and Steve turned away from the car. "I'll be going out again later, so don't shoot me."

He heard Juan chuckle, again, as he walked to the back of the house. Charlie had made a little area for himself close to the back door. Steve caught him lounging in one of the patio chairs.

"Are you comfortable back here?" he asked.

Charlie shrugged. "Can't complain. What's happening when it turns dark? It may get a little cold out here tonight."

"What a wus! Maybe you should go through survival training again."

Charlie didn't laugh.

Steve knew he was pretty worn out. "Kevin will handle the back, tonight. You and Juan set up a schedule for the front of the house."

Charlie smiled. "Sounds great. Any word about Walker?"

Steve shook his head. "No. But he should be joining us soon. He's had to deal with worse things in the past."

He left Charlie and went inside through the terrace door. Carrie was still on the couch in the living room.

The fireplace was going strong. He sat in a chair near her and felt the warmth of the fire.

She stared at him and he could see the fear hiding in the back of her eyes. She was starting to be concerned again.

"I'm going out in a bit. Would you like to watch a little television? The programs here are different."

"No thanks, Gina said she'd bring a dinner tray to my room and after eating, I'm going back to bed.. right now, I'm going to finish that book I started on the trip here." She stood and headed for the stairs.

"Have a good night's sleep, Sis. And don't worry about anything. See you in the morning."

"Okay," Carrie said over her shoulder.

His eyes followed her up the stairs. Would he be able to keep her safe? It bothered him to think about the consequences if he should fail. The fact that he was asking himself that question, disturbed him even more.

A chill slid down his spine. If something happened to his sister and her unborn baby, it would kill him.

He had to shake this mood.

Maybe a drink would help. He went over to the bar and filled a glass with the rest of the champagne. After gulping down half the liquid, he walked to the fireplace and watched the flames glisten off the crystal glass in his hand. The burning log crackled and spit out embers. He wondered where Peter could be at this moment. A sadness coursed through him. He hoped with all his heart that his old partner was still alive, not just for himself, but for his wife and child.

ELEVEN

Raoul, driving a rental car and followed by his private security, pulled up to a huge wood and stone house surrounded by trees.

The mountains with snowy peaks in the background made a picture so beautiful, Marian gasped. "This is such a gorgeous place, Raoul. How did you find it?"

He grinned at her. "I do have a few secrets, my dear."

They stepped out of the car and onto a path leading to the house. As if on cue, a man dressed in the clothes of a servant, opened the massive front door.

"Your new home awaits," Raoul said. "I believe that is our butler. Go on in, I'll get the luggage."

Marian entered a large foyer. She gazed down at the floor, impressed with the beautiful marble.

The butler stood at the open door. "Buonasera, Madame, I hope your ride here was pleasant."

She looked up and stared at the huge beams of rustic dark wood on the ceiling. She could see that they continued on into a grand room off to her right. A stone fireplace took up most of one wall. To her left was a stairway of gleaming polished wood. Realizing she was being rude, she turned and gazed at the butler. "It was a very beautiful drive from the airport. The mountains are magnificent."

The butler smiled.

A servant came out of a door on the side of the

stairway. He walked toward her and the butler spoke to him in Italian. The man nodded.

Raoul and one of the security men set the luggage down in the foyer. The servant picked up Marian's suitcase and headed for the stairs.

The butler bowed. "Madame, if you will follow me, please."

Marian smiled, satisfied with the servants and the beautiful house. She continued to smile as Raoul slipped his arm around her waist and gave her a squeeze.

They walked down a hallway off the grand room, towards the back of the house. The butler opened a door and showed them into a cozy room with a small lit fireplace.

"Shall I serve caffe?" he asked.

Marian looked at Raoul.

"We will wait for dinner," Raoul said.

The butler bowed and closed the door on his way out.

Raoul reached over and locked it.

Marian sank into the comfy cushions of the couch situated across from the fireplace and sighed. "I think I'm really going to be spoiled, Raoul."

"It is now my duty in life to spoil you, my dear." He bent down and kissed her cheek. "Won't this place be so inspirational? You can write a novel about this villa in the Dolomites and two lovers who can't get enough of each other." His eyes smoldered.

Tingles of lust and delight flowed through her. Oh, yeah, this was such a good idea.

Raoul went to a sideboard at the window and took out two glasses. "Would you like a drink?"

Her eyes lit up. "Not really. Maybe, we should've

had coffee up in our rooms."

Raoul eased in next to her on the couch.

"We have two hours until dinner."

"And I noticed you locked the door."

He pulled her close and pressed his lips to hers.

Daniella slipped into her dark green shoes. They were the exact same color as her new low cut dress. Tonight she would show Steve what he had left behind.

It was true that she had not yet forgiven him. Her love had been strong, and he had broken her heart.

How will he explain it all?

At the train station this afternoon, she had fought an urge to hit him with her purse. But, after talking to him for a few minutes, the old feelings had resurfaced and turned her impulses in the wrong direction. She had wanted to kiss him.

It had been a bit hard to take. The man had left her at the altar.

Her fingers adjusted the thin straps of the dress. She had to be careful on this assignment. The people involved in the abduction could have followed her from her meeting with Steve this afternoon. Even though she had been careful driving home, she knew the element of danger was out there. It always was.

She picked up her purse off the dresser and opened it. Her hand felt the gun sitting on the bottom, hidden under a handkerchief. The house was quiet and she heard the clock chime the time. Grabbing her shawl, she hurried down the stairs.

Outside, the cool night air refreshed her senses. Her mind became alert, sharp eyes quickly took in the yard and the street. At the curb, she slipped behind the wheel of her Fiat and pulled out into traffic.

A car came out of an alley and followed her. Another turned off of a side street. Frowning, she kept her same speed all the way to the intersection and stopped for a red light. A glance in her rear view mirror confirmed what she feared earlier, a possible tail.

Daniella smirked. When the light changed, her foot hit the accelerator. Let us see what they are made of.

Steve sat in the back of the Bona Vita restaurant. He picked up an olive off the plate of appetizers in front of him and popped it into his mouth. He glanced around at the small cozy room, and breathed in the aroma of baked bread, pasta, and roasted meat.

He smiled. The Bona Vita hadn't changed much since the last time he was here. His mind wandered back to that evening four years ago when he had proposed to Daniella. He remembered how much he had loved her. The following weekend they had gone to Nice where the unexpected had happened.

His thoughts were interrupted by the laughter of a party of eight sitting at the next table. Steve checked his watch one more time. Why is she so late? He'd give her another half hour.

The front door opened and Daniella walked in. She caught his eye and waved slightly. He watched her weave her way to the back, admiring her lush figure and beautiful face. His heart surged.

She sat in the chair next to him and took off her shawl. Steve draped it over the back of her chair.

"Sorry I am late," Daniella said. "I was followed."

"Do you think you were successful in ditching them?"

"Of course!" Her mouth formed an adorable pout. "I am not stupid. I would not have entered the restaurant."

Steve studied her body language. She was irritated at having to lose a tail and he was the reason for her being followed. Ergo, she was already mad at him.

He picked up her wine glass and filled it with her favorite pinot while she loaded appetizers on her plate. Their hands touched as she accepted her drink.

His eyes locked with hers and he was startled. He saw a promise in them. A promise of forgiveness.

"Sorry about the tail," he said. "They must have seen us together at the station."

"Who are 'they'?" She took a bite of Prosciutto.

"I'm not sure yet."

"You have not changed," Daniella said. Her eyes searched his face. "What is the occasion for this dinner, eh? Surely you did not miss me?"

Steve smiled and grabbed her hand. "Business with lots of pleasure. I would like to apologize for the way I left things hanging in Nice. You were taking a bath when I answered a knock at the door. It was my contact in France. He told me that I had to leave. You know how those Agency people can be.

"The bathroom door was locked and when I knocked, the water was running. I had to go. Lives were at stake and there wasn't a pen anywhere."

He paused, allowing her time to absorb the information. It was the truth, but it sounded so lame. Her eyes were on him, watching his every move. He could feel her energy.

She averted her attention to the menu. He cleared his throat. "By the time I was free, you weren't receiving my calls. I sent flowers and hoped for the best. I let the whole thing drop for a while, but now I realize I should have persisted." He squeezed her hand gently. "You of all people know what my life is like."

Daniella pulled her hand free and gazed off into the crowded restaurant. He couldn't read her at all.

The waiter appeared and they placed their order. As he left, Daniella drained her glass.

She's not buying any of this. Steve picked up his fork and speared another olive.

In a quick movement, she opened her purse and took out a photograph. She handed it to Steve as he chewed his olive.

The little girl in the picture sat on the lap of a man who was old enough to be her grandfather. He smiled. "Who is this adorable little girl? Is she one of your nieces?"

"She is your daughter."

Steve felt the blow in his abdomen. His breath escaped and he gasped for air.

"My...daughter!...Why didn't you tell me?"

"You left me at the altar! We were supposed to get married when we got back from Nice. You wanted out of the relationship. I only told you now because you are here in Milan and we can discuss this."

His gut hurt. He had a child? If it had been anyone else but Daniella, he wouldn't believe it. He was always careful whenever he had sex. His reputation as a playboy had been spread about over the years to give him a good cover, but the fact was, it was greatly exaggerated.

With trembling hands, he studied the picture again. Judging by the age of the little girl, she could indeed be his. Why hadn't he come back sooner? And now he was here only because Peter was in trouble.

Guilt tore through him along with regret and frustration. He would have to deal with this issue along with Carrie and Peter. Life could be so complicated.

If this was his child, there was something he had to

discuss with her, and he hoped she would react well to it.

"There is an inheritance to consider. You know of course that the trust will demand a paternity test. If anything happened to me, I would want her to be taken care of without a big hassle."

"We do not want your money! I have only told you about her because she needs to know her father." She glared at him.

The words had practically been spat in his face, and Steve sensed she wasn't finished chewing him out.

However, the lines on her face softened. Her eyes met his. "I am not stupid. I will cooperate."

"Good," Steve said. He felt relieved, as if he'd just passed some kind of miserable test.

The waiter set the pasta and bread on the table. Steve tried to organize his thoughts. He didn't tell her that he had been shot and left for dead in Nice. If he mentioned it now, she would think that he was lying to her, making an excuse. He scolded himself for not calling her from the States.

"What's her name?"

"Rosella, we call her Rosie."

Steve filled his mouth with spaghetti giving him time to think about how to ask the questions that were going through his mind. He watched her eat her pasta with relish, knowing she was nervous. This subject was going to cause indigestion for both of them.

He swallowed and dared one more question. "Does she live with you?"

"Of course! We have a house on the outskirts of Milan. I have a live-in housekeeper."

"I would like to see her." He braced for another barb.

She shrugged. "Maybe it can be arranged." She grabbed the picture out of his hand and put it back into her purse. "We will talk about it."

Steve knew better than to ask for the picture back. He would probably have to beg for one of his own. His mind raced. He wanted to find out more about his daughter, but Peter's abduction took priority. He had to push all of this personal business aside.

"Sorry to change the subject. What can you tell me about Peter?"

"Vittorio de Luca was his contact. He now heads a small task force set up to search for Peter. We have found very little information. Mara Cavari and Bruno Caminetti were the kidnappers. We do not know who they work for. Do you recognize the names?"

"I remember Bruno from years ago. The woman's name draws a blank."

"Bruno is well known to us in Milan. He is an informer and switches sides depending on the amount of money he can scam. I tried to warn Vittorio... The girl we do not know."

Alarms went off in Steve's mind. Bruno was Peter's last contact. Bruno had been one of Cristo's goons years ago.

He had to find Bruno.

"Can you tell me anything else?"

"Yes. A body was found along the Amalfi coast. It was mutilated and the forensic people are still not sure of its identity. Can you give me Peter's medical information to compare?"

"I'll bring it to our next meeting."

"Peter is a wealthy man, Steve. Have you received a ransom note?"

"No, we figure this is related to revenge. That makes it more urgent to find him as quickly as possible."

"Do we consider terrorist groups? We will have to get Interpol involved...do you think he is dead?" The last of her sentence was delivered in a whisper.

Steve forced himself to think of the inevitable. He had addressed this issue over and over for the last week. It was possible that Peter was dead. Or, they could find the kidnappers and not Peter. He caught Daniella's gaze.

"You're right, he could be dead. That doesn't stop me from going all out to find him. As to the other, if an organization has abducted him, we would have heard something by now, or his body would have turned up."

He thought about the body found in the sea and frowned.

She nodded in agreement and pushed her plate away. Grabbing her wine glass, she eased back into her chair. Her intense brown eyes studied him. Steve had a feeling she was trying to figure out if she could trust him one more time.

"In our investigation we have discovered one surprising fact. Bruno was involved with criminals in other parts of the world. Peter could be anywhere and it could take months to find him." She smiled. "But, we are the best at finding people. Are we not?"

Steve returned her smile. "Yes, we are."

"Meet me tomorrow night at Federico's," she said. "I will have more information."

They finished their meal and passed the time talking about what had happened in their lives since that fateful day four years ago. Steve ended up telling her about being shot and almost dying. He didn't think she believed him, but he felt better telling her anyway.

After paying the check, he walked Daniella outside. The night had turned colder and he wanted to pull her close to him, but knew better than to touch her.

At her car, she opened the door and before she could slip inside, Steve grabbed her arm.

"Daniella..." he crushed her against his chest for a tender bear hug. "Thanks, for meeting me for dinner."

She abruptly pulled away from him and sat behind the wheel, closing the door quickly. "You are welcome. We have to work together on this case to find Peter. I will try to be agreeable."

The motor started and she joined the traffic moving down the busy street. Steve watched her weave her way out of sight. He hoped they would be able to heal the wound between them and find his old partner.

She was the best agent the Italian's had in their organization. They would make a good team. Again.

All the way back to the safe house, a picture of his little daughter with the curly dark hair floated through his mind. Steve became determined to see her.

Peter put his ear to the door. He could hear muffled sounds down the hall. They're getting ready to move me again.

He crossed the room and looked down on the street below. In the darkness, a light from the front porch illuminated the driveway. The doors of the van were wide open. Lorenzo came out and tossed a suitcase in the back.

I love it when I'm right.

Hundreds of lights twinkled in the night as his gaze drifted over the rooftops of Milan. He had recognized the large city right away. He had made several trips here on business for the Agency.

It had now been a week since his abduction. When could he expect to meet whoever was orchestrating this fiasco? Or, better yet, when would his rescuers get here and save the day? Surely someone was looking for him.

He believed that they killed Bruno to confuse

whoever was investigating his disappearance. They were the same height and weight. Oops, had been. Also, Bruno had finished his part and was a liability.

Peter couldn't say he missed the dark Italian, but dealing with him was easier than his replacement. Lorenzo. He still didn't recognize the name or the face. A coldness seeped into his psyche and he immediately turned from the window, sensing the man was staring up at him from the driveway below.

Half an hour later, Mara opened his bedroom door. Lorenzo stood behind her with a gun.

"Where are we going, Mara? Will I finally get to meet your boss?"

The tall man grabbed Peter's arm and squeezed it. "Shut up or I will break your arm."

Peter said nothing as they walked out to the car where he was placed in the front next to Mara. Lorenzo sat behind him and every once in a while he could feel the tip of the gun on his back.

They left Milan behind and drove out into the country. On a lone dark road, Mara pulled off and they all got out.

A helicopter landed in the field in front of them. Lorenzo dragged him across the dirt toward the open door. A disturbing thought crossed Peter's mind. Once in the air, would they throw him out?

He didn't have to worry about that. Mara gave him another shot of a narcotic. His mind drifted in and out of weird dreams. At some point, he felt himself being pulled and carried outside into the fresh air. The smell of the sea assaulted his senses.

TWELVE

The sun peeked out from behind large fluffy white clouds. The tree lined road, leading up to the villa nestled in the Tuscan hillside, was bathed in intermittent sunlight.

Countess Alissa DiBiasi pulled the scarf off her head and shoved it into the pocket of her light tan coat. The outing to a nearby village for lunch and shopping had been enjoyable, but what would she do with herself the rest of the day? If she were in France, there would be luncheons and visits to the spa with friends. Out here, in the countryside of Italy, those options were not available. She hated her life here.

The chauffeur steered the car into the double garage. He popped the trunk and got out to remove the wheelchair. Lorenzo came in from the side door to help her husband into the house.

She wasn't happy to see this man. He had returned last night and his cruel presence was already making her nervous. She hurried past him and across the portico to the kitchen door.

Once inside, she took off her coat and carried it with her to the living room at the front of the villa.

Seraphina, her housekeeper, came in from the bedroom area and reached for her coat. "Would Senora have coffee in the sunroom?"

"No, grazie. Serve an early dinner."

The housekeeper hung the coat in a small closet

close to the front door. Voices filtered into the serene atmosphere and Seraphina frowned as she hurried toward the kitchen.

Alissa sat down on the couch situated near the large picture window. The vineyards outside stretched as far as the eye could see. Her husband, Ricco, had inherited this estate twenty years ago from a rich uncle on his mother's side. The out buildings and this house were over two hundred years old.

She heard the sound of the wheelchair and Lorenzo's steps in the hallway. The cruel man would take her husband to the other side of the house until dinner.

Concern filled her. The arrival of Lorenzo meant some evil plan was about to begin.

Even though Ricco was confined to his wheelchair, his mind was still sharp. The horrible incident five years ago that had crippled him had made him, if possible, more diabolical. She shivered. He had been ruthless and cruel before the yacht exploded; now bitterness was added to that mix. Since that fateful night, they had spent their life traveling between this vineyard and their chateau in France.

Alissa walked out of the living room and up the stairs to her large bedroom decorated in different hues of rose, mauve, and lilac. This room was her sanctuary. She stood at the bay window that faced east. In the garden below, Seraphina searched for flowers for the dinner table. Many were just starting to bloom. Others had grown quickly in the balmy weather of the last several days.

Her eyes lifted and gazed toward the sea. On clear days she could see the water over the distant hill. Today, she wasn't as lucky. It was just as well. Her mind kept returning to Ricco and his helper.

The chest that had blown up with the yacht had not

contained all of the gold and jewels meant for the terrorist organization. Half of it had been sent away in the bottom of a vegetable truck to this estate.

She always marveled at her husband's brilliant mind. He had planned for everything and now they had enough money to live in luxury the rest of their lives.

A sudden coldness made her cross her arms and she hugged herself. A week ago she had overheard a conversation between Ricco and Lorenzo.

The tall thin man had kidnapped someone and they were discussing arrangements for the hiding place. In the old days, Ricco had not been adverse to outright murder. Why would he bother to kidnap anyone now? Why did he want to ruin their safe existence?

A terrible sinking feeling made her hurry across the room for a hot bath. She did not want to dwell on this crime and she definitely did not want to think about the victim.

Inside her private bathroom, she turned the water on in the tub and took off her clothes.

The uneasy feeling was still with her. At the time of the incident years ago, Ricco had been the head of the terrorist organization. Today, he was not allowed to be involved.

She sat down in the hot water. Her husband had been warned and punished after he lost that huge cache of jewels and gold. If he was up to his old ways and they found out, the organization would kill him.

They would kill her, too.

She eased herself under the hot water to get away from an encroaching chill.

Dying with him at the hands of his terrible business acquaintances was not what she had in mind for herself. She would have to find out more about this abduction.

Carrie sat in a lawn chair enjoying the sun on the terrace. It had rained during the night and everything had a fresh look and smell. A bouquet of white roses sat on the table nearby and she relished their heady scent as she gazed at the latest fashion trends in the Italian newspaper.

Milan was the financial and fashion capital of Italy and she was tempted to ask Steve to take her shopping. Someone cleared their throat and she instinctively turned around. She was happy to see Steve.

"Are we shopping?" His voice held a cheerful ring. He eased his lanky body into a chair at the table.

"Yeah," Carrie said. "The clothes look tempting... I can't go shopping, right?"

Steve cleared his throat again. "I hate to be the bad guy, but it's out of the question."

"How long will we be staying here?" she asked her eyes downcast. Not being able to go shopping or to see the tourist sights was depressing.

"I'm not sure. Don't unpack your bag...This garden is Gina's pride and joy. What do you think of it?"

Carrie knew he had changed the subject to avert her attention to something less stressful. He was probably wondering if she was upset. He'd been that way all her life. She was the baby in the family and Steve had always been her protector.

"The garden is beautiful...you have something to tell me, don't you?"

He placed his elbow on the table and leaned his head against his hand. "Yeah, tonight I'll be gone again, don't worry about me or that something awful has happened."

She opened her eyes wide. There must be all kinds of danger involved in finding Peter. It would be a challenge tonight to keep herself busy enough not to worry about her brother, or her husband.

"Okay," she said.

"You're safe here with Kevin and Gina. Juan and Charlie will be outside. You'll be well protected."

Carrie felt like a damsel in a tower. Too bad her hair was short; she could have used it to escape. She visualized that scenario and almost laughed. How silly you are. Your husband is still missing, your brother is placing his life on the line, you miss your home and business in Dallas, and you're making jokes.

After chewing herself out, she felt melancholy.

"Are you still with me, Carrie?" Steve asked. "You suddenly looked a thousand miles away."

"Yeah." Her sigh was audible.

"Good. Because I've decided to beat your butt at Trivial Pursuit. I haven't done that for a long time!"

He walked inside and returned with the game. "Have you been practicing?" she asked.

"No. Have you?" He feigned concern.

"Yeah, Peter beats me all the time." Tears welled up as she helped Steve set up the game.

Peter's head ached and his stomach felt like it could throw up at any time. He could smell dampness and mildew. A few minutes ago, when he'd opened his eyes to total darkness, he'd thought he was dead.

A rapid heartbeat reminded him how overpowering that feeling had been.

Where was he now? He'd lost track of time and space.

His legs moved and he realized his body was beneath a blanket. One hand dropped off the bed and touched the floor, the other reached up in the air. Sitting shouldn't be a problem.

He gingerly sat upright, took a deep breath of the

foul air and coughed.

A loud bang echoed throughout his space. His body jumped.

What was that?

Everything became quiet again

Footsteps moved toward him.

Bits of memories flooded his mind. The tall man was his jailer. A helicopter landed in the dark. Lorenzo dragged him into this cell.

A light lit up the room and it moved with the footsteps. Peter looked around and saw that he was indeed in a dungeon. A cell. Only his bed and a chamber pot in the corner. No chair. No sink to wash up in. The light came through a hole in the upper part of the door.

The footsteps stopped. He heard a key turn in a lock. The door opened and Lorenzo stood in the doorway illuminated by the bright light of a lantern.

"Get up," he said. "I take you to the toilette."

Peter pushed the blanket away and quickly swung his legs over the side of the bed. He stood and a swirl of dizziness passed through him, his body swayed.

"Come!" Lorenzo yelled.

The drug they gave him last night must have been powerful. Peter tried to walk, but only managed to move an inch at a time.

Lorenzo stepped inside the cell and grabbed his arm. "Walk faster!"

His jailer pulled him out into the dank hallway. Peter wondered how soon this hell would end. Surely they hadn't kept him alive all this time to allow him to die in this filthy place.

At the safe house, Steve unlocked the study door, located in an alcove under the stairs. He reached for the phone sitting on the only piece of furniture in the room, a Chippendale desk. He knew the phone was clean and didn't hesitate to dial the number of his contact in Washington. The call was answered immediately by a female agent.

"I have met with the Italians," Steve said.

"Good. What did they have to say?"

"A body was found matching Peter's description."

"Yes. It was Bruno Caminetti. We think they had no more use for him and wanted to throw off the investigation."

"Makes sense," Steve said. "Mara Cavari was Bruno's accomplice. The Italian's don't know anything about her yet and they don't know who the two of them work for. But, I'm sure they'll have more information this evening. I want to go to Rome and check out the hotel where Peter was abducted. If Daniella will agree, I'll have her take care of the reservations. Do you have any other news? How's Walker?"

"The trip to Rome sounds good. We don't have anything to add concerning Peter, and Walker is doing well. He may be joining you soon. Call me same time tomorrow."

"Okay." Steve hung up and left the study. He was glad Walker would be coming back to the team soon. They could use him.

Too bad Bruno was dead. Beating the crap out of the creep had been high on his list of things to do.

He left the house and drove off toward Federico's on the other side of Milan. He hoped the Italians would have more than a few bites of news. This case couldn't get solved fast enough.

From the restaurant's doorway, Steve spotted Daniella perched at a table in the far corner of the large bustling dining room. Old memories swirled around him as he walked toward her.

Daniella in Florence wearing a sexy green dress and gazing into his eyes like he was the only man on earth.

Daniella accepting his marriage proposal and telling him she loved him.

Daniella lying in bed beside him with her dark brown hair splayed on the pillow and her lush lips close to his face.

His heart ached for those carefree days, a time when they were lovers and planned their future together. He had screwed up big time.

Tonight, she had on another green dress. He smiled and grabbed the chair next to her. She gazed up at him, but didn't return his smile. Uh-oh.

"You look lovely this evening." He lifted her hand, placing a quick kiss on the soft skin.

She smiled, eyes sparkling. "You have certainly retained your charm. I have ordered wine for us." She pulled her hand free and picked up the bottle of Chianti, pouring generous amounts into each glass.

"Great," Steve said. He felt pretty good. He'd made it through the tough part, the first few minutes.

"Let us make a toast." She handed him his glass and took her own. "To finding our friend, Peter."

They touched glasses and each took a sip. Daniella set her glass down and moved closer to him. She touched his arm and gave it a squeeze.

Now, he knew why she'd blessed him with a smile in the first place. It was all for show.

Okay, let's make this more interesting. He slipped his arm around her neck, bringing her lips to his.

The kiss produced an old stirring that threatened his calm composure. When she pulled away, he tried to forget the kiss. More moments from the past rushed through his mind.

Dummy. Your plan backfired.

Daniella picked up her glass and sipped the wine. She did not like the way his kiss made her feel. Heaven help her, she would jump into a close relationship with him right now, as if nothing had happened. She glanced around the room trying to rid herself of the desire she felt for him.

This assignment will take all of my resolution and strength.

He grabbed her hand again. "Do you know the identity of the body found in the sea?"

Daniella gave thanks, he was all business. She removed her hand and reached for her fork.

"Yes, it was Bruno."

Steve frowned. "Why do you suppose he was killed?"

Daniella shrugged. "They wanted us to think it was Peter."

"Any more news?"

She could sense he wanted to end this meeting as soon as possible. He would not get his wish, there was much to tell.

"Peter was at a house in Monterosso on the Ligurean Coast. Mara Cavari's grandmother's house. We think they took him there first. Also, we have a suspicious place on the outskirts of this city. Peter may have been there two days ago. Neighbors gave a description of two men and a woman."

Steve sat up straighter in his chair. "Well, I have to admire the planning of this crime. It isn't ordinary. They brought him here to throw off the scent and confuse everyone. Since you have a headquarters in Milan, I would be willing to wager that whoever is in charge wanted to show you his power. How did the witnesses describe the people at the house?"

"The woman matched the description of Mara Cavari. One of the men could have been Peter. The second man is very tall, perhaps six-foot-five, with black hair and dark eyes. The neighbors were terrified of him. They said one look from him could kill, and they watched from behind the curtains. Only two people have agreed to come in and look at photos."

"Do you have any suspects?"

"The description of the tall man does fit someone. His name is Lorenzo. He has many false names and is known to be brutal."

Steve winced and fought back panic. It seemed he was following one step behind a trail of clues. It must be part of the abductor's plan. He frowned. The whole thing reminded him of someone from long ago.

"You know, Daniella, for some reason I've been thinking a lot about Cristo since Peter disappeared. Could there be someone out there who had been close to him and is now using his tactics?"

"Like a Cristo clone?" She laughed at her own joke causing her eyes to sparkle. "The case sounds like him, no?"

"Do you think it's possible that he's alive?"

" There has been no sign of him since his reported death."

"He may have been waiting for the right time to do this," Steve said.

"I will bring this up tomorrow morning at our meeting. You and I will see the house in Milan tomorrow afternoon. Okay?"

He nodded.

Daniella glanced at her watch. "I must go. Rosie goes to bed soon."

She stood and slipped on her short black jacket.

Steve stared at her long luscious hair hanging down her back and resisted the urge to touch it.

Outside, he helped her into her car and leaned in the window. "Do you think I could follow you home and meet Rosie?"

"No. We would all lose precious sleep from the excitement. Let us wait. When this work is finished, you will meet her."

Steve nodded and pulled himself away from the car window.

She was right, he needed to wait until this situation with Peter was resolved, one way or another.

Her car moved down the boulevard and he watched her tail lights until they were out of sight.

THIRTEEN

The next afternoon, Steve followed Daniella into a small house located in an average neighborhood in Milan. He was glad to get out of the car. The drive had consisted of many lane changes at outlandish speed. Nothing had changed in that department.

Daniella still knew only one way to drive, fast.

He studied the immaculate living room and thought they'd be lucky if forensics found one part of a fingerprint. Peter was in the hands of professionals.

"They are well trained," Daniella said. "Their behavior did not draw suspicions. But nothing could hide the physical appearance and temperament of the tall man. Let us go upstairs."

He fell into step behind her and was mesmerized by her walk, his eyes riveted on her firm rear end. He looked away quickly, focusing on the details of the house.

She stopped at the first room at the top of the stairs. "We think this was Peter's room. Nothing was found in here." She turned her head and nodded toward a door across the hall. "We did find a partial print in the bathroom."

Steve walked across the bedroom and stood at the window. He thought about the print. Had it been left on purpose? He turned and caught Daniella's gaze.

"You are thinking what I am thinking," she said. "They left the print for us to find."

Steve raised his eyebrows and smirked. "Yes. It

seems so obvious. Who's was it?"

"Peter's."

"I'm not surprised." He crossed the hall and entered the bathroom.

"The room is small," Daniella said.

He turned and studied her as she stood in the doorway. She was all business today in a navy pinstripe suit. The scent of her cologne reached his nostrils. Working so close to her on this case would be more than challenging. Already, he wanted to concentrate all of his attention on her.

Their eyes met before she stepped back into the hall. He had a feeling she read his thoughts.

Back on the street, Steve sat behind the wheel before Daniella could protest. She gave him a dirty look, as she buckled her seatbelt, not even trying to arrange her short skirt in a ladylike position. Steve thought he could see all the way up her thighs. This really bothered him. His attraction to her could ruin everything. He didn't have time for an affair.

As they drove toward the downtown area, Daniella's phone rang. It was a short call. She hung up and grinned. "One of the neighbors picked Lorenzo as the man at the house. Now, we are certain he is involved in this case. We must find Peter soon; this man is an expert at carrying out any cruel and elaborate plan. He receives intense pleasure from inflicting pain on his victims."

Steve scowled. He wondered what other surprises would pop up. "I would like to go to Rome, Daniella. Can you find safe accommodations for Carrie and my team?"

"When?"

"Tomorrow."

"Yes, I will take care of everything. Do you have airline tickets?"

"No."

"We will take care of that too." She turned her head toward him. "Of course, everything will be billed to your government."

Her large brown eyes with the thick lashes and sculptured brows lit up and she laughed heartily.

Steve chuckled. It was the old Daniella. "I also want to see the house in Monterosso."

"Arrangements will be made."

She was clearly in a friendlier mood and Steve could feel warmth coming from her. What did that mean? "Will you meet us in Rome?"

"Yes," she said.

Steve pulled up in front of a large store in downtown Milan and got out. He hurried down the street and Daniella passed him, swerving in and around cars and a bus.

Peter stood beside his cot and wrapped the thin blanket around his shoulders. He pulled it close to his body to conserve the warmth, but a shiver still passed through him. The dampness and the chill were overpowering.

At the last mealtime, Lorenzo had installed lights in the hallway. The jailer probably got tired of carrying a lantern. This light stayed on all the time, allowing Peter to move around the cell freely.

He paced the small area and tried to concentrate on Lorenzo. The man appeared three times a day to bring food and take him to the bathroom.

The exertion of the continuous movement caused him to stop and inhale a lung full of the rank moist air. This caused a coughing spell. Would he never learn not to do that? The only way one could tolerate the smell was to take in short breaths.

An image of Carrie floated through his consciousness. He loved her so much. His throat constricted as tears formed in his eyes.

Stop thinking about her and get a grip. If he wanted to get through this ordeal in one piece, he had to be tough. Thinking about other things only weakened his resolve and strengths. But he also knew that his wife and baby gave him the will to use those strengths.

A door closed and Lorenzo's footsteps moved toward his cell.

He wondered about the building above him, or if there was one. Did his captor live on the premises?

Was this dungeon buried in a hillside and Lorenzo only came here to feed him? A cold chill paralyzed him. He had a strong feeling of being enclosed with no immediate way out.

His feet shuffled faster. Who knew where this place could be? Better to not think about it right now.

Lorenzo stopped outside. "Stand away from the door."

Peter moved to his cot and turned around to face the cruel man.

Lorenzo opened the door and slid a tray along the floor. "You will have a visitor soon."

The deep voice echoed in the still air.

Peter wanted to laugh. Knowing better than to push this guy's buttons, he forced himself to pick up his tray and sit on the bed. He stared down at the food on his plate. The mushy brown substance was not appetizing. However, the bread accompanying it was fresh and smelled delicious. He took a bite.

Lorenzo still stood in the doorway.

"Will you serve tea and crumpets?" Peter asked, his mouth full of bread. He immediately scolded himself. Not a good move.

The laugh from the tall man held a sinister edge.

"What are these crumpets you ask about? If they are poison, perhaps you will get some. This visitor will not take your insolence. I will enjoy cutting out that smart tongue of yours."

Lorenzo scowled and shut the door.

Peter listened to the retreating footsteps. He took a bite of the brown stuff. It tasted as bad as it looked. Lorenzo was not a good cook. He knew the tall man would return in about thirty minutes for the bathroom break. Afterward, Peter would start to work on a section of the wall hidden by the cot.

Early Wednesday morning, Father Dominick Angelo sat at a desk in his small office at the Abby. He could hear movement outside his door in the main hallway and glanced at his clock. Time for morning prayers.

He picked up a piece of paper and read it again. His eyes consulted his calendar. Friday was his annual meeting in Spezia. He would make a stop on his way back to the Abby.

Father Angelo tucked the paper into the pocket of his robe and stepped out into the hall. He joined the other monks heading toward the chapel. They turned a corner and entered a long corridor with columns and large windows. Father Angelo noticed a group of tourists gathering on the grass outside.

The Bella Roca Monastery sat on a hill overlooking a small town and the Ligurean Sea. It had sat there for centuries. Even though the monks did not give tours of their monastery, the grounds were open to the public. The view was far too spectacular to keep to themselves.

Life at the Abby was peaceful and Father Angelo enjoyed the work he did for his Lord. Chanting filled the air outside the doorway leading into the chapel.

He smiled and stepped inside.

"Remember, my dear, only the restaurant and two shops."

Marian stared at her assistant. Yes, he was just her assistant. Who was in charge here?

Raoul smiled. "It is for security reasons. Even though we have two men following us around for protection, we have to be careful. Do not forget what happened at your estate." He raised his eyebrows. "I will never forget."

"Okay, I see your point. The restaurant and two shops it is. But if the restaurant has a shop, I'm not going to count it."

When Raoul chuckled, she opened the car door and stepped out. She could feel a big argument coming on, and they were due for one. Sometimes she wanted to haul off and pinch him or slug him in the arm. But she couldn't do it to someone she cared so much about. Raoul would lay his life down for her. A little cooperation wasn't too much to ask for, right?

They had chosen this large village in the Fassa Valley for its panoramic views of the Italian Dolomites. She glanced around at the street and storefronts. "I see there's still snow."

"This is one of the favorite spots for skiing, my love." Raoul grabbed her arm and they walked toward the hotel where they would have lunch. "We can come back in a few days for a little fun. They even have slopes for all types of skiers."

Marian nodded her head toward the hillsides close to the village. "Lots of dark green trees, Raoul. The snow doesn't look very deep. Didn't the butler say that this was the off season? Between winter skiing and the summer hikers?"

"Yes, he did. It was a good choice. We lucked out, not as many people. However, I think as long as there is snow, there will be skiing."

He stopped in front of a building in the middle of the street. People were sitting at tables outside under an awning. "We can eat outside or inside, Marian. Which is your choice?"

She shivered. The cool air was working its way through her heavy coat. A glance through the two large windows of the restaurant told her it was warm and inviting inside. "I'll take inside. It's still a little cool out here for me."

They crossed the threshold of an old hotel and walked through the lobby to the restaurant. The large room was crowded, but Raoul had made a reservation and they were led to their table. Marian liked the decor of the room. Rustic charm with lots of wood.

She marveled that this part of Italy was so much like Austria. Earlier, Raoul told her the language was German, not Italian. Marian looked at the menu and was pleased to see both types of food.

"I haven't had real German food for a long time," she said.

"What will you eat?" Raoul asked.

She almost laughed at his expression. "Have you ever eaten German food, Raoul?"

He shook his head.

"Brat's are like hot dogs," Marian said. "Why don't you try one of them?"

Raoul shrugged. "You order for me. I do not trust my judgment."

Marian laughed. This had to be a first. Her making the decisions.

After lunch, she chose a shop that had been recommended by their waitress. It had jewelry and perfumes and most of all darling boutique-style clothing. Marian enjoyed herself thoroughly, spending a great deal of cash. Raoul wouldn't let her use her charge card. Too dangerous. "Security, my dear."

She stared out the shop window and saw Raoul sitting on a bench. His face looked pinched from the cold. He certainly didn't hold up too well in this type of weather. It was a far cry from Florida and even New Jersey.

Carrying her purchases, she went outside and stood in front of him.

His dark eyes met hers. "Where to now, my dear?"

"The day has warmed up a little, don't you think? Let's have an ice cream. See?" She pointed to a shop two doors down.

Raoul stood and grabbed her packages. "Lead the way."

She heard him gasp as she sat down in a chair on a large terrace outside the ice cream store. "Let's sit here and watch the people go by."

His hand gripped her arm. "We will go inside and order our stuff. You can have ice cream, but I will most assuredly have a large hot chocolate."

He steered her inside and Marian hid her smile. She loved every minute of being here with him.

"Carrie, open your eyes! You're missing the Tiber River. That's the Castel De' Angelo on the other side."

She forced her eyes open. Steve sat next to her in the back seat, pointing at something. What had he said?

A beautiful Italian woman named Daniella had picked them up at the airport and was now driving toward their hotel. Carrie gazed out the window at the river with the old stone railing. It was almost a blur.

Many people on motor scooters wove in and out of

the heavy traffic. Most of the cars were very small, and traveled at astonishing speed. That's why she'd closed her eyes. It was too scary.

"Rome is a busy place," Carrie said. "I don't know what I expected, but surely not this!"

Steve nodded. "You'll get used to it."

Carrie gasped and grabbed the edge of her seat as Daniella made a quick turn into a narrow alley without slowing down.

"Your hotel is on the next street," Daniella said. She stopped at the corner of the alley and made a left, but was almost hit by another car which had run a stop sign. Daniella braked and yelled something in Italian out the window. She also gestured with her hands.

Carrie glanced at Steve.

"No one stops at the stop signs," he whispered.

She cringed and nodded. A few minutes later, Daniella came to an abrupt stop in front of their hotel. It was situated on a narrow street with many shops surrounding it.

Steve grabbed Carrie's arm and led her inside. They crossed the lobby and stopped at the elevator. Daniella went to the desk.

Once upstairs in their two bedroom suite, she felt better. Her room overlooked the street and the blue bedspread and white lace curtains lent a certain old world charm.

This should make her confinement more endurable. At least she could watch the foot traffic and small cars and trucks. "For a jail, it'll do."

There was a knock at her bedroom door.

"It's me." Steve opened the door a crack. "I hope you like your room."

Carrie opened the door all the way. "I love my room."

"I have to go out. Don't leave the suite or let anyone inside unless it's Juan or Charlie. They're in room 102 down the hall."

"Okay," Carrie said. Her eyes followed him as her brother disappeared down the hall toward the elevator, then closed and latched the door.

Peter struggled to open his eyes, but his lids wouldn't respond. The eerie quiet prevailed. When would this hell on earth end? Where were his rescuers?

They'd better hurry or all they'll find is skin and bones. He was so tired, he didn't care.

Voices and footsteps broke into the silence. He coughed and sat up on his cot, forcing his eyes to open. He shook his head to clear his thinking.

"They're drugging my food and water," he muttered to himself. His words echoed around him like a soft whisper.

The voices stopped, but the footsteps grew louder. He recognized Lorenzo's step.

In the dim light, he could see the form of the cruel man outside his door. Peter thought about the hole in the wall and fought panic.

Lorenzo unlocked the door and swung it open.

"Come here. I will tie your hands."

Peter wanted to bash the bastard's skull in, but he knew he had to conserve his strength. He controlled his urge and walked to the cell door with his arms out. As his wrists were tied together, he assumed this would be the usual bathroom stop.

Lorenzo gestured and Peter walked out toward the bathroom. When they neared the door, his captor shoved him forward. "Do not stop."

"Where are we going? Are you letting me go? I can't

believe you're doing this. It's been so much fun."

"Shut your mouth."

He was pushed from behind and entered a small room. Peter wanted to gag. Several things must have died in here. It smelled worse than his cell. He held his breath and scanned the room. It was about the size of his walk-in closet at home. The devices hanging on the walls were not your usual decorating items. More like spooky Halloween torture equipment. Where was the body hanging from the ceiling?

His heart skipped a beat when he focused and realized they were the real thing.

Lorenzo gave him another hard push. "Keep walking, pig!"

Peter used a lot of his precious energy fighting off his need to turn around and kick Lorenzo in the balls.

A few steps later, he entered a room with bright lights. It was so unlike the dungeon and the smelly room, he blinked several times to make sure it was real. The paneled walls and modern furniture came into sharp focus. Across the room, his gaze stopped and held.

Sitting in a chair directly in front of a fake fireplace was none other than Count Ricco DiBiasi, code name Cristo. His smile was sinister. Peter blinked a few more times. This had to be a dream or a hallucination.

"Peter, so nice to see you again!" Cristo said. "I hope your stay has not been too stressful for you." He threw his head back and the sound of the high pitched laugh resonated throughout the room.

Chills ran up Peter's spine as he forced himself to act nonplused. "Ricco, what a surprise. So, you are the one behind this charade."

Cristo's smile remained glued to his face. He folded his hands in his lap. His fingers were long and his nails manicured.

Peter wanted to throw-up. He hated this man.

"I thought you'd been eaten by sharks long ago, but then I see you didn't escape all in one piece did you?" Peter stared at the wheelchair and grinned.

Cristo's face turned beet red. His eyes bulged. The man appeared to boil inside. The old nemesis would never have allowed that to happen.

"Yes, I did escape. I almost died from your bullet and the explosion. It has taken me this long to gain some degree of health and seek my revenge." He motioned for Lorenzo to move his captive to the sofa. The big man pushed Peter into the soft cushions.

The wheelchair moved closer until the toes of Cristo's shoes touched Peter's legs. His calm chiseled facial features became a cruel mask.

"I have wonderful entertainment for you and your partner. I hope you do not die too soon. There is a certain amount of suffering I want you to experience first."

He grinned and Peter thought he looked like one of the sharks that should have eaten him years ago.

Now that he was on Cristo's level, Peter could see that not only were the man's legs damaged, but his once handsome face was dramatically scarred. One was especially nasty. It ran from left of his right eye, down to his chin. He winced.

The movement was not lost on Cristo.

"So! You find my body offensive." The anger in his voice rocked the room. "Yours will look worse by the time I am finished with it. And we will see how humorous you are when I bring your mother's corpse here and sit her on the sofa for my enjoyment."

The crippled man scowled and wheeled himself out of the room through a nearby doorway.

Lorenzo grabbed Peter and dragged him toward the torture chamber.

Peter fought to stand on his feet. A strange noise came from in back of him and he turned his head in time to see Cristo enter an elevator.

All the way back to his cell, two questions ran through his mind over and over again. How had Cristo survived the explosion and the bullet? And, was his mother dead?

Lorenzo opened his cell door and pushed him inside. Peter turned and stared into the hard menacing eyes. His hands formed fists and he thought that fighting this man for his life was better than waiting for torture. Now that Peter knew Cristo was behind his abduction, it was time to escape. He had to help his mother.

"Do not get any ideas. You will be killed if you try to escape." Lorenzo grabbed a gun from his holster and pointed it at Peter's chest, a reminder of the power the tall man possessed. He shut the door and walked away, laughing.

Peter paced up and down his cell. He was more distraught than ever. The abductions were not going to stop. His mother and Steve were part of the monster's plan. Could his old partner have been sent to Italy to find him? In a way, he hoped not. He didn't want Cristo to capture him, too. Fear gripped him when he thought about his mother. Had Cristo's goons killed her?

FOURTEEN

Steve stood in the doorway of Peter's hotel room and scanned the small area. There weren't any clues here. He felt desperate. The sense of time running out pressed against him. "I don't know what I thought I'd find. It's as if nothing of importance has happened here. Peter must have been overwhelmed when he answered the door."

Across the room, Daniella turned and stared at him. "The people involved were professionals. Do not forget the house in Milan. There was only a partial fingerprint."

The walls started to close in and he stepped out into the hall. Daniella followed him into the elevator.

"We will release the room."

Steve nodded. "The hotel has been more than accommodating. Thanks Daniella. I needed to see this for myself."

"You will pick up his luggage at headquarters?" Daniella asked.

He sighed. He'd better have Kevin do it and take Peter's things back to the safe house. Kevin would be discreet and hide it away until they found Peter. "Yes, I'll make arrangements."

The doors opened into the lobby and they went out to the sidewalk. The bright sun made Steve squint. He reached into his pocket and took out his sunglasses. "Are you going to the coast tomorrow?"

Her eyes studied each of his features. It was hard to read what was going through her mind.

"No, I cannot. Rosie has a doctor's appointment and I insist on being with her."

"Is she sick?" Steve couldn't help the concern in his voice.

"No. It is a cold or allergies. The doctor will tell us tomorrow."

"So, you will go back to Milan for a couple of days?"

"Yes, I have other duties. I cannot babysit you Americans!"

Steve laughed. He could feel the muscles in his body relaxing. "You have no idea how much I've missed your humor."

She gripped his arm. The light humorous moment vanished.

"You must be careful, tomorrow. I can feel Peter's captors watching our every move." She hurried down the street toward the car.

His hand ran through his hair. She'd only spoken what was already in his mind.

Carrie sucked in her stomach and zipped her skirt. Time to buy more clothes. This was the only thing that felt comfortable.

She heard the suite door close and glanced into the living room. Her brother sat down on the couch. He saw her and smiled. "I have something to tell you before we go to dinner."

"What is it?" She hurried across the room and stood in front of him.

"Tomorrow I'm going to the coast to look at a house. The Italians think Peter was there."

Her eyebrows shot up.

"Remember it may not help us find him, but I'm

thinking I'll discover a lead or two. Don't get your hopes up too high."

"I know. I'm grateful you have leads." Her spirits rose. She wasn't looking forward to one more day alone in the hotel room, but it sounded like Steve was making progress.

"Are you ready to go downstairs for dinner?"

"Yeah." She followed him out the door and against her better judgment allowed herself to feel hopeful.

Marian sat in the gazebo near the pond enjoying the cool crisp weather. She pulled her sweater closer as a breeze filtered through screens of the enclosed building. Raoul wasn't far off; she could see him talking to one of the security men near the house.

Her eyes darted around the estate and stopped at the pond. The countryside here certainly had its charm. Even though Marian had been to the Alps in Austria and France, she enjoyed these mountains just as well. They looked powerful with their light gray cliffs and white spires. Right now they were reflected in the water of the pond. Spread out on a little table nearby, was a carafe of strong coffee and a plate of cookies and bite-sized pieces of apple strudel. She picked up her cup and sipped the strong brew wondering if it would keep her awake tonight. She heard footsteps and turned to see Raoul approaching the gazebo.

"Raoul, check out the pond."

"I enjoyed looking at it as I walked over here," he said. His body eased into the chair next to her. "How strong is that coffee?"

"Pretty potent stuff. Would you like a cup?"

"I should pass; you know how it affects me, my dear."

"Oh, Raoul, this place is so relaxing." She set her cup down and leaned over to kiss him on the cheek. "Thanks."

He grabbed her hand and rested it on his thigh. "It is almost a wonderland, and I am here with a beautiful princess."

He lifted her hand and kissed her fingers.

The kisses warmed up Marian's chilled body. "Is it time to go inside?"

Raoul chuckled. "I cannot kiss your hand without you turning into a sex addict."

Marian opened her eyes wide. "Look who's calling me a sex addict. You knew what that kiss would do to me. It's your fault."

He slipped his arms around her shoulders and drew her close. "I love you, Marian. You are so much fun to tease." He kissed her cheek and then her neck. "Yes, my dear, we should go inside now. I have checked the security and everything is in order. The butler said to leave the dishes out here."

Marian stood and was startled by something whizzing past her head. She thought it was a mosquito and raised her hand to shoo it away. Raoul fell to the floor, pulling her down with him.

"Stay down, Marian, someone is shooting at us."

Several more bullets penetrated the Gazebo before they stopped and a barrage of shots started up at the house.

"Stay put, I will see what is going on outside. Do not move! Do you understand?" He pulled her face around to his and she nodded.

Raoul crawled to the opening and carefully looked out. The shooting had stopped. He could see the security men hiding behind the cars close to the front door of the house. They were staring off toward the front of the property.

His gaze switched to the back of the house. He saw two men approaching from trees several feet away from the back door. If he yelled to the security men to warn them, the two guys in the back would know there was someone to shoot at in the gazebo. The shots fired at him a few minutes ago had come from the front.

He crawled out and dragged himself across the grass. Marian would be safe as long as she stayed in the gazebo.

Half-way to the house, he stopped. The two in the back were about to step onto the porch. Raoul opened fire, hitting one in the shoulder and the other in the leg. At the same time, the firing began again at the front. He saw one of the security men fall and not get up. That left only one man to fend off whoever was out there.

What should he do? Where would be the best place for Marian?

He turned around and headed back for the gazebo. As he entered the small building, the gunfire stopped again. He saw the other security man lying in the driveway clutching his leg.

"Marian, follow me. We will head for the pond." He pulled her bright red sweater off of her and stuffed it inside his shirt. He grabbed the small dark blanket she had used on her lap, and then crawled out the door.

There was little time before the attackers would discover they were missing. At the edge of the pond, Raoul stood up and dragged Marian into a copse of trees nearby. She sat down behind a tree trunk. He crawled to the edge of the trees and looked back at the house. The servants came out the back door, running for the woods. Shots rang out after them, but no one appeared to be hit.

He hurried back to Marian and knelt beside her.

"We can't stay here. They will soon figure out we were in the gazebo. Lucky for us, I carry a map of the area with me. I also have all of our important papers in my pocket. You see, Marian, I trust no one."

After consulting his map, he helped her up. He could feel her body trembling. "Everything will be okay, my dear. We will try to find the village we were in yesterday." He tossed her the blanket. "Wrap this around your shoulders. It will get cold."

Raoul knew they had to move fast, but he could not risk wearing Marian out. She would be too heavy for him to carry. He decided to save the sweater until she started to complain about the cold.

Three hours later, Raoul half-carried Marian to the first hotel at the outskirts of the village. He got a room for them and tucked her in bed. As she dozed off, he opened his map and started to form a plan.

The next day, Steve took a train to Monterosso al Mare. He had never been to this part of Italy before and enjoyed the colorful houses clinging to the cliffs, the laundry hanging outside the windows, and the beautiful coastline.

Monterosso belonged to a string of small towns along the Ligurean Sea called La Cinque Terra. For centuries, the five towns were accessible only by sea and were at the mercy of pirates and conquering nations. Today, a train stopped at each town and there was also a road if you cared to drive.

This town was different from the others in the string; it had its own beach. He walked up the hill from the railroad station and turned to look back at the water and the sand. The view was breathtaking.

Daniella's team had interviewed most of the people in the small town. Only a few had seen Mara when she stayed at the house.

He continued on up the hill and after a couple of blocks, got his bearings and decided he was on the right street. It was steep and the view even better. He glanced up the hill. Squinting, he thought he could see a dark figure on the porch of the last house: the place where the Italian forensic team thought Peter had been held captive. He quickened his pace.

The dark figure became clearer and he could see that it was a man dressed in the clothes of the clergy, sitting on the stoop. When Steve approached the steps, the priest stood up and extended his hand.

"Ciao, I am Father Angelo from the Bella Roca Monastery. Do you live in this house?"

Steve shook his hand. "Glad to meet you Father, but no I don't live here. Are you looking for anyone in particular?"

"I received a letter from one of my old friends. The return address on the envelope was this house."

Steve was tired from his trek up the hill and sat down on the steps. Father Angelo joined him.

"Who is your old friend? Maybe I can be of help."

"The only name I know him by is Ricco," the monk said.

Steve's body stiffened. This whole thing was becoming bizarre.

"How do you know this Ricco?"

"A few years ago, he appeared at the monastery. He wanted a tour of our church and grounds. I had to inform him that it was not possible. We are a very private monastery and do not expose our life to the outside world. I am one of the few who are allowed to come and go, and then only on business."

"Why was Ricco interested in your monastery?"

"He wanted to see the catacombs in the lower part Of the church. They are set back against the wall of the cliff. He pressed a check into my hand and urged me to ask for permission.

"The amount was generous, and the Abbot found no harm in allowing the man to see the lower levels. We accepted the donation and Ricco toured the catacombs."

"Is that the only part of the monastery that he toured?" Steve asked.

"Yes. He left that day very happy."

"Did he visit the monastery again?"

"No. A year later, he called from the town below our church. I met him there and he gave a sizable donation again. He was a nice man and I enjoyed talking to him. Since we have not communicated, I assumed he died. You can see how I was surprised to receive a letter this week."

"Why did you think he might have died? Is he elderly?"

"He is young. Possibly your age. He is confined to a wheelchair and his body is full of scars."

Steve tried to assimilate all of the shocking information. Ricco had survived?

Whoa, wait, it could be another Ricco. But, if the man was Ricco DiBiasi, Peter's abduction would make sense. Why did he send this monk here?

In his mind a huge red flag waved. Could he have wanted me to know about this monastery? The next question "why?" swirled around in his head unanswered.

"If this is not your home, why are you here, my son?"

"A friend of mine stayed at this house recently," Steve said. "He has disappeared and I have come to find out if the people who live here would know where I could find him."

The monk checked his watch. "I must go." He stood

and shook hands with Steve. "Perhaps your friend knows my friend. Good luck in finding yours."

Steve watched Father Angelo walk down the hill toward the train station. His mind was going over and over the information he'd just learned, trying to connect all the pieces.

Raoul scooted closer to Marian. Her head was on his shoulder and the scarf covering her auburn hair was falling off. He reached over and pulled it forward to cover her hair again. His princess was dressed in the clothes she wore yesterday. Last night he had left Marian at the hotel while he went into the village to shop for a lightweight coat and a handbag and scarf. He had bought only a jacket and a hat for himself. New sunglasses for both.

They had boarded the bus early this morning. He hadn't seen anyone suspicious watching them or boarding the bus with them. But Raoul knew their attackers could be sitting across the aisle from him. He had the window seat and turned to look out. He was so tired and he'd give anything to get rid of the ache gnawing at the back of his head.

Traffic was light. A car passed and he gazed down into the passenger seat. A man looked up at him. Raoul panicked. He thought he saw this man the other day at the village when they had lunch. He slowly turned back to Marian, trying not to cause the man to single him out from the other passengers on the bus. After a few minutes, the car continued on. Raoul wiped the sweat off his brow. Would they be waiting for them up ahead in Bolzano? He would look for the man at the next stop.

She sat on the edge of Rosie's bed and finished

reading the bedtime story. Her daughter had fallen asleep three pages ago, but Daniella had faithfully finished the story. She set the book on the dresser and then tucked the blanket around her sleeping angel.

Her hand reached out and touched the brown curls with golden highlights. She admired the nose that reminded her of Steve, and kissed the cheek next to the bowed mouth that could pout just like hers. She smiled at the child that brightened up her busy life. She was thankful to have her.

The phone downstairs rang and she hurried to answer it.

"Pronto."

"Good evening," Steve said. "Hope I didn't interrupt anything."

"No, you did not."

"I won't keep you on the phone long. I wanted to tell you what happened today at the house in Monterosso."

Steve told her about the priest and his letter.

"Do you think Cristo is alive and planned this abduction for years?" Daniella asked. She could not hide the disbelief in her voice.

"It looks that way. And it fits his mode of operation. Why would he go to all of this trouble just to let me know about this monastery? And how could he know I would be there when the monk came looking for him?"

"It does not seem possible," Daniella said. "Cristo is dead. Maybe someone is pretending to be him. I will be in Rome tomorrow afternoon; we can talk more about this."

Steve hung up his phone and sat at the desk in the living room of the suite. He wasn't comfortable with this new development. He frowned and within seconds was knocking at his sister's bedroom door, hoping to hell he was wrong.

Carrie opened the door. She looked like a heroine from a monster movie; white nightgown down to the floor, huge eyes, hair disarranged, fingers digging into her mouth.

"Sorry to scare you, Carrie. I'm going to sleep on the couch tonight. If anything happens, Juan and Charlie are down the hall."

His sister nodded. "I know...room 102." She turned and walked back toward her bed. "My heart's beating about a mile a minute. Don't scare me like that. I thought Peter was dead."

"Sorry again, Sis. I'm beat from my long day. Get some sleep."

Steve found an extra blanket in the closet and tried to get comfortable on the couch. His cell phone rang. It was Kevin.

"Hello, Kevin."

"There's been a serious turn of events. I received a call a few minutes ago. One of the private security men, guarding your couple from New Jersey, called last evening and reported they were under attack. We sent a team there and found the two security men dead. The couple is missing."

Steve ran a hand down his face. Marian and Raoul. "So, they are either kidnapped or on the run. Let's hope it's the latter. Raoul is smart. I did give him your phone number in case he needed to contact someone."

"Maybe he'll call. What will you do now?"

"Tomorrow I'll find a safe line and make contact with my superiors. Call me when you know something."

Kevin hung up and Steve stared at his phone.

Whoever was behind this had good informants. A lot of money had been spent on these people and the hired killers. Deep pockets were involved. He hoped Raoul and Marian were on the run.

There wasn't much he could do at the moment. He dropped on the couch and fell asleep.

Fire alarms woke Steve. His heart beat fast and his mind groped for clarity. He ran to the door with his weapon and looked through the peephole. Smoke filled the hall. He couldn't see anyone outside.

Carrie appeared next to him wearing her robe and slippers

"There seems to be a fire," Steve said calmly. "Lots of smoke in the hallway. Take the blanket off the couch and dampen it in the tub."

Carrie hurried to do as he asked. He opened the door and looked down the hall for Charlie and Juan. He didn't see them and took a few steps toward their room.

Don't leave Carrie alone, his inner voice yelled. As he turned to go back, he was hit on the head from behind.

He heard Carrie scream before he hit the floor and passed out.

FIFTEEN

His head hurt. No, his head had a dull aching pain. Steve blinked his eyes several times. Everything was blurry. He waited a few seconds for his vision to clear, and then scanned his surroundings.

Daniella sat in a chair next to his bed. There was an IV in his arm connected to a packet hanging above his head. A television was across the room.

"What happened?" he croaked. He met Daniella's gaze. "Things are bad, aren't they?"

She sighed and swallowed. Her eyes welled with threatening tears. "Carrie is gone. The fire was a ruse. Only smoke. The two agents on duty opened their door when they heard the alarm. They were shot as they stepped out. The killer used a silencer. The agents died instantly. Whoever it was, hit you and took Carrie."

Steve now remembered everything. He tried not to panic. His sister was in the hands of Cristo or his nasty clone. Was this all part of the plan since the beginning? Had they been led along by the nose?

Guilt seeped through every pore. He had brought her to the fiend. His heart fell and he shook his head with distaste. The headache intensified.

He moaned. Whoever was behind this was someone who knew him well, knew that he was the only one who could find Peter. Knew he wouldn't be able to leave Carrie behind.

What a fool he'd been. "Get me out of this bed!" he yelled.

It was dark and Carrie could smell a musty dampness and rotten garbage. Her mind was confused. Was she still at the hotel? Another breath of the stale putrid air caused memories to flood back. Her mouth opened to scream, but she resisted this powerful urge. Screaming would only draw attention to herself and she didn't want to do that. The horrible man might come back.

She sat on a cot in a small room with a light shining through an opening in the door. It reminded her of the movies she had seen when the prisoners were kept in a cell deep in a dungeon. She shivered.

Voices drifted from somewhere outside her cell. She listened and knew they drew closer. Her mind flashed images of the smoke last night. She shook her head. Where was her brother?

She remembered falling to the floor.

She put her head in her hands and tried to imagine what that would mean.

A face popped into her mind and she felt terror. It was her abductor and she knew she had seen him before. Tears pooled in her eyes threatening to fall. She didn't want to cry. It wouldn't help her at all. One escaped and slid down her cheek.

She wiped it away with a fingertip and made herself relive the events, desperately wanting to remember Steve alive. She had stood at the door in the hotel room holding a wet blanket and waiting for her brother. The door opened and she saw the man. She screamed.

Her body trembled now as it had done last night. He had scooped her up into his arms and carried her down to a waiting van on the street.

She remembered his frigid, sinister eyes. He was tall and thin with long black hair pulled back in a ponytail. He was the man at the hardware store in Dallas. The man in the gray sedan. And he must have been the one to break into her home.

He had tied her hands and feet and stuck a gag in her mouth. As they sped down the street, Carrie heard sirens and people yelling. The van traveled some distance before she was put into a helicopter and brought to this place.

Feeling better now having faced her fears, she stood and paced her cell. Questions still bothered her. Why did they kidnap her? Was Peter anywhere near here? She stopped suddenly in her tracks. The voices were gone. However, she could hear a faint sound. It was familiar, one she should know. Yes. Church bells.

Wherever this vile place is, it's near a church. And the sea. She had smelled the sea when she stepped out of the helicopter.

The voices drifted through her cell again and along with them something else. Footsteps. She hurried to the window to look out, but was pushed back immediately when the door opened. A woman dressed in jeans and a sweater stared at her. She was about Carrie's height with long dark hair and big brown eyes.

Carrie tensed when she saw the gun in the woman's hand.

"So, you are the wife of Peter," the woman said. "Come with me." She stepped to the side and gestured, using the gun as a pointer.

The woman led her to a bathroom. She barely made it to the toilet. Panic seized her. Does the woman know I'm pregnant? She glanced down at her stomach. Now into her third month, she only looked slightly bloated.

No one could know about her condition.

She opened the bathroom door and the woman grabbed her arm and jerked her forward. Carrie cried out in pain and scowled. She rubbed her arm and found herself in another room entirely. It had strange looking things on the wall and smelled rank. She covered her nose with her hands.

The woman shoved her from behind. "Keep going!"

Carrie stepped into the next room. It was warm and had a lit fireplace. Great, she could warm up before they took her back to that awful cell.

"Sit down," the woman said.

She glanced at the couch. A man sat on the end staring out into space. Her hands flew up to her face. "Peter?"

Raoul boarded the train in Bolzano, a city known as the gateway to the Dolomites. He turned to help Marian. They walked down the aisle and found seats together. He sat by the window.

Yesterday, after getting off the bus here, they found a nice hotel on the Piazza Walther, convenient to the bus and train stations. At the time, he had no plan. He could have chosen to travel on into Germany, possibly throwing off the people that followed them. But, Steve and Carrie were in Milan.

From their hotel, it was a short walk to the shops in the city Centre. There they had a great meal and bought new clothes. Since their money was running out and they were traveling incognito, he had to make Marian realize they couldn't shop for her usual stylish clothing. They had to keep it simple. She had balked of course, but reason had won out. The boutiques and designer clothing would have to wait for a later trip.

He gazed out the window, watching the people,

looking for anyone familiar or suspicious. This constant vigilance was grating on his nerves. He was not looking forward to what lay ahead.

After they changed trains in Verona and reached Milan, this vigilance would become more pronounced. He had to keep himself together for just a few more hours. By midafternoon they would be in Milan and he would call the number Steve had given him for the safe house.

Marian squeezed his hand. He glanced at her. With completely new clothes, she looked different and didn't stand out in the crowd. She turned her head and their eyes locked. He could see her utter humility and almost laughed. The princess could hardly wait to get the drab clothes off.

Daniella stepped into Steve's hospital room and sat down in the chair next to his bed. He used the remote to turn the television off and stared at her.

She felt uncomfortable with the worry and frustration she saw reflected on his face.

He's blaming himself for Carrie's abduction and the deaths of the two men.

She had to convince him that everything had been covered and it wasn't his fault. She was disappointed with herself for caving in and feeling sympathy for him.

"How is your head?"

"I've had worse headaches with hangovers," he muttered.

Daniella smiled and took his hand. She stood and kissed him on the lips.

Steve returned the kiss.

When they parted, he smiled. "Maybe I should get whacked on the head more often. That was nice." He frowned and his eyes bore into hers. "I'm sorry I yelled at you. I have no excuses."

She laughed. "You've yelled at me before. This time I understand. Let us forget it."

"Okay. What happened to Charlie and Juan? Were they killed? Or was someone else on duty? Also, how could the abductors have taken Carrie outside and into a van without anyone seeing them? What happened to our men outside?"

Daniella sat down in the chair again. "You know how narrow the streets are. A car drove past the front of the hotel and caused a passing Fiat to crash into our surveillance van. Our men were outside the vehicle checking the damage when they saw smoke coming from the second floor of the hotel. They rushed inside and up the stairs. They found you and the two agents. Carrie was gone.

"The kidnappers had taken her downstairs and out the side door. It was well planned and there were only two of them. The people at the front desk gave a description and the license number of the van that drove away. It was stolen."

"I'm sure they abandoned it long ago," Steve said wearily. "Charlie and Juan?"

Her emotions were threatening to break through her usually impenetrable exterior. She swallowed. "They are fine. It was two of ours that were killed."

It was as though a dark cloud passed over Steve. He scowled and his eyes narrowed. "It has Cristo's signature. He has no conscience."

Daniella stiffened. He had practically spit out the words. She could see that he hated whoever was behind this mess.

After a few seconds, his demeanor changed. Steve clasped his hands behind his head and leaned back into his pillows. "He must have survived the explosion and his injuries from that night long ago. This has to be his revenge or someone is getting it for him. I have a strong hunch that I will be grabbed next. It's the only explanation for me being alive today."

"Why do you think they took Carrie?" Daniella asked.

"To give Peter the ultimate torture. And to make me crazy with worry, hoping I will make one little slip to place myself in their path."

Steve only voiced what Daniella had been thinking hours ago. He would be the next victim. She stared at his tortured face and her heart felt squeezed. Her attitude toward him had now changed. Even though it was against her better judgment, she wanted to resume her relationship with this man. She had never stopped loving him and Rosie should know her father. She took a deep breath and tried to be cheerful.

"If your tests are good, you can check out tomorrow morning. The doctor said the bump on your head is big, but you should be fine."

"The bump on my head is nothing. I feel that I've failed those men who died. I knew whoever was behind this mess would attempt to kidnap Carrie again. I should have done more to protect her."

"Steve, I know it's useless to assure you that you did everything possible to protect Carrie and the agents. You are blaming yourself for something you could not prevent. Do not waste time and strength on these matters. We need all of our energies directed at finding Peter and his wife."

"I know it's Cristo," Steve said.

"After what you said about the monk, I think you are right. It has to be him." She checked her watch. "I have to go. Do not blame yourself. Three of our best men have been killed by this monster, for me it is personal now."

She grabbed Steve's hand and gave it a squeeze. He pulled her down and she kissed him on the lips again. Moving away before he could ask her to stay longer, she hurried out the door.

"Thanks, Daniella!" he cried.

She walked to her car and drove toward headquarters. Daniella was determined that Cristo would be caught and punished.

"He doesn't know who he is up against," she mumbled.

Two blocks later, her phone rang. It was Steve.

Peter thought he was dreaming again. Carrie stood in front of him. Her hand reached out and touched him. It was like water to a man dying of severe dehydration. He almost cried with happiness. When she sat down next to him, and pulled him into her arms, tears formed in his eyes. But he didn't allow them to fall. He wouldn't give Cristo the satisfaction of seeing him cry.

Cristo wheeled himself into the room and stopped at the fireplace. "Well, is this not the heart wrenching homecoming?"

Carrie stood up. She wiped her eyes with her fingers and stared at the man in the wheelchair. After a few seconds, her expression changed from one of shock to comprehension. She took a step toward him.

"Ricco?" she whispered.

"Carrie, my love, have you been enjoying our hospitality?" He laughed, but it came out more like a shriek. Tears ran down his face.

Carrie stared in disbelief.

Just as quickly as it had begun, Ricco's mood changed. He regained his composure. "Sit down on the couch with your husband."

Carrie obeyed and sat down next to Peter. He felt her grab his hand again and kiss it. He stared at her and his mind cleared even more. Many questions rushed in, but he settled on one.

"How do you know Ricco?"

She turned to Peter, confused and afraid. How could Ricco be so cruel? Their business arrangements had always been amicable and she had entertained him and his wife in Dallas last year. She thought hard and remembered that her husband had been out of town that week.

"I-"

"Carrie, your husband is in shock."

She thought Ricco looked like a cat that had swallowed several canaries and was now choking on them. Why had he kidnapped her husband? What was this all about?

Peter squeezed her hand. She looked into his eyes. "Ricco is a customer. My store has been doing business with him for a couple of years. I've met his wife, Alissa."

Peter frowned. "I don't remember you telling me about him."

"I did mention him and his wife once. They came to Dallas while you were away on business."

She saw the horror register in his eyes. It quickly disappeared and was replaced with a steely stare directed at Ricco.

The crippled man laughed. "Peter, enjoy the warmth before you return to your cold, damp, cell. Carrie will accompany me upstairs where I have prepared a room for her." He raised his hands as if to push his captive away. "Don't fret! You won't be alone for long. Soon your partner will be here to share in the torture I have planned for you!"

Ricco's face became distorted with hatred. He nodded to the woman.

Carrie dropped Peter's hand and grabbed his arm. She didn't want to be separated from him again.

The woman tried to pull her off the couch. Carrie wouldn't let go of Peter.

"Come with me!" The woman's voice was harsh.

Carrie's grasp became stronger.

The slap on her face startled her. She knew she didn't have a choice.

The agent stood to help his wife, but was stopped by Lorenzo.

Ricco relished Peter's helplessness. Power flowed through him. He loved the feeling.

The O'Brien wedding picture in the New Jersey newspaper had caused him to add this link to the kidnapping. He had been planning this abduction since he got out of the hospital after the first surgery. Everything was coming together nicely.

Peter's punishment had already started. His mother's dead body should be arriving soon; his wife would be a captive upstairs. The only piece left in the puzzle was Steve, Alissa's ex-lover. He would suffer the most.

"Lorenzo, take our guest back to his cell," he yelled. His body tingled with excitement. He turned the wheels of his chair and rolled to the elevator.

In the other room, Carrie cried out to her husband.

Ricco smiled.

"This room must have cost a fortune," Carrie mumbled. She sat in front of the fireplace, staring at the four poster bed across the room. The satin bedspread with matching pillow shams was a lovely shade of lavender, her favorite color.

The rest of the room was expensively furnished and on the textured walls hung rich draperies. The windows afforded marvelous views of the vineyards and the garden.

Her mind continued to replay the scene earlier with Peter and Ricco. Peter looked so bad. Tears fell as she thought of the dark circles beneath his eyes and his gaunt face. How much longer would her husband be able to hold up? Would he die?

The tears fell faster and she sobbed. She felt so helpless. What could she do? She ran into the connecting bathroom and splashed handfuls of cold water on her face and neck. Soft lavender towels soothed her skin.

She returned to the bedroom and forced herself to concentrate on a plan of escape for Peter and herself.

A knock at the bedroom door startled her. She started to panic.

The door opened and the woman from earlier came in with a large shopping bag. She scowled at Carrie, then shut the door and locked it.

"The car that caused the accident was a blue Citron with French license plates," Daniella said. She opened the car door for Steve and went around to the driver's side.

Steve eased into the passenger seat.

It was now evening. After she had left this afternoon, he'd called her and insisted on checking out immediately, not tomorrow morning. It had taken several minutes to convince her to get him released.

"Was it stolen?" Steve asked. He moved the seat as

far back as he could to accommodate his long legs.

"We do not know." She drove away from the hospital.

Steve glanced into the side mirror and saw Charlie and Juan following behind them. For the time being they were protected.

He inhaled, all of his unsolved problems tumbled through his mind. His sister and his old buddy were somewhere out there suffering who knew what. And, Juan had told him that Raoul and Marian were still missing. He felt like time was running out and he didn't have a clue where they all could be.

"Are you okay, Steve? You are quiet."

"Yes. Where are you taking me?"

"To my apartment. Your agents agreed with me, hotels are not a good choice."

She glanced at him and he raised his eyebrows. "I'm glad I called you and insisted you get me out of that hospital. Being injured can have its perks."

Daniella laughed. "You will be on your best behavior!"

"Where is this place?"

"Near the Piazza Navrona. You remember? I use Uncle Luigi's apartment. He is visiting his grandchildren in Florence and will not return for several months." She came to a stop at a major intersection. "My aunt Maria died last year."

Steve vaguely remembered the apartment. He had been there once when they were a couple. He did remember her aunt and uncle. "Sorry to hear about your aunt."

"Thank you. I am happy she saw Rosie before she died."

The light switched to green and she continued another block before turning into an alley and a parking space.

He managed to get himself out of the car and follow her inside the back door of the old apartment building. They went up two flights of stairs and down a hall to the second door on the left. Steve's dizziness returned as he leaned against the wall to steady himself.

Daniella slipped in the key and they stepped into a small foyer which led into a large living room.

"This is very nice. Has it been in your family long?"

"It has been in the family for five generations. Make a drink for us. Perhaps your memory will return." She headed down a hallway. Steve figured the bedrooms were located there.

His equilibrium had straightened itself out somewhat and Steve felt a drink would definitely help it along.

He found the small bar located in an old highly polished buffet table. Grabbing a glass, he walked to the large cheery kitchen and filled it with ice. Back in the living room, he picked up a bottle of old Scottish whiskey and gave himself a healthy dose. As he took a sip, he hoped the liquor belonged to her uncle and not some old boyfriend. He winced. His mind couldn't handle her loving another man.

He heard her step into the kitchen a few minutes later.

"We will have our drink in here," she said from the doorway.

Steve filled a wine glass with Chianti and joined her.

She stood at the counter near the sink. The business suit had been replaced with casual tan slacks and a dark brown light- weight sweater. Her lush figure had only gotten better in four years.

He handed her the wine and kissed her cheek.

She frowned. "Remember, you are on your best behavior. Did you eat at the hospital?"

"No."

She stepped around him and went to a cupboard

across the room. "Good. I am hungry. I will make pasta. There is no time to eat now. I am too busy with you and your American friends."

Steve laughed as he sat in a chair at the large table in the middle of the kitchen. She filled a pot with water and put it on the stove to heat. When she opened the refrigerator and bent down to grab the tomatoes, he smiled. Memories came flooding back. She had spent many pleasant nights in his arms. He remembered having his way with her in this very kitchen. He tried to push these pleasant thoughts away and go to safer grounds. It was no use. Images of their love-making at this apartment in the middle of Rome aroused him.

With difficulty, he managed to focus on Carrie and Peter. "Any news from your meeting this afternoon?"

"We found Father Angelo's monastery and believe Peter and Carrie are in the catacombs underneath the church. A team is being formed to rescue them."

Steve could hardly contain his frustration. How could they be so stupid?

"Daniella, it's too simple. Cristo has set a trap at this church. He sent the monk to tell me about this monastery. Your group is doing exactly what he wants them to do!"

She turned from the stove, gripping a wooden spoon. The crease of her brow and the pinched mouth reflecting her anger.

"The task force does not believe Cristo is behind this. They say he died years ago. I tried to tell them, but they do not listen. I tried to tell them about Bruno and they did not listen. I can only go along with their plan."

Daniella set the spoon down. Her eyes became pleading. "I need you to cooperate, Steve," she whispered.

His heart melted. He sighed and gave in to her need.

"Okay, I'll go, but it'll be a waste of time. Peter and Carrie are not there."

He couldn't shake the feeling of dread settling into the pit of his stomach.

SIXTEEN

After dinner, Steve and Daniella sat on the couch in the living room.

"Great meal, Daniella, I believe you outdid yourself. If we stay here any length of time, I may need a girdle."

Daniella laughed. She felt comfortable sitting with him, on this couch, in this room, where they'd spent many happy hours. Impulsively, she grabbed her purse.

"I have a few pictures of Rosie. They are for you to keep."

Steve's eyebrows shot up and he moved closer to her as she opened the envelope and removed the pictures. He nuzzled her neck and sniffed. "Ummm. You smell great. New scent?"

He ran his hand up her arm and Daniella almost shivered in delight. She could feel his energy and desire. Her own body was raging and she knew now wasn't the time.

"You have to be on your best behavior," she said dryly.

"Okay," he said. "I won't touch you no matter how much you beg."

Daniella chuckled. She lifted a photo off the pile and handed it to him.

"Our daughter's birth picture."

Steve studied the snapshot of the tiny newborn. He

frowned and his body stiffened.

"I've missed the birth of my first child," he whispered.

Daniella was moved by the emotion in his voice. If she didn't know better, she would swear he was going to cry. She looked down quickly and picked up another photo.

"This one was taken by my mother on Rosie's first birthday." Daniella watched him stare at the little girl with short dark curls and big brown eyes trying to open a gift twice her size.

"I've missed so much."

She could see the tears pool in his eyes. She thought Steve would be happy to see the pictures. Instead, he appeared to be sad. She handed him the last picture.

"This one was taken last week by the housekeeper. Rosie loves to play outside. That doll she's trying to put in the dolly stroller was a gift from my aunt."

"The determined look on her face reminds me of someone." His lips trembled as he stared at the picture.

"Yes. She looks like you when you are trying to figure out the clues in a case," Daniella whispered.

She gazed at his face and gasped. A tear rolled down his cheek. Her arms flew around his neck and she held him to her. "I am sorry Steve, I had no idea you would react this way."

They moved apart and she kissed him softly on the lips. He pulled her closer and kissed her hard. The kiss was long and when Steve released her they held each other.

"Please forgive me," Steve whispered.

"I will forgive you only if you make love to me."

He pulled her to him again and kissed her hair.

"Are you begging?

Raoul stood outside a hotel located in the outskirts of Milan, clasping Marian's hand and scanning his surroundings. Yesterday, after reaching Milan without any problems, he had called the safe house. A man named Kevin told him to go to this hotel.

It had only been a short taxi ride and Raoul had been greeted at the door by the hotel manager. Once in their rooms, Kevin had called back and reassured him of their safety. They had protection. Despite all of that, Raoul had spent a sleepless night.

An hour ago, at exactly six o'clock in the morning, Kevin called and told them to meet him outside the hotel. Not an easy task, Marian had protested the hour and no coffee. But, they had managed to get down to the lobby on time. When he had tried to pay the bill, the hotel clerk said it had been taken care of.

Now, as he stood waiting for who knew what, the hairs on the back of Raoul's neck stood up. He felt like a sitting duck. Where were these people?

"Relax Raoul," Marian said. "We've only been out here four minutes. I've watched the time on the clock across the street."

Raoul's eyes scanned the boulevard. There was indeed a clock on a building facing them. He took a deep breath to calm his nerves.

A large gray sedan stopped in front of them and a heavy set man stepped out accompanied by a thin woman with bright red hair. The man's eyes met Raoul's. "I am Kevin and this is my wife, Gina. Do you have luggage?"

Raoul grunted. "No. There was no time for luggage. But we have a few shopping bags."

Kevin grabbed the bags, his face became serious. "So, you left in a hurry. Possibly, because you had unexpected company?"

Raoul grunted again. "You could say that. It is

possible we were followed."

"Get in the car," Kevin said. He hurried to open the door for his wife, and then placed the bags in the trunk.

Raoul helped Marian into the back and joined her. He grabbed her hand again and looked around as Kevin got into the car. His whole body was on high alert, where it had been since the shoot-out at the house in the Dolomites. Where it had been since he saw the men drive past them on the highway. Where it had been since yesterday when they had entered this big city.

Kevin eased the car out into traffic. "The house is close. Did everything go well at the hotel?"

"Yes," Raoul said. "We were not disturbed."

"Good," Kevin said.

They didn't speak again until they were at the safe house. Standing in the foyer, Kevin frisked Raoul and Marian. He removed Raoul's gun. "I have to do this. Hope you understand."

"There are no bullets," Raoul said. He turned and grabbed Marian's arm. "Marian needs to sit down."

He smiled as she pulled her arm free and slipped it around his waist.

"Follow me; we have rooms ready for you." Kevin walked up the staircase and stopped at the top. He gestured toward the first two doors. "These are your rooms. Let us know if you need anything. I will be downstairs in the living room, if you want to talk." He glanced at his watch. "Gina will serve breakfast in an hour. There is a carafe of coffee and a few pastries in your rooms."

Raoul waited for Kevin to descend the stairs before he led Marian into her bedroom. He shut the door and pulled her into his arms. "You will be safe here, my dear. Please rest. I will be downstairs talking to Kevin.

There is much we need to plan."

Marian nodded and stared up at him. Her eyes were dull and Raoul could see her exhaustion.

"Where's that coffee?"

He pointed at a tray on the other side of the room. "That is probably it. I will see you later."

Raoul stepped into the hall and opened the door across from hers. His accommodations were similar to Marian's. The urge to take a nap tugged at him, but he forced himself to shut the door and head for the stairs.

A few minutes later, the two men sat in the living room in front of the fireplace, coffee in hand.

"I am sorry you had to spend the night in the hotel," Kevin said. "I had to get clearance from headquarters before I brought you here."

Every muscle in Raoul's body was tense. "When can I talk to Steve?"

"He is not close to a safe phone at the moment. Do you know any of the men on Steve's team?"

Raoul eased back into his chair. Kevin was testing him. "Yes, I know Juan, Charlie and Walker."

Kevin smiled. "Good. Juan is driving here from Rome to get you. Steve and his team are there investigating new clues in Peter's disappearance. I do not expect them to come back here."

"We are to wait for Juan and go with him to Rome?" Raoul could not believe this news. More travel.

Kevin nodded.

"They have not found Peter, yet." Raoul shook his head. "I hoped there would be good news for Marian."

"Juan said they were going to check out catacombs at a monastery. They hope to find Peter and Carrie."

"Carrie? Has she been kidnapped too?"

"Yes, I am afraid so."

Raoul was vastly disappointed. Instead of finding

everything solved, it appeared that it was worse. He could not believe all the course of events. Not only had they tried to kill Marian and himself, Carrie had been kidnapped. He ran his hand through his dirty hair. Since the attack at the house in the Dolomites, he had not left Marian's side the whole time, not even for a shower.

He glanced at the man across from him, and decided to take a chance and trust Kevin. "Whatever news you have left can wait. I am exhausted and in need of a shower."

Kevin walked him to the stairs and laid a hand on his arm. "This is a most bizarre case. It may get worse again before it gets better."

Raoul sighed as he walked up the stairs. He was too old for this stuff. How could it possibly get worse?

Alissa walked downstairs to the breakfast room for brunch. Seraphina smiled at her and hurried into the kitchen. She knew the housekeeper was on her way to make the special coffee Alissa enjoyed every morning. She sat down in a chair that gave her a view of the vineyards. The sun was shining and there were people working on the vines.

She heard the elevator and listened to the voices in the kitchen. It sounded as if Ricco planned to join her for brunch. He told Seraphina what he wanted to eat, and then scolded her for not doing his laundry yesterday. Alissa frowned. She hoped he did not come to the breakfast room. His mood was foul.

He wheeled himself into the room and grinned at her. She was immediately suspicious. Usually, he took his breakfast alone, outside on the veranda if possible. And the day was lovely.

"You look beautiful this morning."

"Thank you. Are you joining me for brunch?"

"No. I am waiting for Lorenzo. We have to go into town. Seraphina is packing a lunch for us."

The excitement oozed from him. She became alarmed. He is up to something. She had not seen him like this for a long time.

"We have a guest in the house. Do you remember Carrie, our friend who lives in Texas?"

Alissa tried to associate the name with a face. "Is she the one we visited last year? The one you buy from occasionally for your import business?"

He grinned again. "Yes, I see you remember her. She will be staying in our guest room. The door is locked for her privacy. Seraphina is instructed to give her a brunch and this evening she will join us for dinner."

The wheels of the chair glided smoothly over the wooden floor. He grabbed her hand and kissed it. "I feel wonderful today, Alissa. Almost like before that awful day."

She forced a smile. "Have a good time, Ricco."

He dropped her hand and headed for the garage. At the door, he turned and faced her again. "Oh, I forgot to tell you. The elevator to the basement is locked."

Seraphina rushed from the kitchen with a large basket. Ricco turned again and the housekeeper followed him into the garage. A few minutes later, Alissa heard the garage door open. She hurried to the living room window and watched the van pull out and head down the driveway to the road below.

She was filled with anxiety. Where was Ricco going? The explanation about driving into town was a lie. He hardly ever went there without her.

Seraphina returned and Alissa once more sat at the table in the breakfast room. As the housekeeper served coffee and pastries, she thought about her husband.

He does not want you in the basement.

A chill passed through her. She thought about Carrie, locked upstairs in the guest bedroom. She is a prisoner. Was there someone in the basement, too?

She remembered the look on Ricco's face when he told her he would be gone for a while. She shuddered just thinking about it. It brought back memories from the old days.

Lorenzo parked the car under a tree giving them shade. From this vantage point, they had a full view across a huge ravine and up onto the opposite hillside. Ricco rolled his window down to allow a warm breeze inside. He picked up his binoculars and studied the Bella Roca monastery. He could see two police cars parked at the entrance to the church.

They acted quickly to my clue.

He was thrilled that he could lead them by the nose. He wanted to laugh with glee, but did not allow himself the pleasure.

The only part of the plan that was not working right was Peter's mother. He frowned. The woman had great protection. For the moment he had called off any more efforts to kill her. He did not need her now. Soon, Steve would be part of the little group at the house. The torture would begin tomorrow.

He raised the glasses again, and saw a long line of vehicles driving up the winding road to the monastery. He smiled. How many people do they think they need?

At the entrance to the church, men scrambled out of the cars and trucks. He saw that one stood out among the others. Of course he could not be positive at this distance, but his gut told him it was Steve.

He chuckled out loud. The sound caused Lorenzo to

jump.

Ricco roared with delight.

Steve, Steve, Steve. This is not like you to fall for my clues so readily. He set the binoculars in his lap and stared out at the Ligurean Sea. There could be only one reason; Steve was not totally in charge of this operation. Disappointment coursed through him.

The game may not be as much fun. He rolled up the window.

"Everything is in place. Take us to the helicopter."

Lorenzo started the car as Ricco lifted his walkie-talkie. "We are on our way."

It was past noon, when Steve followed everyone into the basement of the church and became part of the search for his sister and brother-in-law. He was already frustrated. It had taken far too long to get everyone assembled and going in the right direction.

The Abbot of the monastery had been surprised that the police would want to explore the catacombs of his church. It had taken precious time to assure him they meant no destruction to the church's property. His cooperation had increased when told the man who had made the huge donations was suspected of abducting two people and killing numerous others.

A shocked Father Angelo thought the police suspected the wrong man. Steve knew they were after the right man. This search through the catacombs had the very smell of Cristo. He always put drama into his crimes and he loved to play with his victims.They walked through a door and into the area where the catacombs were located. The air smelled of musty dry dirt. The hairs in his nose prickled. He stopped and held his light up to gaze at his map. The area under the church was vast. Noise and movement made him turn his head to the left and he saw Daniella leading a team toward a different area of the catacombs.

Steve went to his right and his team followed him deep into the darkness of antiquity. He thought it would be easy to get lost in here. And if the lights burned out, it would be a dark musty hell.

They passed through a series of cells until they found one very large empty room. A cold feeling of helplessness and doom assaulted Steve's senses. He didn't like this room. He shivered and hurried out into yet another series of cells.

When they reached the half-way mark of the area they were to search, Steve selected three men and sent the rest on farther. He returned to the large creepy room.

"Feel along the walls for hidden doors," he ordered.

The men immediately started to press on the walls. The Abbot had told Steve he would find nothing in the catacombs. Now, Steve began to think the man was right.

This room was a lost cause.

"I'll stay here, everyone else fan out into the adjoining rooms, search for hidden doors or false walls."

Standing alone in the large room, he couldn't shake the eerie feeling consuming him. He felt trapped. People long ago would have wanted an escape route. There has to be another way out of these catacombs. He scanned the walls in frustration.

"Sir?"

Steve turned to see one of the uniformed officers standing in the doorway.

"Yes, what is it? Have you found an opening?"

"Si."

Steve followed him to a nearby small cell. The man

walked to the wall and gave it a push. A doorway slid open. "Shall we follow it, sir? It looks like a tunnel."

Excitement overwhelmed him. He had been right about an escape route. Maybe Carrie and Peter were at the end of this tunnel.

"You and I will need help. Find the other two men and send one to tell the others what we've found."

The man left and Steve stared into the tunnel. He wanted to go inside alone, but knew the task force would insist he wait.

A slight movement in the back of the tunnel grabbed his attention. He put a foot inside and lifted his light to get a better look. A canister landed at his feet and smoke billowed out.

Steve coughed. He was helpless to stop the smoke and it quickly filled the room and the tunnel. He couldn't escape. Feeling ill he fell to the ground.

As his body writhed, he saw a tall man, dressed in black and wearing a gas mask, emerge from the shadows. The policeman from earlier re-entered the room also wearing a gas mask. Steve felt them lift him and carry him into the darkness.

SEVENTEEN

He moaned. His whole body hurt like hell. Was he back in the hospital? Steve took a deep breath of air and coughed. Not the hospital. His eyes adjusted to the dim light.

Where am I? He sat up and held his head in his hands trying to clear his mind.

"Steve, can you hear me?"

The voice seemed to be coming from in back of him. Even though it sounded hoarse, it had a familiar ring to it.

The person cleared his throat. "Steve, can you hear me?"

"Is that you, Peter?"

"Yeah. I thought I recognized you. They dragged you past my door and you mumbled something...can't say I'm glad you're here."

"Where are we?"

"Cristo's basement."

Steve scanned his little room. He now remembered the tunnel in the monastery.

Cristo had indeed survived the explosion.

"Is Carrie here too?"

"She's upstairs. Hopefully she has better quarters than we do."

"He must not hate her as much as he hates us."

Peter laughed. "You're not going to believe what he has planned. And you won't believe his physical and mental condition."

Steve listened as Peter proceeded to tell him a little about their old opponent, the layout of the basement, and his own efforts to escape. His old partner had to stop several times to take deep breaths.

"The hole in the wall is almost big enough for me to crawl through. I've put the bed in front of it to hide it from Lorenzo. He can't see it from the outside, because he doesn't walk past that side of the cell."

"You don't have a weapon by any chance?"

Peter laughed again. "You've got to be kidding."

Approaching footsteps interrupted their conversation. Steve looked through the bars in his cell and saw a tall dark man. He recognized him from the tunnel. "Here comes Mr. Personality."

He heard Peter snicker. "It's Lorenzo."

The tall thin man stood outside Steve's door. "Get up. Come to the door and hold out your hands."

Steve stood, but fell back onto his cot, dizzy from the effects of the gas.

"Come!" demanded Lorenzo. His deep voice echoed in the basement as he opened the door.

Steve stood again and forced himself to walk the few feet to his jailer.

The man's mouth turned down as he tied Steve's hands. "Do not try to escape. I kill you."

Steve decided not to give him any trouble. Cristo had gone to great lengths to get him in this cell, in his basement, and in his grasp. The diabolical man from the past had something more exciting in mind for him and he was ready to find out what it was.

Lorenzo pulled him out into a narrow hallway and gave him a strong push. As Steve took a step, the tall man pushed again. He bit back the urge to respond, his physical strength would be needed for what lay ahead. Several feet later, Steve knew they neared the torture room. It was just as Peter had described. Rank.

His eyes darted around the small room. Peter was right. These tools are real and meant for us.

He entered another doorway. The cozy room with a fireplace felt warm and inviting until he saw his old nemesis.

Ricco's sharp blue eyes stared at Steve from across the room. A sinister smile formed on his lips and spread, lighting up his face like a jack-o-lantern. "Steve! So nice of you to join our little party!"

His body stiffened. He now knew why the man had gone to so much trouble to get his revenge. He was a living miracle. And that miracle had cost a small fortune. Cristo looked like he had been through hell several times.

Poor us. This fiend will not stop until he feels vindicated. Steve couldn't let his captor smell his fear. He smirked. "If I'd known you would be here, Ricco, I would've dressed a little better."

The crippled man lifted a decanter off a nearby table and poured a clear liquid into a crystal glass. "Your stupid insults will have no effect on me, Steve. Would you like a drink? It is vodka and it is your last."

"No, thanks. I'd like to keep my wits about me."

Cristo laughed heartily and a tear ran down his cheek. "You always did have a great sense of humor. Too bad we have to kill you."

His eyes gleamed as he raised the drink to his lips.

Steve sat down on the couch, intent on appearing unimpressed with the former terrorist.

"Lorenzo is a man of many skills. You and your partner will be seeing first hand his talent for inflicting pain." Cristo set the glass down. "But that will come later. Now, I must attend a small dinner party upstairs with my wife and your sister. What a reunion this has turned into! I have not seen Carrie for about a year."

He laughed heartily again and wheeled himself to the elevator.

Lorenzo lifted Steve from the couch and pulled him toward the doorway leading back to the cells.

It took every ounce of Steve's will power to allow himself to be lead through the basement. He wanted to act now. To overcome this tall cruel man and go after Cristo. But he knew he couldn't and it made it all the more harder to cooperate. Vengeance would have to come later.

The door shut and Steve listened to Lorenzo's footsteps drifting away. He started to pace. It was time to make a move.

"Peter, are you awake?"

"Yes, barely. Don't eat the food. I think it's drugged. I had to eat it to keep alive. What did Cristo have to say?"

"He didn't really have information, only threats. As you told me, he isn't the same Cristo we knew years ago. I think he's lost it. He laughed so hard, he cried, and the laugh sounds creepy. I think he belongs in a mental hospital." Steve paused and sat down on the cot rubbing his wrists. "You were also right about the scars. The pain from his injuries and surgeries must have been immense. He blames us for his circumstances and hates us. It sounds like he has something horrible planned."

"I think the items on the wall in the smelly room are a specialty of Lorenzo's."

"Great....What is Cristo's connection to Carrie? From what he said, he intimated he knew her well."

Peter sighed. "You're not going to believe this. For a few years, his import company bought goods from

Carrie. Last year my wife entertained him and Alissa when they were in Dallas. I was out of town and never knew a thing about it."

"That loose end is tied up," Steve said. "From the beginning, I couldn't think why the kidnappers would want to bother with Carrie. Now I know."

"What do you mean?"

"I think the tall guy tried to get Carrie at your house in Dallas. He didn't succeed, so I moved her to your mother's estate."

"My mother?"

"Yes, and we were attacked by four men."

"Where is my mother now?

"After the attack we split up. Your mom and her assistant are on their own."

"Cristo said he was going to bring her corpse here."

"That bastard is dreaming. Your mother has good protection."

"I know Raoul has exceptional skills. He's old FBI."

Steve laughed. "I had my suspicions." He yawned. "What do you think will happen next? Cristo went up to dinner. Does that mean Lorenzo will feed us now?"

"Soon. First we'll each have a bathroom break, and then we'll eat. It's dinner time. They'll wait until tomorrow for the torture. Cristo doesn't have a lot of energy."

"Good," Steve said. "That gives us time to rest. Let's get a nap; I think my body is rebelling against the treatment it's been getting the last few days."

"Good idea," Peter said.

Steve put his head back and felt better than he had in a week. It was all out in the open now.

Carrie stood at the bedroom window and watched the workers leave the vineyard. She hoped that meant that there would be another tray of food soon. Her stomach rumbled.

She thought about her husband downstairs in his prison. Did they feed him? Tears threatened again.

All day she had paced this bedroom, taken naps, looked out the window and thought about her husband and her brother. And of course, her baby.

She was determined to figure out a way to get Peter and herself out of here. During her pacing, she made mental notes about everything she noticed out the window. Maybe it would come in handy soon. At one point, she had tried to pick the lock, but had no success.

She turned from the window when she heard a key in the lock.

An older woman opened the door. "Please, you come to dinner."

Carrie took a deep breath to calm herself and followed the woman into the hall and down the wide stairs. At the bottom, the large foyer offered a view of the dining room.

Ricco and his wife sat at a large table. He saw Carrie and motioned for her to join them. She walked inside and stopped at the table, clutching the soft fabric of her long dress.

He smiled. "Please, Carrie, sit down." He patted the empty seat next to him. "Do you remember Alissa?"

Carrie gazed across the table at the other woman. Dressed in a mauve silk dress, cut very low, she was beautiful. Her black hair was braided and pinned on top of her head, allowing the diamonds strung around her neck to stand out like large sparkling stars.

"Yes, I remember her. She came with you to Dallas."

"Good. Would you like a cocktail?"

"No," Carrie said.

"Seraphina, you can serve dinner," Ricco said.

The housekeeper served the first course which was a salad and bread. Carrie took a bite of the bread. At first, she had planned not to eat any of this monster's food, but she knew that wouldn't happen. Her appetite was overwhelming. She prayed he didn't have it laced with drugs. It wouldn't be good for the baby.

"The blue dress looks beautiful on you. I knew it would. Alissa did not mind cleaning out her closet. Did you, dear?"

Ricco's head turned quickly toward his wife. Alissa met his gaze. A slight smile curved her lips. "I did not mind at all. Tomorrow we will order clothes from my favorite shop in town."

He picked up his fork. "Good! I have news, Alissa. You will never guess who is in the basement as our guests!" His wife's stoic expression was pasted on her face. "It's Steve and Peter, our old friends from the past! Isn't that great?"

Steve was down there too? Carrie stiffened. She tried not to react to the words, but sweat broke out on her forehead and her heart started a fast beat again. She stared at Alissa and saw no reaction to her husband's words; the woman merely added more butter to her bread.

There was silence for several seconds before Alissa lifted her eyes and smiled. It wasn't a joyful smile, rather one that was not caring. "Oh? Why do you have them here, Ricco?"

"I am going to have my revenge on them for putting me in this chair!"

He shouted the words and Carrie stuck her hands in her lap. She intertwined the fingers and pressed hard. The man actually looked deranged. He had been chewing food and some of it flew out of his mouth and landed on the table in front of her. She cringed. He couldn't be sane. Despite her efforts to control her hands, they trembled anyway. She willed herself to remain calm.

"How are you going to get your revenge?" Alissa asked.

"The torture begins tomorrow!" He took a long drink from his wine glass and wiped his mouth with the back of his hand. "Peter will be first. He is weak and it will be fun to see him break."

Tears filled Carrie's eyes. Her lips trembled violently as she stared at her plate. There was no way she could look at the two people at the table. She hated them.

The housekeeper set the entree next to her salad. She stared at the meat and vegetables.

"Ricco, could we discuss this later? I would like to enjoy my dinner." Alissa smiled at her husband. "Perhaps, over a drink afterwards, you can tell us the gory details you have planned for the two agents."

The crazy man glanced at Carrie. "You may be right, my dear. Our lovely guest would not be able to eat her dinner, if my conversation was too gory."

He chuckled and then laughed heartily.

Carrie tightened her grasp on her fingers. She wondered how she could avoid the after dinner drinks.

Steve woke with a start. He had been dreaming and the dream seemed real. Something about a tunnel. He sat up on his cot and gradually remembered where he was. The headache was gone, but his body felt like it had been run over by a truck.

"Peter," he whispered. "Are you awake?"

"Yeah."

There was a familiar noise moving toward them.

"Let me guess," Steve said. "It's our friend, Lorenzo."

"Right on. It's his footsteps. I think we'll be presented with a wonderful meal after he takes us to the 'potty.'"

Steve chuckled and it felt good to even feel like laughing.

The tall man opened Steve's door first. "Come. I tie your hands."

Steve got up off the cot and held his hands out. As he stepped outside the door, the ogre pushed him again. He stopped and turned to face Lorenzo. "Keep your filthy hands off me."

Lorenzo grabbed the front of his shirt and threw him against the wall. "Do not provoke me. I have permission to beat you."

The cruelty from his dark eyes caused Steve to stifle a shudder. He would cooperate. He turned and walked toward the bathroom. Let's get this over with. He and his partner needed to make their plan.

After taking Peter to the bathroom, Lorenzo came back with the food. He shoved the trays into the cells and quickly left.

Steve picked up his plate and smelled the mushy substance. By now, he was hungry and it was tempting to eat something. He slipped it under his cot.

"Lorenzo won't be back until morning," Peter said. "He rarely checks on me during the night."

"We'll have to try our escape tonight, then," Steve said. "I'm sorry to report help will be slow in coming. We had no idea where this place could be."

He heard Peter drag his cot across the floor.

Steve went to his little window and waited. A second later, his old partner stood at the cell door.

"I lost more weight than I thought," Peter said with a grin.

Steve was appalled at his brother-in-law's condition and tried not to react. Peter's body was gaunt, dark circles were under his sunken eyes, and his face sported a week's worth of whiskers. He looked dirty and Steve could smell his body odor.

Peter's grin vanished. "I look like hell don't I?"

"No comment. Can you open this door?"

Peter tried, but it wouldn't budge. "You need a key. I can't think well enough to work on it. Probably take too long. Do you have any suggestions?"

Steve shrugged. "It would be nice if I could make a hole in my wall. But I think the best thing to do is for you to get out of here and find help. Contact Daniella and let her know where this place is located."

The thought of Daniella gave him hope. She would not rest until she found them. This he knew. But, another feeling swept through him, pangs of jealousy. He wondered how well Peter knew her. This feeling was a complete surprise. He realized it didn't matter and forced himself to concentrate on the problem at hand. "Maybe you should explore the basement, and then we can decide on our next move."

"Sounds good."

Peter found his way to the stinky room. He was hesitant to go into the living quarters. Cristo was well known for his thoroughness and there could be hidden cameras. Besides, using the elevator would be stupid.

Cristo liked to have alternate plans. There had to be stairs somewhere. Peter rushed to the bathroom and felt around for a hidden door. Nothing. He tried to think, but it wasn't easy to keep his thoughts going in one direction. He concentrated hard and remembered that Lorenzo always came from the direction of the bathroom. Wait. No. Lorenzo came from a different direction twice. When he pressed his memory, he decided it must have had something to do with Carrie and Steve.

Peter hurried back to Steve. There had to be another exit somewhere close to his partner's cell.

A few feet away from Steve's door, he reached for a decorative ring hanging under a wall sconce.

"Anything yet?" Steve asked. He stood at the door. His eager face reflecting a desperate hope.

"Maybe." Peter pulled the ring and a doorway opened into a narrow corridor.

Steve let out a whistle. "Great."

Peter followed the space a short distance to a stairway. This makes sense. Cristo would not have brought his prisoners into the house and down the elevator.

He turned around and retraced his footsteps and stood outside his partner's door again.

"There's a stairway."

"Be careful, my friend," Steve said. "I have no idea where we are, but look for the monastery on the hill. That's where they grabbed me. If you can make it to the monastery, they'll help you."

"A monastery? What were you doing at a monastery?"

"We were looking for you and Carrie. We found a relationship between the monastery and Cristo. When we found out about the catacombs under the church, we hoped he had you confined there. We had to follow the clues... It was only a trap, set many years ago and I was the prey."

"He certainly went to a lot of trouble to get us here," Peter said.

"Yeah, and you'd better go now. You may be our only hope of spoiling his plans."

Peter nodded. "Daniella may find you before I can

get help. She's pretty smart."

"That she is," Steve whispered. "Good luck, Buddy."

Peter turned and went back toward the stairway. Steve's words echoed in his mind as he fought a wave of despair and hopelessness. He was already feeling tired again. He knew he had to get help for Carrie and Steve, but first he had to escape from the house.

He climbed the stairs and stood at the top. There wasn't any light, so he felt all over the landing and decided there were two doors. One to the outside and the other to the house. He thought about the choices and was afraid to select one.

You're wasting time; just pick one, his inner voice screamed.

He opened the one on the right and set off an alarm. The noise was extremely loud and he instinctively covered his ears. He ran out the door almost falling off of two steps leading into a garden. His senses were assaulted by the crisp night air and the crunch of dirt under his feet. His weak legs felt like they would collapse at any moment, but he pushed himself on.

The garden flowed into a huge fenced yard and Peter saw a gate at the far end. He forced himself to run faster, and when he got there the gate was locked. He knew he couldn't stop now, so he hurled himself up over the gate and landed on his right arm as he fell into bushes on the other side.

The amount of adrenaline coursing through his body made him stand up. He scanned the area to get his bearings. Which way should he go? A door opened and voices drifted from the house. To the left, there was an open field. The voices became louder. Peter took off. Someone fired a weapon and he dodged bullets as he ran through the open field. One of the bullets struck him and he fell to the ground.

Again, adrenaline from his exertion, plus the pain from the bullet gave Peter the strength to push himself up and continue running. At the edge of a ravine, more shots were fired and when he turned to look back, he lost his footing and fell headlong into darkness. He tumbled and tumbled until he came to rest out in another open area. He looked around and crawled into the protection of the bushes in back of him.

Carrie heard the alarm and rushed to the window. It was dark and she couldn't see anything. Within seconds, flood lights came on and she could see over the wall. Someone was running toward a ravine. Her pulse quickened. Is it Steve or Peter? She grabbed her fingers and started twisting them. She didn't know which one she wanted it to be, her husband or her brother. No one should ever have to make that choice.

Lorenzo and another man stepped out of the gate and fired a round of shots. The fleeing form fell down and then picked itself up as Lorenzo and his partner ran from the gate. Carrie recognized the person as he fell down the steep ravine. It was her husband. She screamed.

The sound of a key in the lock made her turn. "Oh, no, they're coming for me now."

When Alissa entered the bedroom, Carrie was relieved. She turned back and gazed out the window again. Tears ran down her face and into her mouth and hair.

Alissa stood next to her.

They watched Lorenzo and the other man shine their lights into the ravine. Carrie's numb body was riveted to her spot.

EIGHTEEN

Alissa stared out at the scene in the garden. Lorenzo had gathered a group of men. All had lanterns and weapons.

Which one escaped? She figured it must have been Peter. He had been the clever one in the old days. Ricco had been boasting at dinner about how Peter looked beaten and weak. Alissa smiled. These agents always seemed to get things done. Maybe now this terrible nightmare would come to an end.

Melancholy hit her hard and weighed her down. Ricco was getting worse. Sometimes he scared her because he appeared so unbalanced. Tonight, as he told her of his fiendish plans for his prisoners, fear had almost overwhelmed her. His demeanor had an air of lunacy.

She glanced at Carrie. She didn't like this woman. Her innocence and sweetness reminded Alissa of herself before her years with Ricco.

"Get back into your bed," she said harshly.

Carrie turned her head and their eyes met. "Please help my husband!" she pleaded. "Please help us!"

Alissa pulled the curtains together at the window. "Get in bed. If Ricco hears you pleading for your husband's life, he will come up here and verbally torture you. He is good at that. Right now they cannot find whoever escaped. Be thankful."

Carrie stopped crying and slipped beneath the

covers. Alissa covered her with the quilt and left the room.

Steve sat on the edge of his cot. The burst of excitement and anxiety had passed and he felt exhausted. After the alarm sounded, he had felt helpless and kicked the door in frustration. His foot still ached from that act of stupidity.

The first shots fired had scared him. When others followed, he knew Peter had made it outside the perimeters of the house.

All he could do now was wait. He stretched out on his cot and closed his eyes. A few minutes later, the sound of Cristo's wheelchair on the dungeon floor caused him to sit up and take notice. He braced himself for the inevitable hate-filled words the maniac would hurl at him.

Cristo stopped outside his door and Steve heard the key in the lock. When the crippled man pushed open the door, Steve saw the barrel of his gun.

"Stay where you are," Cristo ordered. "Your partner has escaped, but my men are out searching for him. Peter will not get far. He will be dragged back here to meet his end with you."

Steve gazed at Cristo and remembered the night on the yacht. The bullet he had taken and the effects of the explosion would have killed any normal person. Why had fate spared this worthless creature?

"Tomorrow morning the torture will begin," Cristo continued. "You can think of your friend, as your body is pulled and twisted. The pain will be so bad; you will beg us for mercy."

Steve ached to kill this man with his bare hands. Hatred started to take hold. He stood up and clinched his fists.

Cristo reached for the door. "Do not be foolish, Steve. I hold the power. I still have Carrie."

The wheelchair eased out and the door shut. Steve heard the lock click and listened to the sound of his jailer going back to the elevator. He grabbed the rag that was his blanket and once more stretched out on the cot. There was nothing he could do for Peter. Or Carrie. A good night's rest would be needed to get through a day of Lorenzo's torture.

After leaving Carrie, Alissa returned to her bedroom. She tried to sleep, but could not forget the issues at hand. Finally, she got up and walked down the hall. From the top of the stairs she stared at the darkness below, and then descended into the living room. She moved across the room, enjoying the strange sense of security the darkness gave her. Her feet stopped at the couch and her gaze focused out the picture window. Men with lights searched the vineyards.

"It will be a long night, Alissa."

Startled, she reached over and turned on the lamp next to the sofa.

Ricco wheeled into the living room.

"Which one escaped?" she asked. Her voice trembled a little, and she tried to calm her rapid heartbeat.

"Peter. He must have used every waking hour and every ounce of energy to dig a hole in his cell wall. He placed his bed in front of the hole. I think he hid the dirt in his clothes and released it when he went to the bathroom."

In the soft light of the lamp, her husband's face looked like a piece of red marble chiseled into the features of a man. A cold feeling made her shiver. Desperation overtook her.

"Ricco, can we leave this place? Your men will not find him. He is too smart. If he reaches the authorities, you will be found." The thought of the police arresting both of them terrified her.

"We will not leave here yet! I am not finished with what I want to do!" he screamed. "Do you feel compassion for these men who almost killed us five years ago?"

"No, Ricco, I do not. I understand your hatred for them, but now the situation is different. You risk being caught!"

"Where is your faith in me?" He spun his wheelchair around and headed for the doorway. "I have to rest now. Later today, Steve will pay for his partner's escape."

Alissa watched him leave and wondered if he could live through this ordeal. He had endured so much pain and agony just to be able to function as he did now. She felt pity for him. It was a shame to survive so much and waste what little of his life he had left on revenge.

She sat on the couch for a few more minutes, and then went back upstairs, shaken to the core. Her senses had not picked up Ricco's presence. Little slips like that could cost her dearly.

Daniella stood before the assembled task force. The faces of the men and women reflected fatigue and determination. She knew they wouldn't want to quit before they found the American agent, but it was well past midnight.

"Everyone is dismissed. Go home and sleep. Meet here in exactly ten hours." One by one the group left. She started toward her car. Raphael, her assistant, walked with her.

They had searched the catacombs and found the tunnel. It had come out on the other side of the hill. The task force had scoured the area and found tire tracks leading to the north. A car had been found ten miles from the tunnel. The trail ended there.

Daniella suspected a helicopter was used to transport Steve to a hiding place. He could be anywhere in the world. But, if her hunch was right, Cristo would have his prisoners nearby. In the past, he liked to stay close to the action and watch the futile efforts to find him.

Cristo was smart. No, he was cunning. She had to admire that about him. It would be a challenge to hunt him down.

She sat behind the wheel of her car. Raphael got in next to her. "Has there been any communication from the American team?"

"Si, Juan Castillo is waiting for us in a little town about ten kilometers. It is on the way to our hotel."

"Good," Daniella said. "We will coordinate our efforts with theirs."

Peter stopped and crouched down in another cluster of bushes. He took a deep breath and filled his lungs with fresh air, then let it out as slowly as he could. At this moment in time, he felt the searchers were gone. He sat down to rest. Fatigue pulled at his mind and his spirit. A dull aching pain in his left leg reminded him he was hit. He leaned back against the base of the large bush and took another deep breath.

His fingers found the wound on his calf. It was small. This would complicate everything. He tore a piece of his filthy shirt and wrapped it around the painful area. He knew his socks and pant leg were soaked with blood, but nothing could be done until sunrise.

After sitting for several minutes, he crawled through the bushes until he came out at the very end of the ravine. It was at the top of a hill and he could smell the sea.

You're losing it man. He scanned the dark night. There were no lights anywhere, only darkness and silence. The moon was covered by clouds. He knew the men had not given up. At dawn, Cristo would send them out again until they found him dead or alive. Peter laughed. Come and get me.

A breeze came up and he smelled the sea again. He hadn't been hallucinating after all. If he was still in Italy, the sea would be to the east or the west. His eyes looked up at the sky. The clouds obscured his vision of the stars, his Eagle Scout training would have to wait until later. Right now, he'd use his sense of smell. With much effort he stood and took another deep breath. He headed toward what he hoped was water.

Raoul shook Marian's shoulder. "Wake up. We have to leave now."

Marian rolled over. "What time is it?"

"It is very early. Kevin woke me up a few minutes ago and told me that Steve has been kidnapped. Juan cannot come for us. We will fly to Rome."

She moaned and sat up in the bed. "How much time do I have?"

"Not much, my dear. We have to leave in ten minutes. Kevin has arranged for us to fly in a special plane."

She threw the covers off and stood. "I can do it. Go get yourself ready."

Raoul left her and packed his clothing into a small

suitcase Kevin had provided. He would have to squeeze Marian's things inside, too. Whatever didn't fit, would go into a shopping bag. Anything else would stay behind.

The door opened across the hall. "I'm ready, Raoul."

"Bring your stuff in here." He gestured toward the suitcase.

Within minutes, they were packed. He grabbed her arm and they hurried downstairs. Kevin waited for them in the foyer.

Raoul followed Marian out the door and wondered when this all would end.

Juan opened the door of his hotel room located near the monastery. He let Daniella and Raphael inside. It had been a surprise to hear that Steve had been kidnapped, but the American team wasn't shocked. Their boss had told them it was a possibility. He and Charlie were ready to work with Daniella to find their boss and the others. Walker would be joining them, soon.

He gestured toward the couch and a chair. Daniella and Raphael didn't move.

"We cannot stay long. What will you do now?" she asked.

"Walker will meet Peter's mother and her assistant when they get off the plane in Rome. He'll bring them here so we can keep them close to us. Charlie and I will search the area for Steve. We plan to interview townspeople along the main highway, close to the sea. They may have seen Cristo and his wife at some time or heard of them."

Daniella turned and headed for the door. "Please keep in touch with us. I would like to share information on the search. That way we will not be following each other around the countryside."

Juan smiled. He had worked with Daniella years ago and knew she was good at her job. "I'll call you if we find anything."

The Italians left and Juan called Charlie. "Get a nap-we leave in five hours."

When dawn broke over the mountain, Father Angelo rose from his bed and fell to his knees in prayer. He felt heartbroken that his friend was such a scoundrel. It was depressing to be involved in this mess. His guilt made him feel responsible. Deep inside, he knew his only way of restitution was to find the agent who had disappeared yesterday.

After morning prayers, he would take one of the cars and search for the poor soul.

Peter lay on a grassy area on the slope of a hill. The darkness had vanished. Had he been sleeping? He looked around him. The top of the hill was only several feet away.

He raised himself on one knee. Using his hands to balance, he stood on both his feet. His wounded leg rebelled with a jolt of pain. Sweat broke out on his forehead and a coldness swept over him.

Thinking he might pass out, he forced himself to move to the top of the hill. And he was rewarded. Down below was a main highway.

Instead of being elated, he frowned. It would take the whole day to reach it. His body would require many periods of rest.

"I won't make it," he whispered.

He started down the hill anyway. As he went, the terrain below became clearer. There were dirt roads running down to the highway. Maybe he could find a ride. This thought was encouraging.

He felt another stabbing pain in his left calf and stopped to lift the dirty rag off his wound. It didn't look good. He needed water to clean it. Water. He swallowed. He was so damned thirsty.

His eyes scanned the hillside and couldn't see any water. There wasn't even a shed or any buildings between here and the highway.

He walked several more feet, trying to conserve his energy . He laughed. What energy?

Thoughts of Steve and Carrie back at Ricco's house helped him to move a little farther before stopping to rest. Would Steve survive his torture until help arrived? Would Ricco treat Carrie badly because her husband had escaped?

He sat down again. His right arm ached from the fall off the gate. He'd give anything for a few aspirin. Taking deep breaths, he gazed down the hill and felt a surge of hope. There was a dirt road running east and west about half a mile from where he sat. What luck. He would head for that road.

A few minutes later, he stood and walked several more feet.

The crack of the whip echoed in the little room. Steve bowed his head and grimaced. Instead of crying out, he let out a breath and took another. The pain was excruciating, but he had experienced worse. He chuckled. This was nothing compared to the beating and the bullet he took four years ago.

The chuckle wasn't lost on Cristo. The vile man wheeled closer to him.

"You laugh! Lorenzo will change whips. The barbs on the new one should give you a new thrill."

Steve cursed his own stupidity.

Lorenzo left the foul smelling room and Steve was alone with his tormentor. He heard the wheelchair move closer.

"Your partner has managed to evade us. But he will be caught. I have everyone out there looking for him."

Steve's back hurt like hell. He took a deep breath. Peter had escaped and remained on the loose. This was good news. "You will not find him, Ricco. Right now, he is telling the authorities where you are. Face it, you're doomed."

He turned his head and looked down at the man. Cristo's face was a nasty shade of purple and red.

"We will see who is doomed," Cristo hissed.

His dulled senses didn't see it coming. A knife dug into his foot. Steve screamed in pain.

The wheelchair moved and he turned his head to watch it disappear into the living room. Taunting the crippled man had not helped him. Now, he had to deal with this wound as well as the ones on his back. This morning, before they dragged him to this place, he had decided he would try to escape, too. The wound in his foot would compromise any escape. He breathed deeply and closed his eyes. A little rest would be nice.

Voices startled him. His body jumped. He heard the wheelchair moving toward him. Lorenzo entered the room with Cristo. The tall man held another whip. Steve cringed.

Juan opened the door and let Walker and Charlie inside.

Walker grinned and stretched out his hand. "Good to see you, partner. Our friends are in a room two doors down."

Juan shook hands. "Good. Did you have any

problems?"

"No. And no one followed us."

"Maybe Cristo isn't interested in her anymore," Charlie said.

"That would be my guess," Juan said. "Charlie and I will go up the coast and look for Steve."

Walker put his hands on his hips and stared at Juan. "I know you want me to stay here and watch our friends... I want to go south and look for Steve. Can't you get someone from the task force to help us out? Like you said, Cristo may not be interested anymore."

Juan shrugged. "That sounds like a good idea. I'll call Daniella."

He grabbed his phone and dialed. Daniella answered on the first ring.

"This is Juan."

"Hello, Juan. Everything okay?"

"Yes, Walker's here and he wants to be part of the search for Steve. Can you help us out with our friends down the hall?"

"I am sure that can be arranged. Talk to the manager of the hotel. He is reliable."

"Thanks."

"Juan, keep in touch."

"Will do."

Juan hung up and looked at Walker. "She says to talk to the hotel manager. He can be trusted. You and Charlie talk to him. I'll go down the hall and check on our friends."

NINETEEN

Raoul heard the knock and rushed to the door. Marian was asleep on the bed and she needed her rest.

"Who is it?" he whispered.

"Juan."

He opened the door and the agent walked inside.

"Marian is asleep," Raoul whispered.

Juan glanced at the bed. "Do you want another room?"

Raoul shook his head. "I will not be separated from her. Not until we get home. Is there any news about Steve?"

"No. We're going out to look for him. The hotel manager will take care of whatever you want. I suggest you stay put. We're not sure if they're still after you or not."

"Okay."

Juan put his hand on the door and opened it. He glanced over his shoulder. "Did Walker give you his phone number?"

"Yes."

"Call if you need him."

Walker and Charlie appeared outside the door. Juan joined them and Raoul watched the agents disappear toward the lobby. He and Marian were on their own, again. He stepped back inside and shut the door.

"Who was that, Raoul?"

He turned at the sound of her voice. "It was Juan, my dear. The agents are going out to search for Steve."

Marian sat up and stared at him. "Any news of my son?"

"Evidently, not. Juan did not say."

She got up and walked toward the bathroom. "I'm going to get a shower. Why don't you take a nap? Later on, we're going to search for my son."

She shut the bathroom door. Raoul tensed. Nap? Who has time for a nap? He knew there would be no rest until Peter and Carrie were found.

"Wake him up!" Ricco shouted.

Lorenzo grabbed Steve's arm and shook him.

Steve opened his eyes and immediately closed them again.

"Wash off his back. It's full of blood. I want to see his wounds."

Lorenzo picked up a basin of water and tossed it on Steve. The blood and water splashed down to the floor.

Ricco's eyes scanned Steve's back. "Take him to his cell. I want him to rest. When he wakes up we will resume his torture with something else."

Lorenzo started to untie Steve's ropes.

"I will have lunch with Alissa. Come upstairs after you get him in the cell. Give him water. I do not want him to die, yet."

Ricco turned and steered his wheelchair toward the elevator. He glanced at his watch. Good, Alissa should be down for lunch soon.

Alissa sat on the couch in the living room. She

raised her head from her magazine and stared at the woman across from her. Carrie had been allowed to come downstairs as long as she behaved herself. So far, the American woman had not moved from her chair.

"Would you like to have lunch downstairs?"

Carrie met her gaze. Alissa could see the worry in her eyes and it frightened her. Would all of this torment make her sick? Right now they did not need a sick person to care for. Ricco was down in the basement torturing Steve.

"No. Thank you. I would prefer to eat upstairs...Will you come up and tell me the news about Steve and Peter?"

"Yes. I will tell you what Ricco tells me. Seraphina will bring you a tray."

Carrie stood and walked toward the stairs. Alissa did not want to help Peter's wife, but she understood how Carrie would not want to hear the gory details of her brother's torture. Or, how Peter was found dead or alive.

She followed Carrie up the stairs and into the bedroom. Alissa looked around. What did the woman do up here all day? "I will have Lorenzo bring a television into the room for you."

"Thank you," Carrie said. "Do you have any books, besides magazines?"

Alissa smiled. "Not many. Seraphina will bring you what she can find." She stood at the door. "I will come up later and tell you what I have found out."

"Thank you," Carrie said.

She shut the door and hurried down the hall. At the top of the steps she heard voices coming from the kitchen. Ricco appeared in the doorway. He smiled up at her. "Come to the dining room. I want to tell you about my morning. Seraphina will serve our lunch in a few minutes."

Her husband could not wait until dinner to gloat. Alissa needed a cheerful place to hear the depressing news. The sunroom would be a good spot. She started walking down the stairs.

"I would like to eat in the sunroom," she said.

His happy face fell.

"Please Ricco, the sunroom."

"Oh, very well. Come now." He turned his wheelchair and moved into the kitchen.

Alissa stood at the foot of the stairs for a full minute. She had to gather her thoughts. Ricco would read every line and expression on her face. He would know her feelings about his captives. She forced a smile and walked toward the kitchen.

The sunroom, situated next to the kitchen, was bathed in sunlight. Her spirits rose a notch, but she was careful not to show it.

Ricco sat in his wheelchair at the table, waiting for her. Happiness oozed from him. A chill passed through her. Could Steve be dead?

She sat next to him and stared out the large windows. The weather outside was gorgeous. The birds were taking a bath in the fountain and the sky was filled with soft white clouds.

"Why are we eating in here?" he asked. His voice was harsh.

"The sun is shining and the day is beautiful," she said. Ricco needed more warmth in his life.

"I do not care about the day. I only want to eat and then have a nap. My business in the basement is not finished. Steve has a strong body. He is resting now. I want him to live long enough for Peter's return."

"Have you found Peter?"

The happiness left Ricco, again. "No. The men have not found him yet."

Seraphina and Lorenzo entered the room carrying trays of food. The housekeeper set the dishes on the table and left. Ricco's assistant stayed behind.

"Is our prisoner resting?" Ricco picked up his wine and took a sip.

"Si. I have given him water and wrapped his foot."

"Good. Come back in half an hour. I want a nap." He set his wine glass down and picked up his fork.

Alissa watched Lorenzo leave. She was numb. His foot? What had her husband done?

Ricco chuckled. "Poor Steve. Even after being beaten with a whip for an hour, he still could not keep his mouth shut. He had to taunt me."

"What did you do?" Alissa studied the pasta on her plate.

"Why, I did what anyone would do! I stabbed him in the foot!" Ricco laughed.

She picked up a crust of bread and stuffed it in her mouth. Chewing would prevent her from commenting. He stabbed Steve. Well, she knew Ricco wanted him dead. What did she think would happen? He would die from laughing?

"After my nap, I will have Lorenzo use that contraption that pulls the fingernails out. It will be more than enjoyable to see him scream again." Ricco dug into his pasta. "I will eat fast. Lorenzo will return soon."

She swallowed her food and used her fork to move the vegetables around on her plate.

"Alissa! I have a wonderful idea!" Ricco smiled and stared at her. "When I go back downstairs, you will come with me."

She inwardly cringed. There was no way she would go down there and watch him kill Steve. And he knew it. He was only baiting her.

"What a great idea, Ricco," she said.

Minutes later, Lorenzo returned. The tall man followed Ricco down the hall.

Alissa listened to the retreating wheelchair and knew she had to act now. She had to help Steve escape. But, helping Steve would sign her death notice. She would have to go with him.

Fear gripped her. Could she go through with this plan? Steve was an old friend. They went way back. He had been her contact on her first and only case with the Agency. Ricco's case.

Her mind rebelled. She did not want to deal with this now. She took a deep breath. There was no choice. If Ricco killed Steve, how would she deal with the guilt?

What about Peter's wife? The woman had to stay here; there simply was no time for her. Ricco would not harm Carrie. He would want her alive until Peter was found.

Her mind cleared and she made her decision. She would help Steve escape.

Alissa walked out of the sunroom and up the stairs. She saw Seraphina take the vacuum into one of the rooms down the hall. The housekeeper turned the machine on and Alissa went into her bedroom and shut the door.

She sat down on the bed and clasped her hands in her lap. She had to find a key to the basement. Seraphina would have a key. However, the housekeeper could not be trusted. The simple woman adored Ricco.

Alissa stood up and walked to her closet. Steve might need a blanket to lie on in the car. She reached up and pulled down a light-weight throw. She tossed it on the bed and walked over to her dressing table. She opened a drawer and stared down at her key ring. The key to the basement was not on it.

Anxiety caused her to lose her concentration. She sat on the bed again. Her mind cleared.

Steve had to be behind more than one door. She would need Ricco's key ring. How could she get it? No. Wait. There was a better choice. Lorenzo had every key to every lock on the estate. An idea formed. Seraphina has help today. The part-time maid could prove to be useful. Alissa opened the door and glanced down the hall. The maid came out of Carrie's room.

Marian sat in the front seat of an old car. Raoul came out of the hotel with a map in his hand and several bottles of water. She hadn't had to beg him to take her out looking for Peter. He probably had realized it was useless to protest in the first place. The monastery would be their starting point.

Raoul slipped behind the wheel. "The manager says the monastery is about half an hour away. It is above a town. He says we can drive up to the grounds, but only for the view. They do not give tours. The view is supposed to be magnificent."

"That sounds good. But, can we have lunch in the little town first? I'm starving."

Raoul started the car and glanced at her before pulling out onto the street. "My dear, you are not starving. People in third world countries are starving."

She rolled her eyes. "You're right. How about ravenous?"

He laughed. "Better. Maybe you could use that word as a title to your next novel."

"Oooooh, I like that, Raoul! Would it be a love story or a third world country story?"

He laughed again. "That is entirely up to you, Marian. Now, do not talk to me for a few minutes, I have to concentrate on the hotel manager's directions."

Steve lay on his cot and every inch of his body hurt. Luckily for him, Cristo had to nap often. Earlier, when Lorenzo untied his hands, his body had fallen into the cruel man's arms.

"You are lucky Ricco wants you to live, I would kill you now." The voice was harsh.

At that moment, Steve welcomed a fast death.

Lorenzo had half-dragged his limp body back to the cell. He tried to raise his hand, but the effort was exhausting. His eyes closed and he remembered the cleansing of his wounds. It was something he didn't look forward to again. Lorenzo had poured alcohol on them. Steve had cried out in pain and the tall man had laughed.

A sad thought came to mind. There was a chance he would never see Daniella again, or meet his daughter. Melancholy set in and he fought it off with all his might. He forced himself to think of positive things, like maybe an escape attempt.

The ludicrous thought made him want to chuckle. But his body couldn't do it.

Rest. Rest would be all he could do for himself now. He closed his eyes and thought about Rosie.

Alissa stood in the kitchen. The maid was in Lorenzo's bedroom coaxing the horrid man to get in the shower with her. From the sound of things going on in there, the maid was truly earning her money.

It was the only way to separate him from his keys.

Her head turned when she heard a noise in the hall. Carefully, she peeked around the corner. Lorenzo and the girl came out of his bedroom and entered the bathroom.

As soon as the door closed, Alissa tiptoed down the hall and pushed Lorenzo's door open wider. Two steps into the room, she grabbed the set of keys sitting on the dresser. Water started running in the bathroom and Alissa rushed out of the bedroom and headed for the basement stairs. Yes, she knew about the stairs to the basement. She had seen Lorenzo use that door many times.

The blanket waited for her in the hall. She grabbed it and carefully opened the door. Light from behind her showed steps going down into darkness. She stepped inside and reached out for the rail with one hand, the other pushed the blanket between her knees. Her free hand shut the door. Grabbing the blanket again, she took slow steps down into darkness. At the bottom, she placed her hand on the wall and walked until her toe touched something. Reaching out, she found the doorknob.

Once outside of the dark room, she leaned against the wall and took a deep breath. She coughed. What a terrible smell. How did Peter and Steve endure it?

A dim light hung above her head. She could see a door with a small window directly in front of her. Gazing through the opening, she saw someone lying on a cot. It had to be Steve.

She examined the lock. It looked new. She searched for the right key. It took her eight keys before she found the right one. Swinging the door wide, she stared at the form on the cot. "Steve, Steve, wake up."

Steve heard his name. He groaned and tried to sit up. He wasn't sure if his body moved or not. He tried it again. Open your eyes, dummy.

No. No. He must be dreaming. Someone was in his cell.

"Steve, Steve, wake up."

The voice was familiar.

"Who are you?" he croaked.

"Alissa. I have come to help you escape."

He fell back down. It had to be a dream.

She was horrified. That could not be Steve. This man looks like he is in the throes of hell. They had less than two hours to get out of the house and down the road toward town.

She lifted him to a sitting position. "Steve, wake up."

He mumbled a few words. She slapped his face and he opened his eyes.

A container of water sat close to the cot. In the shadowed light, it appeared to be clean. She put it to his lips and he drank a little. She added more until he could take an actual sip.

"Alissa?" His voice sounded scratchy, like a sore throat.

"Yes, Steve, take a drink of this water."

Steve took a drink. Alissa put the water down. Too much might make him sick. She stood and moved his body so he could lean back against the wall. Something dark was on his blanket. She picked it up and studied the dark spots.

"Watch where you put your hands, I'm bleeding," Steve said.

She threw the blanket down. "We don't have time for this!"

"You wouldn't have a few aspirins would you?" He tried to chuckle, but coughed instead.

"I've come to help you escape. I didn't bring aspirin."

"You're taking a big risk," Steve whispered. He rested his head on the wall. "Where are Ricco and Lorenzo?"

"My husband is napping in his room. He naps for two hours at this time of day. Lorenzo is being entertained on the other side of the house by the maid. I have paid her dearly and hope she will not betray us. She will not have to work for many years on the Euro that I gave her."

"Let's see if I can stand and walk," Steve said.

Alissa helped him to his feet. He stood a few minutes.

"Better help me sit back down again." He almost fell over, but Alissa caught him. "Look around outside for something I can use to lean on."

She helped him sit down, then went out of the cell and looked around. This was going to waste precious time, but Steve was too big for her carry.

TWENTY

"How far to the next town?" Raoul jerked the car a little to the left to avoid a hole in the dirt road.

"According to the map, we should already be there," Marian said.

"Are you sure you are reading it right?"

"Yes, Raoul, I think I'm reading it correctly. However, I can't read Italian and my ESP has stopped working."

"No need for sarcasm, Marian." Raoul pulled over to the side of the road and grabbed the map. He tried to figure out where they were. He did not have any luck either.

"We're hopelessly lost, aren't we?" Marian asked.

"Time to stretch our legs." He opened the door and got out. She followed. He put his hands on his hips and looked around. Yes, they were lost.

"There is a chance we may not find the monastery, my dear."

She wrapped her arms around his waist and gazed up at him.

He knew he had to keep looking. He pulled her closer and kissed her forehead. "Have you thought about what we will do when we find the monastery? The whole task force could not find Steve. What makes you think we can find Peter and Carrie?"

She laid her head on his chest. "Back at the hotel it

had sounded like such a good idea. It's been so frustrating. Carrie and Peter could be lying out here somewhere needing help. I suppose I just needed to try!"

Her eyes filled with tears and Raoul turned his head and mumbled a curse. She would cry all the way back to the hotel. He would not be able to stand it.

He pulled her tighter and rubbed her back. He loved her so much. It was like an addiction. When he was away from her, she was always on his mind. When he was with her, he stayed as near to her as he could manage.

"Okay, we will have another look at the map."

She smiled and slipped her arms around his neck. Her body moved closer to his. Raoul laughed.

"Do not start this stuff now, Marian. We are on a mission, no time for sex."

Marian chuckled. "Who said anything about sex? I think you're reacting to your own wishes."

"Where is the map?"

She let go of his neck and turned around. "It's in the car. I'll get it."

He followed her. Together they studied the map.

"Do you hear that sound, Raoul?"

"What sound?"

She turned around and pointed down the road. "It's coming from that direction. I think it's a church bell!"

Raoul listened. Yes, it was very faint, but he could hear a church bell. He grinned. "Get into the car, my dear. We will drive in that direction. It will be your job to watch for the monastery above us."

Several miles down the road Marian started clapping and carrying on. "There it is! There's the monastery!"

Raoul saw a sign pointing to a road. "Let us hope this road is not too steep."

He turned and went about a half mile before the

road became one lane. And to make matters worse the curves were pretty sharp.

Marian grabbed the car door. "I don't like this road. Maybe we should go back down and talk to the people in the town instead."

"Too late. We are committed."

Around the next curve, they hit a car. Even though Raoul had managed to get over a little, the front of the other car was damaged.

"Are you okay, Marian?" She looked fine, a little shocked maybe, but fine. "You stay in the car; I will take care of everything."

The words were barely out of his mouth, when she opened the door and got out. Raoul followed her to the other car.

A portly man sat behind the wheel. He held a handkerchief up to his nose.

"Are you okay?" Marian said.

The man said something in Italian. Raoul could figure out a few of the words. He reached for the latch and opened the door. "I think he said he is okay." He helped the man out. "Do you speak English?"

The man nodded. "Yes. I am Father Angelo." He looked at the damage to his car and then at their car. "Your car does not look good."

Raoul got behind the wheel of his car. The motor did not start. He tried and tried. Marian and the priest stood outside and looked through the window.

"I will call my friend in town. He will come up and get your car," Father Angelo said.

Another car came around the curve and stopped in back of Raoul. The driver got out and came up to see what was going on. Raoul shrugged. What could he do? "That would be great, Father. Call your friend."

It took Alissa eight precious minutes to find the long

board. She carried it back to Steve. "Can you use this?"

Steve studied the board. "Yeah, I'll have to lean on you, though."

She placed the board against the door. Steve stood up. His legs gave out and he dropped back onto the cot.

He took a deep breath. "Let's try again."

She helped him stand and he grabbed her shoulder to balance himself.

Alissa handed him the board and with her help, he walked the short distance to the door and back to the cot. He sat down. "I have to rest a minute."

"We do not have much time." She glanced at her watch. "Ricco will be down here in one hour and twenty minutes."

"Help me up again."

Steve walked to the door and continued into the passageway. He leaned against the wall. Sweat dripped off his face. "Give me another minute."

Alissa cringed. This would take forever and she did not know how to get to the garage from here. "Steve, you cannot go up the stairs. Is there another way out of here?"

"I only know about the elevator." He thought a minute. "You have to help me up the stairs. There is another door up there. The one Peter used to escape. It has an alarm."

"It is our only hope."

He wrapped his arm around her shoulder and she moved for the door.

Daniella pulled up to the airline terminal in Rome and parked the car. She hurried to the plane in the hangar and got into the passenger seat. Sergio, her pilot, was already getting ready for take-off.

"Did you make a flight plan?" she asked.

Sergio's sharp brown eyes darted to her face. "Of course."

The plane started moving out of the hanger and toward the runway.

She touched his arm.

He chuckled. "I made a broad sweep of your entire area. You were no help." He glanced at her and smiled. "Trust me."

She sat back in the seat and got ready for take-off. Sergio was an experienced pilot. He had done this many times. She could rely on his judgment.

They spent fifteen minutes walking up the stairs. Steve had proved to be a great spy. He found the light switch. That had made things so much easier.

Now, standing at the top, Alissa was confused. Which door did she come out of?

"I have no idea which door Peter used," Steve said. "Do you know where you're alarm system is located?"

"Of course not! That is why I have servants."

Steve shrugged. "Which door would you like to have? The one that goes inside the house or the one with the alarm?"

Alissa knew she was wasting precious time. "The one into the house. Ricco has a spare wheelchair in the hall closet. I could wheel you to the garage."

"Where would Ricco and Lorenzo be?"

"Ricco is in bed and hopefully Lorenzo and the maid are occupied." She shrugged. "The stairs are close to the kitchen. And the kitchen is closer to the garage."

"Tell me exactly how we would do this," Steve said.

"I will open the door and check to make sure no one is in the kitchen and the hall. Then, I will hurry to the closet and get the wheelchair and bring it back here."

Steve looked around the landing they were standing on. "There is no room to bring it in here. I will have to get into it in the hall. What happens then?"

"We hurry through the kitchen to the side door. We go out onto a breeze way and into the garage."

"How fast can we do that?"

"With no complications, a few minutes."

"Okay, get the chair."

Alissa opened the door she thought she came out of. The alarm didn't go off and she checked the hall and the kitchen. No one. She stepped out and shut the door. She hurried to the closet and pulled the wheelchair out. Opening it up, she rushed down the hall with it.

At the door to the stairs, she froze. She could hear voices. Someone was coming toward her. She pushed the chair into the kitchen and folded it up, slipping it into a spot between the stove and the pantry.

Seraphina and the maid came down the hall. Alissa checked her watch. Thirty minutes until Ricco will get up from his nap.

The two women saw her. She smiled. "Seraphina, the woman upstairs needs a television. When you see Lorenzo please tell him to put one in her room. And find a few books for her to read. She may need only English print."

Seraphina looked at the maid and scowled. "She has been with Lorenzo. I found her coming out of his bedroom."

Alissa was horrified. Where was the fiend now? She was afraid to ask, but she had to.

"Where is Lorenzo now?"

The maid looked at her with fear in her eyes. "He is in the fields. A man came to get him. There is a problem."

Relief reinforced her. "Seraphina, in one hour, please bring a tray up to the woman's room. Make refreshments for two. I will be there."

Seraphina showed surprise. She nodded.

Alissa walked into the living room. The two women went upstairs.

She rushed to the kitchen and pulled out the wheelchair, unfolded it and hurried to the door.

Steve must have heard her coming and he opened it before she could turn the knob.

Within seconds he was in the chair and they were rushing through the kitchen and out the door. She glanced around as they went down the breeze way and into the garage.

Her hands trembled as she opened a back door and helped Steve get inside the car.

She glanced at her watch. Ten minutes left.

Marian stood outside of a shop and licked gelato off a cone. She didn't know where Raoul was. He had left her there and taken off with the priest.

She sat down on a bench. What a day this had turned out to be. She had started out with such hopes to find some kind of clue to help find her son and daughter-in-law.

They had gotten a ride into town with the priest. His car was not as damaged as theirs. They all managed to get their car as far off to the side as they could so that Father Angelo's car could go around it. The man that had come up behind them backed down the road. Marian had held her breath watching him do it. Thank heavens they hadn't managed to get too far up the hill before the accident.

A car stopped on the street and Raoul got out. "I see you found something to eat. Good."

Father Angelo got out and went into a store a few doors down.

"Both vehicles were totaled. We got another car." Raoul sighed and put his hands on his hips. "It's in his name and he insists on driving."

"We should be thankful it was him we ran into. He seems to have connections."

"It would be nice if he can read a map better than we can. That winding road we were on was the old way to the monastery. Father Angelo had taken it only because he thought it was a short cut."

The priest came out of the store carrying a bag. He smiled at Marian. "I have water and food."

Raoul grabbed her arm. "Let's get in the car, we have wasted valuable time."

Alissa buckled her seatbelt and pushed the button for the garage door to open. She glanced in the backseat at her passenger, Steve had his eyes closed. She checked the back window to see if anyone was coming toward the garage. It was clear.

The car sped out and turned, then drove down the driveway to the dirt road.

"How are you, Steve?"

When he didn't answer, Alissa took her eyes off the road and turned her head. She looked in the back seat. Steve opened his eyes and focused on her.

"I'm doing better." he said.

She didn't believe him. She turned back to the road. "I am sure they heard us drive off. We will have about fifteen minutes before they can get to the car. Ricco will insist on going, so Lorenzo will have to take the time to help him."

She slowed down to turn from the driveway onto a dirt road leading to the sea. She saw Steve looking out the window.

"Alissa, do you hear a plane? Do you think it's looking for me?"

Once on the dirt road, she stepped on the gas. She glanced in the rear-view mirror and saw a cloud of dust following them.

"I do not hear a plane." She shrugged. "But it is possible there is one looking for you. Ricco does not have a plane, only a helicopter."

"If it is help, they'll see the car and radio ahead." Steve took a deep breath as if to clear his mind or gather courage. "Where's Carrie?"

Ricco opened his eyes and glanced at the clock on his night stand. It was almost time to get up.

He heard a commotion at the front of the house. He reached over and pushed a buzzer that sounded in the kitchen. It was loud enough for anyone in the house to hear.

Seraphina appeared at his doorway. She was taking deep breaths and her eyes were huge.

He was immediately suspicious. Something had happened. "What has happened?" he asked.

Her eyes met his. "The Senora has left in the car."

"Did she say where she was going?" This was not like Alissa. She only went places with him or Lorenzo.

"I do not know. Someone was in the car with her."

"Was it Lorenzo?"

Seraphina shook her head. "He is helping with the vines."

A chill passed through him. It could not be. He refused to believe it. "Get Lorenzo, now!"

Seraphina ran away from the doorway.

He sat up and cursed.

Daniella saw a car speeding down a dirt road toward the sea. Why was this person in such a hurry? She had a feeling this car could be connected to Steve's disappearance. The monastery was only an hour or two away.

She scanned the area and saw a house and vineyard. The car could have come from that villa. She signaled Sergio to circle back. The plane made wide turn.

She grabbed the camera and took pictures. As they flew over the house, two vehicles drove off the property and followed the car. She motioned for Sergio to follow the three vehicles.

Lorenzo hurried into the bedroom.

Ricco was livid. He wanted to scream at his assistant. Instead, he waited.

"It took you too long to get here! Alissa has taken the car and the prisoner is not in his cell. Seraphina summoned the field manager and he gathered several men. They are following her."

The news was bad. His wife of twelve years had helped his prisoner to escape. How could she do this?

"Get me out of this bed!" he yelled.

Within minutes Lorenzo had him dressed and wheeled him into the living room.

Ricco heard a lot of noise outside.

Lorenzo ran to the window. "The workers are leaving. I told them to go home."

"Get Carrie and bring her here!"

Lorenzo ran up the steps.

He did not want to believe that Alissa helped Steve escape. The prisoner could not have done it without her. Of course, Peter could have found help and the agents rescued Steve and took his wife. Deep inside he knew that didn't happen. His wife had betrayed him.

Ricco knew what he had to do. He wheeled over to the telephone and called the helicopter. As he hung up, he almost panicked; they had ten minutes to leave this house.

Lorenzo pulled Carrie down the stairs. "I hear an airplane, I think it is circling the villa."

Ricco listened and he too heard the plane.

"Take Carrie to the van and tie her in it. Then, go to the basement and set the bomb."

Lorenzo nodded and half dragged Carrie toward the kitchen.

Ricco wheeled himself down the hall and into his bedroom. He stopped at a large bookcase next to his desk. He took a key out of his pocket and inserted it into a lock located in a cupboard. He opened the cupboard door and pulled out a valise. After putting it in his lap, he pushed a button and the cupboard closed. He wheeled himself into the kitchen and waited.

Lorenzo pushed Carrie into the backseat of the van. He tied her hands and feet together. He looked into her large moist blue eyes and snarled. When she showed fear, he laughed.

After shoving her down onto the seat and locking the van doors, the tall man rushed back into the kitchen and then down the stairs to the basement.

He went to an area close to the restroom and uncovered the explosives stored there. He found the mechanism and switched it on. They had half an hour to get away before the villa blew up.

He used the elevator to go upstairs and into the kitchen.

Ricco was waiting for him.

"It is done."

"Good. Drive to the rendezvous point."

"I need your keys."

Ricco stared at him. "Why?"

"Alissa took mine while I was in the shower."

Ricco reached into this pocket and pulled out his keys. The tall man grabbed them.

TWENTY-ONE

"We are low on fuel. We must go back to Rome."

Sergio turned his head, waiting for instructions. Daniella did not want to go back to Rome yet. "Fly over the villa one more time."

Daniella called Rafael. "Send a team to intercept three cars." She gave him the directions. "Have you heard from the Americans?"

"No. They have not called. I have sent someone to their hotel."

"Good. Let me know about the cars."

She signed off and reached into her bag for her camera. If this was the place Cristo held his prisoners, she would need pictures.

A few minutes later they moved closer to the villa. A van drove out of the garage. It turned and sped off in the opposite direction of the cars.

"Sergio, we need to follow that van!"

"Only if it goes toward Rome!"

Daniella realized her dilemma. She nodded. "Do what you must."

She called Rafael, again. "There is a van traveling on the same road as the three cars. It is going in the opposite direction. We cannot follow it."

"We will send a team to intercept it."

"Drop a team off at the villa, as well. Call me later with an update."

Sergio was able to follow the van a short distance.

When it turned off the road and headed north, he continued on to Rome. Daniella watched the van for as long as she could. Her instinct told her that the cars, the villa, and the van were important.

Father Angelo parked the car in front of a church. Marian and Raoul watched the monk go into the rectory. This was the fourth little town since meeting the priest. Earlier, they had eaten lunch while the good father talked to the people at the hospital on the other side of town.

So far, there had been no news of any strangers being found in the surrounding area.

Raoul looked at Marian. The heat was getting to her. Her face was flushed, she was fanning herself with her purse, and she rolled her eyes at him. He noticed the two small bags of souvenirs sitting beside her. "Let us make one more shopping trip, while the good Father visits his friends."

Marian smiled and opened the door.

They stood on the curb looking around.

Raoul gestured to his left. "That looks like the main part of the town."

Marian started walking. "It would be nice if we could find a store with clothing and jewelry instead of pottery and old stuff."

Raoul laughed. "Marian where is your spirit of adventure?"

"It got lost in the last town."

"The people were nice and the gelato was good."

"Yes. You're right. The gelato was good."

"I was impressed that you ordered a different flavor than the previous town. Three gelatos in one day must be a record of some sort." He turned his head away from her to hide his smile.

He heard her intake of breath and wanted to laugh.

"Are you counting my gelatos?"

"Of course not. How many gelatos you eat is no concern of mine."

"Are you insinuating they should be a concern of mine?"

He grabbed her hand and pulled her close to him. "My only concern is you, my dear. This town looks a lot bigger than any we've been in today. Why waste precious shopping time on the subject of gelatos? I think we may find something more interesting on the next street."

Marian looked up at him and laughed. "Sometimes I think I'm your entertainment. Just remember, you work for me. And I can have as many gelatos' as I want."

Raoul picked up the pace. "Sure, my dear, and I, your favorite employee, will carry your new purchases."

They both laughed and after two blocks found a dress shop.

Marian made a bee line for the colorful cotton dresses hanging on a rack against the back wall. A shop girl approached her and Marian shooed her away. Of course, the girl came up to him. He was the other customer in the shop.

"May I help you find a gift?"

Raoul watched Marian select a dress off the rack and move over to the shoes. The sales girl was staring at him.

"You seem to have a wide selection of clothing and accessories. We did not see any stores like this one in the previous towns. Business must be good."

The girl smiled. "Yes, it is good. We have special clients we order for and we buy a little extra for our regular customers. And of course, for the tourists."

Raoul smiled and turned on the charm. "Who are these special clients? Movie stars?" He waited for her laugh.

"No movie stars. One of our clients is a countess."

Raoul raised an eyebrow and made definite eye connection. "Does she live around here?"

The girl turned her head and watched Marian at the jewelry counter. "She does not live far from here. Her husband has a large vineyard."

Raoul decided that maybe this countess might know about the people who kidnapped Peter and the others. "Can you give me directions to her villa?"

The girl threw a suspicious look toward him. "I do not give out information about my customers."

"One of our friends has disappeared. We are searching for him now. Perhaps this countess has seen him. He is an American."

"The countess is very beautiful. It is hard to tell if she is American. Her husband is Italian. It is possible she could have met your friend."

Raoul reached inside his pants pocket and took out his pen and small notebook.

Marian couldn't believe her luck! There was so much to choose from she couldn't decide which items she really wanted. She held the dress out from her and thought this was perfect to wear tonight after this long tedious trip through the back towns and horrific heat.

She glanced at the sandals. They were pricey. But she had to have them. Out of the corner of her eye, she could see Raoul and the sales girl. Her assistant was writing something on a piece of paper. Was he getting her phone number? Horrified, she made a motion to get the girls attention.

The girl ran over to her. "Have you found something

you like?"

She thrust the shoes and dress into her hands. "Yes, I have." She felt like adding, "have you?", but didn't. Before she followed the girl to the counter, she grabbed four pairs of earrings off a rack.

Marian took out her wallet and watched Raoul stroll outside. The dirty old man! He didn't fool her one bit.

She paid for her purchases and joined him at the curb.

"I see you found a few things, my dear," he said. He reached over for her bags. She stuffed them into his hands.

Raoul raised an eyebrow. "Something bothering you? Did they not have everything you wanted?"

"No, they didn't have everything I wanted. However, I noticed they had something you wanted!"

He looked back at the store.

Marian started walking toward the car. "I've had enough shopping."

He walked up beside her. "The sales girl gave me some important information, my dear."

"I bet she did," she muttered.

He grabbed her arm and stopped her progress. "What is wrong with you Marian? The girl told me about a countess that lives nearby."

"Oh? Great, a countess." She frowned and started walking again.

Once more, he caught up and stopped her. "The woman is an American. She lives in the country."

"So?"

"Marian, if you were going to kidnap someone, would you not want to take them out into the country somewhere? Away from prying eyes?"

It dawned on her then. "You think Peter might be there?"

"I do not know, but it is a place to start."

Father Angelo pulled up at the curb. They got inside the car. He smiled at them. "I have a clue!"

Alissa slowed the car and made a quick turn onto the paved road heading for the nearest town. Her town. The one where she had dared to make a few friends and have lunch. She felt pity and disgust for her husband. What a combination of feelings. Once, Steve had asked her why she stayed with Ricco. She had not told him about their little son Luciano. She remembered how he had felt in her arms the day he was born. He had been born premature and his lungs were not good. Two days after she went home from the hospital, he died.

He had been such a beautiful baby. The grief had been devastating for both of them. Ricco said it was the worst thing that had happened to him in his life, including the death of his mother and step-father when he was a child.

They found comfort and solace in each other for a few years. That was before she found out how cruel and ruthless he could be.

The explosion of the yacht and the trauma that followed had numbed her. Ricco had been in such pain. The doctors did not give him much of a chance. They did not know his strong will for revenge.

Living in France had been a blessing. She loved it there. She had many friends and could travel the country without fear of detection.

One day Ricco told her to pack a few bags. He had inherited a vineyard in Italy. His strange moods increased once they were in the villa. Lorenzo came to live with them. Before, he only came for short visits. She shivered. The man frightened her.

Now, she could not go along with Ricco's craziness.

She increased her speed.

"Are we there yet?" Steve asked. He laughed. "That bit of humor is lost on you isn't it?" He tried to laugh again, but stopped.

Alissa turned her head and glanced at him. She was shocked by the pallor of his skin. His face was contorted with pain.

She panicked. He looked awful and his voice was not strong. What if he died before she reached the hospital? Her foot pressed onto the accelerator.

Ricco popped into her mind again. He had been right about Steve. They had indeed been lovers years ago. She was not in love with him, but she cared for him very much. Tears welled up in her eyes. She did not want to see him die.

She choked back tears. The little town was just over the hill.

"We are almost there, Steve. Hang on a little longer."

A car with blinking lights came over a hill ahead of them. Alissa recognized it as official police. She stopped and honked her horn.

"There is a police car coming, Steve."

"Get out and wave them down," Steve croaked.

She followed his order. When the car neared her, it stopped and two men got out. One looked like an American agent.

She leaned into the car. "What do we do now?"

"Come back here and help me, Alissa."

She opened the door close to Steve. His body looked so contorted. Like he was a puppet on strings and the puppeteer had dropped him.

He watched the two men. "Alissa, do you know any of those men?"

"No."

"The American is named Walker. He is on my team.

I suppose the other man works for the local police. Do not volunteer any information. Let me handle it all."

"Okay, Steve."

Walker reached the car door and looked in. "Where've you been Steve? We've been looking all over the country for you." He glanced at Alissa. "I see you're not alone."

"Very funny, Walker."

Walker laughed and said something to the other man. The man left and walked toward the police car. "I'm going to drive you to the hospital." He looked at Alissa. "Get in the back with Steve." He picked up a bottle of water off the floor of the car. "Give him a little of this on the way."

Alissa got in the back seat. Steve leaned against her. Walker took off down the road.

"Walker, this is Alissa DiBiasi, Ricco's wife. She is not to be arrested or held for questioning. You drop me off at the hospital and once I'm inside, drive her wherever she wants to go. We owe her."

"The road should be coming up soon," Marian said. She sat in the back seat reading the map.

Raoul glanced over at Father Angelo. "Maybe you should slow down."

Father Angelo, broken out of his thoughts, looked over at Raoul and drove past the turn off.

"What did you say?" he asked.

"For Pete's sake, you just drove past the road!" Raoul yelled. Between Marian and the monk, his nerves were wearing thin. Maybe it was the way they drove in Italy. Now, they had gone past the turn off to the vineyard and would lose precious time turning around.

Father Angelo slowed down. He stopped the car

several feet later, and Raoul could not see a good spot to turn around.

The portly man took out his handkerchief and wiped his forehead. "This is a good place. We will have a drink of water. I am thirsty again. The dust is bad for my throat."

Raoul wanted to scream, but he chocked it back and only nodded. It was useless venting his frustrations at the priest. He could not help it that he didn't move fast, and when he did manage to move fast, went past the turn off.

All three got out of the car. Raoul decided he needed to relieve himself. He scanned the area for the best place and walked toward a thick brushy area above the road. He looked over at Marian and motioned toward the bushes. Marian nodded. She turned her back and looked out toward the sea and took deep breaths.

Father Angelo opened the trunk and lifted out a large water container. The bag of water and food he had started out with this morning was gone and he had bought a very large container at the last town.

Raoul saw him fill his cup and take big swallows. Sweat rolled down his face.

He was just about to the bushes, when he saw a colorful object about ten feet away. After he finished his business, Raoul went over to the colorful object and found Peter lying in the dirt. He was shocked. Peter appeared to be dead.

Raoul felt for a pulse and smiled. He called his name.

Peter opened his eyes. Raoul stood up.

"Marian! Bring water! Hurry!"

Father Angelo and Marian ran up the hill. They carried a cup of water. When Raoul saw them, he became frustrated. "It's Peter. We'll need more water."

Marian cried out when she saw her son. He looked terrible. She sat down and cradled his head in her lap. Raoul dipped his finger in the cup of water and wetted Peter's mouth. Her son's chapped lips moved, but he didn't taste the water.

"Let us get him to the car," Raoul said.

Father Angelo helped Raoul carry Peter to the car and put him in the back seat.

Raoul's eyes scanned her son's body. Marian knew he saw the bloody pants. "Is there a wound, Raoul?"

Her assistant nodded. He took off his shirt and handed it to her. "Tear this into strips. Father, we need more water. Do you have something bigger to put the water in?"

"Yes." The priest ran to the trunk. He returned with a large glass. Raoul looked at it. It would have to do. "Fill it up."

He grabbed the bloody pants leg and tore it open. Raoul took the glass from the priest and poured its contents over Peter's calf. He handed the glass back to the priest.

Father Angelo filled the glass again. This time Raoul focused the water on the bullet wound. Yes, he had recognized the kind of wound. Silently, he cursed. It looked bad. Infection had set in.

He took the strips and wrapped Peter's leg. Carefully, he searched his body for anything else that needed attention. There were many bruises along with small scratch marks. His hands were bleeding. "More water."

Father Angelo filled the glass again. Raoul cleaned

Peter's hands and wrapped them. "We have to get him to the doctor."

Marian got into the car next to her son and cradled his head in her lap. They moistened his lips again and Peter's tongue responded. He licked the water. Slowly, his eyes opened.

"Give him a sip now," Raoul said.

Marian placed the cup at his lips and raised the back of his head. The water ran down Peter's chin. She placed the cup again, and this time he opened his mouth. She gave him a small amount of water.

Raoul slid behind the wheel. He glanced in the back seat. Marian had tears running down her cheeks, as she calmly cleaned her son's face with the rest of the water and a strip of shirt. He took a deep breath and swallowed to chase away the emotion. Father Angelo ran around and got into the passenger seat.

He turned the car around and headed back to the last town. "If I remember right, Father, the last town had a hospital."

"You are correct, my son. A good hospital. And a very good doctor. He is my cousin."

TWENTY-TWO

Carrie sat in back of Ricco in the helicopter and watched Lorenzo fold the wheelchair. Where would they take her now? She was so frightened. Her hands trembled and she squeezed them together in her lap.

Lorenzo sat down beside her. She turned her head toward the window and tried not to cringe. She knew better than to react in any way. Both of them were so unpredictable and cruel.

Earlier, before they drove out of the garage, Ricco told Lorenzo to untie her hands and feet. If it had been up to the tall horrible man, she would still be trussed up like a Christmas turkey.

The two men had argued all the way from the villa to this clearing. She didn't know what they said, because they spoke only in Italian. The worst time had been when the plane was flying overhead. Ricco had screamed several times at Lorenzo.

The helicopter took off and her eyes drank in the beautiful countryside. Down below, people were enjoying their ordinary lives. Up here, Carrie wondered if she was going to have a life to enjoy.

Where was Alissa? Did she and Steve escape? Both of the men had mentioned their names many times. They were the only words she could understand. Was her brother still in the house waiting to be rescued? Somehow, she didn't think Ricco would have left him there. An awful thought entered her mind. Had they killed him? She quickly pushed it aside.

Tears welled up in her eyes.

The other heartache, which had now become a dull constant nagging in her mind, wanted its fair share of worry and tears. Her husband. Where was Peter? The thought of him lying in a ravine waiting for help that would never come, tormented her.

Ricco reached down and picked up a set of earphones. He put them on, adjusting them over his ears. She stared at the back of his head. It had been spared the torture of the rest of his body. He appeared perfectly normal from the back.

She wondered if he ever had been something other than crazy.

Ricco was pleased. Everything had been covered. Lorenzo wiped the van clean and emptied the glove compartment. If something had been left, it would not matter. They would not be coming back here again and they had carried nothing with them when they left the house, except his brief case.

It will be as if we have vanished. If things had gone as planned, he and Alissa would be on their way to the chateau in France. There he had another identity and life.

A sadness flowed through him. Alissa had betrayed him. The authorities would know about the chateau. Circumstances dictated that he go to the island. No one would think to look for him there and his wife knew nothing about the island home. Only Lorenzo and the pilot knew of this getaway. He smiled to himself and felt smug. This place would be safe and he would spend the rest of his life with Carrie. He stifled a chuckle. And Peter's baby.

He told the pilot to change course. Minutes later, the

helicopter made a turn and headed toward the sea.

Steve winced with pain as Walker helped him out of the car and into a wheelchair. A nurse pushed him toward the doors of the hospital emergency room. He looked back and saw Walker getting back into the car with Alissa.

The wheelchair continued into the building and down a hall. Another nurse came from the opposite direction and joined them. They turned into a small room and the women helped him out of the chair. He barely had the strength to get up on the table, even with their help.

He laid his head back and watched them cut his clothing off his body. His shirt was bloody from the open sores Lorenzo had inflicted on him that morning. He raised his head and saw the bandages on his foot. They were bloody also.

Well, what had he expected?

He put his head back down and closed his eyes. He'd been in worse shape before and lived.

Juan stepped up to the reception desk in the emergency room. He showed his badge to the woman at the counter. Charlie stood next to him.

"We are here to see Steve Crawford."

The nurse smiled and nodded her head. She motioned to another woman and told her to watch the desk.

"Please follow me."

They walked down a hall and turned into a small room. Steve lay on an examining table. His body appeared lifeless. His skin was pale and his breathing labored.

Juan was shocked. When Walker had called the

hotel earlier and left a message for him to come to this hospital to take care of Steve, he'd wondered what condition his boss would be in. He hadn't expected this.

Steve's body moved and moaned. The nurse stepped closer and touched his arm. She turned and joined Juan and Charlie.

"Your friend is doing well. You can visit for a few minutes. The doctor is in surgery now. He can speak with you later."

She went out the door and Juan walked up to the bed. He touched Steve's arm. No response. "Steve, it's Juan. Steve." Still no response.

He glanced at Charlie who had elected to stay in a safe place at the doorway. Coward. He touched Steve's shoulder this time. "Hey, Boss!"

Getting no response again, he joined Charlie in the doorway. "He's out of it. I have to speak to the nurse. You stay here in case he wakes up."

Juan hurried down the hall.

He marched up to the desk. "I can't wait for the doctor. You have to tell me about his condition."

The woman stared back at him. He knew she didn't know if she should divulge the information or not. Juan reached into his pocket for his cell phone and dialed Rafael's number.

"Rafael, we have found Steve. He's in a hospital."

"What is his condition?"

"I don't know. The doctor's in surgery and the nurse isn't giving me any information."

"Give her the phone," Rafael said.

Juan handed the woman the phone. Within minutes she handed it back to him.

"Your friend is scheduled for surgery," she said. "He has a wound in his foot. His back has many welts and cuts. Some are infected. His body is weak."

"Did you hear that Rafael?"

"Si. You stay with him. I will call you back. Where is the town located?"

"It's the first one north of the villa. Walker said they intercepted Steve and a woman on the highway close to the dirt road. I'll wait for your call." Juan hung up and headed back down the hall to Steve's room. Charlie stood at the bedside.

Their eyes locked. Juan could see the fear. "Any improvement?"

Charlie shook his head. "Let's go outside. I need some fresh air."

The plane touched down and headed for the terminal. Daniella had not heard from Rafael or the Americans for a while. She knew all three cars had been intercepted. Steve and a woman were in the first car. The American agent named Walker took control of the scene and her agent had continued on with the rest of the team.

The other cars contained workers from the villa. They were detained and Rafael was questioning them.

Where was Steve?

Sergio parked the plane. She grabbed her large purse off the floor and smiled at the pilot. "Thanks. Stay close. We might need you again."

He nodded. "My home is nearby."

She got out of the plane and walked toward her car. Her cell phone rang and of course, it was at the bottom of her purse. She struggled and found it. It was her second in command.

"Rafael, what news do you have?"

"Steve Crawford is in a hospital located in a small town near the villa. He has a serious wound in his foot. He needs surgery."

Her heart beat fast. Steve was alive. He was wounded. "Where are you?"

"Ten miles from the hospital. The workers have not given us any information of value. They knew nothing of the people they worked for. Everyone lived off the grounds. One of the workers said that one night they were called to come in early. A group of men were searching for someone. Do you think Peter O'Brien and his wife escaped?"

"Peter could have escaped. We will hope he took Carrie with him." Daniella could not think of them right now. She must do something for Steve. She wanted him close to her. "Rafael, go to the hospital. I will order a medical helicopter to pick up Steve and bring him to Rome."

"I will leave now."

"Wait. What happened to the van? What about the villa?"

"The van disappeared. We think they used a helicopter to escape. The team at the villa found no one and nothing of interest. They are waiting for me. I will know more after I see with my own eyes."

"Call me from the hospital."

Rafael hung up. Daniella ordered a helicopter for Steve. She hoped Peter and Carrie would turn up soon.

Raoul entered the small town and drove as fast as he dared toward the hospital. It helped that they had spent so much time here earlier in the day. Peter's life could depend on how fast he got help.

A few minutes later he pulled up at the hospital emergency door.

"Look, there's Juan and Charlie!" Marian said.

Father Angelo and Raoul got out of the car. Father

Angelo ran inside to get help. Raoul opened the door and faced Marian and her son. Peter looked worse.

Juan and Charlie ran up to the car. They stood beside Raoul and stared at Peter. A nurse and a doctor came out with a gurney, followed by Father Angelo.

Raoul and the agents stepped away from the car and let the medical team get Peter out.

"I tried to call agent Walker, but could not get a connection," Raoul said.

Juan nodded. "We had big problems staying in touch today. Walker left us a message at the hotel. Otherwise, we wouldn't be here."

"What is Peter's condition?" Charlie asked.

Raoul frowned. "Not good. He's got a bullet wound in his calf. He also is severely dehydrated. There could be other things that are not obvious."

Juan shook his head. "I didn't recognize him."

"He's lost weight," Raoul said. "Who knows what hell he's been through."

The doctor and nurse took Peter into the emergency room.

Raoul rushed to help Marian out of the car. Her face was wet with fresh tears.

He pulled her into his arms and held her tight. "We will get through this, my dear."

"I know," Marian whispered.

Raoul slipped his arm around Marian's waist and started to walk toward the emergency room door.

"We'll be out here a few more minutes," Juan said. "Steve's being prepared for surgery."

Raoul continued walking, but turned his head and stared at Juan. "You found Steve?"

Juan nodded.

He pulled Marian tighter. "See my dear, things are getting better. They found Steve and he is alive."

She sighed. "That's great, but where's Carrie?"

The helicopter landed in a field on the outskirts of Livorno on the Tyrennehan Sea. Ricco prepared to get out of the helicopter. He needed to use the toilette. He hated the thought of going behind a tree or a rock. He looked down at the ground and studied the terrain surrounding the landing site. It was full of small pebbles. He would not be able to wheel himself to a decent spot. He would need help.

Lorenzo brought the wheelchair over and lifted him out and into the chair. He glanced up at Carrie.

"Leave her inside for now. Have the pilot wait while you take me behind that big rock." He pointed toward a huge boulder about twenty feet away.

His assistant spoke to the pilot. Ricco thought about Carrie. He could feel her fear. He knew most of it was because of her baby. When Lorenzo was stalking her, he'd seen the Baby Bunting woman go up to the front door.

He felt the chair being pushed from behind. It moved slowly toward the boulder.

"Lorenzo, when we are finished with this business," Ricco said. "You will walk into town and meet the limo. Here are the directions. Make sure the yacht is ready before you come for us." He reached into his pocket and pulled out a piece of paper. "Let Carrie relieve herself, then handcuff her to my wheelchair. Where is the water and food?"

"In the helicopter. I will get it when I bring the girl. What will we do with her?"

"She will go with us. Alissa is gone. Carrie will be my new wife."

Lorenzo followed a path to the road. He did not care how far he had to walk. He needed time away from the crazy man and his captive. He knew he had to call the boss in Naples. Ricco's behavior must be reported. This affair with the agents and their families was a failure.

Alissa's departure would not be taken lightly by the organization. She helped the agent escape and there would be actions taken.

He dialed Antonio's number.

"Lorenzo, it has been too long since you called. What is happening? We are hearing rumors."

"Ricco's plan for the agents and their families is a failure. One escaped during the night and Alissa helped another to escape today. Ricco has O'Brien's wife and he intends to keep her. Forever."

"Where are you now?"

"We are in Livorno. We will take a limo to the yacht. The plan is to go to Positano for a few days before we go to Elba."

"Follow the plan. Contact me when you get to Positano."

Lorenzo frowned. He did not like this. Will they kill Ricco? What about the woman? Is this an attempt to rescue an American agent's wife? Why would the organization bother?

He could kill her and dispose of her body. No one would ever find her. He smiled. That would please him very much.

Carrie and Ricco sat beneath a tree close to the big boulder. She was beside herself with fear and apprehension. This man who had been so charming and alive in Dallas was nothing more than a tyrant. He had kidnapped her and the two people she held dearest.

She glanced at him. In the sunlight, his scars looked so much worse. How had he gotten them? What had happened to him and why did he hate her husband and brother?

Her role in this was so confusing.

He turned his head and their eyes locked. Carrie expected to see craftiness or cruelty, but it was her old friend staring back at her.

"What has caused you so much pain, Ricco?"

"A life of disappointments and power, Carrie. Alissa has left me and turned to the other side. My vineyard is ruined. I cannot go to my chateau in France, it is lost. I must make a new life for myself."

Carrie thought Ricco had enough money and influence to live a comfortable life. She knew he still wanted his revenge.

His eyes glistened in the sunlight and Carrie shivered.

"You will now share all of my money and power with me. You will be by my side forever," Ricco said.

A chill passed through her again. There was no way she would live with this monster FOREVER. Instinct told her to approach him in a gentle manner. It wouldn't do to make him mad. "Ricco, please, let me go. I love my husband and we're going to have a baby."

"I know. It will now be our baby."

Fear clutched her. He knew about the baby all along. Was that why he had brought her here? To take her away from everything she held dear in her life? Just to punish her husband and brother?

Why was he even bothering with them?

"Why do you want to hurt my husband and brother?"

He stared at her for several seconds. He shook his

head. "It is a very long story. The two agents put me in this wheelchair and ruined my life."

"Ricco, please think this through. If you take me along with you, yes, it will bring a lot of pain to my husband and brother. But won't it bring more pain for you, also? Every day you'll be reminded of them and the people who would be searching for you. My brother is very good at finding people and he never gives up."

He turned his head and looked away from her. She said nothing for a few minutes. When he turned back, the cruelty was gone from his eyes. She could see torment and sadness.

"Did you know I once had a son? He died two days after he was born. I will never have another child of my own."

In that moment her fear was replaced with compassion. "I'm sorry for your loss, Ricco. Please don't keep my husband from seeing his son. The hatred you feel for him is a result of both of your careers. Leave the families out of it."

He put his head back and rested it on the tree trunk. "I am tired. My body needs to rest. Lorenzo will be back soon."

He closed his eyes and Carrie felt relief. She wouldn't have to talk to him for a while. Her mind moved to her other problem. How could she escape?

Juan glanced at his watch one more time. Steve's surgery would be in one hour. The doctor was with Peter right now, and he would most likely go into surgery right after Steve.

Rafael walked into the waiting room. Juan stood up and waved at him. He joined them.

"A medical helicopter will be here in twenty minutes.

Steve will have surgery in Rome."

Juan exchanged looks with Charlie.

"Peter O'Brien is here, too. Marian and Raoul found him alongside a road and brought him here," Juan said. "He's being looked at right now."

Rafael placed his hands on his hips and stared at the floor. A few seconds past. He looked at Juan. "There should be room for him to go too, if the doctor thinks he can make it to Rome." He paused and stared at Juan. "We found no one at the villa."

Juan understood all too well what he meant. Carrie wasn't there. He nodded. "We figured Ricco took Carrie with him."

Marian and Raoul came in the emergency room from outside.

"If Peter goes to Rome," Juan said. "We'll need another car. His mother and her assistant are here."

Rafael shrugged. "We will find transportation for them."

The ground shook. A muffled sound broke the silence in the room. It lasted several seconds.

"What was that?" Charlie said.

"It felt like an earthquake," Juan said.

Rafael pulled out his phone. "Communications are down." He faced the agents. "I must go. Let me know if there is a problem with the helicopter. I think the villa blew up."

Juan watched him go out the door. Raoul and Marian rushed over.

"Do you think that was an earthquake?" Raoul asked.

"Rafael thinks it could have been the villa where everyone was held," Juan said.

Marian cried out. "Do you think Carrie was still there?"

"No, Carrie wasn't at the villa when the team

arrived. We don't know where she's at right now," Juan said.

Walker walked into the hospital. Juan was glad to see him.

"I think the villa just blew up," Walker said.

"That seems to be the overall opinion," Juan said. He paused. This seemed as good a time as any to relate the news. "There is a helicopter on its way here to pick up Steve. There's room for Peter, if the doctor lets him go."

Marian's hands flew to her face. "Thank heavens. I was so worried he wouldn't have the right medical attention here. Have you heard anything from the doctor yet?"

"No," Juan said.

"What about Marian? Is there room for her on the helicopter?" Raoul asked.

"Probably not. Rafael will help with your transportation. We have two cars. One belongs to the Italians. I'm thinking you two can go along with Walker. Charlie and I have some unfinished business here before we can join you all in Rome."

"Can I see Steve and Peter?" Walker asked.

Juan started. He'd forgotten about Walker being out of the loop. He hadn't known about Peter being found. "Yeah, man, Steve's down the hall, but you'll have to wait to see Peter. The doc's working on him right now."

He started down the hall with Walker on his heels. "Marian and Raoul visited with him a few minutes ago. We have to keep it short."

"Gotcha."

Juan stood in the doorway while Walker hurried into the room. Steve was still doped up. He glanced at his watch. He had to talk to the doctor before the copter arrived.

Walker left the bedside and returned to the door. "How bad is it?"

"He'll make it. He's been worse."

They went back to the lobby. Marian and Raoul were sitting on the couch talking to Charlie. Juan walked up to the desk.

"A helicopter will be coming for Steve Crawford. If the doctor thinks he can make it, we're taking Peter O'Brien, too."

The nurse frowned. "When will the helicopter be here?"

"Twenty minutes."

She turned and hurried into another room. Several minutes past. Juan wondered what was going on. Finally, she emerged and joined him at the desk. "The doctor is still with Senor O'Brien. We have started to get Senor Crawford ready for the helicopter."

Juan thanked her and joined the others. Marian was sipping coffee, Raoul had his head back on the couch, and Charlie was talking to Walker. They all came to attention.

"Now we wait for the helicopter," Juan said.

A commotion began at the desk and outside the hospital. The doors opened and a man ran inside. He spoke to the nurse at the desk. She ran to the door she'd been to earlier for Juan.

A few seconds later two nurses came out with a wheelchair. They rushed outside.

In the stillness of the waiting room, they heard the ambulance siren heading away from the hospital.

"I think this place is about to get busy," Charlie said.

TWENTY-THREE

Daniella sat at her desk in her apartment. She had a lot of paperwork to fill out before tomorrow's task force meeting in Milan. She rubbed her temples and thought a major headache was on its way. They had no leads on Cristo and the O'Brien's. They had appeared to have vanished into thin air, like Steve from the monastery

Her cell phone rang. It was Rafael.

"Rafael, I hope you have good news."

"The villa blew up. The phones have been out. One man is dead and several are wounded. The dead man was standing close to the front door when the explosion happened. Two of our men drove three injured to the hospital. We wait now for the ambulance. I sent another man south to the nearest available hospital. He is taking another of the lesser wounded. We hope they will have more than one ambulance."

"I will send a medical team down there to help. Any news about Peter and Carrie O'Brien?"

"Si, Senor O'Brien has been found and is in the hospital. The Americans did not know about his condition. If the doctor says yes, he will go with Senor Crawford on the helicopter."

Daniella felt relieved that Peter was alive. She glanced at the clock. "Very good, Rafael. Call me in two hours with updates. I want to know when Steve gets here."

Rafael hung up. Daniella felt exhausted. She knew she had to stay up and drive to the hospital. She would want to be with Steve. She hoped Peter would also be there. Now, only one victim remained. Carrie O'Brien. This could be the most difficult person to find. Cristo could keep her locked up somewhere for a very long time.

Earlier she had said good night to Rosie. Her daughter had been happy for her to return tomorrow. A sadness washed over her. So much time away from her daughter bothered her. She leaned back into her chair. It was times like this when she wished she had someone else to help her. Like Steve.

Ricco sat next to Carrie in the limo. She had her head back on the seat, watching out the window. They were close to the marina, perhaps ten minutes away. He had to make a decision about her and her baby before they boarded the yacht. Would he leave her here in the city or take her with him?

If it were possible, his hatred toward the agents was stronger than before he tried to extract his revenge. The anger had built up until he had to vent it on someone. That person had been Lorenzo. He glanced at his right hand man, sitting in front with the driver. For some reason he was having his doubts about him.

Carrie's breathing took on more of a rhythm. He turned and stared at her. She was sleeping and her angelic face was beautiful. Her beauty was different from Alissa's. This woman's beauty came from within her. He needed someone like that in his life now.

He frowned. He could punish the agents in one swoop by killing Carrie and her baby. But he wanted her for himself. He didn't have to kill her to get the results he craved. Let them worry the rest of their sorry lives. Let them feel the pain of never seeing her again, or knowing the child.

How sweet it sounded. He could achieve his revenge. He frowned, again. The baby spoiled everything.

Even though his hatred for the agents was paramount, he had something bigger to deal with. The organization would have heard about his fiasco by now. They had warned him several times to behave. If they found out he had an American agent's wife and child, he would pay dearly. He was sure his behavior had already been discussed by the council, the group of men that ran the organization.

The council was not afraid of the Italian government or the United States government. They preferred having not to bother with them. Two governments snooping around would mean a slowdown in business.

He still wanted Carrie. She would board the yacht.

Juan stood at the car and watched the attendants put his fellow agents on the helicopter. The small hospital did not have a heliport, so they had transported the patients to the outskirts of town.

At the last minute, the doctor had given his okay for Peter to go with Steve. Although he was in bad shape and hadn't gained consciousness yet, the doctor thought he would have a better chance in Rome. Marian and Raoul had accompanied him to the helicopter. His mother looked awful. It was a good thing she had Raoul in her life.

They had Steve doped up for the ride. Talking to him had been a challenge. He had no clue as to what was going on. Juan knew Steve would bounce back from his wounds. Peter on the other hand, was a different story. It would take months for Peter to get over his ordeal.

The attendants hurried back to their car. The helicopter's blades began to spin. Marian and Raoul moved closer.

"We want to leave right away," Raoul said.

Juan turned to them. The anguish on their faces was hard to take. He swallowed to get rid of the emotion he felt.

"Walker has the car ready whenever you want to go. It would be a good idea to check into a hotel when you get there. I know you'll want to be at the hospital all the time, but you may need somewhere to go to clean up and rest. Peter won't be able to go home for a while."

Marian leaned on Raoul. He pulled her tighter against him. "Good advice, Juan."

"Well, let's get in the car and head back."

Twenty minutes later, he and Charlie watched Walker drive off with Marian and Raoul. Juan sighed. "Tonight we get a good rest. Tomorrow we'll head north and look for Ricco and Carrie."

Charlie walked toward their car. Juan followed.

"He knows we'll be hot on his trail. The only bad thing is, we don't have a trail to follow," Charlie said.

Juan opened the passenger side door and got in. Charlie slipped behind the wheel.

"We may not have a trail now, but we will. Ricco could be anywhere, but he always stays in the same place. Italy." Juan paused for a minute to think about Ricco's history. When the yacht blew up, it had been off the coast of Positano. Ricco had also lived outside Rome.

Charlie drove north out of town. "Do you think he bought another yacht?"

Juan laughed. "Good thinking. That's where we'll start. We'll check out the coast. It's possible he Will be close to Positano.

Charlie glanced at him. "Better get some sleep, we have a long drive ahead."

Ricco stood in the salon looking out at the harbor. He bought this boat when he and Alissa had moved to the villa. Lorenzo kept it docked on Elba.

Carrie had not wanted to board with them. It was the first time she'd opposed anything he had wanted her to do. She tried to escape, but Lorenzo had put a stop to it. Now, she was in one of the staterooms, crying.

He knew this situation brought her much pain. He didn't care. She was his now. Her brother and husband would pay.

Fear surged through him. Again, he wondered how he could keep this from the council. The plan to go to Positano for a few days bothered him. It was too close to Antonio's home. His cousin was on the council. He had been a good ally over the years. Now, Ricco did not trust him.

He and Carrie would stay on board while Lorenzo went ashore for supplies. Most people would notice a crippled man in a wheelchair and a pretty blonde with blue eyes. Alissa's stateroom was filled with clothing and toiletries. His wife had loved to shop. Carrie would not need anything for weeks.

As the boat left the harbor and into the sea, Ricco smiled. He thought about the island. Not Elba. Another. He chuckled. They would never find him.

Daniella paced up and down the waiting room at the

hospital in Rome. Rafael had called her when the helicopter arrived. He had been in touch with the pilot all the way to Rome.

When she got here, both agents were being prepped for surgery. Now, all she could do was wait until they were in recovery to find out the extent of their injuries.

The Americans were handling the family matters. Her part would be finding Carrie. She knew the American agents were searching now. Rafael had turned the villa clean up over to another and he would start the search for Carrie after he had some needed rest.

There were no clues. Today, she would send agents out within a two hundred mile radius of the villa to ask questions. Maybe some small bit of information would surface.

Time was important. She would only have about a month to devote to this case. There were other matters of importance to work on. The task force was small. Like all countries, not enough money to go around.

She picked up a magazine and tried to concentrate on the pages. No use. The thought of Steve being beaten and stabbed bothered her. What would have happened if he had died? She could not think of life without him now. Not with Rosie in the picture.

A woman had helped him escape, and that had to be Alissa DiBiasi. Why did she take the risk? Did they have a past?

She put the magazine down and leaned back into the sofa. She closed her eyes and rested. She had called Vittorio and he would cover for her today at the meeting. He would give an update to the task force.

Peter focused on the ceiling. Where the hell was he?

It wasn't his stinky cell in the dungeon. He looked around and realized he was in a hospital. The last thing he remembered was falling down. He remembered being exhausted and not being able to get back up. It was dark. Oh, and yes, the sea. He remembered smelling the sea.

Someone had found him. How lucky could he get. His jubilation was short lived. His pulse quickened. Sweat broke out on his forehead. He tried to move in the bed. He had to tell someone about the villa. About Carrie and Steve. A nurse hurried into the room. She came to the bed.

"Where am I?" he asked.

"You are in a hospital in Rome."

"Please, you must contact Daniella Franco. She works for your government."

He felt the strength rush out of him. He closed his eyes and before he drifted off, heard the nurse talking to him. He thought she said that Daniella was there to see him.

Daniella reached up to Steve's forehead and touched his hair. She could see a few gray hairs mixed in with the blond. She ran her knuckles softly across his cheek. The doctor had told her that Steve would be able to sit in a wheelchair this afternoon. He said Steve's body was strong. Something she had always known. His will is stronger. He would never give up until his sister was found.

She sat in the chair next to the bed.

"Don't stop. That caress felt good." Steve's mouth formed a lopsided grin. His eyes opened and met hers.

She stood and kissed his mouth. "How long have you been awake? Were you waiting for me to make a fool of myself? Throw my body across yours and weep?"

Steve managed another grin. "How are you, Daniella? Have you found any of my relatives yet?"

She sat down again. She was near exhaustion and hoped she would make sense. "Peter is here. He had surgery. Marian and Raoul found him on the side of a road near the villa. Cristo escaped and took Carrie. No one was at the villa before it blew up."

Steve's eyes opened wide. "The villa blew up? Sounds like Cristo. I'm not surprised he took Carrie. I'm just thankful he didn't kill her or blow her up in the villa...Where is 'here?'"

"You are in Rome."

"How is my daughter? I thought a lot about her while I was in Cristo's dungeon." He reached out and grabbed her hand. "I want to become a part of both your lives. I'll get a position here in Rome."

"Is there one available?"

Steve tried to shrugged, but all he could do was move his arms. "What's wrong with me?

"Your back is full of welts and some are infected. The doctor was able to operate on your foot. He said there would be a long recuperation. The damage was extensive."

Steve scowled. "Great. I'll probably have a limp."

Daniella laughed. "This is nothing. We will worry about the foot, later. We have to find Carrie."

Carrie paced up and down her stateroom. She knew Ricco didn't trust her now. Trying to escape may have been a bad decision, but she had to try.

During the night, she had slept very little. This morning, she had looked out the window and been surprised to see a beautiful old city, perched on cliffs above the water. Breakfast had been on deck with

Ricco. It would have been wonderful to enjoy the delicious breakfast, the beautiful view, but Ricco had spoiled it. He had fussed at her for not eating enough. He was worried about her baby. He still persisted with the idea that she and her baby would be his.

She walked into the bathroom. Alissa had left enough creams and perfumes and hair product to last at least a year. The closet was full of clothes.

Would she ever get off this yacht?

She heard a noise outside and hurried to the window. A boat pulled up and moored. A few seconds later, men with guns boarded. Her hands flew up to her face and covered her nose and mouth. Alissa came aboard with them. Her mind raced. Were these Ricco's men? She rushed to the stateroom door. She knew it was locked. She'd tried it many times. She pressed her ear against the door and heard shouting.

She ran back to the window in time to see the men helping Ricco onto the boat. Alissa joined them. Where were they taking him?

There was a knock at the door. She was afraid now. Lorenzo didn't get on the boat with them. She would be at the mercy of the tall horrible man. She froze.

The door opened and Lorenzo stood in the doorway. Carrie's heart was somewhere up in her throat.

"You will get dressed for town. We go ashore in one hour."

He closed the door and she was alone. The relief was short lived. Now the questions began.

Were they going to release her? Or, would she be joining Ricco on shore? The most important question- why had Alissa returned? Did she love him after all?

She went to the closet and picked out something to wear.

The nurse left the room. Peter knew she would

return in one hour with his noon meal. She told him not to be too excited about it. At this stage of his recuperation, he wouldn't be getting great food. Terrific. It was just as well. He wasn't hungry.

The nurse did give him some happy news. There were several people here to see him.

His heart flipped when his mother and Raoul entered the room. He wanted to cry, but choked it back.

His mother hurried to the bed. Tears ran down her cheeks. She had always been the emotional kind of mother. While other children had mothers that didn't react to every childhood disaster, he had one that cried at everything. Good or bad.

She kissed his cheek.

"Hi, Mom," he managed to say.

Raoul stepped over and took her hand. He sat her down in the chair next to the bed. How did they get here so fast?

His eyes met her assistant's. He nodded his head toward him. "Raoul."

"We've been so worried about you, Peter," his mother said. "We are thankful we found you when we did."

He was incredulous. "You..you..found me?"

She nodded. "Me and Raoul and Father Angelo."

"Who's Father Angelo?"

Raoul stepped in. "He's a monk we met. There is too much to tell you and the nurse said we could only stay a few minutes or so. Do you have any questions?"

"Where's Carrie?"

His mother started crying again. Raoul went over and comforted her. Peter braced himself for bad news. He hoped she wasn't dead.

"That awful man took her with him!" his mother cried.

"They have no clues. They only know she is

probably alive. She wasn't at the villa." Raoul continued to console his mother.

Cristo took Carrie with him? Peter became tense.

"Where's Steve?"

"He is here, in the hospital. Someone helped him escape," Raoul said.

"If he's here. That means he's hurt."

Raoul nodded. "Someone beat him with a whip and the welts are infected. He was also stabbed in the foot."

He clinched his fists. He wished this was a dream and his mother and Raoul would come later with wonderful news. He wished his wife would come in with them. He held back tears.

The nurse stepped in and cleared her throat.

"We have to go," Raoul said. "We will come to see you this evening."

His mother stepped over and hugged him. She ran her hand over the top of his head. "Get some rest. Let the nurses and doctors take care of you. I know you want to get out of the bed now and find Carrie. But you have to get stronger."

He nodded. She was right. He watched them leave. He was glad they could only stay a few minutes. Those minutes had been horrible. Now he had to concentrate on what they had told him. He closed his eyes for a second to gather his strength.

"You did well, my dear," Raoul said. He stared down into her bloodshot eyes and marveled that she had held together so well on this awful trip from hell.

She sniffed. "Thanks, Raoul, I tried not to be too overwhelming."

Raoul smiled. He knew how overwhelming she could be. He guided her toward the elevator. "We will go to the hotel and rest. Come back in the evening and visit Steve. The nurse said he is doing well. She said Daniella has been with him."

"A rest sounds good. I could use a cup of tea and a long hot bath. I don't have to worry about my son, but Carrie is still with that awful man." New tears formed and Raoul tried to think of something to distract her.

"Your publisher called while you in the restroom. He wants you to write two novels using your adventure here to find your son."

They reached the elevator and waited for the door to open.

"Oh, I can't think of that right now. Not until Carrie is found and the baby's okay. Peter would have to go off the critical list and we'd probably have to go home, before I could concentrate on work...did he give you a due date?"

Raoul laughed. "You have to finish your work in progress first. He has given you a year."

Marian smiled and stepped into the empty elevator. She slipped her arms around Raoul's waist and kissed his lips.

He returned the kiss. Then pulled away. "Not here Marian. Too public. We would not want you to be on the cover of an Italian tabloid."

She laughed. "I'm looking forward to our resting time, Raoul."

He smiled. Did he know how to motivate her or what?

"Hey, partner."

Peter turned his head at the familiar voice. Steve was in the doorway sitting in a wheelchair. A nurse stood behind him.

"Hey," he said.

The nurse wheeled the chair up to the bed.

"We only get to visit a few minutes. They weren't going to bring me in here, but I have no visitors. I think they felt sorry for me."

The nurse left the room.

"I can share my two. Mom and Raoul were here."

Steve raised an eyebrow. "What did they tell you?"

"Cristo took Carrie. You're in bad shape. My mom cried like I was on death's door. They mentioned something about a monk helping them find me." He sighed. "That's about it."

"Daniella has been here all night. She just left about an hour ago. The Italians have already started looking for Cristo and Carrie. Juan and Charlie called Daniella this morning and told her they were concentrating their search along the coast."

Peter nodded. "He could be anywhere."

"She's really confident they'll find him and rescue Carrie."

Peter wanted to believe it, but he didn't. "He'll use her to give us the worst possible nightmare. Not knowing where she and our baby would be. Knowing he had her and we didn't."

"It won't be for long. I'm sure he won't kill her. He's alone. Alissa helped me escape. I told Walker to take her wherever she wanted to go."

Peter met Steve's eyes. "Yeah, we owed her."

Steve smiled.

The nurse came in and placed her hands on the chair.

"Looks like my ride's here," Steve said. "I'll see you later, probably this evening."

He watched his friend/ partner/ brother-in-law leave the room. They had shared so much the last seven years. It was nice to know that Steve would always be in his life.

Suddenly, he was tired of his job. The danger and implications had filtered through to his wife and baby. It would not happen again. This would be his last assignment. He had made up his mind when he was in the cell in Cristo's basement. If he lived, he would turn in his resignation. It would be after Cristo was put away. He had to be part of that.

He ate the gruel that was offered and drank water to wash it down. The nurse had told him that tomorrow he would get to have toast. Yay, toast.

"Ahem."

He glanced at the doorway. Steve wheeled himself into the room.

"You must be better," Peter said. "No nurse to help you."

Steve stopped at the foot of the bed. He had a big grin on his face. "They made me wait until you had finished your meal before disturbing you."

Peter chuckled. "Yeah, my meal. It was great."

Steve frowned. "I have news. It's good news."

"Oh yeah, if it's good, why are you frowning?"

"Because I don't want to add to your excitement. Carrie is safe. She turned up in Positano. Daniella is on her way up with her right now."

His heart beat fast. "You mean she's here? In the hospital?"

Steve laughed. "Yes. Isn't it great?"

All he could do was nod and smile.

"Carrie told Daniella that a boat pulled up to the yacht and Alissa and a few armed men came aboard. They left with Ricco. Lorenzo took Carrie to Positano and dropped her off."

He was speechless. What could he say? His wife was safe.

"I think the organization took control of Cristo. Perhaps, he's swimming with the fishes as we speak," Peter said.

"That would be great. But, I think not. The fact that Alissa was there and he wasn't killed on the spot, tells me they took him somewhere." Steve shrugged. "Maybe they wanted to kill him away from civilization. Alissa probably has to atone for helping me."

"Would they kill her?"

"I hope not."

Steve turned his chair around. "I'll check to see if the girls are out in the hall."

Peter couldn't believe his wife was here. He had finally come out of his bad dream. Things were really going to be okay.

Steve went out of the room and Carrie stepped in. He almost lost it.

She rushed to the bed and kissed his lips. Tears ran down her cheeks. He didn't mind. He wished he could do the same. Being a man sometimes had its limitations.

She hugged him, then stepped back and wiped her eyes. He couldn't talk. The emotion was just too much.

"I can't believe we're together again. The doctor says we have to stay here a couple of weeks before you can be transported to the States," Carrie said.

He grabbed her hand. "I'm so glad to see you." Then, he thought of the baby. Had she been able to keep the baby with all the stress? Did they still have a baby?

"How's the baby?" he asked.

She grinned and lifted her top. "Still there and growing. I had a mini-physical downstairs in the emergency room."

He pulled her hand and she bent down and kissed

him, again.

"The doctor said I can leave tomorrow," Steve said.

Daniella smiled. "I will pick you up and take you to my apartment. You are not leaving my sight again."

Steve grinned. "You'd better rephrase that. I have to leave in three days for the States. I was able to make a call to my contact and he is pretty sure I can get transferred over here soon. I have to close everything up in Texas."

"Do you know where?"

"Rome."

Steve stood up from his wheelchair and pulled Daniella close. He kissed her neck, then her lips. He knew he had to be the luckiest man alive.

TWENTY-FOUR

One Year Later

"What did the doctor say about your foot?"

Steve sipped his espresso, and then set his cup down on the colorful mosaic tiled table. He glanced around at Daniella's garden. It was a pleasant day to be spending with the woman he loved.

"Steve?"

Her tone was pressing. Steve made eye contact. "He said there wasn't anything else to be done right now. It's still healing."

"You must tough it out, as you American's say. You are just tired of not being on the job. Sitting behind a desk is not for you."

He nodded. "Tell me about it."

Much had changed for Steve since Cristo's escapade. He now spent every other weekend with Daniella and their daughter. Right now Rosie was at a friend's house for the morning leaving a special alone time with Daniella.

He didn't want to admit the foot scared him. He hated the damn limp. If he was in the field, he worried he wouldn't be able to chase someone down if he had to. He was limited. Something he had never had to deal with over the years. He always bounced back after his various wounds.

He glanced at her again. Her head was turned and she was staring in the direction of Rosie's bike parked across the courtyard. Something was bothering her. He wondered when she would tell him. Was her job getting to her?

"What's wrong Daniella?"

She turned. Her long brown hair moved with her. Her sensual eyes held his. But they weren't sensual right now, they were worried. Her cute mouth was not bowed, it turned down. "We have to find Ricco DiBiasi, now. The task force wants to close his file. How is Peter?"

"Peter is doing well. When we talked last week, he said he was almost back to before the kidnapping." He stared into her eyes. "You and I know he'll never be that good again. He still wants to leave the Agency."

"All the more reason to do this now. Ricco's body has not turned up anywhere. He has vanished. The trail has been dead for months."

He held her hand. "What do we do first?"

"Call Peter, tell him to come to Rome. We start there."

"Good morning, Daddy! It's time for breakfast."

Peter lifted his head off the pillow and stared at the doorway where his wife and child waved at him. Peter waved back. The baby laughed. Peter's heart melted.

They came into the room. Carrie handed him the baby. He sat him on his chest and grabbed his little hands. Carrie propped her pillows up and sat on the bed resting her back against the pillows, knees up.

He slipped his hands beneath the baby's torso and lifted him in the air. The baby laughed. Drool came out of his mouth and dripped onto Peter's chest. When he brought him down, he kissed the chubby cheeks and sat him on his stomach again.

The baby looked at Carrie and whimpered.

"Are you hungry, Brettie?" she asked. She held out her hands and Peter passed his big boy over to her. She set the baby on her abdomen. Brett straddled her body. She leaned forward and kissed his neck and wiped his moist mouth. She pulled a baby bottle from her robe pocket and offered it to the baby.

Peter scrunched his pillow in back of his head watching his wife and baby. "He seems to be hungrier this morning."

Carrie stared at him.

Peter thought she looked beautiful. She had taken on a softer, more mature look since the baby was born. Brett Steven O'Brien had brought them closer together than he could ever have imagined. Fatherhood was wonderful.

"He's always hungry, how can you tell he's hungrier?"

"His mouth is moving faster today. How much weight did the doctor say he gained?"

"You know how much he gained! He's going to be a very big boy." She smiled and stroked the blond hair on the top of Brett's head.

"I have the weekend off. What would you like to do? Drive out to the cabin at the lake?"

She opened her mouth to respond, but the phone rang.

"Hold that thought," Peter said. He hurried down the hall and into the study.

She could hear him talking. After he hung up, he didn't come back to the bedroom right away and she became suspicious. They had been so happy this last year since their return from Italy. Peter had healed from his leg wound and he did lesser jobs for the Agency. Carrie sold her business to her assistant. Now, she was a full time mother and wife.

The baby gurgled and Carrie lifted him to her shoulder and patted his back. They were so blessed to have him.

She looked up and saw her husband standing in the doorway watching her. Their eyes met and she knew he would be going back to Italy. Steve and the Italians hadn't found Ricco.

"When do you leave?"

"Tomorrow morning, very early."

He walked into the bathroom and turned the shower on.

Carrie rose from the bed and carried her sleeping son to his crib. She laid him down, covered him with a blanket, and sat in the rocking chair next to the crib. Her hands flew up to her cheeks. A strong urge to cry formed tears in her eyes. Even though she didn't want Peter to go, she knew he had to do it. He needed closure. They all needed closure.

She took a deep breath and left the room, shutting the door gently before hurrying down the hall. The walk back seemed to take forever.

Peter stood at the foot of the bed with a towel wrapped around his waist. His suitcase was open with several items already packed. She stopped next to him and he pulled her close. She laid her head on his chest. Immediately, she felt safe and secure. Comfortable in his arms. She wished they could be frozen in time.

"There are no clues since Alissa's disappearance months ago. Steve said he needs me. I have to go."

Carrie sighed and bent her head back to stare up into his face. His handsome face that looked at her with love. "I know. Be careful. We want you back in one piece." She smiled and touched his cheek. "And don't make me go to Italy and bring you back!"

Steve scanned the passengers walking through the terminal in Rome. When he saw Peter, he didn't make contact, but started walking. Peter followed him to the nearby train. They boarded and Steve sat a few seats down from Peter. After the train traveled for several minutes, he moved to the seat across from his old partner.

"You're looking well," Steve said.

"And you also. Why the drama? Couldn't you just pick me up in a car?"

"Sorry, I want everyone to see you. I want our friend and his cronies to know you're here."

Their eyes met.

"Thanks, Steve; I'm really feeling secure now."

Steve laughed. "It was Daniella's idea."

"You probably blame everything on her. How is she?"

"Doing well. In a few days we'll fly to Milan. I have a surprise for you there."

Peter raised his eyebrows. "I hope it's a nice surprise."

Steve shrugged. "You'll have to wait and see."

After a short ride on the train, Peter followed Steve onto a bus and rode to the Castel de Angelo located near the Vatican. He barely glanced at the former refuge for popes before Steve grabbed his arm and guided him to a waiting car. They sat in the back and the car sped off.

"I see you have assembled the best team," Peter said.

Juan turned around and grinned. "Great to see ya, Boss."

"Yeah," Walker said from the passenger seat. "How was the flight?

"Not as tiring as the last two hours." Peter glanced at Steve and everyone in the car laughed. "What's the plan now?"

"We have a safe house. We take you there and drop you off. I'll come in a couple of hours and we'll go to dinner. You know the night life gets started late here. People have a siesta, remember?"

"Yeah, I remember. A siesta sounds great."

Antonio Leonardo sat at his desk in his large opulent office. He picked up a note from his second cousin, Renaldo. A special meeting of the Council had determined that Ricco should be killed. The American agents were together again and it could only mean that they sought to find his nephew. The organization could not risk the investigation. There were too many projects out there. Too many sleeper cells that could be discovered and too much jewels and money floating around to finance the enterprise.

He stood and walked to his window over-looking one of the most popular streets in Naples. He did not want to kill his nephew. Yes, the man was insane, but he had helped to create the organization. He had made it grow into the power it was today. He deserved more than to be shot in the head and left in a ditch along one of the rural roads in Italy. Like a dog.

The phone rang. He picked it up and answered as he pushed the button to scramble their conversation. It was something he had always done since the new technology had become available. One never knew who was listening to your conversations.

"Pronto."

"Bueno."

He recognized Lorenzo's voice. "Where are you?"

"On the yacht in Portofino waiting for Alissa and Ricco. We are going to Elba. Peter O'Brien is in Rome."

Antonio knew Lorenzo was in Portofino. He always had a man on him. He frowned. Alissa has heard the news. They were already on the move.

"You are right. The Americans are in Rome, gathering a task force to find Ricco. Go to Elba. Do not allow Ricco off the yacht. He must never get off the yacht. Sail around the area for several days, and then go off to Greece. He will be safe there sailing around the islands. Call when possible with reports. At some point you may have to kill him. The Council is concerned."

He hung up and leaned back in his office chair. The stage was set.

The blonde woman's high heels clicked on the tile floor as she hurried down the hall of the sanitarium. She paused and looked into each room as she went. They had moved him again and now she had to find him quickly because there was little time to act. An hour ago she heard that Peter had arrived in Rome.

Halfway down the hall she found him. She stood in the doorway and watched him staring out the window at the bird feeder. A small bird was eating the seed and Ricco was enthralled.

"The bird is building its nest again, Alissa."

She was always amazed at how he knew she was there when he had not even turned around to look at her. "We have to pack your bags and move you. The agents have teamed up again. Peter arrived in Rome today."

"It will take them a while to find us here." He turned around to face her. "I am considering allowing them to know where I am this time. Do you think they would be surprised? Or disappointed?" He tilted his head back and laughed heartily.

Alissa cringed. The medicine could only do so much. "I'll be right back. We will need help to carry your things to the van."

She left the room and he could hear her high heels clicking again. He turned and stared at the bird feeder. He thought about the two agents and what had happened a year ago. He became furious when he thought about how they had escaped him. But he had outsmarted all of them, except Alissa and the Council.

After they took him from the yacht, he had been put on board another boat and taken to Antonio's house outside Positano. On the way they had passed the home he and Alissa had lived in when the yacht exploded. It was still beautiful, perched above the sea. His heart had fallen and by the time he'd reached Antonio's, his will to survive had diminished. He was willing to do anything they asked.

He thought about Carrie. It had been hard to let her go. He was not given a choice.

He could see Antonio's face now. It had been filled with rage. Two days later, Lorenzo and Alissa put him into a private sanitarium in the Alps. He left there only once, to come here.

He could hear Alissa returning and other voices moving with her. She was good at getting help. He smiled ruefully. When Alissa turned up in Positano, he had wanted to kill her for helping Steve escape. However, when Antonio told him that Alissa had been ordered by the Council to take care of him, he felt better. She had no choices either; she would have been killed if she had refused.

The footsteps and the voices were getting closer. The anticipation of getting out of this place filled him with excitement. He wondered where they would take him.

As soon as he knew where they would go, he would make a plan to escape. At that time, he would kill her for helping Steve. That would please him very much.

He chuckled again. Watch out, Alissa. Don't miss a step; it could be your last. He laughed and looked out the window again.

Alissa shut the van door and got behind the wheel. Driving vans had never been something she'd longed to do in the past. But since Ricco had to be moved and Lorenzo had to get the boat ready, it had been up to her to get her crazy husband out of the sanitarium. She drove off toward the road that would connect with the autostrada.

Ricco sat in the seat next to her. She could see him out of the corner of her eye. His body was stiff and he was staring straight ahead. Her heart raced. He knew. She fought a surge of panic. Surely he would be happy to go to the island again. She focused on the driving and felt better. A few miles down the road, she was startled when Ricco broke the silence.

"Where are you taking me, Alissa?" His voice was a cold monotone.

"It is a surprise."

"You know I do not like surprises."

"I am taking you to a special house in France."

Alissa hoped he accepted her lie.

"I do not believe you."

Alissa knew her husband had never forgiven her for fouling up his plans for Steve. But as it turned out, she had saved his life. He had threatened her then and she still believed he could do her harm.

"Would it please you to go somewhere more isolated?" They had several more hours of driving before they reached the yacht. All she had to do was keep him in a good mood until Lorenzo could help her.

He turned his head. "You know I do not like surprises. You also know I do not tolerate lying."

She stifled a shudder. The element of surprise was usually a good approach with her husband. He tended to make different plans of escape if given too much information. Should she try another lie? Why not?

"I do not know where we are going. Lorenzo has kept it a secret."

"I do not believe you." He took a deep breath as if to calm himself down.

Alissa started to feel uneasy.

"Tell me why you moved me from the other sanitarium in the Alps?"

Alissa forced herself to remain calm and concentrate on the road. The doctors had found a good treatment for him at this last sanitarium. Ricco could think better. She didn't know if this was a good thing or a bad thing. She thought it best to tell him the truth.

"The Council contacted me and told me to move you. They wanted you closer to Naples... someone told them that the Italians would start looking for you soon, and they were going to ask the Americans to help."

"You should have told me!" Ricco flung the words out. Spittle ran down his chin. He was furious. His eyes bulged and his face was a bright shade of red.

The veins in his forehead stood out and his hands turned to fists.

The urge to hit Alissa was great. In all of the years of their relationship, he had never struck her. And he never would. He was disgusted with himself. That damn sanitarium had made him soft. He took another deep breath. "When were you going to tell me? Right before the Council put the bullet in my head?"

Tears ran down her cheeks.

He looked out the window and thought about his situation. She had foiled the plans by reacting quickly to the news of the agents' reunion. His lips moved into a slight smile. He might not kill her after all.

Peter wrapped the towel around his waist and stepped out of the bathroom. Steve had arrived ten minutes ago and woke him up from his siesta. His partner waited downstairs in the large living room.

He walked to the Armoire and selected his clothes for the evening. The safe house, located near the Forum in Rome, was perfect. Roman hotels did not have the allure they once had.

He dressed and hurried downstairs. They had plans to meet Vittorio and Daniella at a restaurant. But first Steve was going to fill him in on why he brought him here in the first place.

Steve sat on a gold couch in a centuries old living room. Beautiful paintings hung on the walls including a tapestry. The furniture made the antiques in America look fake. The drapes on the large window were pulled for privacy.

"Good evening," Peter said.

"Back to you. Would you like a drink? The bar's over there." Steve pointed to an ornate baroque buffet sitting in the corner.

"Sounds good." Peter helped himself to a Bloody Mary and sat in a brocade chair across from his old partner. "Why am I here, Steve?"

"Daniella has passed on to her informants that you and I are looking for Cristo. She hopes to stir the pot and wait for something to pop up."

"Do they have any idea where he might be?"

"Not a one. Every lead has reached a dead end. This is our last chance to find him. Daniella wants to clear her files, and I just want to be able to relax."

"While we're waiting for the pot to spit something out, why don't we go over the files?" Peter asked. "We have one hour before we meet the Italians. Let's make the most of it."

"I thought you'd suggest that." Steve grinned. He got up and went over to the buffet and opened a cabinet door. He pulled out a large brief case and walked back and sat down in the same spot.

"Vittorio can't make dinner tonight. We'll go to Milan tomorrow and meet with the Italian's the next day."

"There's a strong feeling of urgency on their part," Peter said. "Isn't there?" He couldn't help the sarcasm. It was the very same attitude that had caused him to be kidnapped and Dimitri killed.

Steve laughed. "Such sarcasm! Do I detect some bitterness?"

"Not some. A lot. I don't trust them."

"You're right, things haven't changed much." Steve became serious. "Let's get something straight from the beginning, partner. We'll be on our own on this. Daniella will cooperate with her counterparts. We do not have to do that. We will call the shots."

Peter had his doubts. He sipped his Bloody Mary and thought about all that was at risk again. He was determined to be in control of his own life this time. He had to trust Steve.

"What's in the file?"

Steve took the contents out of the huge file and spread it across a glass table in front of him. Peter got up and sat next to him.

"Where do you want to begin? This is every piece of information I could gather from our files and Daniella gave us what she could find. They want him found. They were very helpful."

"Let's start at the beginning."

TWENTY-FIVE

Lorenzo waited in the small parking lot near the village of Portofino. Earlier he had been surprised to hear about the agent returning to Rome, he thought the business with Ricco was finished. After talking with Antonio, he made a quick call to Alissa. Ricco must stay aboard the yacht. She understood.

He omitted telling her that the Council wanted to kill the crazy one. He chuckled inside. It would be his privilege to do the job.

A van drove into the parking area. Lorenzo waited. A blonde woman stepped out and opened the back. She removed a wheelchair and pushed it to the passenger side of the van.

It was them. He waved when she looked his way and waited for her to bring Ricco closer. As she pushed the wheelchair toward the walkway, Lorenzo saw a man get into the van and drive off. He knew it was headed to its new owner somewhere in the Italian Alps.

Alissa did not make eye contact. She continued walking past shops and restaurants to the yacht parked on the other side of the harbor. Lorenzo followed her. When she stopped at the yacht, he quickly put Ricco on board and pushed him across the deck and into the salon.

His old counter-part in crime was inside his favorite yacht again.

Ricco looked up and smiled. "Lorenzo, it's been a while."

Lorenzo smirked. "Where do you wish to go?"

"Wheel him to his stateroom. It has been a long trip," Alissa said.

"We are not in the sanitarium any longer!" Ricco screamed. "I will do as I wish." He began a coughing fit that lasted a minute or two. He removed the handkerchief out of his pocket and wiped his mouth, then took a breath before speaking. "The stateroom is a good choice. I am tired... Later I want to have dinner on the deck...look around for our chess set."

Lorenzo made eye contact with Alissa. She nodded her head. He wheeled the crazy man to his stateroom. Alissa followed and went into her own quarters.

He pushed Ricco to the bathroom. The crippled man could still help himself with his bathroom duties. He shut the door and went to the window. The yacht began to move out of the harbor. There was no turning back now.

Ricco came out of the bathroom. "Tell me what you know."

"The American agents are gathering to find you. The Council wants you dead. Antonio has confined you to this boat for your safety."

"Where are we going?"

"Elba."

"For how long?"

He shrugged. "A day or two. Then on to the other islands."

"And then?"

"When the American's get close, we go to Greece and sail around those islands."

Ricco smiled. "I like the plan. It is a very big world. We can get lost as long as no one sees us."

Lorenzo nodded.

"Help me onto the bed. I must rest."

Steve filled two glasses with wine and handed one to Peter. They were sitting at a table in Raphael's Restorante, waiting for Daniella.

"Do you think she'll have any trouble finding this place?" Peter raised his glass to his lips.

Steve munched on olives and bruschetta. The men were hungry and had already ordered.

"She's taking a taxi. It was her idea to meet here. She likes this restaurant because of the good wine they serve."

"She's right." Peter set his glass down and helped himself to the salami and cheese. "One of the things I like best about Rome is the food and wine."

"Me too." Steve looked at his watch. "Daniella should be here any minute."

"What did she tell you when she called earlier?"

"Someone called in with an anonymous tip concerning a sanitarium near Florence. She sent a team there. Cristo had definitely been at this hospital for the last three months. A woman arrived this morning and checked him out. The staff identified his picture, but had trouble with Alissa's."

Peter raised an eyebrow.

Steve chuckled. "Who knows, maybe she did disappear. Maybe she had enough of him and wanted a better life."

"I'm surprised he's lived this long. His terrorist organization must think of him as a liability by now."

Steve thought for a minute. This idea had crossed his mind many times in the last year. Why would Cristo's cronies allow him to live? One thing was for sure, the man was definitely nuts. Alissa had put him in his proper place.

Daniella entered the restaurant. Steve drank in the sight of her as she smiled and walked to their table. The plum colored suit looked stunning on her as she extended her hand to Peter. Steve beamed and helped her into her chair next to him. He could still smell her scent when he sat back down. He knew he loved her very much, and lately he'd been thinking about marrying her when this mess with Cristo was finished.

"I see you two have ordered. Did you order for me also?" Her mouth tightened and formed an adorable pout.

Steve nodded his head as Peter poured wine into Daniella's glass. She filled her own plate with salami and brushetta. Both men watched as she lifted her glass to her lips and took a sip. "Ummmm. This wine is wonderful."

Steve glanced at Peter. His partner suppressed a smile.

"How was your flight from Milan?" Steve asked.

"Good."

"Tell us about the information from the sanitarium," Peter said.

"The people involved were low key. The woman came to visit every day. The man was treated for paranoia and schizophrenia. They were not able to make a total diagnosis of him. He was cold and refused to communicate. He perked up and became a different person when the woman came to visit."

"It must have been Alissa. I can't imagine anyone else affecting him that way," Peter said.

"I agree with you," Steve said. "She probably had plastic surgery and bleached her hair. Perhaps, she uses wigs."

"She would have plenty of money at her disposal," Daniella said. "We think Ricco had several accounts. The money we confiscated last year was substantial, but we always suspected he had other accounts scattered around the world. Maybe even other identities. He used an alias at the hospital." She sipped her wine again.

"Peter and I have been going over the old files and we've come across something that puzzles us." Steve reached into his pocket and removed a picture.

Daniella studied the photo for a few minutes. "Where did you get this and when was it taken? He and Alissa look young on here."

"We found it buried in Cristo's file. We think it was taken around the time he first came on the scene," Steve said.

"Who are the other two people?" Daniella asked.

"We think the man sitting next to Alissa is Antonio Leonardo, a crime boss residing in Positano. That's his wife sitting next to him," Peter said.

"The puzzling thing about the picture is the crest hanging above them," Steve said. "Could it be a family crest? The picture was taken at the DiBiasi's villa outside Rome. We recognize the view from the window."

"The crest doesn't look familiar to me. Can I keep the picture?" Daniella said. "How do you recognize the view?"

Steve smiled. "You can keep the picture. We made several copies. We recognize the view because we've both been there. Probably not long after the picture was taken."

"It was during my first assignment, when Steve and I became partners," Peter said. "Cristo was already a prominent figure in the growing organization."

"Peter spent a weekend at the estate. And was enamored by the vivacious Alissa." Steve grinned at his brother-in-law.

"You'd better not mention that to Carrie," Peter said.

"She wasn't impressed with Alissa when she was a prisoner last year."

"Don't worry pal. There's no way I want to ever remind Carrie about last year. I'm still having nightmares over the torture equipment." Steve glanced around for the waiter. He knew Peter had his own nightmares about his captivity. The best thing his ex- partner had ever done was to quit the Agency full time. The small job he had now was just to keep his foot in the door. Steve saw the waiter and motioned for him to bring the food.

After dinner, they dropped Peter off at the safe house. As Steve pulled away from the curb, he grabbed Daniella's hand and kissed it. "I missed you."

"I missed you also, my darling."

Steve headed for his house in the hills. "Will it be too late to call Rosie when we get to the house?"

Daniella looked at her watch and smiled. "I think we can call. She stays up later. She convinces the housekeeper to read one more book."

"That reminds me of someone else I know."

Their eyes met. Hers were filled with love.

Ricco sat on the deck eating breakfast. The sun was out and the warmth did wonderful things to him. The freedom he felt was like a magic elixir. His body was alive. His mind was sharp.

He took a bite of egg and raised his head to stare at the land mass in front of him. Elba. He longed to go up to his house on the other side of the island. The secret house. He and Lorenzo had spent many days there after the explosion. They always went when Alissa had her spa treatments and shopped in Paris with her friends. The house had belonged to his mother and step-father. Many memories were there.

He felt sad that the house would not become his home base after all. It sat above the Marin De Campo over-looking the beautiful harbor and sandy beaches.

This afternoon they would sail to the other side. He needed to get his fill of the house before they left.

Alissa walked out of the salon wearing a long sheer dress with many bright colors. He wanted to laugh. She is enjoying the yacht like in the years before the explosion. In fact, he thought he recognized the dress.

Her new face was even more beautiful than her real one. Of course, she could not do much about her mannerisms. Anyone that knew her well, might be able to recognize her.

She sat down across from him. "Are you going for a swim later, Ricco?" He handed her a plate of pastries. She took one and set the plate down. The cook served her espresso and fruit. Alissa always ate fruit in the morning.

"I am thinking about it. Maybe it would be good for my legs."

She shrugged. "It is worth a try."

"After being in that sanitarium for so long, I am ready to try many things." He stared at her and raised an eyebrow. He liked her new look, it reminded him of Carrie.

She smiled. "They did find a medicine that helped. You seem more calm and happy."

His eyes darkened. "I am happy because I am not confined to that hospital... You put me there!"

He saw her shrink back. He laughed inside. The old ability to scare her had returned. And she was right. The new medicine did work.

Peter followed Steve into the foyer of a large house located in the outskirts of Milan. The home had a cozy feeling and the aroma was wonderful. "Something smells good."

Steve pointed straight ahead to a room that looked like a kitchen. "She's cooking for us."

Daniella stepped into the foyer wearing an apron. She smiled at them. "Welcome to my home," she said. "Steve, please serve drinks while I set the table."

"Okay." Steve led Peter into a moderate-sized living room off the foyer.

"What will you have? I know there will be wine with dinner, so you may want something different now."

"Make anything." Peter's eyes scanned the room. "Daniella has a beautiful home. Has she lived here long?"

"The house has been in her family for generations. She moved here about six years ago."

Peter took his drink from Steve and they both sat down on the couch. A loud noise sounded from upstairs and both men raised their eyebrows. A child started crying and then stopped abruptly. A few minutes later, Daniella appeared in the doorway holding a pretty little girl by the hand. The child had brown hair with blonde highlights and was rubbing one of her eyes.

"Peter, we will have to give you your surprise now." She looked at Steve. "The housekeeper had to leave early. Can you keep her busy until the food is on the table?"

Steve smiled. "Sure can. Rosie, come her and sit on my lap." The little girl stared at Peter and hurried to Steve. She climbed on his lap and put her arms around his neck. Steve hugged her and kissed her cheek. "What happened upstairs?"

Rosie started to reply in Italian, but Steve stopped her. "Peter is American. We need to speak English."

He winked at Peter, knowing the man was fluent in

Italian.

"Daddy, is he the man that is married to Aunt Carrie?"

Peter dropped his drink on the floor.

"Uh-oh Daddy. I will get the mop!" She hopped off Steve's lap and ran toward the kitchen.

Peter stood up. He had spilled half of his drink on his pants. "You should have told me ahead of time! What a shock."

"Sorry, pal, we were going to tell you at dinner. The plans changed... Rosie is our child." He locked eyes with his brother-in- law. "It's a long story."

"Carrie will be so surprised," Peter said. "I think the whole world will be surprised."

Rosie ran into the room carrying a big towel. Daniella followed her with a dust pan and a mop. "Rosie said you had an accident. You were more than surprised?"

Peter laughed. "Yeah."

Daniella handed him the towel. "When you are finished cleaning up, dinner is served."

Peter unpacked his bag. His mind couldn't stop thinking about the adorable little girl down the hall. When Steve told him he had a surprise in Milan, he had not in his wildest dreams thought of a child.

He smiled. She had entertained everyone at the dinner table this evening and appeared to be intelligent and witty. Carrie will love her.

Steve and Daniella appeared to be in love. He should marry her and settle down. Peter knew this was not an easy task for his friend. Their line of work was very hard on relationships. Daniella had the same profession and understood the pitfalls, but that was not a guarantee for a successful marriage.

He carried his personal items into the bathroom and set them on the sink. Maybe after they caught Ricco things would calm down. He knew his old partner could not let go of his feelings for revenge.

He picked up his phone and dialed his home number. He had to tell Carrie the news.

The night was clear and the stars were so close you could almost touch them. Ricco sat on the deck and enjoyed the night air that circulated around the yacht.

The lights on Elba were also like the stars in the sky. His childhood home had grown in population since the last time he was here. And of course, he always stayed at the house, his mother's house.

Ricco had been born in Naples, the only son of a rich merchant and his wife. His mother was from Elba; his father belonged to a large family in Positano. When Ricco was seven, his father was gunned down on a street in Naples. They had been shopping and Ricco witnessed the shooting.

After his father's funeral, he and his mother moved to Elba. It was a time of great sadness; his father had been a dynamic personality. He himself remembered him vividly.

On Elba, his mother created a new identity. When he was ten, DiBiasi came into their lives. His mother fell in love with the large happy Italian. They married and Ricco came to love his step- father. He was everything his father had not been. The man taught him to sail and bought him his own sailboat when he was fifteen. That boat had opened up his life and boosted his self-confidence.

Two days after his sixteenth birthday, his mother and step-father died in an accident. His life sunk to a new low.

He turned his chair around and stared out across the sea. All day he had felt the pull of his favorite place in the world. All day he had lifted the binoculars to his eyes and glanced at its tall peaks. It was too dark now to get one more look. Tomorrow they would be there.

The two agents hurried inside the building that housed the headquarters for the Italian equivalent of the United States FBI. They rode the elevator to the third floor and met Daniella in a conference room. Vittorio sat at the end of a very long table and smiled when they walked into the room.

"Ciao, my friends," he said. "Welcome to our world!" He laughed heartily. The sound resonated in the large room.

"Thanks," Steve said dryly.

Peter shook Vittorio's hand. "Good to see you again, my friend. I hope you have new information for us."

Vittorio shrugged. "Maybe yes and maybe no."

They sat across from him as Daniella took her seat at the head of the table. "Would you like espresso?"

Both agents shook their heads. "We had a big meal at the Bona Vita restaurant," Steve said.

Daniella rolled her eyes and smiled. "We will get right to business. One of my assistants is working on the picture you gave to me last night. We are sending a team down to Naples tomorrow. Maybe Ricco has ties with the Leonardo family, or Leonardo is an old friend. We will see.

"Interpol has the description of the woman who took Ricco out of the hospital. They have not responded with any information. Our sketch artist is working on a likeness of her based on the description. While you two are in Milan, we would like both of you to work with this artist. We need fresh drawings of Ricco, Lorenzo, and the 'old' Alissa. You can provide more details."

She paused and glanced at Vittorio. "Vittorio will be joining his team on the west coast around Livorno. That is the last place Ricco was seen before he disappeared. Even though the area was searched extensively at the time, we will start over from that point." She grinned widely. "Something could turn up. Ricco could have another yacht!"

Everyone laughed.

Daniella looked at her watch. "That is what we have going on right now. The artist will be expecting you in twenty minutes...Any questions?"

Peter cleared his throat. "I have a thought. Ricco plans things well in advance. Look how he befriended the monk years ago, later to bring him into my kidnapping. My guess is that he is in a place where he thinks we would not look for him." He shrugged his shoulders. "That could involve another yacht. He would be mobile and could be anywhere."

"As I see it," Steve said. "We have two things working for us that he cannot control. He cannot hide his wheelchair or his right hand man, Lorenzo. Of course, we don't know for sure that Lorenzo is with him."

"The wheelchair is our biggest lead," Peter said. "Someone has seen him. And Ricco may not be in control."

There was a definite moment of silence as everyone thought about what was said.

"Maybe the sketches, if circulated enough, will give us a lead," Daniella said. She stood and grabbed her briefcase. I have another meeting in five minutes and it's down the street. Sorry to run."

Steve watched her leave the room. He looked at

Peter. "I suppose we'd better find the sketch artist."

Vittorio headed for door. "Follow me, please."

TWENTY-SIX

The yacht sat in a tiny cove surrounded by clear, greenish-blue water. Ricco adjusted his binoculars and focused on Montecristo. It was six square miles of solid granite. In 1989, the Italian government had declared this island a national park. They only allowed one thousand people a year to go ashore.

He studied the three gray peaks rising out of the morning mist and longed to relive the adventures of his youth. He remembered roaming the hillsides with the goats, climbing as high as he dared, and best of all, watching for the deadly vipers and peregrine falcons. For an adventurous boy, it was heaven.

The best part of the island was the caves. He spent many days exploring caves, seeking to find the treasure. Now, he knew there was no treasure, but at the time the legend became his mantra.

Before his step-father died, Ricco had taken his name. It was an important step; he wanted to separate himself from the Leonardo family. As it turned out, when DiBiasi and his mother died, his uncle became his guardian. Antonio had insisted he come to live with him. It was the beginning of the end of his carefree innocence.

Antonio started a new terrorist group. Ricco had no choice but to join the organization. One of the first things he did was to kill a rival crime boss, the one responsible for the deaths of his mother, father, and step-father.

Montecristo had remained his secret for many years. Right before he kidnapped the agents, he sent Lorenzo to set up a base in one of the caves. At the time it was a precaution in case they needed to escape from the world. He now saw the wisdom in that decision.

Alissa sat in a deck chair. The island appeared to be a place only Ricco could love. She shivered. What desolation, all rock and no trees. Who would ever think to look for him here?

"What do you think of Montecristo?"

She turned her head toward her husband. He had wheeled himself closer. "It has its own beauty. When did you first discover it?"

"In my youth. It belongs to a chain of islands called 'The Pearls of Venus.' It is said that a necklace slid from the neck of Venus and fell into the Tyrrenhian Sea. As a child I sailed all of the islands. My favorite has always been Montecristo."

Alissa knew better than to ask why he had kept this island a secret. She knew there were thousands of things she didn't know about this man. And she didn't care.

Ricco held out his binoculars. "Here, take a look. This cove we are sitting in is the only part of the island that is inhabitable. There is a ruin of a thirteenth-century monastery."

Alissa didn't want to look at the horrid place. She forced herself to take the binoculars and raise them to her eyes. She focused on the building with the arches.

"The monastery was used for target practice by the Germans during world war two," Ricco said.

"The valley inlet is nice," Alissa said. She moved the

binoculars to the left and up into the mountainous part. Something moved! She pulled the binoculars away from her eyes.

"Something moved up on the hillside!"

Ricco laughed. "It is probably one of the many goats that live there."

He took the binoculars and laid them in his lap.

The boat started to turn and Ricco wheeled his chair away from his wife and toward the end of the boat. The yacht was heading on to Giglio and Giannuti.

Ricco's behavior was starting to bother Alissa. Last night off the coast of Elba, he sat in the salon and stared out at the sea for hours. Now, she knew what he had been staring at. It made her uneasy because she knew his mind moved fast, and she could tell he was planning something. She hurried into the salon not stopping to sit down on the beautiful sofa overlooking the water. She was tired of the water.

Continuing on down the hallway leading to the bedrooms, she sighed. The yacht was very comfortable, but it was her jail. She and Ricco were imprisoned on this boat.

If not for the agents pursuing them, it wouldn't be bad to live on the yacht and sail around the world. She knew it was inevitable, the agents would find him or the Council would kill him. With all that pressing on him, Ricco acted like he did not have a care in the world. What infuriated her the most was that at times she thought he wanted to be caught. He loved the thrill of danger.

She entered her quarters and hurried to the bathroom, pulling off her bikini. As she slipped it into the clothes hamper, she paused. Her husband loved this island called Montecristo. Did Ricco know all along that his code name was Cristo? Had Ricco been instrumental in giving himself that code name?

A shiver went up her spine. She remembered the first time she'd met her husband. It was at a party at one of the chic restaurants in Rome. She had been a spy then, and Ricco was her number one priority. He had been very handsome and charming.

Steve was her contact and he warned her about getting too close to Ricco. She did not listen until it was too late to turn back. She had fallen in love with him.

She became a spy to avenge her fiancé's death. Charles had been a spy on assignment in Rome. He arrived in the morning and by dinner time, he was dead. It had devastated her. She had wanted revenge. So she signed up and talked them into sending her to Italy. In the first months, she had allowed herself to become close to Ricco because she didn't believe he killed Charles. Over the years, she watched and waited for someone to appear on the scene that she could connect to her dead fiancé. No one stood out.

Steve thought someone in Ricco's group or even Ricco himself had killed Charles. She did not believe it then and she did not believe it now.

A knock sounded at her door. She pulled her robe over her naked body and answered it. Ricco smiled up at her as if he knew what she had been thinking. That was impossible. Wasn't it?

"What do you want Ricco?"

He held a bottle of champagne in his hand. He leered at her. "I thought we could share a glass of Champagne, and get to know each other again."

She was shocked. Since the explosion their personal life had not existed. Now, he wanted to be friendly or...intimate? Whatever he wanted might prove to be interesting. She opened the door wide and allowed him inside.

"Juan, haven't heard from you for a day or two.

Where are you?"

"Hey, Boss, we're in Portofino. Yesterday we took the sketches that you sent and showed them around the shops and restaurants. No one recognized Alissa or Ricco. But they did recognize Lorenzo. And they remembered a beautiful blonde pushing a man in a wheelchair."

"When was that?" Steve asked.

"Three days ago. Lorenzo bought provisions and ate at an outside cafe."

"What did he buy the provisions for?"

"A yacht. People saw Lorenzo and the captain hanging out for a couple a days before they left."

"Any suggestions on where they might be headed?"

"Your guess is as good as mine. They could be going to the south of France... maybe down the coast."

"And, of course, they could be anywhere," Steve added. "Juan, you and Charlie come to Milan, now. We have an idea that Cristo might be somewhere around Naples. How soon can you leave?"

"We'll be on our way in one hour."

Steve hung up. Portofino. It was the perfect place to throw everything off. He headed downstairs to the living room of Daniella's house. Peter had gone off early to meet with a few of his old contacts. Rosie was due home from pre-school any time. Daniella was at her office downtown. He and Peter would work on the case while Rosie napped.

He thought about what Juan had said. The south of France was a definite possibility. It sounded good. So did Naples and Positano. Somehow, he didn't think Cristo would escape to such obvious places. Even though he might be tied to the Leonardo crime family, Ricco had always been his own man. If he went to France, Interpol might get involved. No. Cristo was still in Italy. And he would be in a new place, close to home.

He picked up the phone and called Walker.

Daniella studied Steve's photo one more time. This time she used the magnifying glass and tried to make out the words on the crest. She thought one of the words was "Monte" something. She set the photo down.

Over the last two days, she and her assistant had gathered information on Italian family crests and so far found none that could even be remotely like the one in Steve's picture.

She reached across her desk and picked up another folder full of information and photos. She thumbed through them and sighed. It was getting late and she wanted to leave. She was tired and her feet hurt. A hot soaking bath would be great.

She threw the folder on the desk. It landed with a thud. Guilt overwhelmed her. Steve was counting on her to come up with a clue. Or even a match to the crest.

Quickly picking up the file again, she decided to finish this group of photos and then leave. She studied each one carefully. Three photos later, she froze when she found the Leonardo family crest. Her pulse quickened. The crest was almost identical to Ricco's. She had found a big clue.

She stuck the photos into her brief case, grabbed her purse and headed for the door. At last, a very valuable piece to the puzzle. She could hardly wait to tell Steve.

Twenty minutes later, she stepped into her foyer. She sniffed. Smelled like someone started dinner.

"Hello!" No answer. She listened and heard voices coming from outside. She walked to the terrace window and looked out. Steve and Peter stood on the brick patio watching Rosie ride her tricycle. Her daughter was laughing and showing off. Her heart flipped a little. Rosie looked so happy.

This was a good time for a bath. She hurried up the stairs and set her briefcase on the desk in her study. Her bedroom with connecting bath was across the hall. A few minutes later she had thrown her clothes off and was soaking in the tub. She did not hear Steve come up the stairs.

She felt his presence and glanced at the doorway. Their eyes met across the bathroom. He held a glass of wine in his hands.

"I thought I'd find you up here," he said. He walked in and handed her the wine. "Bad day at the office, dear?"

"Where is our daughter?"

"Downstairs entertaining Uncle Peter. He's reading "Sleeping Beauty" for the fifth time." Steve laughed.

"It is good preparation for baby Brett." She put the glass to her lips and sipped the wine, then laid her head back on the edge of the tub.

"How long until you wish to dine?" Steve asked.

"Give me thirty minutes."

Steve raised his eyebrows. "Must have been a really bad day."

Daniella closed her eyes and made a humming noise that must have been a response to his remark. He tried not to laugh.

He turned and hurried down the stairs and into the small kitchen. He turned the heat down on the pots and pans, dinner wouldn't be too great if it was burned. He heard laughter in the living room and peeked around the corner. Rosie was still on Peter's lap holding her closed book. Her eyes were sparkling and her smile was teasing.

"That is not how the story ends, Uncle Peter." Her tone was scolding.

"That's how my mother used to tell it," Peter said. He picked up his niece and set her on the floor.

"Well," Rosie said with one hand clutching her book and the other resting on her tiny hip. "That's not the way Italian people tell the story."

Peter roared. Steve stifled a laugh. Rosie ran from the room and up the stairs yelling for her mother.

"What did you say to her?" Steve joined Peter in the living room.

"I said that Sleeping Beauty lived happily ever after with her Charge cards and Rolls Royce." The two men laughed.

Ricco wheeled himself into the salon. Alissa sat on the couch waiting for him. On the coffee table in front of her was a bottle of wine and two glasses. The cook had prepared wine and cheese and antipasto. Dinner would be much later.

He smiled at her. Their time in her bedroom this afternoon had been revealing. He enjoyed the old feelings. The medicine had indeed worked wonders.

She poured the wine and handed him a glass. He tasted it and smiled. "Lorenzo has not forgotten what I like," he said.

"No, he has not," Alissa said. She picked up a small plate and arranged a little of everything on it, then set it close to him.

He picked up a piece of cheese. "Would you like to play a game of chess before dinner?"

She nodded. "Since we are tied three games each, one of us will be a winner today."

Ricco smiled. Their tournaments only lasted seven games. It was all he could stand. He let her win the three games just to have someone to play with. Lorenzo had no mental ability for the game and the cook and captain were too afraid of him to play. Tonight he would win.

Lorenzo walked into the salon.

Ricco met his gaze. He could tell the tall man had news. "What is it?"

Lorenzo glanced at Alissa. "You may want to hear this in private."

Ricco felt so good, nothing could spoil his mood. "Alissa can stay. Do you have news?"

"I called my friend in Portofino. He said there were men showing my picture around the town. He thought they were Americans."

Ricco froze. "Did they have one of Alissa and me?"

"Yes."

"Her new face?"

"Yes."

Ricco couldn't move. He couldn't think straight. How had the agents known about the sanitarium? That was the only place, except Portofino that would connect him to Alissa's new look."

"Someone must have told the Americans about the sanitarium. They found out about it too soon." Could the Council have anonymously given a tip? Was this how they wanted him killed?

"What do you want to do?"

He had two choices. Plot a course for the Greek Islands or go back to Elba. They could not know about Elba. He did not want to be out around the other islands. They were sitting ducks for surveillance planes.

"Tell the Captain we want to go back to Elba as fast as he can manage it. We will decide what to do on the way."

He turned his chair around and headed for his bedroom. He needed to rest before dinner. Perhaps he would need a little help resting.

"Alissa, bring my wine."

After dinner Daniella raved and raved about the meal. "Not too bad for two old agents," she teased.

She helped clean up and Steve put Rosie to bed. When he joined Daniella and Peter in the living room, he could tell she was ready to talk shop. Her brief case sat beside her on the sofa.

"Looks like you have some information for us," he said.

Daniella nodded. "The research on the Leonardo family has turned up a few interesting points. One member was gunned down on the streets of Naples. His wife and young son were with him when it happened. The child's name was Ricco."

Steve and Peter exchanged glances. This could be the break they needed.

"How old would the child be today?" Steve asked.

"The son would be Ricco DiBiasi's age now."

"It must be him," Peter said. "The pieces all fit."

"I found the Leonardo crest today. The crest in your picture is similar. Yours has a few different words." She reached into her brief case and pulled out the pictures of the crests.

Steve grabbed them and held them out in front of him. Peter moved closer to take a look.

"We now know Ricco is tied to the Leonardo crime family." She handed Steve the magnifying glass. "I think the word 'Montecristo' is on Ricco's crest," Daniella continued. "We should intensify the search in the Tuscan Archipelago."

"Perhaps we should go out there ourselves. It would be great to get away from the office and out to sea," Steve said. "What do you think Peter?"

Peter nodded his head. He appeared to be deep in thought.

"Good," Daniella said. "We will start with Elba, it is the largest of the islands and we can take the ferry."

"Steve, Cristo had been instrumental in picking his code name," Peter said. "If he was able to infiltrate the Agency to that extent, he surely must know that Alissa was an agent. Why did he stay with her all these years? Did he really love her or did he use her to find out who his enemies were?"

"I always suspected that he killed Alissa's fiancé. And now it appears he could have known Alissa was connected to Charles...Cristo's tentacles have always reached pretty far."

"I will make arrangements for us to go to Elba," Daniella said.

Steve glanced at his partner. "That sounds good, but we'd better wait for our team to get here. They're on their way now." He cleared his throat. "Daniella, Juan called this afternoon. He and Charlie showed the sketches around Portofino today. Lorenzo, Ricco, and Alissa were there. They have a yacht."

Daniella picked up her coffee and sat back into the couch. She stared at the large family picture on the wall in front of her. Steve knew she was tossing everything over in her mind. She took a sip of her coffee and made eye contact. "He could be anywhere. He could be on the French Riviera. Or in order to throw us off, he could have gone down to Sicily."

"Peter and I have decided he wouldn't go that far. With your new info about the crest and the man being gunned down in Naples, I think you are on the right track. We should go to Elba and see if that leads somewhere."

"Good. We will do that. However, I will call Vittorio and get him moving. He will need to send people all the way up to the coast of France. We must follow through on all clues." Daniella yawned. "Oh, sorry. I am tired. I will make the call to Vittorio now, but we will not do anything else until your team is here."

Steve stood and helped her off the couch. "Going to bed is a good idea. We'll need good rest from here on out. We know he's got something planned."

"He always has something planned," Peter said. He was half way up the stairs. "See you in the morning."

TWENTY-SEVEN

Off the coast of Elba near Portoferriao, Alissa prepared to join Ricco on the deck for breakfast. She had not slept all night, worrying about the agents. Finally, she decided to tell Ricco she wanted to go back to France.

If not for the Council's demand that she stay with her husband and care for him, she would be in Paris now, lunching with her friends and enjoying the theater.

Did she dare defy the Council?

A sense of futility filled her. She had no choice. The agents were getting close and she did not want to die alongside Ricco.

She pulled a cotton dress over her head and walked to her dressing table. She grabbed her hairbrush and ran it through her long blonde hair. Thoughts of France filled her mind again and she laughed. Would her friends recognize her?

She set the brush down and stepped over to the big closet. Her new look would fool anyone, of this she was positive. She paused amidst her search for the right sandals; Steve would know. A chill passed over her at the thought of being caught again.

All the more reason to leave Ricco, now.

Steve had been the only positive thing in her life years ago after Charles. Helping him escape Ricco's wrath, paid back the many times he had helped her in the past. But, he had saved her again by letting her go. In her heart, she knew he would not be so generous again. On the other hand, the Council would not allow her to be caught. They would kill her first.

She shuddered. She would still take her chances with the Council. After all, she had always cooperated with them.

Thinking of Steve made her face something she had repressed for a while. She knew her husband loved Carrie. Ricco had a different look in his eyes when he gazed at Peter's wife. A look Alissa had never seen before. The look of utter adoration.

It was difficult for her to imagine that Ricco could adore anyone other than himself.

Her shawl lay on the dressing table, and she grabbed it as she headed for the door. Once in the hall, a fear started to rise within her. What would she do if he denied her?

The sun was shining and the air pleasant. Ricco sat at the table spread with his usual breakfast of eggs and pastries. She smiled at him as she took her seat opposite his.

"Good morning, Ricco."

He looked up at her and smiled. "Yes, it is a good morning. Did you sleep well?"

She shook her head. "No, I did not. The agents worry me."

The cook came out with her espresso and set it down in front of her.

Ricco picked up the plate of pastries. "The cook spared nothing this morning. How can you not eat a croissant?"

She shook her head. "No thank you."

He lifted an eyebrow. "What will you do today? Since the agents are so near, having your hairdresser and manicurist come on board is out of the question."

Her eyes met his. "I am thinking that I would like to go to France."

He laughed. "Surely, you are making a joke."

Emotions flooded through her. How could he laugh? She swallowed to gain control. "If the Americans capture you, they will take care of you. If the Council finds you...you die."

Tears ran down her cheeks. She grabbed her napkin and carefully wiped her eyes.

Ricco's face turned pink. His eyes bulged. She could tell he was raging inside.

"Give me some credit, Alissa! I do not plan to be captured by the Americans. And I do not fear the Council. Do not forget, half of them are my relatives. My close relatives."

She blew her nose and sniffed. "I know you are clever. I cannot watch all of this unfold. I need to get away."

He picked up the pastries again and offered them to her. He smiled, but it did not reach his eyes. "We will discuss this later. I have to think about it."

She took a croissant and set it on her plate, feeling lucky they had gotten this far without him killing her. She sipped the espresso and thought about what she would take with her.

Ricco sat in the salon by himself. Alissa had run off to her quarters presumably to get away from him. She wanted to leave. And he did not blame her. Did he need her to be with him to the bloody end?

They returned to Elba last night. Lorenzo had advised him not to be on the deck with people out there looking for him. He did not care.

His hatred for the Americans welled up inside of him again. The feeling was so fierce he thought he would explode. What had happened? How had they gotten so close, so fast? He knew someone had tipped them off about the sanitarium. And he knew who it was. His cousin Renaldo. The weasel had always wanted him out of the picture.

It had been only a matter of time.

He picked up a glass vase off the coffee table and threw it across the room. It shattered into tiny pieces.

How, he hated them all!

He wheeled himself to the large window and stared out at the busy port. Maybe he should let Alissa go. If the Americans catch her at the ferry landing, the yacht will be long gone. And of course, she will have no clue what his plans are. No one knew, not even Lorenzo.

He sighed. She would only slow him down.

Ricco wheeled down the hall and found her in her bedroom. She sat on the bed, crying, like a child. The memories came swirling back and they were strong. The memory of their son, the day he was born, and the day he died. The happy times before the yacht exploded. He and this woman had shared a thrilling and sometimes, tragic, life. It would be hard to let her go. He forced himself to not be sentimental.

She grabbed a tissue and blew her nose. He folded his hands in his lap and stared at her. "Lorenzo will take you to the ferry. If you hurry, you can be packed and gone quickly. Do not try to contact me after you leave. It will be the best for both of us. Your personal accounts have enough funds to last you the rest of your life. And if they kill me, you will get it all."

She stared at him with swollen teary eyes. He almost felt sorry for her. He wheeled over and took both of her hands in his. "I have loved you all of these years, Alissa. It is hard to say goodbye. We will meet again if things work out right."

Alissa began to cry again. He wheeled out of the room and down the hall to his own quarters and shut the door. He knew his end was near. It would be hard to get away from the agents this time. His wheelchair was a hindrance.

His hands gripped the sides of the chair. He would give it all he had. They were not invincible. He knew he could outsmart them. Kill them all. His hatred came to the surface again.

He wheeled over to the bell to summon Lorenzo. They had a lot of work to do.

Steve answered the door at Daniella's house and let Juan and Charlie inside. It was early afternoon and the two men had slept in this morning having arrived very late last night.

"Hey, Boss!" Juan said.

Steve almost expected a high five. Juan was always upbeat.

Somebody had to be.

Charlie nodded as he came through the door.

They followed him into the living room.

"Hope you two are rested. We have a lot of ground to cover in very little time," Steve said. "By now, Cristo has heard that we know about the yacht and Portofino. Best of all, he realizes there is a description of his wife's new appearance. He's probably connected the dots, meaning someone gave him away."

Peter came into the room from the kitchen. He shook Juan and Charlie's hands. "Good to have you guys along. Do you want something to eat or drink?"

Juan looked at Charlie. His partner shrugged.

"No thanks, we're good," Juan said. He made eye contact with Steve. "Who do you think ratted on Cristo?"

Steve shrugged and gestured for them to sit down. They all sat down.

"No one seems to know who could be behind it...If I had to guess, it would be one of Cristo's own people in his old terrorist organization." He glanced at his watch. "Daniella had to go to her office. She should be back soon. We'll all be flying to Marina di Campo airport on Elba. Walker has a car and will pick us up. So far, he's shown the sketches around one side of Elba with no results."

"What are the accommodations like?" Juan asked.

"We decided to stay in the town of Marina di Campo. You guys will stay with Walker on the boat we've rented in the small harbor. Peter, Daniella and I will be at a hotel nearby, where we'll set up a home base," Steve said. "Here's the name of the hotel. Our rooms are close to one another."

Juan took the paper and studied it. "What have the Italian's done so far? Did they search the islands for Cristo?"

Steve shook his head. "They only sent one guy out to Elba. He never made it to the other islands...Remember; we only just found the connection to this part of Italy." He shrugged. "We could be wasting our time."

Antonio Leonardo sat at his desk in his office in Naples. He tried hard to concentrate on business, but could not stop thinking about his problem. Last night, Renaldo called and asked to come by in the late evening. At the agreed time, the two of them retired to his library for privacy. The information was dour. The Council knew Ricco was not dead. They made threats to Renaldo. If his nephew made headlines or harmed any of the agents, he Antonio, would pay the dear price.

He took a deep breath wishing this problem would go away. He glanced at the clock. Lorenzo would be calling in today.

He got up and walked to the bar on the other side of the room. His hands worked fast grabbing a glass and pouring himself a generous drink.

Instead of returning to his desk, he chose to sit on the couch. His shoulders relaxed and he leaned back into the cushions and took a sip. Everything was in the hands of Lorenzo. He knew this man could be trusted to follow his orders. Still, even though his nephew was a lunatic, Ricco was very cunning. He could cause untold and unwanted problems. It could tear the organization apart. He took another sip and contemplated his next move.

The phone on the desk rang. His body responded quickly. It was Lorenzo. He pushed the scrambling button before answering.

"I hope you have good news for me, Lorenzo," he said.

Lorenzo laughed. "Your hell is not over yet, Antonio. I am at the ferry on Elba. Alissa is on her way to France. The agents are too close for her comfort. She does not want to die with her husband."

Sweat broke out on Antonio's forehead. The Council must not hear of this. "What does my nephew have planned?"

"We have a small boat in the harbor. No one knows about this boat. It has been here for many years. I have loaded supplies and will take Ricco off the yacht. We will go to Capraia. The yacht will continue on to the Greek Islands. If all goes well, we will meet the yacht in Greece."

Antonio took a sip of his drink. The plan sounded good. "Be sure to call me again tomorrow and let me know where you are... and Lorenzo, he is not to be taken alive. You are not to die for him. You will take care of him and get yourself out of there... I need you for something we are preparing to do in the Middle East. I leave you to the details. Do you understand?"

"Yes, Antonio, I understand."

Lorenzo hung up and Antonio stared across the room. He raised his glass and finished off the drink. There was nothing to do, but play this out. In any case, he would have to address the Council, soon.

Lorenzo walked down the boardwalk at a small marina in Portoferriao. He had used valuable time to get rid of the yacht's dingy. It was on its way off the island. Ricco's small boat was at the end of this boardwalk. His eyes darted around looking for anything out of the ordinary.

He slowed his pace a little as he approached the boat. It had been several months since he had been here. Everything appeared to be in order. He went on board and started the motor. As he eased out of the slip and toward the sea, his thoughts returned to Antonio. He did not tell him about Montecristo. The crazy one did not trust his uncle. If pressed too hard, Antonio might give him up. Lorenzo chuckled. Ricco was always prepared for the unexpected.

Yesterday, while Alissa and Ricco were enjoying the Montecristo cove, he had used the dingy to take supplies and furniture to the cave. The Park patrolled the island, but no one had passed through the hidden opening. He knew where the many traps were set waiting for anyone that discovered it.

He steered the boat toward the yacht.

Ten minutes later he tied the rope and stepped onto the deck. Ricco wheeled himself out of the salon. He had a duffle bag on his lap.

"Are you ready?" Lorenzo asked.

Ricco nodded. "Was my uncle surprised? Did he like the plan?"

Lorenzo grunted. "Surprised? He was scared. I have never sensed his fear in all these years. The Council is breathing down his neck. He liked the plan."

Ricco smiled. "Get me on board. Let's be off before the Americans come ashore."

He helped Ricco onto the boat and got him situated down below, then headed toward Capraia.

Alissa, wanting to blend in with the crowd, followed a family off the ferry in Piombino. As she neared the main street, her eyes searched the area for a taxi.

She knew she had to be careful. Even though no one would recognize her as Alissa DiBiasi and she had her French papers with her, the agents were smart. Inside, she smirked. Her new look was very French and today she wore a red wig along with her green contact lenses. When she landed in Paris later, she would hurry to her apartment and assume her other identity, again. Her own world. A world Ricco knew nothing about.

Her mind flashed back to her last moments with her husband on the yacht. When he had hugged her goodbye, he had whispered something in her ear. Something that had frightened her. "I know you were a U.S. agent. I killed Charles."

She had stood gaping at him as he wheeled himself away. Lorenzo had grabbed her and forced her into the dingy for the ride to the ferry. Her urge to run after Ricco and demand an explanation had to be stifled. Once on the ferry, she allowed herself to think about what he had said.

How could Ricco have known about her job as an agent? How could he have killed Charles? This revelation made her look at her life with him in a different way. Why was she still alive? Her best answer was a startling one. Maybe he did love her.

The ferry whistle sounded and brought her out of her thoughts. A cab pulled up and she settled in the back seat. The driver loaded her suitcase, and then pulled away from the curb. She made herself relax. She was safe. Wasn't she?

Daniella stopped at the door and slipped the key into the lock. It opened right away and Steve followed her into her room. She went over to the connecting door and opened it wide. Walker had dropped them off out front. He and Juan and Charlie continued on to the boat in the harbor.

She opened the draperies and gazed out at the harbor below. "This is a lovely hotel, Steve. I like its Mediterranean style...And I like the view from this window!"

Steve shut her door and walked into his room with his own bag. He came out and stood behind her, placing his hands on her shoulders. "You really need to get out more."

She turned and slipped her arms around his waist. "I am too busy."

"Too busy to take a vacation?" He pulled her in close. "Or too busy with the people in your life, like me?"

Daniella chuckled. "Well, I am not one to take a vacation. My job is demanding, especially when I have to help Americans find terrorists."

He bent his head and kissed her lips lightly. "I'd go on a vacation with you anytime. And wouldn't care about the destination."

She moved her arms around his neck and his mouth covered hers. He wanted to show her how much he loved her. It was hard to tell her, there never seemed to be the right moment. And working on a case was not the right time.

A knock at the door made them pull apart. Steve felt his frustration level rising. They weren't supposed to meet anyone for two hours. Who was it? He moved away and heard the knock again. It came from the other room.

He hurried to his own door. Peter stood in the hall clutching a suitcase. "My room won't be ready for an hour. Can I leave my bag with you?"

"Yeah, come on in."

"Do you want to go down to the bar for a drink?"

Steve figured the private moment with Daniella had passed. He might as well give her some time to herself. "That sounds good."

Peter came in and set his bag down.

"I'll be right back," Steve said. He went into Daniella's room and closed the door.

She sat on the bed with her shoes off.

"It's Peter, his room's not ready. I'm going to the bar and have a few drinks with him. Where do you want to eat?" He glanced at his watch. "We have one hour and forty-five minutes until we meet."

"Let's eat here in the hotel. I will join you at the bar in thirty minutes. I have a few people to call."

He kissed her on the cheek. His body told him he wanted to stay and do more than kiss her. It would have to wait until later.

"See you then," he said.

He and Peter walked into the bar downstairs and saw Juan and Charlie occupying two seats.

"Everything okay with the boat?" Steve asked. He

stopped next to Juan.

"Yeah, it'll do. Beats some of the places we've had to stay in," Juan said.

"Let's get a table," Peter said.

They found a table and Peter and Steve ordered drinks. "Daniella will join us in half an hour or so. It depends on how many phone calls she has to make," Steve said.

"We're meeting Walker at a restaurant on the promenade in a few minutes," Charlie said.

"Good, we can have our own little meeting. Headquarters has notified me that we need to close this up fast. There's a problem in France," Steve said.

"Have they been creative with your job description, again?" Peter asked.

Steve frowned. "I have a new job description. They've given me a promotion of sorts. I'll still be based in Rome, but not confined to Italy. They don't like me in one place."

Juan laughed. "What's new?"

"Laugh all you want, buddy," Steve said. "You and Charlie are permanently on my team, again."

Charlie and Juan looked at each other. "What about Walker?"

"He's been reassigned."

The table became silent. Steve knew this wasn't great news for Juan. He had recently married and lived in the States. Steve hoped he would be able to work things out with his new wife. Charlie on the other hand was still a bachelor, but this was his first experience in Europe. There could be reluctance on his part. He shrugged these minor details off. There was bigger news to tell them.

"I've got something else to report." Steve didn't want to tell them this, but he had no choice. "David Westgate is our new boss."

Juan drummed his fingers on the counter. "You have to be kidding!"

Steve shook his head.

"I'll have to request a transfer. You can start that proceeding right now," Juan said.

Charlie looked from Steve to Juan and back again. "Who's David Westgate?"

Steve knew this wasn't going to be easy. He knew Juan would have the reaction he did. Hell, his own reaction was worse. He'd cursed headquarters over and over for hours after hearing about it.

"He used to be on our team," Peter said. "He almost got us killed, but was deemed a hero by the higher -ups. It's not good news for you all."

Out of the corner of his eye, Steve saw Daniella move across the bar. He cursed under his breath. They all needed to talk about this a little more. "Daniella's here. Let's not mention this to anyone, including her."

Steve got up and found another chair. He placed it next to his. He glued a smile onto his face as the love of his life reached the table.

Daniella stopped and placed her hands on her hips. "Okay, what is the matter? You all look as if your drinks were poisoned."

Juan and Charlie stood up. "We have to meet Walker. See you at the meeting."

They turned and headed for the exit. Peter also stood.

"I'll go along with them. Give you two some privacy." He winked as he left.

Daniella sat down. "What is going on? They are upset."

Steve motioned for the waitress to come over. "Don't worry about it. It's nothing."

TWENTY-EIGHT

The small boat slipped through the opening of the cave. Lorenzo shut off the motor. It was dark and eerily quiet. The only light was the large lantern hanging from the helm. Ricco sat on deck and watched Lorenzo steer the boat to the stone platform. He was amazed at how the cave wound deep into the rock.

Memories of his teen years assaulted him. His boat had been smaller than this one, large enough for only himself. He had found this cave the first time he sailed to Montecristo and to his knowledge no one had ever found it after him.

Lorenzo jumped off the boat and tied the rope to a mooring Ricco had used on his own trips. The tall man returned and hurried down below. A few seconds later, he came up with another lantern. He lit it and left the boat, again, walking several feet across the stone platform. He placed the lantern on a table. The light did wonders for the cave. The whole platform came to life. His assistant had done well, there was a bed for his naps and the table had chairs. Ricco was pleased. Everything looked perfect.

Lorenzo set up the wheelchair on the platform. He came back on board and picked up Ricco, carrying him off the boat.

"Do you want the chair or the bed?" Lorenzo asked.

"The bed will do for now."

His assistant placed him on the cot and went back to the boat.

Ricco felt the chill of the cavern creep through his body. He felt relieved when he saw Lorenzo coming toward him with two blankets. They would live on the boat, but Ricco wanted the option of being outside too. He would not be able to stand the chill for very long. He realized they would have to leave this haven periodically; the oppression of his surroundings would close in on him.

"How long do you think it will take for the agents to find us?" Lorenzo asked.

Ricco frowned. "By not going to Capraia, we have thrown Antonio off. I do not trust him. He might figure out we came here, but it will take him awhile. The agents are less predictable. They could be here now."

"Will they be thrown off by the clues we left for them?"

"Not for long...we will stay here in the cave for three days. If no one has come to the island by then, we will sail to Corsica."

"The agents are smart. But they do like for you to lead them by the nose."

Ricco laughed and it echoed in the stillness of the cave. "We will hope they have enough clues to follow to keep them off our trail."

"Who wants a drink?" Steve asked. He looked around the room and no one acted like they wanted one. "Too much pasta?"

No one laughed at his feeble joke.

Daniella picked up her briefcase and took out a folder. "It has been a long day and we are all tired, no? Let us get started. Vittorio reports, there are no clues in France. He believes Ricco is in Italy. It is

possible they left the yacht and traveled by train.
Croatia would be a good destination for him.
Tomorrow a team leaves for Venice.

"Antonio Leonardo received a call today from Elba. We do not know what was said, he scrambles his conversations. We know his cousin Renaldo visited him at his home in Positano last night. Vittorio thinks the organization is putting pressure on Leonardo concerning his nephew. There is a rumor they want to kill him." She stopped and looked around the group. "Any questions or comments?"

"I agree with Vittorio," Steve said. "Ricco has to be in Italy. It fits his pattern."

"If Renaldo paid a visit to Leonardo, Vittorio is right, the organization must be putting pressure on Ricco's uncle," Peter said. "The call from here, in Elba, makes me think we're onto something."

"What is your plan for tomorrow, Daniella?" Steve asked.

"I think we should concentrate on our immediate surroundings. I will fly over Pianosa, Capraia, and Elba. My photographer is busy in other parts of Italy, so I will take the pictures myself. What is your plan?"

"Walker will finish Elba. Juan and Charlie will take the ferry to Pianosa. And Peter and I will go to Capraia. We'll meet tomorrow night, same time, and same place."

Some minutes later, Steve closed the door on the last of the team to leave. Daniella had retired to her room. He walked over and stood in the doorway. She came out of the bathroom in her nightgown. She looked at him as she sat on the bed and took off her jewelry.

"Did you call Rosie, earlier?" Steve said.

Their eyes met. "Yes, she is fine. She was very excited about a party tomorrow. The housekeeper says she wants to wear her new dress."

"The one I brought to her from Rome?"

Daniella stood and pulled the covers back. "Yes. It is two sizes too big for her." She slipped under the covers. "I told Rosie she had to save the dress for when we return."

Steve sat on the bed and took his shoes off. He didn't need an invitation to sleep with her. It was already part of their routine. Just like a married couple. There was no place he would rather be at this moment in time.

"Maybe we can buy her a dress here, before we leave for home," he said.

"That is a good idea."

Steve got into bed and pulled her over to him. He kissed her lips and then her neck. "I think I like us working together."

She snuggled closer to him. "This is a nice arrangement. It reminds me of our little trip before we were to be married."

He raised his head and looked down at her. "The ending will be so much better. I have no intentions of leaving you again."

Lorenzo grabbed the oars and turned the dingy around. He paddled toward the opening of the cave. When Ricco woke up this morning, the first thing he wanted him to do was to go up to the fortress and scan the island. Lorenzo was hesitant about leaving the cave in daylight. Ricco assured him it had to be done.

It took a few minutes to reach the mouth of the cave. He sat in the dingy and listened. Not hearing any noises, he tied the dingy to a rock and jumped out.

One of the reasons the cave was hidden so well, was the way the rock opened to the side and not straight out into the sea. To someone in a boat, the rock would appear to continue on, they would not have a clue there was a cave there. And the wonder of it was how large the opening was. Their small boat had fit through fine. The opening was concealed by the grass and bushes hanging down from the rock above and a growth formed at the base of the rock. Lorenzo wondered how Ricco had managed to find this perfect place so many years ago.

He pulled a bush aside and looked out. He saw nothing. He eased out a little, scanning the area for anything, anyone. Nothing. He hurried from his hiding place and hid between two large rocks. When he thought the time was right, he ran to the next rock or bush and so on until he had climbed to the highest peak on the island. He hid in the ruins of an old fortress and took out his binoculars. He scanned the water surrounding the island and focused on the little cove. Nothing. There was no sign of the park rangers moving around yet. All appeared to be still.

He studied the land as he made his descent to the cave. The conditions on the island were so remote and rugged, if the agents found them here, it could be the end. He remembered Antonio's words and fought an urge to leave the crazy one in his cave, alone.

By the time he reached the dingy and turned it around, he knew he would not leave Ricco. The man had saved his life many years ago.

In the evening, Steve opened the suite door and allowed a waiter to wheel in a cart filled with food. He knew everyone would be hungry. He also knew the team depended on him to feed them most of the time.

Oh well, he was their boss.

The waiter stopped at the buffet and started unloading the cart.

Steve went into his own room and brought out his briefcase. Peter would be here any minute and he wanted to go over a few things with him before the others came.

He sat on the couch and opened his file. Today, after they returned from Capraia, he had called his office in Rome. Westgate would be coming in three days. Steve wanted to be prepared for whatever this guy had to throw at him. Peter knew David Westgate better than anyone Steve knew of. And they weren't friends.

The waiter finished his job at the buffet and wheeled the cart away from the table and settled it in the corner of the dining area. Steve got up and signed the ticket, then watched him walk out the door.

The suite had been a great find. It was meeting their needs. The large dining table accommodated the whole team at once, and he liked that. Daniella's bedroom and bathroom were separate from this living room area. All in all he thought that Marina di Campo had been a great choice to set up their base.

Daniella came in carrying her large bag and purse. He could tell it had been a long day.

He got up and hugged her after she set her bag and purse on the desk.

"Would you like a glass of wine?"

"Yes."

"Long day?"

"Yes, again. The plane ride took up the whole morning and then I had to drive to the ferry and meet with several of my agents."

Steve stepped over to the little bar area and poured her a glass of pinot.

"I have a few calls to make before the meeting." She took the glass. "Something smells wonderful in here." She glanced toward the buffet. "I see you have ordered for us. Good. I am starved."

"At first I thought you were referring to me smelling so good. It's sad when pasta and sauce smells better than you."

She snorted. "You can be very silly."

"I like to keep the moments as light as possible. Peter will be here in a few minutes. Should he and I go into my room and talk?"

She looked at him and laughed. "You were with him all day. Are you not tired of his company?"

Steve became serious. "If he was a woman, I would expect you to be jealous. But he's a guy and something new has come up since we came back from Capraia."

He pulled her into his arms and kissed her hair. He loved her scent. It sure beat pasta and sauce by a mile. How did she work all day and still smell so good when she came home?

She stepped out of his embrace. "Do not start with me. Everyone will be here soon."

Steve watched her take her wine and briefcase into the bedroom and shut the door.

A few minutes later, Peter arrived. He let his ex-partner inside and motioned toward the couch. "We need to talk."

Peter sat in one of the chairs. "What's up? Didn't you have enough talking time today?"

Steve handed him a drink and sat on the couch. He shook his head.

"Daniella had basically the same comment." He took a stiff drink, trying to fortify himself for the discussion ahead. He cleared his throat, and then proceeded. "I called my office in Rome and Westgate will be here in three days."

Peter raised his dark eyebrows. "Not good news. I had hoped to be gone before he ventured over here."

Steve shrugged. "Maybe you will be. Cristo might turn up tomorrow."

"Wishful thinking on your part."

"What can you tell me about Westgate?"

"Aside from what I told you today?" Peter said. "That he is narcissistic, demanding, and untrustworthy?"

"Yeah, what was it like to work with him?"

"Well, for one thing, he wasn't my boss. For another I was the agent in charge when we worked together. He tried everything he could to undermine my authority. So watch your back. You won't have trouble with your team, but he could throw a wrench into any case you might be working on...and where you're concerned, it didn't help that you stole his girl away from him."

Steve set his drink down on the small table in front of him. "It's possible he holds a grudge. But he did get her back and they're married. Hopefully, she won't be with him."

"Yeah, Daniella's pretty sharp. She'll know you had something going on with her."

"I'll have to deal with it when they get here. We have three days to find Cristo. If we don't, Westgate will try to run everything and Cristo will get away. And when he does, Westgate will close the book and be on to something else. We have to find our nemesis now!"

"I agree."

A knock sounded and Steve went to answer. He let the rest of the team inside.

"Don't sit down. Pick a chair at the table. If you already ate, eat some more." He went to Daniella's door and rapped on it, then opened it slightly.

"Everyone is here, Daniella." He saw her reclining on the bed in her robe.

She waved at him. "Start without me, I am on the phone with Vittorio."

Steve closed the door and joined the others at the table. "Daniella's on the phone. Let's start."

She joined them a few minutes later, and Steve made a rule that no one could talk about the present case while eating. Between Juan and Peter, the amusing escapades from past cases filled the time.

After dinner they retired to the sofa and chairs.

"These are the photos I took today." Daniella handed Steve a handful of pictures. "As you can see there is not anything that looks like the description of Ricco's yacht. Vittorio is convinced that Ricco is in Italy or Turkey. He thinks the yacht is gone."

"What do you think Daniella?" Peter asked.

"I do not have an opinion."

"Ricco could be anywhere in the world," Steve said. "But all of our clues point to right where we're at. I want to close this area up before going on to something else."

"I agree," Peter said. "And I want to rule out Corsica, Sardinia and Sicily."

"We cannot help you do this," Daniella said. "Vittorio is tiring of the hunt. He has other pressing problems."

"We will proceed on our end," Steve said.

"If he is not here, where would he be?" Juan said.

"Greece," Peter said. "He could get lost to the world sailing around those islands."

"Knowing Ricco, it wouldn't surprise me if he ditched the yacht," Steve said. "I want to finish what we've started here. We haven't explored Montecristo yet."

"What did you find on Pianosa, Juan?" Daniella asked.

Juan shrugged. "No clues. You have to get special

permission to go on shore. We talked to the security people on the island. No one had anything to contribute."

"Peter and I found a clue on Capraia," Steve said. "We found a few people who recognized Lorenzo. He had been on the island on the same day he picked up Ricco at Portofino."

"The problem is, was that before or after?" Peter said. "I think it was after."

"After would fit more into our theory about the Archipelago," Steve said.

Juan grinned. "Clues from Cristo?"

Steve nodded. "Yes, planted clues. He's known for that."

"And of course, we have to follow them," Peter said. "It's part of his game."

"Anyone have anything else to add?" Steve glanced at all of them and decided they didn't. "Good, what do you have planned for tomorrow, Daniella?"

"I will fly over Montecristo, Giglio, and Giannutri."

"Great," Steve said. "Juan, you and Charlie go to Giglio and Giannutri. See what you can find there. Peter will go to Gargona. Walker and I will stay on Elba and interview a few people of interest."

Peter stood up and put his hands in his pockets. "I'm gone. Have to call Carrie. Brett had a playdate today."

Charlie snickered. "A playdate? Isn't he a little young?"

"Things have changed since you were a kid, Charlie," Juan said. "They start socializing at a younger age, now." He stood and stared at Steve. "We gotta go too. The trip to Giglio and Giannutri starts very early." He headed for the door.

Charlie followed Juan. "But, Juan, the kid is only a year old!"

Juan opened the door and Charlie turned and waved at everyone as he stepped out the door.

"Thanks for the meal," Peter said. He too headed for the door. "I hope I find something on Gargona."

"Me too, "Steve said. "Cristo would be great." He watched his ex- partner close the door, and then turned to Daniella. She was still on the couch studying her pictures.

She looked up and smiled. "I think Ricco is not on the yacht and the yacht is not in the Archipelago."

"I think you're right." He stepped over to the phone and called the desk. When he hung up, he stared at her. "I have to wait for someone to come up and take the cart."

"I will help you clear the table."

He extended his hand to her. "That's a great idea."

Ricco was stretched out on a bunk in the back corner of the small galley. He could not fall asleep. Lorenzo's snoring echoed in the small boat, and no matter how many blankets they put on the bed, he could not get warm.

He sighed. It was not the blankets or the snoring that was keeping him awake. He was afraid to go to sleep. Last night he had a bad dream about his father's death. One minute he was looking at the colorful toys in a store window, the next the sound of gunshots, then his father lying on the street, blood flowing from his body. It had been years since he'd had this dream. When he woke from it, Lorenzo stood over him. He had cried out. Afterward, it had been difficult to fall asleep, again.

Tonight, he had another problem to add to the list. When he closed his eyes, all he could see was the explosion on the yacht.

Fear gripped him like the mouth of a wolf on the throat of a lamb. What if the agents are successful in catching him? Would they kill him? Something inside him wished they would. It was hell to feel such a lack of control.

Anger roiled inside him. He would not let them take him alive.

TWENTY-NINE

Last night, he had to take a sleeping pill. Now, his mind was groggy. He did not like his mind to be groggy. Ricco grabbed his hands and held them still. The shaking had begun earlier and he knew he needed to leave the cave before he lost his self-control.

Lorenzo walked across the platform from the boat. He sat down in a chair across from Ricco. "Do you want me to go out and check for boats?"

Ricco shook his head. "Not necessary."

Lorenzo stared at him.

"This will be our last night in the cave," Ricco said. "I cannot take it anymore. It is worse than the cells in my former basement."

"What do you think to do?" Lorenzo asked.

"We will go to Corsica and Sardinia. Do you still have an uncle on Corsica?"

"Yes."

"We will talk him into giving us a place to stay. That way we can get off this boat for a while. I need to find out what is going on with the agents."

"What about your uncle and the Council? They want you to stay on the boat."

Ricco slammed his fist down on the table. "I do not care about the Council! They do not know where we are."

Lorenzo shrugged. "It will not hurt to go to Corsica. We can come back here if we need to." He got up from the table. "I will go up and look around. We do not want surprises tomorrow morning."

The dining room in the hotel was not busy. The group had decided to meet at this location rather than the suite. Steve and Walker were the first ones at the table. Steve ordered appetizers and they both ordered a drink.

"I don't like leaving the team," Walker said.

Steve winced. He and Walker had been discussing this all day. "You know there is nothing I can do about it."

Walker turned his head and looked out the window at the sea and the bay below.

Steve felt helpless. What could he say to make it better? Nothing. Westgate had some reason for sending Walker away. His eyes darted toward the dining room door, hoping one of the other agents would show up about now to help break the tension. He grinned when Daniella entered the room.

The waiter came over and set the appetizers on the table and Steve grabbed a glass. Daniella stepped up to the table. Her beautiful eyes were bright. He wanted to kiss her on the lips, but knew it wasn't appropriate. He helped her into the chair next to him.

She set her large bag on the floor. He poured her wine and handed her the glass.

"I saw Peter in the lobby, he is waiting for Juan and Charlie," she said.

"Good. We can end this early. I have a hunch we'll be going to Montecristo, tomorrow." Steve handed her a small plate.

Their eyes met. He had a distinct feeling that she had something to say about tomorrow.

Peter and the other two agents entered the dining

room. Steve grabbed another glass. He glanced at the waiter and nodded. The agents sat down and the waiter disappeared into the kitchen.

"This is nice, but not as cozy as the suite," Peter said.

"Do you want cozy or a full course meal?" Steve said.

"The meal will be nice." Peter accepted his glass and took a sip.

Juan and Charlie passed on the wine. They each took a bottle of water.

While they all filled their plates with the appetizers, Steve started everything off. "Yesterday, Walker found a woman that recognized the DiBiasi name. She said her grandmother lived across the street from them many years ago. Today, we dropped by and had coffee with her and her grandmother."

"The old woman remembered when the parents died and the boy had to go to live with his uncle," Walker said. "It was a sad day. The boy did not want to leave Elba."

"The house was never sold," Steve said. "People would come a few times a year to keep the grounds up, but no one stayed there until a few years ago. A crippled man and his helper were there often, but kept to themselves. The grandmother recognized Lorenzo's picture."

"She said she never got a good look at the man in the wheelchair," Walker added. "We got the address and found the home. It is above the sandy beach right here in Marin Di Campo."

"No one was home," Steve said. "A neighbor came out of the house next door and told us it had been over a year since anyone had stayed there."

Steve let everyone digest the information while he ate his food.

Peter was the first to respond.

"Sounds like we're on the right track."

Juan nodded. "It has to be our guys."

"What did you find on Giglio and Giannutri?" Steve said.

"We found Alissa's purse and scarf," Juan said.

"And someone recognized Lorenzo," Charlie said.

Everyone was quiet, eating and drinking. Steve liked the quiet. His blood was rushing through his body with anticipation. He knew Cristo had been here and he knew he was now on Montecristo.

"So, where's the yacht?" Peter asked.

"The yacht has been found," Daniella said. All heads turned in her direction. "Vittorio called me right before I came downstairs to join you. It was found in the Mediterranean Sea near Crete. There was only the captain and the cook. No Ricco or Lorenzo."

"Well, this has certainly been a productive day," Steve said. "Did you find anything on Gargona?" He looked at Peter.

Peter shook his head. "It was a bust."

"Great, well, we should plan to go to Montecristo. Juan, you and Charlie split up, one to Corsica and the other to Sardinia. Walker, you go to Sicily. The rest of us will explore Montecristo."

"The boat leaves before dawn," Daniella said. They all stared at her. She shrugged. "I made arrangements for Marco to bring several agents and a boat for our use."

"I suppose Ricco's captain and cook aren't saying anything of importance?" Steve grinned.

Daniella shook her head. "No they are not...And we need to find Ricco soon. My orders have changed. If we do not find him within forty- eight hours, I must go home."

Steve's face fell slightly. They had to find Cristo in

the next two days or face Westgate's interference and Daniella's orders to go home. He almost sighed. Sometimes fate could really stir things up.

Steve stood at the patio door in the suite, staring out at the night. The weather was balmy. He walked out and looked over the balcony at the promenade below. Lots of people were strolling on the seafront walk, famous as a meeting place in the evening. He and Daniella had just returned from their own stroll.

He was immediately surprised by two arms embracing him. Daniella laid her face on his back and squeezed his waist. "It is a beautiful scene, is it not?"

He turned and pulled her close. "Not as beautiful as this scene."

She laughed. "You are so full of compliments this evening. I enjoyed the walk on the promenade."

He smiled. "Me too. Let's sit down." He motioned to the loveseat with soft cushions. They sat close to each other and Steve grabbed her hand. He held it close to him. He knew he had to tell her about Westgate. Now, not later.

Her head turned and their gazes locked. He could see concern reflected in her eyes. He loved her so much.

"What is it Steve? What is bothering you? Are you thinking of tomorrow and the danger?"

"No, I'm thinking of you." He bent down and claimed her mouth. She moaned. He pulled her closer. All thoughts of tomorrow and Cristo and Westgate disappeared. All of his concentration was on her. Her mouth, her hair, her body, her essence.

Staring into those wonderful brown eyes, he brushed a few strands of her thick brown hair off her face and gathered all his strength. He tried to tell her how much he cared. "I know we agreed to not talk about our private life until this business with Ricco was finished. But I have to tell you something, right now, right here."

He kissed her forehead and slipped his arm around her shoulders, drawing her in closer to him. "This last year has been wonderful." His voice cracked and he almost panicked. He took a breath and went on. "I have enjoyed getting to know my daughter and most of all I have loved every minute with you."

Daniella pulled herself away from him. He could see the glistening of tears in her eyes. "I love you, cara mia. In two days I will be home. If we catch Ricco tomorrow or the next day, you will be home with us. If we do not, Rosie and I will wait for you."

Steve lowered his head and kissed her throat. His hand moved over her body, possessively. He wished this night would never end.

Lorenzo sat up on his cot and stared across the galley. The crazy one was talking in his sleep, again. Ricco was not the only one tired of this cave. He, himself, hated the cave. But most of all he hated being the nursemaid to this man. Leonardo must be contacted when they land in Corsica. Leonardo must decide Ricco's fate. He, Lorenzo, could not. He owed this man and he could not kill him.

Ricco shouted out and Lorenzo moved across the room and stood over the cot. He wondered what the crazy one saw that made him so afraid.

At dawn, Peter stood on the deck of the small ship and watched the decoy team head for shore. Earlier, everything had gone smoothly. Marco and his men had been on time and he, Steve, and Daniella were waiting, having packed and checked out of the hotel before turning in the night before.

Peter removed the glasses and looked around at the island. The still water was a beautiful turquoise color. The only noise was from the gulls as they circled the rugged coastline. The sun had come up shortly after he came on deck, but a slight mist still hung around the pinnacles of stone that dominated the island.

A sickening feeling was settling in his stomach. Today they might find their nemesis. Today, someone would have revenge. He hoped it was him and not Cristo.

"I wonder if Cristo is watching the decoy party, too."

He almost jumped at Steve's voice. His ex-partner could be quiet as a mouse at times, but Peter should have heard him. He shook his head. He was losing his edge. Another reason to quit after catching Cristo.

Peter put the binoculars back to his eyes and watched the team go ashore. "If so, he won't be fooled. He's expecting us."

"What do you think of Cristo's island?"

"I don't think much of it. It kind of reminds me of him. Cold, hard, isolated, etc."

Steve chuckled. "The other islands have more beauty. His attraction was and is the caves."

Peter turned and stared at Steve. "I agree. Are we going to explore those caves today?"

"Odd you should ask. Daniella wants us to join her and go over our plan."

Peter laughed. "What plan?"

Steve walked toward the door leading to the galley. "Don't laugh. I told her you had the plan."

They joined Daniella in the dining area. She had a map of the island spread out before her on a large table. She looked up as they came into the room. "Did the team land?"

Peter helped himself to the coffee sitting nearby. "Yes, the decoy team has landed."

Daniella smiled. "Good. What is your plan?"

Peter gave Steve a dirty look for good measure. But he wasn't upset that his brother-in-law had passed the buck. "Steve and I will take the dinghy and search the coastline for caves."

"Great idea." Steve said. He grinned and glanced at Daniella. She rolled her eyes.

"When will you do that?" Daniella asked.

"After lunch."

"Sounds good," Daniella said.

"While we're checking out the caves, are there any other animals we should be looking out for besides the goats?" Peter asked.

Daniella looked up from her map. "Did Steve tell you about the viper of Montecristo?"

Peter put his coffee cup down on the table. He stared at Steve. "No, he didn't. Is that a snake?"

"Yes, a very deadly snake."

His body shuddered. He hated snakes.

"Not to change the subject," Steve said. "but we never discussed the clues Cristo left on Giglio and Giannutri."

"No, we did not. I assumed it was to throw us off and make us think he had left the Archipelago," Daniella said.

Steve grinned. "Me too."

"Me three," Peter said. He got up and filled his coffee cup again. He didn't want to offend Daniella, but Cristo had actually left the yacht to buy time. The Italians would have waited at least one or two days until they decided there were no more clues.

Lorenzo sat Ricco in his chair on the platform. They

had just finished eating breakfast. Their last meal in this miserable island.

Ricco smiled up at him. "After everything is made ready, go up and take a look. I would like to get an early start.

His assistant shrugged. "Everything is ready."

Ricco grinned. "Later today we will be in Corsica."

Lorenzo nodded. Tonight he would meet with his uncle and convince him to take them in for a few days. He got up and headed for the dingy. Within minutes he was outside the cave and climbing to the fortress. He scanned the sea surrounding the island. Nothing. He carefully moved down the hill to study the cove. When he put the glasses to his face, he almost dropped them. A boat sat in the tiny harbor. He focused on the villa hidden in the trees. He could see men talking to the foresters and the guard. Movement caught his eye and he saw more people walking up the hill. He lowered the glasses and put them away. His descent to the cave didn't take long. His heart hammered as he got in the little boat and rowed toward the platform. The crazy one will not like the news.

He joined Ricco at the table. A large map filled the space. "There is a boat the size of your yacht in the cove. I saw men talking to the foresters. Others moved up the hill."

Ricco sat back in his chair and stared at Lorenzo. His eyes bulged out. His mouth formed a straight thin line. Lorenzo knew his anger was rising. He knew the crazy one wanted to lash out at someone or something. He knew he wanted to kill someone.

"They have found us too soon!" he shouted. "Could they not have waited one more day?" Ricco slammed both fists onto the table.

Lorenzo took a step back to give him more space.

He did not want to be the brunt of this man's anger. It would force him to kill the maniac.

Ricco bent his head and covered his face with his hands. "Were the clues not good enough to throw them off?" He clasped his hands and raised his head. His body shook. He slowly looked up at Lorenzo, a peaceful expression on his face. "They will find nothing. We will leave at midnight."

Lorenzo grunted. He turned to walk back to the boat.

Ricco cleared his throat and spoke. "We will not go to Corsica now. If that is the agents in the cove, they are too close. Corsica will not be safe. We will go to Sicily. I have a cousin on the island. After a short stay we will look for the yacht."

Lorenzo nodded and finished his walk to the boat. Once down in the galley he started to make adjustments for a longer trip. He knew Ricco would plan where to stop along the way for supplies. His only concern was the Council. Leonardo would have to be contacted as soon as he could manage it. Leonardo must make things right with the Council. If not, there would be very much trouble when they settled on Sicily. Ricco had more than one relative on the island. And most of his relatives did not like him.

Steve adjusted his scuba equipment and jumped off the boat and into the water. Peter followed him and they swam for the rocks on the coast. They surfaced and swam several more feet before pulling themselves up and sitting down on large rocks. Steve took out his map. He had talked to people who were familiar with the caves on the island and had made a map of where the known caves were. Their plan, however, was to cling to the coastline and explore any openings they found. As they rested and looked at the map, Peter heard a rustling in the bushes, he became nervous, and he wondered if it was a viper.

Steve chuckled. "You won't last long if you think every noise is a viper."

Peter scowled. "If you had told me there were snakes, I would have gone with Walker."

Steve shrugged. "Sorry. Didn't think about it." He gazed at the map once again. "We'll only be able to search this side of the island today. Tomorrow we can finish the job."

"What are we going to do if we find his cave? Go in with our small pistols blazing?"

Steve shook his head. "Don't be sarcastic. We'll swim back and get help. Oh, and form a plan."

Peter gave him another bad look. "Let's get on with it. Where's the first cave?"

Steve folded the map and stowed it away. He dropped down into the water. "It's about five feet away."

All afternoon, Steve and Peter searched the caves and found no evidence of Cristo. In the early evening they retired to their cabins for rest before dinner. Steve had wasted no time falling asleep. He had a plan in his mind that he would share with the others and if they wanted to participate, that would be okay.

His alarm on his watch woke him a half hour before he and Peter would meet with Daniella. He quickly dressed and went down the hall to Peter's room. He knocked at the door.

"Who is it?" Peter asked.

"Steve."

"Are you alone?"

Steve raised both eyebrows. "Yes."

"Come on in. I'm too tired to get up."

Steve opened the door and stared at his ex-partner.

He knew Peter was still recovering from his ordeal with Cristo. But, he couldn't help his concern. Peter wasn't bouncing back. He grinned at him, lying on his bunk.

"Is this the man that runs five miles a day and works out at the gym? What has our Agency come to? A bunch of wimps?"

Peter laughed. "I think it's the heat and the rocks."

"Well, wash up. Time to eat."

He shut the door and hurried to the dining area. Daniella sat at the table waiting for them.

"Peter's on his way."

She smiled. "Good."

Steve helped himself to a drink and sat down next to her. "I'm worried about him. I don't think he'll stay with the Agency too much longer. His strength is not what it should be."

"Perhaps it is time for him to retire. No?"

Steve shrugged.

Peter walked into the room and sat down next to Steve.

Daniella cleared her throat. "The decoy team covered half the island and saw no sign of Cristo. How was your search?"

"Not any better. The caves we saw were small. Cristo would need something large. He would need a means of escape. I think he has found one big enough for a small boat," Peter said.

"I agree," Steve said. "And if he is here, he saw the decoy team today."

"If he is in one of the caves, what do you think he will do? Will he try to get away and go somewhere else?" Daniella asked.

"He may try to leave tonight," Steve said. "He always has an alternate plan. We'll have to be watchful. I'm going to rest for a couple of hours. My guess is that he will try to leave around midnight. If something happens, I can radio in to whoever is on duty. You two can catch up on your beauty sleep for the big day tomorrow."

Daniella raised an eyebrow and gazed at Peter. "Okay. If Ricco does not make an escape tonight, what is your plan tomorrow, Steve?"

"Same as today except on the other side of the island."

"If we don't find the cave tomorrow, we can circle the island for several hours. Then, at midnight, I'll try again. If they don't make a move, we leave and go home."

"Daniella smiled. "We have a plan. What is your opinion Peter?"

"I like it."

THIRTY

The alarm on Steve's watch woke him around eleven. He put on his scuba equipment and walked up the steps to the deck. He was surprised to see Daniella and Peter standing near the rail, both dressed in scuba gear.

"Did you really think we'd let you do this alone?" Peter asked.

"We all don't need to go," Steve said. "What if his boat is spotted? Someone needs to be here to give the orders to follow him."

"Peter and I have discussed this while waiting for you. Marco is to follow any boat that appears to be leaving the area. I will have communication with him." Daniella patted her radio.

Steve sighed. "What is our plan?"

"We'll row to the northern end of the island and drop off Daniella. From her perch she should be able to see anything that moves out to sea. You and I will proceed around the island with the inflatable dinghy. If Daniella sees anything she'll signal with her light."

"How will she know where we are?"

"We'll radio when we start around to the other side. And we will keep in contact every five minutes. If she doesn't hear from us, she will know we're in trouble."

"And if she doesn't call us, we'll know she's in trouble."

"Right."

Steve peered over the railing and saw the dingy tied up to the boat. It seemed like a good plan. "Okay, let's go!"

They rowed to the northern shore and dropped off Daniella. Steve checked his watch, it was midnight.

Ricco sat on the boat in the galley. He and Lorenzo had double checked everything. They were ready to go to Sicily. He felt like he had a heavy weight on his shoulders. He had no clue where the agents could be, they could not be in the Archipelago or they could be right outside waiting for him. He felt relief that he was leaving the cave, but it would be sad to say goodbye. And he knew he would never come back again.

Ricco looked at his watch it was midnight. Lorenzo appeared on the stairs. He had just returned from checking the boat in the harbor. "Are you ready? All is clear; the boat is in the harbor."

He nodded. "Remember, when you reach the entrance, turn the motor off and listen for any sound. Go outside and wait thirty minutes. If you feel comfortable about leaving, pull out of the cave."

Lorenzo nodded. He vanished and within minutes, Ricco heard the motor start. It was very loud inside the cave. Ricco panicked for a moment. Surely the whole world could hear this motor. His fears were abated within minutes. They were at the opening to the cave very quickly. The motor shut off.

Peter had started the rowing and each time they talked to Daniella, they switched. It was Steve's turn and Daniella called.

"Nothing here," she said. "How about you?"

"Nothing here," Peter said. "We're getting close to

the end of the island. Will call you when we get there."

"Okay

Steve held his hand out for the radio. Peter gave him the radio and the night vision glasses then took the oars.

Steve looked ahead. There was very little moon tonight, but aided by the glasses they should be able to see something. He hoped. Daniella also had a pair of the glasses.

The rowing was slow. Very slow.

Lorenzo felt good about leaving the cave. The agents were on the other side of the island, so they would not hear or see them when they left. He had waited the half hour. There was no sign of anyone.

He took a few minutes to open the cave entrance large enough for the boat. He went back aboard and switched on the motor, then pulled out of the cave.

"Steve, I heard a noise, are you around the corner yet?" Daniella's voice came in loud and clear.

"We're there now," Steve said.

Peter grabbed the oars and they finished the turn. As they rounded the bend, they saw Daniella's light.

Steve grabbed the oars and started rowing again.

As he came out of the cave, Lorenzo saw a faint light off to the left. He immediately turned the motor off. The boat drifted away from the rocky coast. He listened, but heard nothing suspicious. He hurried to the galley.

"What is it?" Ricco asked in a low voice.

"I saw a faint light off to the left."

"Go back into the cave. Now."

Steve continued to row. After a few feet, Peter touched his arm. The boat stopped.

"I see something up ahead," whispered Peter. He handed over the goggles.

Steve glanced through the goggles. What he saw accelerated his heart beat. There appeared to be a small boat. He immediately called Daniella.

"We see something. We're going to take a look."

"Okay, Steve."

A few seconds later both agents went over the side.

Lorenzo left Ricco and grabbed the helm. He heard a noise on the other end of the boat. He took his gun out of his pocket and walked toward the noise. He took two steps and stopped. One of the American agents stood close to the railing. The agent held a large bright light and was pointing a small gun at him. Lorenzo laughed.

"Don't try anything, Lorenzo, drop your gun."

Lorenzo snickered. "No." He almost dropped the gun when he felt something slam into his back.

"You heard Steve. Drop the gun."

Lorenzo dropped the gun. Steve came forward with a rope he'd found at the end of the boat. He started to tie Lorenzo's hands.

"I'll go below," Peter said.

After securing the tall cruel man, Steve hurried to the cabin to help Peter.

Steve stood at the top of the stairs and looked down into the dark galley. Where was Peter? He had a light. Why wasn't it on?

He went down two steps. A light went on. He saw

Cristo standing over Peter with a gun in his hand.

His partner lay unconscious on a small couch.

"Come, Steve, join our little party," Cristo said. "Are you surprised? Even Lorenzo doesn't know I can walk. I have fooled everyone, even the stupid doctors and nurses at the insane asylum."

Steve slowly walked down the steps. He sat on the couch next to Peter and noticed his partner was still breathing.

"You have surprised me a little Steve; I had not given you enough credit. But, Of course, I planned for this. Who is the person with the light? Is it your girlfriend? The mother of your child? Will she be joining us?"

Steve was shocked to hear that Cristo knew about his daughter. He made a little move on the couch and the madman shot him in the leg. He sat patiently as his hands and feet were tied to Peter's. He watched the man leave the cabin with no apparent disability.

Ricco almost laughed when he walked up the stairs and onto the deck. Lorenzo's mouth hung open and his eyes bulged. He cut the tall man's ropes.

"Let us not waste time talking. Get the dingy over the side of the boat. I'll go below and set the charges."

Lorenzo stared at him. "Are you going to blow up the boat? How will we get away from here?"

"We will go back to the cave! That is the beauty of the plan. The authorities will think we have left or are dead along with the agents. The girlfriend saw our boat, but she did not see where we came from, the opening can be made even more secure. Put the dingy over the side of the boat. Now!"

Lorenzo left to do as he was told. Ricco hurried

below to set the charges. As he walked past the two agents, Steve glared at him. Peter was still out cold.

"Do not worry, Steve, it will be over soon." He chuckled as he stepped into the galley.

"Don't get your hopes up too high, Ricco, we may have the last laugh."

Ricco opened the oven and cackled. The bomb sat perfectly inside it. While Lorenzo had been on deck, he had been down below making his bomb. He smiled at his genius. After he set the timer for ten minutes, he hurried up to the deck.

"Lorenzo!" he called. No Lorenzo. He looked over the side of the boat and saw the dingy tied up and waiting for them. "Lorenzo! We do not have much time."

He took a step toward the helm and that is when he saw her. Daniella stood a few feet away on the deck with Lorenzo at her feet. Ricco could tell he was dead. She held a gun with a silencer in her hand and it was pointed at him.

"What is your hurry, Ricco?" she asked.

Ricco grinned. "Your two friends are down below, tied up. I have set the timer on my little bomb for ten minutes." He glanced at his watch. "We have seven minutes to get away from the boat."

When he told her this, she showed no emotion. Ricco sensed her disbelief.

"Poor Steve, I had to shoot him in the leg. He will not make it off the boat in time. Too bad!"

Daniella could not take the chance that this maniac was baiting her. She motioned for him to move over toward the steps. When he didn't move she shot him in the arm.

Ricco was surprised. "You are much more ruthless

than I thought."

"Stop wasting time. Move down the steps, or I will shoot the other arm."

Ricco moved to the steps and started going down. When he reached the last step, he made his move. He turned around and grabbed Daniella's gun. It went off. Daniella kneed him in the chest and he fell down onto the floor. She saw Steve and Peter on the couch and ran over to them using her knife to cut them free.

"Hurry, Steve, Cristo has a bomb!"

She reached under Steve's arm to help him up and he grabbed her gun and fired. As Daniella stood up, she saw Ricco lying in a pool of blood, lifeless.

Together they lifted Peter. Steve hoisted his partner onto his shoulder and they rushed up the stairs and onto the deck. They ran to the side of the boat and jumped into the water. They swam. Within minutes, the boat blew up.

Steve saw a light heading in their direction. "Is that Marco?"

"Yes, I did not leave anything to chance."

Daniella hurried down the hall and entered the hospital room. She didn't stop until she reached the head of the bed. Steve reached out and grabbed her hand. They had been successful in getting rid of Cristo for good. It was a major accomplishment in this world of so many reverses.

She bent down and kissed him on the lips. "When do you have to go?"

Steve squeezed her hand. How did she know? It had weighed heavily on his mind since he had received the summons a few days ago. He had wanted to tell her many times but somehow it hadn't seemed right. Now he had no choice.

"They want me back as soon as possible. In fact, because of my injury, they are arranging for me to fly on military transport."

Daniella didn't say anything. It was as she suspected. She hated him. She loved him. She wanted him. But it was out of her hands.

"Maybe we should say our goodbyes now, Steve. I wish you the best." She withdrew her hand from his and walked out of the room. She didn't want to look at him.

Carrie heard a car pull up outside the house and ran to the window. She had just put the baby in his crib for his afternoon nap. Her plans to take a long soaking bath just came to a halt as she watched her husband step out of a cab. Immediately, she was down the hall, and then the stairs, taking two steps at a time. She met him at the door as he walked in and was in his arms in a heartbeat.

Peter held his wife for a few seconds. He thrilled at the feel of her against him. He pulled away and kissed her. "I've missed you so much. We're never going through this again. I've quit the Agency."

Cristo was dead. There was no threat. He felt wonderful. He pulled Carrie into another tight embrace, kissing her face and neck and then just holding her.

Tears ran down Carrie's cheeks. "I have some incredibly good news. I'm pregnant!"

Peter gazed into her eyes and knew life couldn't be better.

Daniella opened the letter she had almost thrown into the trash. It was from Steve. Three months had gone by. She went to work every day and tried to get on with her life. It helped to have Rosie and her home here in Milan. But it was going to take a long time to get over Steve. Rosie constantly asked about him and the house held so many happy memories.

She started to read the letter and tears began to spill out of her eyes. She had just blown her nose and wiped away tears before she had even opened this letter. Halfway down the page she threw the letter down and sobbed. He wasn't coming back. The letter was postmarked Washington D.C. but she knew he was not there. He would be somewhere in the world helping to find the terrorists that had the world by the throat.

Tomorrow was Christmas Day. She and Rosie would spend it at home alone. Her parents were off in Switzerland visiting her brother and his family. She had declined to go with them, it was too depressing.

The doorbell rang. A sound drifted upstairs and she smiled through her tears. She could hear Rosie's laughter.

"It is only the delivery boy from Federico's," yelled the housekeeper."

"Okay, I will be right down," she called back.

Tonight she was hosting a Christmas Eve dinner party before going to Midnight Mass.

She had invited only a few people from work and church. She did not feel the Christmas spirit. It was so unlike her to allow herself this self-pity. She could blame Steve for that. She loved Steve. No. She hated him.

She eased off the bed and opened the closet. Daniella took out her new dress and stared at it. She did not feel like wearing it. She put it back. She hated him. She slipped out of her robe and reached for the dress again.

"That color always did look good on you."

Daniella froze. Could it be him? She slowly turned her head and saw Steve standing in the doorway. His blue eyes held love and warmth. And she wanted to run into his arms. But she did not. She wanted him to kiss her passionately. But she would not go to him.

Their eyes locked. Steve knew she was angry. He also knew that he loved her very much and would always love her. He had realized during the last three months that he couldn't live without her and Rosie. He rushed into the room and pulled her into his arms. He kissed her passionately. And when she pulled away, he grabbed her and kissed her again.

"I love you, Daniella. I don't want anyone else in my life except you."

"I hate you! You have made my life miserable!" Tears ran down her cheeks. She moved away from him.

"Okay, I deserve all of your hatred. But, Honey, I love you. I've come back to marry you, if you and Rosie will have me."

Daniella stared at Steve. He thought she hadn't heard him correctly. She did not move a muscle. Steve reached into his pants pocket and pulled out a small jewelry case.

"I was hoping you would be happy about this. I took the liberty of buying you an engagement ring. While I was at it, I bought a locket for Rosie. There are pictures of you and me inside."

Daniella's tears stopped. She was moved by his gesture and held out her hand for the jewelry case. The locket was pretty and she could see the pictures of herself and Steve. Lying next to it was a ring. She looked up into Steve's face and she could see that he did love her. She loved him.

"How long are you here this time, Steve?"

"I've managed to get my old job back in Rome. Maybe you could get a transfer and join me there?" He took the ring out and put it on her finger.

She slipped her arms around his neck and kissed him passionately. She loved him and he loved her. Could they be engaged? If it was a dream, she did not want to wake up.

A peal of laughter drifted up the stairs.

"I think we'd better go down and rescue our company from the clutches of our daughter," Steve said.

Daniella dressed and they walked down the stairs. The living room was filled with people. She could see Rosie sitting on her Uncle Peter's lap and smiling at Baby Brett. Carrie grinned at her when she walked in. The holidays would never be the same again.

One week later, Steve and Daniella were married.

www.ingramcontent.com/pod-product-compliance
Lightning Source LLC
Chambersburg PA
CBHW062010170626
46813CB00001B/98